The Drain

Copyright ©2011 James V. Pagano
All rights reserved.

ISBN: 0578099365
ISBN-13: 978-0-578-09936-1
Library of Congress Control Number: 2011946198
CreateSpace Independent Publishing Platform
North Charleston, South Carolina

The Drain

James V. Pagano

2012

ACKNOWLEDGEMENTS

Once again I want to thank Linda Hart, PhD, for her editing expertise, R. Payne Cabeen for the artwork, and my wife, Lani, for her forbearance during the many hours I hogged the computer trying to get this finished.

Walter Family Tree

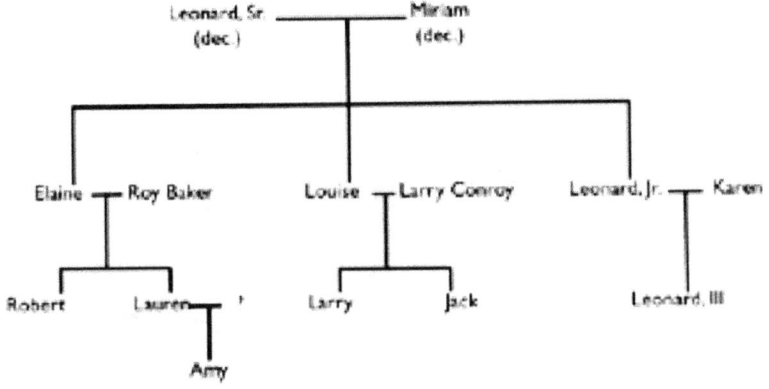

Chapter 1

"Code blue, ICU. Code blue, ICU."

The garbled overhead page was just loud enough to be heard by the ER unit clerk. She waited a few seconds.

"Code blue, ICU. Code blue, ICU."

A patient in the intensive care unit was having a cardiac arrest. It was the ER doctor's job to respond. At the moment, Dr. G. B. 'Fish' Hooks, M.D., FACEP was in treatment room 6 with the door closed, wads of cotton in his ears, trying to repair the chin laceration of a three-year-old boy who was screaming his head off and doing everything in his power to get free of the sheet wrapped around his body and the two nurses trying to hold him still.

"Code blue, ICU. Code blue, ICU."

The clerk realized that no one in the ER but she knew someone was trying to die down the hall. She grudgingly got up. She opened the door to room 6 and the wailing, which had been tolerable with the door closed, spilled out into the emergency room, echoed down the corridor, past the triage desk, and into the waiting room, where the screaming child's parents, already anxious, now became convinced their son was being murdered.

The child was in no pain and hadn't been since the laceration was anesthetized ten minutes earlier. But, he was seriously pissed off at the entire situation. The sheet, the two nurses, one draped over his lower body and the other holding his head, the towel over his face, strategically placed to both keep the wound area more or less clean and to keep him from seeing what the man in the blue scrubs and white lab coat was doing with the weird tools, all of it.

"Dr. Hooks," the clerk said. No response.

"DR. HOOKS!"

"WHAT!?," he replied, looking up.

"Code blue, ICU."

"Fuck," was the mumbled response. The chin wound was about an inch long, and deep. He'd already repaired the subcutaneous layer with absorbable sutures and was just starting on the skin. Another five, maybe eight minutes and he'd be done. He put down the needle holder and forceps, removed the sterile gloves, and pulled the cotton from his ears.

"Let him up and let the parents know what the deal is," he said before leaving the department.

This was the third time on this shift he'd been called to a code in the Unit. Each of the two previous times the victim had been the same ninety-two-year-old man with end-stage heart disease, diabetes, and kidney failure who'd acquired the nickname 'The Un-dead'. Un-dead only because his children refused to let him go and insisted that 'everything be done'.

As he made his way to the ICU, conveniently located in a corner of the hospital farthest from the ER, Dr. Hooks contemplated both the scene he was about to enter and the one facing him when he got back. The Un-dead was doubtless trying to get a good look at the afterlife, his children were doubtless praying to keep whatever was left of him in this one, and the child with the chin laceration would have to go through the entire ordeal again from scratch, including the anesthesia, because the lidocaine he'd injected earlier would, by the time he got back to the ER, have worn off.

As he punched in the code to unlock the ICU door he was approached by several family members of The Un-dead, officially Mr. Walter, who by now had come to believe he was capable of performing miracles.

"Please, Dr. Hooks, fix him," the eldest daughter, and spokesperson of the Walter clan pleaded. He stared at her for a moment, trying to find something to say that she might be able to understand.

"You know, there's only so much we can do, and we've pretty much done it already," was the best he could come up with.

And he was right. During the first code blue Mr. Walter had been intubated. A tube had been placed into his trachea and attached to a ventilator to assist his breathing. That had stabilized him for a while. The second code was called because he'd dropped his blood pressure to the point he was no longer perfusing his vital organs. Dr. Hooks started him on a Levophed drip. Levophed is a powerful drug that causes constriction of blood vessels and stimulates the heart muscle to beat faster and stronger. This has the effect of supporting a patient's blood pressure. For a while. It also has the effect of decreasing blood flow to certain organs, like the kidneys, and can cause kidney failure if used for too long a time. In the case of The Un-dead, who already had marginal renal function, it was too long already.

Inside the ICU it was organized chaos, as usual. It was a ten-bed unit and there were currently eight patients in residence. The lights were always on, heart and blood pressure monitors, oxygen sensors, ventilators, and telephones beeped, flashed and rang. Dr. Hooks walked directly to bed 7, Mr. Walter's room. There was a crowd around the bed. Two nurses fiddled with IV lines and rummaged through the crash cart, as the large metal storage container, painted red and filled with an array of medicines and pieces of equipment useful in a code blue, was called. Two respiratory techs monitored the ventilator and guarded the patient's airway, while a third, probably a student, performed chest compressions. Two LVN students, young women in their first year of nursing school, stood in a corner with expressions of both fascination and mild disgust on their faces.

"What happened?" he asked as he waded through the crowd to the bedside.

"Blood pressure dropped to thirty, then no pulses. We gave him a milligram of epinephrine and called the code. It's been a few minutes so it's time for a second dose," the nurse responsible for Mr. Walter's care responded.

Dr. Hooks was silent for a moment.

"Doctor?" the nurse added, waiting for an order.

"Hold CPR and check the rhythm."

Chest compressions cause spikes on the cardiac monitor, especially if performed vigorously. The respiratory tech student was pounding away on poor Mr. Walter with gusto so it was impossible to know whether the activity on the monitor was coming from Mr. Walter's heart or was merely an artifact produced by the compressions. He stopped, and the blips on the monitor continued.

"Check for pulses," Dr. Hooks said, placing his fingers over the patient's carotid artery at the side of his larynx. "I've got nothing. How about you?" he asked the nurse who had her own fingers on the patient's femoral artery in his groin.

"Nothing."

"We're done."

Everyone in the room turned toward him. An awkward moment passed.

"But he has a rhythm," the nurse argued.

Dr. Hooks let out a sigh. Chest compressions, he knew, were the most important part of a resuscitation. Stopping them, even for thirty seconds to check for a pulse, could cause whatever perfusion pressure you'd managed to generate to drop precipitously. But he also knew that Mr. Walter, The Un-dead, was a goner.

"Look," he said, staring at the nurse, "he's got a rhythm but no pulse. That's called PEA, pulseless electrical activity. In some cases that can be due to a treatable condition. In this case it's because

Mr. Walter's heart isn't strong enough to move his blood around. He's on the maximum dose of Levophed already. More epinephrine, which is basically the same drug, isn't going to help. Nothing is going to help. He needs to be dead."

He let that sink in for a moment. Medical professionals are trained to save lives. They are not trained to stand idly by while someone, even The Un-dead, tries to flee the scene. But Dr. Hooks had learned over the years that knowing when to stop was just as important as knowing when not to.

"Turn off the ventilator. I'm going to start hanging some crepe in the waiting room."

Dr. Hooks walked out of the ICU and was immediately besieged by Mr. Walter's family. He was prepared. He ushered them into the small waiting room outside the ICU and had them sit.

"OK. As you all know it's been a tough day for Mr. Walter. We put him on a breathing machine and we've given him every possible medication to try to sustain him. We're running out of options."

The eldest daughter began to sob.

"We're still working on him," he lied, "but it isn't looking good. If he doesn't respond in the next few minutes we'll have to stop. It's the best thing. Really. We don't want to resuscitate his heart if he is going to end up with permanent brain damage."

He moved his eyes from one relative to the next, making sure they'd heard him. Then he went back into the unit. During the brief time it took to inform the family the patient's rhythm had deteriorated. The electrical spikes slowed, then stopped. Mr. Walter was no longer The Un-dead.

He waited a few minutes longer before going back out. It gave the family enough time to digest what he'd told them, but not enough for them to begin cultivating unrealistic expectations. They were still in the waiting room.

"I'm very sorry," he began. "We did everything we could but we weren't able to get him back this time."

The sobbing intensified.

"The nurse will be out in a few minutes to let you in so you can be with him. I have to get back to the ER."

As he walked back down the hall he thought about all the Mr. Walters he'd treated over the years. Patients with no quality of life subjected to all manner of invasive and uncomfortable treatments in the name of mercy. Most doctors had gotten better about communicating with patients and families in advance of a crisis. Had this been the case with Mr. Walter he would have been a no-code, either from the time he was admitted to the hospital with congestive heart failure, or, certainly, after the first code was called. Dr. Hooks made a mental note to have a talk with Mr. Walter's attending physician the next time he saw him.

When he got back to the ER it was a mess. Three trips to the ICU had made it impossible to keep up with the patient flow and now it was almost five PM, heading into the busiest time of the day. He had two more hours before the end of his shift, and he knew he'd be there for at least an hour or so afterward finishing up. He couldn't let the night shift guy walk into a complete disaster.

"Let's finish the chin lac, and get the work-ups started on the new ones," he barked to the charge nurse. "Christ!" he mumbled to himself as he reached for a new pair of sterile gloves.

Chapter 2

Gilbert Bass Hooks was the eldest of four children born to Gilbert Sr. and Marlene Bass. The family resided in Lakewood, a once-idyllic community in Southern California not far from the ocean and, more importantly, near the McDonnell-Douglas plant where Gilbert senior made a good living building airplanes.

Young Gilbert fantasized about growing up to become an engineer, like his dad, or possibly a professional surfer. The fantasies came crashing down in the early 1990's when the aviation industry, and Mc-Donnell-Douglas in particular, imploded. His father managed to hold on to his job but many of his co-workers did not.

Gilbert was in high school at the time, a good, though not particularly motivated student. A conversation with his guidance counselor got him thinking seriously about his future. Surfing was not an option, unless he was prepared to starve to death. Or drown. He was good, but not world-class good. Engineering was O.K. but all he really knew about it was what his father did, which was not really an option.

His counselor took him down the list of possibilities, things he felt the young man had the aptitude to achieve. Law, an MBA degree, CPA, all solid but not particularly exciting. Medicine? Hmm. He'd never seriously considered becoming a doctor, but as he mentally juggled the various options the possibility became more intriguing. "What the hell," he thought.

This was not exactly the attitude shared by the majority of pre-med students who tended to pursue their dream with an almost religious fervor. Getting accepted to medical school was a long-odds bet. His obliviousness to the fact, or at least his apparent lack of concern, proved to be advantageous.

He'd done well enough in high school to be accepted to UCLA. There he kept his head down, took the right courses, got the right grades, and eventually secured an interview at the UC Davis medical school. He'd never been to Davis, a small agricultural community in northern California. What he found when he got there was a distinct lack of distractions.

His first interviewer was a young doctor, a member of the house staff of the university medical center, as doctors-in-training are called. He was in his final year of an Internal Medicine residency. He sized Gilbert up. A little over six feet tall, athletic build, sandy hair falling over his ears, hazel eyes, slacks and sport coat. Gilbert had considered a suit for the occasion, but the reality was he didn't own one and couldn't really afford the investment.

"Mr. Hooks," the doctor began, shaking the young applicant's hand, "I'm Dr. Winston. Have a seat."

"You can call me Fish," Gilbert replied.

The doctor looked at him, unsure what to say. Gilbert sensed his unease.

"It's what most people call me. I got the nickname when I was in grammar school. I was never crazy about Gilbert, my middle name is Bass, which is my mother's maiden name, and, you know, my last name is Hooks, so by, like, the third grade kids started calling me all sorts of things. Fish stuck and I was O.K. with it."

The doctor smiled. The guy was relaxed, if nothing else. "O.K., Fish, lets start with this. Suppose I told you that I've already decided to put you on the acceptance list. You're in. But, now I'm telling you that the most you can ever expect to earn as a doctor is twenty thousand dollars a year. You still interested?"

Fish looked at him. It was his turn to smile.

"Look," he began after a pause, "I've never made twenty thousand dollars in a single year. But, there are probably a few things I could do to earn that much eventually, and none of them would be as hard as becoming a doctor. Medicine is great, but if I'm going to make the sacrifices necessary to do it I'm going to want more than what I could make, you know, giving surfing lessons or something. I don't expect to become a millionaire but I'd like to have a decent life. So I guess my answer is no."

He was taking a chance but felt that honesty was important, especially considering what he was signing up for.

Dr. Winston studied him for a moment, then laughed. "You're the first honest person I've interviewed today. As far as I'm concerned, you're in. And you *will* make more than twenty thousand dollars a year some day."

And that was that. He left for Davis the following fall, accompanied by the rest of the family; Gilbert Sr., Marlene, his brothers Danny and Billy, and his little sister, Marla. She was fourteen at the time and he was her hero. She kept a stoic front as they got him organized in his new apartment and when she hugged him goodbye. He didn't find out until years later that she cried pretty much the whole way back to Lakewood.

The four years that followed were more of a grind than he'd anticipated. Two years of books and classrooms, on the quarter system, as many as seven or eight courses crammed into a quarter so you were constantly studying for a test. Then two years of clinical work, on the wards, dealing with real patients, sort of. Ridiculous hours, dealing with the 'real' patients who ended up on the teaching service, the nursing home residents, the poor, the uneducated, running around all night doing the sorts of menial tasks the interns were too busy or too tired to do. Drawing blood, starting IV's, chasing down lab results, trying to stay awake the next morning when the attending arrived to do rounds.

But somehow this seemingly insane system worked. As the years passed he felt the changes, absorbed the knowledge. He learned he could push himself much farther than he'd thought possible the day of the interview. He was becoming Dr. Fish, if not quite Dr. Hooks, yet. Bleeding was a symptom, an illness was a problem. He could take a step back, objectify things that would have seemed disgusting or appalling a few years earlier.

He also realized he needed to make another big decision. Getting through medical school, as important as it was, didn't qualify you to practice medicine. You needed at least another year of internship for that, and, really, you needed to do a full residency in one or another specialty to be truly proficient. The question was, what sort of residency did he want to do?

He liked doing procedures, like suturing lacerations and inserting various tubes and catheters. He hated medical clinic day, listening to a series of patients going on about their diabetes, blood pressure, hemorrhoids or whatever. He liked the energy of the ICU. He had no interest in psychiatry, though he did have a somewhat odd affection for crazy people. Radiology was interesting, but a little too much sitting in the dark looking at pictures all day. Surgery was great, but not great enough to justify ten years of training after medical school.

Emergency Medicine seemed about right. You got the cuts and broken bones, you got the diabetics and hypertensives when they were out of control, you got to look at some x-rays, see a few kids, and deliver the occasional baby. Plus there were the assorted crazies, drug-induced or otherwise. Best part, when the shift was over, you got to go home. There was no office to maintain, no nurse or secretary to hire. You could take your skills with you and work anywhere.

Emergency Medicine was the newest of the medical specialties and there were only a limited number of residency programs. Fortunately, there were two in Los Angeles. He applied to both, the one at his alma mater, UCLA, and the other at USC, the cross-town rival and arch-enemy. USC responded first and he jumped at it.

Being home again was bittersweet. His parents still had the house in Lakewood, but his siblings were no longer living there. Billy, two years younger than he, was living in Silicon Valley working at some kind of tech start-up, Danny was finishing up his undergraduate work at UCLA and was about to enter law school, and Marla, now eighteen, had exercised her newly acquired adulthood by moving to New York City. She was working in some restaurant at night and going to acting classes and auditions during the day, living with a room mate in a tiny four story walk-up in the Village, and loving every second of it. The world, or at least the Hooks' part of it, had changed and he hadn't been there to watch it happen.

The residency program was a four-year affair. One year of hellish internship rotating through various services; Medicine, Surgery, OB-GYN, Pediatrics, eighty or more hours a week being treated like a criminal because you were the 'ER guy' and not one of their own, and two months in the ER, where you were tortured but at least you felt at home, followed by three more years of increasingly pleasant, if you could call it that, work, as you became the senior house staff member.

When it was finally over he was officially Dr. Hooks, MD, ER doctor. He had his choice of jobs, and chose one at Saints' Hospital in the San Gabriel Valley. His decision was based on a number of factors. First, he was tired. The ER at Saints' was eight beds with a volume of about forty patients a day. Manageable without being boring. It wasn't a trauma center, so he was insulated from the gangbangers, gunshot wounds, traffic disasters and other 'trauma center criteria' injuries that he'd seen so much of the previous four years. Plus, he liked Dr. Riegel, the director.

And this is where he was on a Thursday evening more than eight years later, finishing his charts, an hour and a half after the official end of his shift. He was Dr. Riegel's co-director. He had to set the right example for the young guys. He wanted to say he was getting too old for this shit, but that was the director's line. Besides, he wasn't. Yet.

Chapter 3

"Hey, Fish, glad you're still here."

Fish looked up from his computer into the familiar face of Dr. William Riegel, the ER contract holder and medical director.

"Hey, yeah, I got behind with the charts. Spent half my shift coding this old guy in the ICU. Fucking ridiculous. What's up?"

"I just got out of the Board meeting. Couple things I need to talk to you about. Come down to my office when you get done here."

The director turned and walked down the corridor, Fish staring at his back. Dr. Riegel tended to be somewhat inscrutable, and sometimes indecipherable, so it was impossible to know what he could possibly have on his mind. Fish shrugged it off and got back to work. Twenty-five minutes later he rapped at his boss's office door and let himself in.

"Have a seat. Want some coffee?" Coffee is to those who work in the ER what tea is to the Japanese, donuts to the cops. It is the mystical substance upon which a significant part of life is based. There is a reverence about it. Except unlike the other essentials ER coffee generally sucks.

"Uh, no thanks," he replied, taking a seat opposite Dr. Riegel.

"So," the director began, "it's a funny business we're in. You work hard, try to do the right thing. Bullets coming at you from every direction, fourth and inches all day long. You get what I'm saying?"

Fish had had enough of these conversations over the years to realize it would be of no use to tell him 'no, I have no fucking idea what you're talking about'. He merely nodded in the affirmative, certain whatever it was would become fairly obvious soon.

"Good," he continued, "because something came up at the Board meeting, couple of things actually, that we need to talk about."

Fish just looked at him, waiting for what was beginning to sound like something he'd prefer not having to hear.

"So, the old guy you were coding all day, Mr. Walter I think his name is?"

"Y-e-a-h?" Fish replied, trying to get a fix on where this was headed.

"Well, it turns out that he's some big shot, or was anyway. Owns car dealerships. Used to until today. Big time Catholic, you know, grammar school at St. Mary's, high school at St. Ignatius, church every Sunday."

"And so now he's in heaven," Fish interrupted, "and everything's good."

"Christ, Fish, I don't know where the hell he is. That's not the point. The point is how he got there."

There was silence as the two doctors stared at one another. Dr. Riegel looked at his young colleague wondering how he could not understand the gravity of the situation. Dr. Hooks looked back, wondering if maybe this time the old guy had finally lost it and considered whether or not he should call another code blue.

"How he got there? He fucking died, that's how he got there! That's how everybody gets there, if there is a There to begin with! Jesus!" Fish finally shouted.

"Whoa, calm down. I know how he got there. The problem is the ICU nurse who was taking care of him isn't as clear on the subject."

Fish narrowed his eyes.

"According to her," Dr. Riegel continued, "the guy had a rhythm, you just looked at him, checked for a pulse, and said he needed to be dead. Then you had respiratory turn off the vent. Nurse said you went out, talked to the family, made them think you were actually trying to save the guy, then went back into the ICU, by which time the guy really was dead."

"WHAT?!"

"Yeah. Turns out the nurse is a big Catholic, too. Knew Mr. Walter from church. Tells the daughter you just let him go. Daughter goes nuts, complains to the director of nurses, she goes to the C.O.O., you know the wimpy guy administration hired to help improve business, he goes to Sister Dolores and she blind-sides me at the Board meeting and makes it sound like we're running around the hospital killing people. That's what."

Fish stared back in amazement, unable to respond for a moment. "And you believe that load of crap?" he asked.

"Of course not. The guy shouldn't have been a full code in the first place. The only reason he was in the ICU was because Sheldon, you know, his cardiologist, was getting pressure from the family, and Sister Dolores wanted him to go through the motions, run the whole play book, give him both barrels. Then you waltz in there and tell everyone who can hear that he needs to be dead. So it gets back to Sister Dolores, and you know what a mean bitch she can be, and she waits until the Board meeting and then goes directly up my ass with it."

Fish started to smile. He couldn't help himself. Sister Mary Elizabeth Dolores was the mother superior of the Sisters of Ineffable Sorrow as well as President and Chairman of the Board of Saints' Hospital. She was formidable, of indeterminate age, probably in her sixties, and it was her job to keep Saints' running. She took the job seriously.

"And now you're going up mine?"

"That's how it works."

"So now what?"

"So now the Board wants to refer the case to Peer Review."

"For what? The guy was dead. I just happened to be the one who had to tell him he was dead."

"Relax. I'm on that committee, too. Nothing's gonna happen but there needs to be an investigation."

"Are we going to send every unsuccessful code blue to Peer Review now?"

"No. But we're sending this one."

Fish shook his head in disgust.

"Look," the director said, "there's more to it. This guy Walter gave money to the hospital. A lot of money."

Dr. Hooks let that sink in for a minute. "So this is all about money?"

"Oh come on. Everything's pretty much all about money. Especially now, when nobody has any. Which brings me to the other thing I need to tell you."

Fish looked up but said nothing.

"Saints' is in serious financial doo-doo. The hospital's lost money four of the last six months. That's why they hired that guy Doyle, the COO. He's supposed to be some kind of financial genius, gonna turn things around, stem the tide."

"What's that got to do with me?" Fish asked, not seeing the connection.

"Maybe nothing. But you gotta figure a lot of things are on the table now that weren't a year ago. Just keep that in mind. For now just go home and let me deal with Sister Dolores and the Peer Review committee."

Fish shook his head again, got up, and walked back toward the ER. "What the fuck was that all about?" he mumbled to himself.

Chapter 4

Barring any unusual traffic it was about a twenty-minute drive from the hospital to his home in Los Feliz. It was an area to the north and east of downtown Los Angeles, an old community, once quiet and sedate, which had recently become hip. Being hip wasn't what attracted him to the place. The hills, old Spanish style homes mixed in with newer, modern structures, the multitude of new bars and restaurants, and the lack of pretensions were the draw. Plus the fact that he was no more than thirty minutes away from just about anywhere he might want to go.

Dr. Riegel's cryptic remarks were still banging around in his head as he started the trip but by the time he got home he'd managed to lock them away. As he pulled up he noticed the lights were on.

"Micky?"

Michelle Riley was, he finally had to admit, his girlfriend. Though she had her own apartment she had the keys to his place and spent most of her time there. They'd met in the ER a little over two years ago. She was a new nurse and fourteen years his junior. It took a near-fatal car accident for him to realize that those were insufficient reasons not to date her. Not to mention that it was she who initiated the relationship by following him into the shower one afternoon during his convalescence.

Prior to the accident Fish had not been a one-woman kind of guy. He enjoyed the company of women but had no interest in the entanglements of a serious, long-term relationship. Almost dying changed his attitude about a number of things, and though he hadn't intended his relationship with Micky to be any different from all the rest, when it started getting serious he found himself uncharacteristically content. More than content.

"Mick?" he yelled a little louder.

There was no one home. He dropped his briefcase in the hall-way and hung his lab coat on the back of a dining room chair as he made his way to the kitchen. As he began to open the refrigerator, in search of a well-deserved beer, he saw a note attached to the door by a magnet in the shape of a butterfly. A bit of territorial girlishness that made him smile.

"At the Step with Marla. Come on over if you're not too tired. L, M."

Why not? He had Friday off and a drink with Micky sounded a lot better than one alone. He pulled off the scrubs, took a quick shower, and put on his regular off-duty uniform of jeans, T-shirt, and leather jacket.

"Much better," he said to no one as he walked out the front door and got back into the Lexus.

Chapter 5

The Thirteenth Step was a bar that served food, or a gastro-pub, depending on your point of view. The owner, Tommy Traina, preferred 'bar'. The food writer for the LA Times had called it a gastro-pub, which seemed a little too frou-frou for Tommy, but the review had been positive and business picked up after it was published.

The place was originally called Al's Bar, after Al, the guy who'd owned it for close to thirty years, and it was located in Silverlake, about three miles south of Fish's place in Los Feliz. This was true hipster-ville with a substantial population of actors, musicians, gays and lesbians. Al was not a hipster. Not even close. He had no interest in changing the feel of the place to accommodate a younger clientele and when he thought the time was right he put it up for sale. When that time came it was no surprise that someone like Tommy would want to buy it.

Tommy was a musician, a guitar player to be precise. He'd had a modicum of success in the business, having written the top ten Indy hit "Bite Me", which fairly summed up his worldview. It was a worldview that made it difficult for him to secure steady work, reluctant as he was to compromise on just about anything. Realizing that "Bite Me" was possibly the pinnacle of his career he did what many of his fellow musicians failed to do. He took his royalties and invested them in a different business.

His first act as owner was to change the name to The Thirteenth Step. This created a serious backlash from the recovering alcoholic and substance abuse community. Tommy was unfazed. He believed that political correctness was the un-doing of America and was committed to fighting it tooth and nail. "Besides," he said, "recovering alkies aren't exactly my target demographic."

Next he gave the place a facelift. The neon beer signs came down, or at least most of them. The St. Pauli Girl, all smiles and boobs, was just too good. Likewise the Bud Lite poster of the three young women in the skimpiest of bikinis, backs to the camera but faces turned towards it, in some alpine ski resort, on skis, no less, also got to stay. In place of the others he hung photo's of himself, a shade under six feet tall, rock-star thin, with long black hair, hazel eyes, and Italian good looks, his touring band, his gold record for "Bite Me", and in the short hall leading to the rest rooms a fourteen by twenty-two inch framed color photo of the Betty Ford Clinic.

When asked about the photo Tommy would just laugh and say he thought it was funny. Whether or not he had any sort of deeper attachment to the place remained a mystery. While performing he wasn't a big enough star to attract constant media attention. It would have been fairly easy for him to come off the road at the end of a tour and slip in for rehab instead of the usual vacation to Jamaica or Costa Rica.

There was nothing wrong with the actual bar. It was an old slab of polished mahogany, twelve stools in front, (Tommy made a note to add one more in keeping with the place's new name), and a large back bar with plenty of room for bottles and glasses. The mirror in the center added a sense of depth.

The bar was situated on the wall opposite the door. In between was an open area for tables and to the left of the door he'd built a small stage from which live music would be performed on Friday and Saturday nights. To the right of the bar were the restrooms and a small kitchen which Al had used as a storage space. Tommy cleared it out, cleaned it up, and installed new appliances. Being of Italian descent he had an innate appreciation for good food. Beer nuts and pretzels, tasty as they were and the only edibles provided by Al, were not exactly what Tommy had in mind.

Lastly, he began interviewing for a cook. He placed an ad in the local paper and a sign in the window. The ad caught the attention of Marla Hooks. She'd recently relocated to LA, having given up the idea of becoming an actress in New York. Her plan on returning had been to enroll in culinary school and pursue her other passion, cooking. Actually, that was only half of her plan, and only one of her passions. The other part of the plan was to pursue her budding relationship with Dr. Bob Graber, one of her brother's younger associates.

Part two of the plan was working out as well as she could have hoped. She and Bob had become exclusive and saw almost as much of one another as her brother and Micky. Almost, because Bob was a junior member of the ER physician team and worked a regular schedule, including nights, weekends, and holidays on a rotating basis with the other doctors. Fish, as the associate director, worked days.

Part one had gotten derailed by a scary bit of Hooks family drama. It began as a bout of 'indigestion'. Her father, Gilbert Sr., had just finished a large Sunday dinner prepared by her mother, Marlene. It was the thousandth or something anniversary of their engagement so she'd gone all out, Southern style. Fried chicken, mashed potatoes, gravy, greens, and a big piece of homemade apple pie, a la mode, of course. The kind of food they had every Sunday back home in Alabama and now saved for special occasions.

Having grown unaccustomed to such rich fare Gilbert thought nothing of the mild stomachache and heartburn and simply took a swig from the bottle of antacid that had been sitting in the bathroom medicine cabinet for, seemingly, ever. It helped, a little. Later that night he was awakened by a different kind of pain. It was more of a pressure sensation and now it was in his chest. Refusing to believe it was anything other than his gastrointestinal system's payback for his dietary indiscretion he tucked another pillow under his head and waited for it to go away. It wasn't until he found himself feeling short of breath an hour or so later that he woke Marlene.

She wanted to call 911 but he wouldn't allow it. "Paramedics'll show up with the lights flashing and the sirens blasting, wake up the neighbors, make a big scene, all for a case of heartburn," was his view of the situation. The Hooks' were not the sort of people who 'made scenes'. He did agree to seek a professional opinion, though, and allowed Marlene to drive him to Sunset Community Hospital. It was a small hospital with a smaller emergency room but had a good reputation in the area.

When they arrived and Gilbert described his symptoms to the triage nurse he was whisked immediately back to the treatment area. Dr. Lee, a young man three years out of his emergency medicine residency, appropriately ordered an EKG, chest x-ray, and blood tests. It was his opinion that there was more than indigestion at work. The EKG confirmed his suspicion. There were elevations of the ST segments, the spaces between the spikes on the cardiogram, in three different leads. Mr. Hooks was having a heart attack.

There are ways to deal with a blocked coronary artery, to open it back up, restoring blood flow to the area of the heart being suffocated by the blockage. There are thrombolytic drugs, 'clot busters', that can be administered intravenously. There are systems in place in LA County to insure that patients like Mr. Hooks got to the right hospital with the right staff and the right equipment where emergency angiography could be performed. A catheter is placed in the femoral artery in the groin and threaded into the main coronary artery. Contrast dye is injected and the blockage is seen on the fluoroscope. The catheter is then moved to that spot and a stent is placed inside the small artery to relieve the blockage. The treatment of myocardial infarctions, 'heart attacks', has come a long way.

The problem, though, is that these treatments are time sensitive and Gilbert had waited too long to seek care. His symptoms had begun nearly eight hours earlier. He was no longer a candidate for thrombolytics. Had he allowed Marlene to call the paramedics, they would have done the EKG on the spot. The ST elevations would have been noted, and Gilbert would have been transported to a hospital certified to provide state of the art care for his type of problem.

Now, though, he was in a small ER, being treated with oxygen, aspirin, nitroglycerine, morphine, and a diuretic, waiting for the ambulance to arrive that would transport him to the closest heart center. The blocked artery had caused damage to his heart muscle, which was no longer beating with its usual intensity. Blood had backed up into his lungs causing congestive heart failure, which was why he was short of breath. He wasn't dying, but his condition was serious.

As soon as Marlene got the report from Dr. Lee she called Marla, ordering her to notify her brothers. It was a little after five A.M., which meant it was just after two A.M. on Maui, where her oldest brother was vacationing with Micky, Danny, and his new girlfriend, Ashleigh. After three rings she got a sleepy "Hello?"

"G?"

"Marla?" He knew it was his sister. No one else called him G. He refused to answer to 'Gilbert' and she'd refused to call him 'Fish'. "What's the problem?"

"It's dad. He's having a heart attack. He's at Sunset Community but they're going to move him to University. You need to come home."

He'd been in Hawaii for eight days. The trip had been planned for twelve. He'd taken the time off partly in response to Dr. Riegel's suggestion that he do so, and partly because he was burned out. The accident, the surgery on his leg, the months of rehab and the months of dealing with the malpractice case against him had taken their toll. Even though the suit had no merit, and even though it had been de- cided in his favor, it had given rise to an antipathy towards medicine, patients, and bullshit in general he'd previously not known. He need- ed time to sort out his feelings, and to make some decisions about his future.

And he had. Only two days earlier he'd decided enough was enough. No more administrative work, kissing the butts of senior medical staff members, board members, and Sister Dolores. No more being on-call. No more Saints' Hospital, for that matter. Fuck it. He was going to work on his terms. Locum tenens. Two weeks in Hawaii, two months in New Zealand. Wherever the surf was breaking, and just enough to pay the bills. No more fantasies of getting rich, either. He planned to tell Dr. Riegel when he got back home. He was glad he'd de- cided to wait, because the phone call from Marla changed everything.

As soon as he hung up he called Sunset and spoke to Dr. Lee. The situation wasn't great, but from what he could gather his father would survive. He'd probably need a catheterization and possibly a stent or two in the next few days. He'd need cardiac rehab. He'd be on several new medicines. But he would be alive. No way, Fish knew, could he go gallivanting around the world right now.

He also knew that his sister's plans were about to change. His mother would need help and emotional support. Marla would have to postpone culinary school, at least for a while.

It was almost a year later as he drove to the Thirteenth Step. He was still working at Saints', he was still the associate director of the ER. There really was no better job for him in LA. He had scheduling priority and his director's stipend. Short of acting on his Locum Tenens plan, this was as good as it would get. As he predicted, Marla put off going to school. She'd been living at his place, waiting for classes to start. She was still living at his place, sort of, when she wasn't at Bob's, and she was the chef, or cook as her boss called her, at the infamous Thirteenth Step.

She'd seen the ad, and despite her initial discomfort with the name of the place she'd gone in for an interview. She and Tommy hit it off and he hired her on the spot. How hard could bar food be, he figured. More important that she had the right attitude.

Marla thought she'd work there for six months, maybe a year. It would be good experience. But she was getting a reputation as a chef to watch. The review in the Times referred to her as creative, daring, 'a fresh new face on the local food scene'. She agreed with 'creative', she was less sure about 'daring', unless the very fact she worked at a place like the Step qualified her as such, and as for her face, that was for others to decide. Regardless, she was having fun and learning new things. So although her father was out of the woods she continued to postpone school.

She was making the rounds of the room when her brother walked in. She was also keeping a protective eye on Micky, who was sitting at the bar. It was ladies night, which, considering the local population and Tommy's somewhat warped sense of humor, had evolved into a lesbian free-for-all. The regulars knew Micky and left her alone, except for some playful flirting. The newcomers could be a little more aggressive. Marla saw that Tommy was behind the bar. Micky was safe.

"Hey, G!" she yelled when she saw her brother walk in. She ran over and gave him a hug.

"Micky's at the bar. Tommy's taking care of her."

"Hey, yourself," he answered with a grin.

He made his way through the crowd of mostly familiar faces, exchanging the 'Hi's' and 'How ya doin's' and found an empty stool next to Micky. Empty because Tommy had asked the woman sitting in it to move. He gave her a big kiss and took his seat.

"Thanks, Tommy."

"No problem, Doc." Tommy poured a draft without waiting for him to ask. "Hungry?" he asked, sliding a menu down the bar.

Marla created the food, but Tommy named it, and though many of the menu items remained the same their names changed depending on the occasion and Tommy's mood. Reading the menu was part of the fun. Fish scanned the simple typewritten sheet. It was ladies night, after all, so the three-ounce Kobe beef slider with a profusion of alfalfa sprouts poking out from beneath a whole-wheat bun was the Fer Her Burger. The special cocktail was the Lawnmower, basically a mojito strained into a martini glass with a splash of Crème de Menthe and a maraschino cherry. For those with a sweet tooth there was the Lickety Split, a mini version of the classic banana concoction.

"Jesus, Tommy," he said with a laugh, "you've out-done yourself. A burger would be great. And some of your famous French kiss fries."

While Tommy placed the order he leaned in close to Micky. "Lickety split?" he whispered in her ear. She buried her face in his neck to hide the blush and punched him on the arm.

"Stop that," she said, though there was a distinct lack of conviction in her tone.

Chapter 6

Fish awoke the next morning a few minutes after six. He reached over for Micky but found her side of the bed empty. He lifted his head and heard the sound of the shower running. "Damn," he mumbled, flopping back onto the pillow. He'd been hoping for a little fool around time before she had to leave for work but he'd overslept. He considered a sneak attack in the shower but thought better of it. Not enough time. "Hmm."

He waited a few minutes for his anticipatory erection to subside, then got up, pulled on his sweatpants and T-shirt and shuffled off to the kitchen. The house was a single story structure, two bedrooms, two and a half baths, living room, dining room, study, and kitchen in about three thousand square feet. It wasn't huge but the rooms were good sized and the layout was such that the bedrooms were on opposite sides of the house, so whatever was going on in one was generally not audible to whomever was trying to sleep in the other.

He turned on the coffee machine then went out to fetch the paper. There was a small yard on either side of the walkway leading to the front door planted with a variety of perennials and clumps of festuca. Today the paper was in the part of the yard to the right of the door. The question was never whether or not it might be in the bushes, only which bushes would he have to wade through to get it. The city allowed him to use his sprinklers on Monday, Wednesday, and Friday. Today was Friday. So in addition to the bushwhacking he got the added annoyance of wet slippers and sweatpants.

Back in the kitchen he took a seat at the small table and glanced at the front page of the Times. Something about the president taking on the banking community, something about the housing slump, nothing particularly new or interesting. The Times was your basic liberal news publication and Fish had come to regard what it printed with a bit of skepticism. He didn't expect the editors to be overly supportive of the banks or overly critical of a liberal president. Truth was, he didn't really give that much of a shit. He was more interested in the sports section, the puzzles, and the obituaries.

This latter fascination had been acquired during his convalescence. After falling asleep at the wheel while driving home from a night shift, and rolling his SUV a few times, he'd had a number of months to ponder a number of things. Prominent among them was the idea of mortality. Not just his, though that was big, but the whole notion that life was indeed short and that each of us had a tenuous hold on it, at best. Though he was only thirty-seven years old, actually thirty-eight in a few months, he understood that he was by no means too young to just keel over one day. Heart attack, brain hemorrhage, get hit by a car, the list of possible catastrophes went on and on. The truly amazing thing was that he'd managed to stay alive as long as he had.

The coffee machine sputtered, indicating it had completed its task. Fish got up to pour himself a cup as Micky emerged from the bedroom, dressed for work in a light blue scrub suit, the top adorned with a few printed flowers.

"Hey", he said, pouring a second cup for her. "I missed you this morning." He helped himself to a handful of her butt as he gave her a good-morning hug. Micky was a little over five-foot-seven, a hundred twenty five pounds. She had long legs, small but perfectly shaped breasts, fair skin and honey blond hair. Despite the fact they'd been together nearly two years he found her irresistibly sexy. That she looked a lot like his sister had been a little creepy at first but after doing some introspection he realized his attraction to her was not a case of transference.

"Hmm, I know," she purred. You looked so peaceful I didn't have the heart to wake you up."

She wiggled free and took a seat at the table. He joined her and began flipping through the paper.

"Whoa! Look at this," he said when he got to the obits. He turned the page so she could see it. There was a large photo of a man, maybe in his fifties, and a full page spread.

"Who's that?"

"It's The Un-dead!"

"Who?" she asked, putting her cup down.

"The Un-dead, Mr. Walter, remember, the guy I told you about?"

She thought for a second then understood.

"You mean the old guy you coded a bunch of times yesterday? But you said he was ninety or something. This guy's not even seventy."

"Yeah, it's him. Mr. Leonard Walter. They always use an old picture if it's an old guy. Makes him look better."

Micky gave him a glance indicating it was a little weird that he would know these things. He ignored it.

"Hm. Riegel was right," he said after skimming the article.

"Right about what?"

"About Mr. Walter being a big deal. Self-made jillionaire. Had seven car dealerships. Fords and Toyotas. First guy to 'see the potential of the smaller Japanese cars in the U.S. market'. Invested in real estate. Philathropist. 'Died after a long battle with diabetes and heart disease. Survived by his two daughters, Elaine Baker and Louise Conroy, his son Leonard Walter, Jr., and his adoring grandchildren, blah, blah, blah.'"

"His grandchildren are named Blah Blah Blah?" Micky interrupted with a giggle.

"Very funny. 'Funeral services to be held at St. Mary's church.' Hmm, next Tuesday."

"Why the 'Hmm'? You thinking of going?"

"Probably not a great idea, remember? According to Dr. Riegel the family thinks I'm responsible for bumping him off. I'm surprised they didn't list that as cause of death. 'Died after multiple code blues in the ICU of Saints' Hospital at the hands of the evil Dr. Hooks.'"

"OK, that's just silly," she said getting up from the table and placing her now-empty coffee cup in the sink.

"Yeah, it is. But the case is going to be reviewed at the next Peer Review committee. Sister Dolores put it on the agenda. Riegel said it's just politics. I hate fucking politics."

"I know," she replied with a sympathetic lilt. "It'll be fine. You know it will, and I've got to get going or I'm going to be late."

She gave him a quick kiss good-bye and turned toward the door.

"I've got a Department of Medicine meeting today at noon. I'll stop by the ER."

"K, bye!"

Chapter 7

Shortly after being pronounced dead Mr. Walter's remains were whisked away by the discrete and efficient staff of the Tate and Valentino Mortuary. There he received the full court press he'd earlier been denied by Dr. Hooks. Blood was exchanged for formaldehyde, hair cut and styled, nails buffed, wrinkles injected with collagen, and final makeup meticulously applied. By Sunday morning he looked a good twenty years younger and much more alive than he had three days earlier in the ICU. He was ready for viewing.

The inner circle of the Walter family were first to arrive. Elaine led the way, followed closely by Louise, then Leonard Jr. The grandchildren, five in all ranging in ages from thirty-two to forty-one followed, accompanied by their immediate family members. At a discrete distance behind them was Consuela Sanchez. Known as 'Connie' to the others she had been Mr. Walter's caretaker for almost sixteen years.

It was noon. The funeral home would not be open to the public for another hour. The family was early due to Elaine's insistence that they spend a little quality time with the deceased. It would also give them the opportunity to make sure things had been done 'the way Leonard would have wanted'.

What Leonard wanted was to be cremated and have his ashes scattered in equal parts over his seven car dealerships. When his wife died several years earlier there'd been an elaborate service and solemn burial attended by a who's who of family, friends, employees and those who had in some way either been touched by his largess, or who held hopes that at some point in the future they would be. OK. No big surprise.

But enough was enough. He realized that although some of the mourners had actually known his wife and had been fond of her the vast majority were there primarily to kiss *his* ass. Fine. He understood their point of view. He was rich and it couldn't hurt to show the rich guy some respect. You never know what could happen.

But when it came to his own funeral such a display made no sense. He would by then already be dead. The will would have been written, signed and sealed. No one who hadn't already gotten a piece of the Walter action was going to somehow get one now. So why put everyone through a more-or-less pointless exercise? Why not just give his employees the day off, have a small service for the immediate family, and call it a life?

And, if anyone thought they could favorably impress the surviving family members by making an appearance it only showed how distant their orbit was from the Walter nucleus. His children had grown up wealthy, and as such children often do, they'd shown an impressive lack of self-determination and drive. Each of them had been content to shuffle through life working at one or another of his businesses, making enough to get by and more than they actually deserved, waiting for this very day to arrive.

He had specified in his advanced directive that he wanted a low-key send off. The attorney had made this known to Elaine. She had made it clear to the attorney that Leonard was *her* father and though she appreciated his humility it would be she who determined how his passing would be memorialized.

"Besides," she'd added, "we're Catholics and we insist on a proper Catholic funeral."

It's true that Leonard was, or had been, a Catholic, and a good one, too. But he hadn't taken all the tenets of his faith literally. He went to Church every Sunday because he enjoyed it. The stained glass, the incense, the organ music. It was comforting. But that it might be a sin to eat meat on Friday seemed a bit arbitrary and he was loath to comply. He still confessed his transgression prior to Mass, but when the act was decriminalized by a later, more progressive, Pope, he demanded that his confessor give him credit going forward for the countless Our Father's and Hail Mary's he'd been required to recite as penance.

He held similarly unconventional views about death. If, he figured, the body was merely a vessel for the soul, then once the soul had moved on the body was nothing more than a collection of chemicals in the shape of an ex-person. It required no special handling. Spreading it around the car lots was, in his opinion, just fine. His attorney advised him that there might be a legal problem with disposing human remains in such a manner.

"OK, fine, whatever. Just keep it simple."

Bouquets of flowers and extravagant wreaths had been arriving at Tate and Valentino since news of his death and the site of his penultimate repose had hit the paper. Sympathizers seemed to be in competition with one another and there appeared to be a few different categories in which they could choose to compete.

First was the 'Largest and Clearly Most Expensive' category. The finalists here were Elaine, Louise, and Leonard Jr. Their entry consisted of a three by four foot portrait, in oil paint, of Leonard Sr. in his prime, surrounded by concentric circles of an innumerable number of flower species in shades of white and lavender, smaller flowers in the inner circles becoming increasingly larger toward the periphery. Interspersed with the foliage were 8 x 10-inch head shots of the siblings, the grandchildren, and Amy, the only great grandchild yet to be produced. She had been born out of wedlock to Elaine's only daughter and despite her dubious provenance she had been her great grandfather's pride and joy. The fact that a picture of her father was not available was a deciding factor in Elaine's demand that only direct descendents of Leonard Sr. be allowed on the wreath.

Across the top, written in some sort of green plant material was 'Leonard Walter Sr.' Across the bottom, 'Our Angel, now with God'. Had the thing been mounted on a car it could have been entered in the Rose Parade.

In the 'I Can't Really Afford This But I Can't Afford Not To' category were a dozen or so smaller wreaths submitted by various key employees. Sales managers, head mechanics, property managers, the lawyer, the accountant. They each understood that something special was required, not to improve their position, but, hopefully, to maintain the status quo.

In the 'Most Tasteful' category there were two standouts. One was a small wreath in white, green and a golden yellow with 'Rest in Peace' inscribed at the bottom submitted by the Sisters of Ineffable Sorrow. The other was a simple glass vase filled with white and red roses and a spray of baby's breath. It was from Consuela.

The mortuary was divided into several chapels, most small and intimate. But the one chosen for the Walter wake was the Grand Salon. It was arranged like a normal church with aisles on either side and two rows of pews separated by a central aisle leading to a raised platform in front. The platform was the room's focal point, and in the center of it was the current guest of honor, Mr. Walter, lying in an ornate gilt coffin, surrounded by the steadily growing profusion of vegetation.

The walls of the room were oak paneled and stained a muted reddish brown. There were chandeliers hanging from the twelve-foot ceiling, assorted candelabra, and a bank of votives giving the room a warm and subdued glow. The dark carpet with the subtle paisley design absorbed much of the sound.

Having surveyed the room and approved the layout it was time for the viewing. The family slowly made its way to the platform, climbed the two steps, and gathered around the head of the coffin. With an almost theatrical flair the funeral director raised the lid.

There was a gasp, a muted whistle, a 'Wow', a 'Holy Shit', and a sob, this from the caretaker.

"He's perfect," Elaine finally declared.

Mr. Walter would likely have disagreed.

Chapter 8

Saints' Hospital was located in the middle of the San Gabriel Valley, about twenty miles from downtown Los Angeles. It was a middle class, blue-collar neighborhood, and though it had its share of low-life's it was by and large not a bad place to live. Most of the people had jobs, many owned homes, and, most importantly as far as Sister Dolores was concerned, the majority had some kind of health insurance.

It was this demographic that had allowed the Sisters of Ineffable Sorrow to carry out their mission of mercy with such success. The many with insurance provided the revenue to pay for the care of the few without.

The hospital was not a full service facility. There was no pediatric ward, no psych unit, no open-heart or neuro-surgery. No bells, no whistles. It was the kind of place that dedicated itself to taking care of the common medical and surgical problems that common people commonly came down with. Diabetes, pneumonia, heart failure, appendicitis, gall bladder problems, kidney disease, broken bones, not to mention delivering babies. There was plenty to do without cracking someone's chest open or removing the top of his skull, and the staff at Saints' did it well.

Plus, there was the Emergency Room. This was Saints' portal to the community. An eight-bed oasis of healthcare, open twenty-four/seven, available to anyone who chose to come. It was the essential expression of Christian charity.

"It's killing us."

Timothy Doyle, COO, was trying to give Sister Mary Elizabeth Dolores a crash course in medical economics.

"Things are not the same as they were fifteen, twenty years ago," he continued. "The population has changed, the kind of insurance they have has changed. We have these managed care HMO plans that barely pay us enough to cover costs. Medicare payments are getting denied more often. Then there's Medicaid—total joke, and the truly uninsured. The state used to give us some money to cover them but that's gone now. Are you seeing where this is going, Sister?"

She stared at him, stony-faced, as the skin of her neck, as much of it as you could see peeking out of her habit, began to change colors. It had been a pasty white when the conversation started. It was now pink. By the time she was able to formulate a response it had become a definite red, and the redness had spread almost to her eyelids.

"Listen to me, Doyle," she growled, "I've been running this hospital for over twenty years. I know how it works. I understand the math."

She paused for a moment, then leaned forward. There was a desk between them. The COO was beginning to appreciate how helpful that might be.

"I don't need some TWERP LIKE YOU TELLING ME HOW TO RUN A HOSPITAL! YOU SEE WHERE *THIS* IS GOING?" She was now shaking her right fist and was nearly half way across the desk.

"Sister Dolores, PLEASE," he implored, shrinking back in his chair. "We need to consider every option."

"Well consider it considered. We're NOT closing the ER. Now get out of here and think of something smart we can do. For a change."

Truth was, closing the ER wasn't a particularly stupid idea, from a business perspective. As much as the ER was the hospital's portal to the community, it was the community's portal to the hospital. Anyone who walked in seeking care was entitled to receive that care until they were 'stabilized'. No financial questions asked. That was the law. And the definition of 'stable' was intentionally vague.

So a patient with abdominal pain couldn't be declared 'stable' until you were reasonably certain there was no surgical emergency. This meant a physical exam, lab tests, IV fluids, medicines, and probably a CAT scan of his abdomen before you could even ask to see an insurance card, if there was one to see.

Same thing, only worse, with a chest pain patient. If there is even an inkling the pain could be heart-related the patient would need at least twenty-four hours of observation, multiple blood tests, repeated EKG's, and finally a cardiac stress test before being declared 'stable for discharge'.

And patients are more mobile than they used to be. If they live close to Memorial, the big trauma center in the dodgy part of town, and go there with their belly ache only to find it's going to be a four-hour wait to see the doctor, they'll simply drive down the road to Saints', where the wait is almost guaranteed to be much shorter. Being in a nice neighborhood no longer protected you from the unwashed masses.

The only way to avoid having unwanted guests was to close the doors. This is exactly what over two dozen hospitals in California over the past ten years have done, a large percentage of them in the greater LA area. What Timothy Doyle, COO, was suggesting was hardly novel. It was just the last thing Sister Dolores wanted to hear.

She waited a full ten minutes before picking up the phone. It took that long for the blood to drain out of her head and her blood pressure to drop below Def-Con 3. She dialed the number and got an answer after the first ring.

"Hello?"

"Bill?"

"Sister Dolores?"

"Yeah. Yeah, yeah, good to hear your voice, too. Got a minute? (Pause.) The meeting doesn't start for almost half an hour. (Pause.) Yeah, it's important. My office. Five minutes? Fine."

Getting summoned to the principal's office wasn't Dr. Riegel's idea of a good time.

"I hope this isn't about that Walter guy," he muttered as he locked his office door behind him.

Chapter 9

The meeting with Sister Dolores proved to be every bit as unpleasant as he'd feared. She talked, he listened. Fifteen minutes later he walked out with his head spinning. He sat through the Department of Medicine meeting paying almost no attention to the proceedings. Fortunately Fish was there, sitting next to him, and was able to provide whatever information was needed for the agenda items involving the ER.

"You OK?" he whispered half way through the meeting. His boss had been acting more strangely than usual since their cryptic conversation the previous day about The Un-dead. He was getting genuinely concerned.

"Huh?"

"You all right? You don't look so good."

"I'm fine. We need to talk. I'll tell you about it when this is over."

When the meeting ended, finally, Dr. Riegel pulled his young colleague aside.

"Got a call from Sister Dolores this morning."

Fish waited patiently.

"And you know what she told me?"

Of course he didn't, but saying so was unnecessary.

"She told me a lot."

Fish was certain she had.

"We need to discuss it."

Ah, he thought, we're getting closer.

"When I'm done, later this afternoon. How about 5:30. I'll meet you at the Step. OK?"

Ever since Marla took over the kitchen the Thirteenth Step had become the unofficial office away from the office for the ER staff. Dr. Riegel appreciated the sensibility of the place, or rather the lack of it. Like Tommy he had no patience for mincing words or political correctness. Bob Graber was there whenever he got the chance so he could spend some time with Marla. Micky and Marla were practically best friends and de-facto roommates. It just made sense that the Step was the place to be.

At 5:30 sharp Fish walked through the doors. It took a few seconds for his eyes to adjust to the low light of the room. As they did the door opened behind him and Dr. Riegel stepped in. He was a stickler for punctuality.

"Lateness is a sign of a weak character, or arrogance, or disorganization, or just being a fuck-up," he once told his doctors during a staff meeting when one of them walked in ten minutes after the scheduled time. "And I don't want to work with somebody who's a fuck-up. Understand?"

They did.

Tommy saw them from behind the bar.

"Hey it's Fish and the Kingfish!" he said loudly. He'd given Dr. Riegel the title the first time they'd met and he learned that he was Dr. Hooks' boss. "Let me buy you boys a beer," he added, doing his best impression of George 'Kingfish' Stevens.

"Thanks, Tommy," they answered in unison. They took a table near the small stage. It was Friday, so there would be live music, but it wouldn't start for a few hours. Tommy brought the beers and a small bowl of pretzels.

"Want me to tell Marla you're here?" he asked as he set the glasses down.

"No, that's OK. We have some business to talk about. I'll pop my head into the kitchen later."

"Cool," Tommy replied. "I'll leave you alone."

They each took a gulp from their glasses. Fish spoke first.

"OK, so what's the big deal, what's the big mystery?"

Dr. Riegel stared at him for a moment.

"Remember when I told you about the financial problems the hospital is having?" he began. Fish nodded. "And about how there may be things on the table that we never thought would be?" Fish nodded again.

"OK. So here it is."

Dr Riegel then went into detail about his one-sided conversation with Sister Dolores. Fish sat with his eyes wide and jaw slack. When his boss was done he continued to stare while his brain processed the information it had just uploaded.

"So when Doyle suggested closing the ER to keep the place from going bankrupt what did she say?" he asked finally.

"She told him to fuck off. Well, probably not 'fuck off' exactly, but whatever the Sister Dolores version of 'fuck off' is."

Fish sat back in his chair and crunched on a pretzel, obviously relieved.

"Don't let that make you feel better," Dr. Riegel warned.

"What do you mean? She told him to fuck off, or whatever. We're safe. Right?"

"We're safe for now, but this isn't over. Sister Dolores is committed to the ER. It's important to the work she's trying to do, you know, care for the sick, the poor. But it's getting harder to do. There's no money in taking care of sick people."

Dr. Riegel let that sit out there for a minute, as though it was just a matter of time before Fish would understand what he was saying.

"Huh?" Fish grunted, when he realized there was no further explanation on the way.

"Look. People don't want to pay for the kind of healthcare they actually need. They think it should be free, because they need it. Like air. How can you charge someone for air when everybody has to breathe? But they have no problem digging into their pockets to find their last dime to pay for healthcare they don't need. Stuff they just want. Like plastic surgery. The same gal who'll gladly put down twenty grand for a boob job will pitch a fit when you ask her for the fifty-dollar co-pay for her ER visit after she wrapped her Mercedes around a telephone pole because she was too busy talking on the phone to see where she was going. You following me so far?"

Fish was, in fact, following him. He nodded to indicate as much.

"Good. That's why a lot of doctors are moving out of their area of expertise, or 'expanding the scope of their practice', more likely how they'd describe it, to do more of the things they can actually get paid for. You know, like gynecologists giving Botox injections, Ear-Nose-and-Throat guys doing cosmetic eyelid surgery. "Who needs to be up all hours of the day and night delivering babies when you can do 9 to 5 in the health spa, cash on the barrel head? It's kind of a shame, but bullshit pays, taking care of the gardener who ran his foot over with the lawnmower doesn't."

"So-o-o?" Fish asked tentatively. He wanted to know more but was afraid of what he might hear.

"So," the director said, taking a long swig from his beer glass, "this guy Doyle was hired to increase revenue and he's not going to do that by bringing in ten more homeless, uninsured patients a day through the ER. Sister Dolores told him to find some paying customers, recruit new doctors to the staff, guys with that kind of patient base."

"Like who," Fish asked, genuinely curious.

"Good question. I don't know. I'm glad it's not my job."

"Fish drank the last of his beer. "And what happens if he can't find these guys?"

The director sighed. "I've known Sister Dolores for a long time. She's one hundred percent behind the ER. But, she's one hundred and fifty percent behind the hospital. If Doyle strikes out with his recruitment campaign, comes up empty, and we're getting close to the buzzer, down by five points, he's gonna go for the Hail Mary."

Fish motioned to Tommy behind the bar. The conversation had just moved into two-beer territory. He waited for the refill before speaking.

"Huh?"

Tommy had wisely brought two beers to the table. The director took a gulp, then set his glass down and leaned toward Fish.

"He'll take another shot at the ER. He'll tell Sister Dolores that something's gonna have to happen or the hospital's going belly up. She's smart. She doesn't need him to tell her what she already knows. She'll fight it, but if it's a choice between losing the ER or going down with the ship I think you and me'll be heading for the lifeboats."

Dr. Riegel drained his glass, placed a ten-dollar bill on the table, and stood. "Gotta run. The wife's cooking dinner. If I'm late none of this is gonna matter 'cause she'll kill me. When are you back at the hospital?"

"I'm relieving you on Monday."

The director still worked shifts. Actually, half-shifts. Once, maybe twice a week. He'd start at seven AM and get someone to come in at one in the afternoon to do the second half. Twelve-hour days were more than he had the patience for, and though he was still a first-rate clinician the nurses were happy to see him go because by around 12:30 he'd start getting a little grouchy.

"Great, see you then. Have a good weekend. Thanks, Tommy," he said as he walked past the bar and out the door.

"See ya', doc."

Fish sat at the table for a while longer, sipping his beer and mulling over what the boss had said. He couldn't imagine Sister Dolores closing the ER but he agreed that if closing it would allow her to keep the rest of the hospital open, she just might do it. He also thought about his 'good weekend'. He'd stopped to visit with Micky before leaving the hospital. She reminded him that it was her weekend to work and that she'd be staying at her place the next couple of nights. The missed opportunity earlier that morning, oversleeping, now assumed serious proportions.

One of the problems with 'going steady' was the lack of a bullpen. When the starting pitcher was out of the lineup you were out of luck. (Jesus, he thought, I'm starting to sound like Riegel.) Having never had a real steady girlfriend before Micky he'd never been in this predicament. He thought about it some more and realized he wasn't really interested in a 'reliever'. "Hmm," he said.

He stood and put his own ten dollars on top of the director's. They almost always paid for the 'free' beers. Tommy was generous. They didn't want to take advantage. Plus, they'd developed a sort of proprietary interest in the place and didn't want to damage the bottom line. He walked toward the kitchen. A visit with Marla, and maybe a free burger, seemed like a good idea.

Chapter 10

It wasn't a great day for surfing but the way Fish saw it even mediocre surfing was great compared to most other things he could be doing. He sat on his board staring out toward the horizon, ostensibly waiting for the next set of waves to roll in. But in fact it was more of a meditation. The smell of the sea, the gentle bobbing of the surfboard, the white noise of the surf breaking behind him, had always had a mesmerizing effect. It cleared his head. Gave his thoughts a chance to ebb and flow, to rearrange themselves in ways his conscious mind may not have considered. It was like dreaming in a way but without the fantasy and symbolism that made dreams interesting, or frightening, and mostly just confusing.

It was early Saturday morning. On even an average surf day he would have been surrounded by other surfers and wanna-be's, jostling for position, competing for every wave, trying to intimidate one another. It could get tense at times. Fortunately, conditions were practically flat and most people had chosen to sleep in. The few in the water with him were mainly people he knew by name or by face and they left him alone.

His thoughts drifted from his conversation with the director, to his relationship with Micky, and to the idea of what, actually, was he doing with his life. Only a year earlier he'd decided to let it all go. Well, not all of it but he'd come to the decision that the job part of it was expendable. He'd become tired of the politics and the demands made on him by an increasingly hostile work environment.

The patients were becoming angrier and less appreciative, the administrators were referring to patients as 'customers', the other members of the medical staff were taking themselves off the ER back-up panel in droves making specialty consultations increasingly difficult to obtain, and the government was wading into the middle of it all flailing wildly in an attempt to legislate uniform healthcare for everyone but in fact making the entire situation worse. And, as always, the lawyers were sitting on the sidelines waiting to capitalize on the misfortunes of others.

A year ago he would have cheered the news that Sister Dolores was thinking of closing the Emergency Room. What, he wondered, had changed? There was his father's heart attack, sure. That's what caused his rebel fantasy to come crashing to the earth before it had even gotten launched. But that was a year ago. His father was fine now.

Was it the money? Had he gotten used to the regular paycheck, the director's stipend, money earned by going to meetings, fielding patient complaints, being on-call? Money, he thought now, earned doing the very things he once hated doing most? Or had he changed in some fundamental and subtle way. Had he come to actually enjoy doing these things and was merely reluctant to admit it to himself?

And what about Micky? He'd been seeing her for almost two years and though she'd never brought up 'the future' he was certain that at some point that conversation was going to be had. What about the future? Until Micky he'd never thought about having a steady girlfriend. He realized that now he was going to have to deal with the idea of a wife. And kids. Well, maybe not now, but eventually. Probably sooner than later. "Holy shit!" he said out loud.

"Hey, Fish! Wake up!" The shout stirred him from his hypnosis. It came from a guy he knew from the beach named Dale who'd paddled up on his right. "This is as good as it's going to get this morning. Let's go."

What Dale was referring to was an actual set of waves bearing down on them, two, maybe three feet tall. Fish barely had time to react. He got his board turned around and began paddling. The first wave of the set was already by him before he got up to speed, but the second lifted his board. He stood, and all those other thoughts were immediately dismissed. He was surfing. Nothing else mattered in that moment.

He spent the rest of the morning hanging out with Dale, catching a few decent rides, exchanging small talk. By noon he was tired and the tide was beginning to recycle. It was time to quit for the day. He had no plans for the evening, which suited him fine. Micky would be working on Sunday but he knew she had the next few days off. He was fairly certain he'd be able to talk her into spending Sunday night at his place. One of the advantages of having Marla share his house was her teaching him how to cook. He was getting good at it, in a limited menu kind of way. He'd spend part of the afternoon putting together a meal he knew Micky'd be unable to resist. He just hoped she wouldn't be too tired for dessert.

Chapter 11

Five days after the final code blue and two days after being put on display the lid was closed on Mr. Walter's coffin. It was time for the grand finale. The wreaths and bouquets had already been transported to Saint Mary's church where they filled the altar and cascaded down the side aisles almost half way to the doors. The mourners were filing in, the pews were filling up, and it looked as though Leo's funeral would be a standing-room-only event.

Back at Tate and Valentino the family members were being assigned to various limousines lined up behind the hearse into which Mr. Walter had already been deposited. In the first car were the children, Elaine, Louise, and Leonard Jr., accompanied by their spouses. The next two cars contained the grandchildren, their spouses and Amy. Two additional limos followed carrying assorted cousins and more distant relatives. There had been no room for Consuela and her family who were left to drive to the church themselves.

When everyone was properly situated the caravan began the five-mile trip to Saint Mary's. Elaine, with the help of John Wright, the family attorney, had arranged for a police escort. Traffic was stopped, red lights were run. Mr. Walter and his entourage had clear sailing.

There was little conversation in the first limo. Thoughts were doubtless on the life, and death, of their father. Thoughts were also doubtless on their father's money. Mr. Walter had not been a profligate man. His children got what they needed but had not been overindulged. He had hoped this would foster in them a sense of self-determination. It hadn't.

His daughters knew their father would not allow them to starve or go homeless, so when it came time to choose husbands they opted for looks over either brains or ambition. Neither Roy Baker nor Larry

Conroy was much in the mover or shaker departments, but each was handsome and affable. Both had been given jobs by Mr. Walter shortly after announcing their engagements.

Things had been slightly more difficult for Leonard Jr. His father insisted that he graduate college. It was an experience that he himself had been denied and he wanted his son to be an educated man. Leonard Jr. managed to put together enough credits in a sufficient number of related courses to earn a bachelor's degree in sociology from the local state college. It wasn't exactly what Leonard Sr. had had in mind. He'd hoped his son would get a degree in business, or economics. Or that he would discover a love of knowledge and pursue a graduate degree, maybe in law, or accounting, or that he'd get an MBA. Something, anything useful. But he was forced to admit that his son had complied with the letter of the law, and upon graduation Leonard Jr. was added to the payroll.

Things were a bit livelier in the second and third cars. The grandchildren felt no particular compunction to maintain a degree of solemnity or decorum. Like their parents they had done little with their lives, and given their genetics it wasn't clear how much they would have been able to accomplish had they tried. The death of Grandpa was, they believed, the beginning of new and very comfortable lives for each of them. Though they hadn't seen the will, and really had no good idea of the size of the estate, they passed the time speculating how much was there, and how much each was likely to receive.

The exceptions were Lauren, Elaine's daughter, and Amy, Lauren's daughter. Both sat quietly, each absorbed in her own thoughts, oblivious to the chatter around them. Lauren was thirty-two, the youngest of the grandchildren, conceived by accident a bit late in her mother's life. She'd been a free spirit as a child, with a vivid imagination and an irrepressible curiosity about the world around her.

Unlike her older brother and her cousins she could barely wait to get to college, and when the time finally arrived she opted for the University of California campus in Santa Cruz. The college was tucked away in the northern California redwoods, between the Santa Cruz Mountains and the ocean. It was an idyllic setting and lent itself to flights of fancy. Still, it enjoyed a solid academic reputation skewed though the curriculum might have been toward the most liberal of the liberal arts.

It was perfect for Lauren who spent her time there studying poetry, dance, and wine appreciation. She became interested in wine the day after she recovered from her first hangover. She'd spent a long night partying with friends drinking what was advertised to be wine but was, she was convinced, some sort of toxic mixture of bad grape juice, grain alcohol, and red dye numbers 3 and 5. Rather than being put off by the experience she instead committed herself to learning everything she could about the 'enemy' in order to forever be its master.

She rarely came home during those years, and not at all during her final semester. So, when her parents arrived for her graduation they were mortified to discover she was six months pregnant. More appalling still was Lauren's refusal to name the father. Her parents brought her home that same weekend.

When news of the pregnancy was eventually divulged, as was inevitable, the rest of the Walter family was properly outraged and humiliated. All except Lauren, who was eagerly awaiting the birth of her child and motherhood, and Leonard Sr. He'd wanted a great-grandchild before he died and he was delighted that the person to give him one was Lauren. That there wasn't a father attached seemed to him a minor distraction, considering the qualifications of the other potential sires in his clan.

Amy was now ten. She was fiercely independent, with her mother's wild streak, her grandfather's determination, and something else, a ferocious intelligence that put her at the top of her class and above the slights and condescension shown her by the rest of her relatives as punishment for the circumstances of her birth. She truly could not have cared less about their opinions, of her, or of anything else for that matter.

When the convoy finally arrived at the church the women were escorted to their places in the front two pews. The men donned white gloves and took their places on either side of the coffin. Mr. Walter weighed in at about a hundred and sixty pounds. The coffin, though, added almost two hundred more, built as it was to outlast the pyramids. The pallbearers bravely hauled the load up the twenty granite steps where it could then be placed on the rolling platform for its trip toward the altar.

Elaine had insisted on a high mass, complete with sermon, communion, organ music, and live vocals, in addition to the actual funeral service. In all it lasted close to an hour and a half. Midway through Amy thought she heard a noise coming from the casket. She leaned toward her mother and told her so.

"It's probably your great-grandfather doing somersaults," was Lauren's reply.

Eventually the words ended, the funeral was over, and Leonard Walter Sr., was rolled back down the aisle accompanied by a familiar dirge from the pipe organ. The pallbearers performed their task once again, this time down the stairs, and the coffin was reinserted into the hearse. From here on in it would be strictly a family affair.

The limousines followed the hearse to Majestic Acres, again accompanied by a phalanx of motorcycle cops, to a choice spot near the top of the hill with a commanding view of the valley and the San Gabriel Mountains beyond. A few more prayers were intoned, the casket was lowered into the ground, dirt was tossed onto it by each of the family members, and Leonard was laid to rest alongside his wife. It was pretty much exactly the scenario he'd tried to avoid.

Chapter 12

While Mr. Walter was getting the funeral he didn't want Dr. Hooks was dealing with the patient he couldn't move. About and hour into his shift the paramedics dropped off a man who'd been injured at a construction site. The injury involved a skill saw and the index, middle, and ring fingers of his left hand. There were several problems, including damage to two flexor tendons, multiple jagged lacerations, and a fracture of the tip of the index finger. Fish had anesthetized and cleaned the wounds, ordered the appropriate x-rays, applied clean dressings to the hand, and administered a tetanus shot and a dose of intravenous antibiotics.

That's all he was qualified to do. Flexor tendons have a tendency to heal poorly and no sensible ER doctor would attempt to repair one. The patient needed a hand surgeon. Unfortunately the patient, Mr. Ruiz, was a day laborer, working off the books, not covered by his employer's work-comp policy. He had a Medi-Cal card, California's version of Medicaid, but the one hand surgeon on staff at Saints' Hospital didn't take Medi-Cal patients. In fact, he didn't take call for the ER at all.

In an effort to make emergency care available to everyone the federal government had passed legislation mandating, among other things, that a hospital with the ability to provide a certain type of specialty service, like hand surgery, must make that service available to everyone. This means that a patient with a hand injury at Holy Smokes hospital down the road with no surgeon available can be sent to Saints' ER to be seen by the hand surgeon on call for Saints'.

So, the person doing the right thing by taking ER call to support his hospital and the local community was now expected to be on call for the entire San Gabriel Valley. It took about five minutes for the hand surgeons, plastic surgeons and orthopedists to realize what was going to happen. Then they resigned from the call panel. They were no longer obligated to respond. Not just at Saints', but at every small to medium-large hospital in the area.

Now, instead of being able to pick up the phone, make one call, and get the patient the care he needed, Dr. Hooks had to play a game of dialing-for-doctors. He started with his own hand surgeon, who politely declined. He called Memorial, the local trauma center. They were too busy and had no available operating rooms. So they said. He called the County transfer line. They said Saints' had a hand surgeon on staff and that he should take the case. Fish explained that the hand surgeon was not on ER back-up. And around it went. For hours. Meanwhile the ER got bogged down, the waiting room filled up, and everyone got frustrated.

"Fish, what the fuck?" Dr. Riegel had the day off but had come in to do some administrative work. It was a Tuesday afternoon. The ER should not have been this big a mess. Especially with his associate director working. Dr. Hooks explained the situation.

"Did you call administration?" the director asked.

"Why, you think Sister Dolores can do the surgery?" was the sarcastic response.

The director just shook his head and walked to the nurses' station. He picked up a phone and called his boss. After a brief conversation he found his associate. "She's working on it. She'll call you back." Then he walked back to his office.

The patient had already been sitting in the ER for over seven hours. In general, the sooner injuries like Mr. Ruiz's get definitive treatment the better the result. But there was nothing Dr. Hooks could do to expedite the matter. Hopefully, either the County would eventually call back and accept the transfer or Sister Dolores would perform some kind of minor miracle.

Fish couldn't just call an ambulance and send Mr. Ruiz to Memorial, where he'd eventually get the surgery he needed. Not without making a formal transfer request and getting the OK from the surgeon there. Even though it would be in the patient's best interest. And though Memorial did have a hand surgeon on call for their ER, and therefore was obligated to help, they had played the one card they had to avoid the transfer—they had no open operating rooms. Allegedly.

The only other option was to explain to the patient that he should sign himself out of the ER 'against medical advice' and take himself to Memorial or the county hospital. Once there they'd have to deal with him. The problem, though, was that the county transfer people already knew about Mr. Ruiz, and if he suddenly appeared unannounced at another hospital they would immediately suspect Dr. Hooks of pulling a fast one. Questions would be asked, in English and Spanish. Mr. Ruiz, already a little unnerved by the entire experience, would likely crack. He didn't need the county to start poking into his immigration status, after all. He would admit that the good and kindly Dr. Hooks had done the only thing he could to help him.

The good and kindly Dr. Hooks would then get sued by the federal government for a violation of EMTALA, the federal patient transfer law. He would need a lawyer, which his malpractice carrier would not provide, because his policy, or rather the one purchased by Dr. Riegel to cover all the ER doctors, specifically excluded from coverage violations of federal patient transfer laws. He would face a fifty thousand dollar fine, which would also come out of his pocket, plus a possible investigation by the state medical board.

Then, because the hospital would get sued as well, he would get dragged in front of half a dozen committees wanting to know what the hell he was thinking. The hospital could be removed from the list of hospitals approved to treat Medicare patients, a group of seniors most hospitals could not survive without. And though that would likely not happen for a first offense, the expense and bad publicity would be sufficient for Sister Dolores to consider asking Dr. Riegel to ask Dr. Hooks to find another place to work.

"No fucking way," Fish mumbled when his charge nurse suggested the maneuver.

Forty-five minutes after the director spoke to Sister Dolores, she called down to the ER. "Get Dr. Hooks," was her greeting. Fish got on the phone with the usual trepidation he experienced whenever he had to deal with her directly.

"OK, listen," she said, not wasting any time. "Benson, our hand guy, is gonna take the case. I had to promise to pay him Medicare rates plus guarantee him priority scheduling for his surgical cases for the next two weeks. Try to do a better job getting these cases transferred, OK? Before we go broke?" Click.

Fish stared at the phone for a minute. "How did *I* become the bad guy?" he asked rhetorically as he handed it back to the clerk.

Chapter 13

"John? Yes, hello, it's Elaine Baker."

The lawyer had been expecting the call. Not because it had been scheduled but because it was a week since the funeral and Leonard's will had not yet been made public.

"Elaine! What a nice surprise. Yes, the memorial service was lovely. I'm sure Mr. Walter is smiling in heaven."

John Wright saw no point in reminding her that her father wanted no fuss, no muss.

"It's been almost a week since the memorial," Elaine continued, "and I think the family has done a remarkable job of healing itself after our terrible loss. I think it's time that we turn our attention to some important business."

He remained silent for a moment, amused at how transparent his client's daughter could be. "What sort of business are you referring to?" he finally replied.

"Why, the will, of course! There are businesses to be run, serious financial decisions to be made. We need to know what my father's wishes are, or were, so that we can carry on where he left off."

"Oh, yes. Of course. I was going to call you about that this afternoon," he lied. He'd been instructed by Leonard to let them squirm.

The old man had done a lot for his children over the course of his long life. He'd gotten little return on his investment. If there was any chance of being able to look down from above after he died, Leonard thought, he wanted the view to be as entertaining as possible.

"When I'm dead, and after they give me some kind of carnival of a funeral, which you know they will regardless of what I have to say about it, they're going to want to get at the money. Make 'em wait," he'd instructed.

"So," Elaine said, a more relaxed tone in her voice now, "when do you think we can get a reading and begin probate?"

"How about Tuesday, two weeks from tomorrow? It will give me time to notify the heirs. Your father was very specific about how he wanted this done. He wanted all the heirs to be present. I think it is only right that we respect his last wish."

It was Elaine's turn to be silent. Waiting another two weeks wasn't exactly what she had in mind, but saying so, she knew, would be unseemly, even by her standards.

"That will be fine, John. I'll wait to hear from you about the time and place."

The call ended and John Wright sat back in his chair, remembering that meeting with Leonard. He'd been a little surprised by his client's insistence that he 'let 'em squirm'. He'd underestimated the degree to which his client had been disappointed in his children. Nevertheless, he'd drawn up the will and knew that despite all that Leonard had left them in very good shape. That's why he was more than a little surprised when at the end of the meeting the old man handed him a sealed manila envelope.

"What's this?" he'd asked.

"It's my will."

Mr. Wright stared at the envelope, a look of bewilderment on his face. "But..."

"Yeah, yeah," Leonard said, cutting him off. "I already have a will, the one you drew up. I made a few alterations. Old one's no good now. I had a guy at Shaeffer-Deutsch write it up. Didn't want you to know about it in case the family starts trying to get details before the formal reading. You know, 'plausible deniability'."

"Uh..." Mr. Wright began, but didn't know what to say and just left it hanging there.

"Look, John, here's a list of everybody getting a piece of my estate," he said, handing him a separate sheet of paper. "I want each and every one of them here for a formal reading. You're still my executor. This stays sealed until the reading. Whatever's in here is as big a mystery to you as it is to them. Better that way."

The lawyer looked at the list of names. Everyone was still there. He switched his gaze to his client's face, searching for something that might add a little clarity to the situation. Nothing. He opened his mouth but before he could say anything the old man raised his hand.

"Nothing else to discuss." Leonard then grabbed and shook the limp hand of his confused attorney, turned, and walked out of the office.

Chapter 14

Peer Review Committee met monthly, on the fourth Wednesday, at noon. Lunch was provided. The members were a collection of physicians, all prominent members of the medical staff, one from each of the medical specialties practiced at Saints'. Plus Sister Dolores. As chairman of the governing board she was a non-voting member of all medical staff committees.

The first ten minutes were devoted to filling plates and eating. Dr. Riegel surveyed the entrees. Chicken and fish. You would expect a hospital cafeteria to be committed to healthy dining. But the chicken was chicken Cordon Bleu, a healthy chicken breast stuffed with ham and cheese, breaded, then deep-fried. The fish was a filet of indeterminate species, similarly breaded and fried. Dr. Riegel was amazed that the chef hadn't found a way to roll it around a clump of shrimp mousse. No matter, because either selection was guaranteed to shorten you life span by several days.

As he pondered his options he wondered how a hospital, of all places, could be so oblivious to the fundamentals of nutrition. He wasn't sufficiently paranoid to believe the kitchen was trying to increase business by fostering heart disease, but the thought had nevertheless crossed his mind on more than one occasion. Fortunately there was a salad bar. As he filled his plate he noticed Sister Dolores having her own difficulties. She looked from one choice to the other, hesitated for a moment, and took one of each.

He waited for her to find a seat, then placed his salad in front of the one to her immediate left. She shot a withering glance at his plate.

"You on a diet or something?"

"Who, me? Nah. I had a couple of donuts a little while ago, wrecked my appetite." Telling the truth and criticizing the cafeteria, he knew, would only make her crankier than she already was.

The meeting was eventually called to order. The chairman, an older general surgeon named Carter, who was also the current Chief of Staff, began ticking off the agenda items. Previous minutes were approved, old business was addressed. This consisted in large part of cases that had been dragging on for months. Doctors being reviewed for dubious therapeutic choices, overutilization of services, keeping patients in the hospital too long, (meaning any number of days longer than Medicare would pay for, regardless of medical necessity), and bad behavior, like yelling at a nurse or throwing an instrument in the operating room.

In each case a letter had been sent to the physician under review asking for an explanation. Eventually a response had been provided and often it was of the sort that took great umbrage with the committee's obvious lack of accurate information and its alarming malice. This would generate another letter. The more egregious the malfeasance the more voluminous the correspondence. Eventually an understanding would be achieved, the offending physician would agree to amend his ways, and the case would be closed. Rarely was the offense such that it would warrant a restriction of privileges.

Finally it was time for new business. There was a single case for review and it involved the care, or lack of it, rendered to one Leonard Walter by the ER doctor, Gilbert Hooks, known to the committee members as physician 9027. Anonymity was important in meetings such as these.

"So, Bill, you want to tell me what this is all about?" the chairman asked the ER director.

"Sure. It's noth...."

"It's about Dr. Hooks telling the ICU nurse taking care of Mr. Walter, who happened to be one the biggest donors to our foundation, that he needed to be dead and that he wasn't going to try to resuscitate him," Sister Dolores said, cutting him off.

"Excuse me?" the chairman replied, taken aback by the outburst but more so by the naming of the doctor under review.

"You heard me. The family is terribly upset. We need to do something about this. We owe them an apology," Sister Dolores said, wiping greasy breadcrumbs from the corner of her mouth. She had attended the funeral the previous day and had gotten an earful from Elaine as she tried to offer her condolences. Sister Dolores enjoyed dishing it out but was less enthusiastic about taking it.

"Dr. Riegel?"

"With all due respect to Sister Dolores," he began, "this is a non-issue. This guy Walter was old, really old, and sick. He coded three times that day. Physician 9027, who happens to be Dr. Hooks, as Sister Dolores pointed out, responded to all three codes. Fish is a damn good doctor. Saved the guy's life twice. Intubated him the first time, put him on a ton of meds the second time. Kept him going all day, gave the family a chance to get used to the idea that he was dying. Finally he codes a third time. He's on maximum doses of pressors, he's already on a vent, and he goes into PEA. His nurse had given him an amp of epinephrine before Fish got there. He's got no pulse, he's not breathing on his own. The nurse is expecting the full court press. Fish explains to her that it's not going to work and the best plan is to just pass the ball around for a few minutes until the clock runs out. He goes out to prepare the family, then goes back into the ICU and it's game over."

The chairman took a moment to digest what he'd heard. "Anyone here have a problem with the way this case was managed?"

There was a low rumble from the members, the tone of which suggested that they did not.

"Well *I've* got a problem with it!" Sister Dolores shouted, a few small bits of food escorting her words. "I'm trying to keep this place going and I've got doctors with the sensitivity of sand paper! I spend all day coddling this family, trying to show them how important Mr. Walter is to us, and then Hooks blurts out that he needs to be dead! Do you people have any idea what kind of shape this hospital would be in without donations to the foundation? Carter, you're on the board, you know the financial problems we're having."

"Yes, Sister, I do. Tell me something. Did Dr. Hooks tell the family that Mr. Walter needed to be dead?"

She waited a moment before responding. "No. He told the nurse, and everybody else in the ICU who wasn't deaf."

"I see. Then how did the family hear it?"

"I don't know," she said with a huff, crossing her arms over her chest.

Dr. Riegel had been biting his tongue, trying to let the chairman work things out, but the feigned ignorance was too much.

"Oh please!" he said, a little louder than necessary. "You do too. You told me yourself the nurse blabbed it to the family. She knows them from church."

"Yeah? Maybe so, but if Hooks hadn't said it in the first place she couldn't have blabbed it."

"Oh, Jesus," the director mumbled under his breath.

"Watch it," Sister Dolores warned him.

"Sorry."

"OK," the chairman said, trying to take back control of the meeting. "What do we want to do here? Any suggestions?"

"I think we need to send Dr. Hooks somewhere for some sensitivity training," Sister Dolores suggested.

Dr. Riegel grabbed his forehead. "No. That's not going to happen. This is a hospital. It's not Mr. Rogers' Neighborhood."

"I agree, I think," the chairman said. "How about we send Dr. Hooks a letter?"

"And tell him what, that he needs to keep his fat mouth shut?" Sister Dolores asked.

"C'mon. Enough." The director knew it was time to get this over with.

"We're not sending Fish anywhere and we're not putting a negative letter in his permanent file. We all know, and that includes you, Sister, that his care of Mr. Walter was appropriate. What was *not* appropriate was the nurse shooting *her* mouth off and the family's insistence on making the guy a full code in the first place. Sheldon should have had the guts to say 'NO', to you and the family, and let Mr. Walter die in peace with a little dignity.

"So what we're gonna do is this; I'll talk to Fish and tell him to be a little more professional in the way he addresses the nurses. You, (turning toward Sister Dolores), will speak to the director of nursing and have her educate her staff about what they should and shouldn't be telling family members. Then it's case closed. If not I'll refer the whole business to the ethics committee and we'll be talking about this nonsense for the rest of our lives."

He looked around the room. No one seemed to object. Sister Dolores grumbled but left it at that. Besides, the meeting had already run twenty minutes long.

"Fine," the chairman said. "I need a motion to adjourn."

"So moved," Dr. Riegle said as he got up and began walking out. He wasn't in the mood to wait for someone to 'second' his motion.

Chapter 15

"We would call it 'The Center for Addiction Recovery', or 'CARE'."

It was the first Thursday of the month, one week after the Peer Review Committee meeting, and Timothy Doyle, COO was trying to explain his latest plan for putting Saints' Hospital back in the black. His audience was the Medical Executive Committee. This group was composed of the medical directors for each of the clinical departments, the CEO, COO, and Chief Nursing Officer. Its function was to represent the medical staff as a whole and forward recommendations to the Governing Board for final approval.

New physicians applying to the staff were vetted by the Credentials Committee, and if their files were found to be acceptable they were referred to the Executive Committee for consideration. Once approved there they would go to the Board for a rubber stamp OK. Mr. Doyle was making his case on behalf of Dr. Gerald Byner. Dr. Byner's application to the staff of Saints' Hospital was languishing in Credentials Committee and Mr. Doyle was using his 'Administrative Report' to give it a boost.

"Dr. Byner is applying for membership to our medical staff. He has a unique program for the rapid detoxification of drug addicted patients and is looking for a hospital in our area in which to establish a satellite center."

Dr. Byner, 'Jerry', was in fact a recovering drug abuser himself, a habit he acquired during his practice as an anesthesiologist. When he was caught snorting coke in the doctors' dressing room of an upscale Westside hospital in LA his privileges were suspended and he was referred to the Physician Wellness Committee. From there he was sent to a State-approved diversion program where he underwent his own not-so-rapid detoxification and many hours of counseling and rehab. Eventually he was declared 'cured'. He was readmitted to the staff and allowed to resume his practice under the close scrutiny of a designated proctor.

While in rehab he'd learned about a process called 'rapid detox'. An addict would be admitted to the ICU, placed on a ventilator, dropped into a drug-induced coma for twenty-four hours, infused with a variety of chemicals, and awakened the next day no longer an addict. Clean and sober. Just like that.

The price for this miracle was about a hundred grand, a third of it going to Jerry, the rest to the hospital. Cash. Blue Shield didn't want to hear about it. Run of the mill street junkies need not apply.

He'd tried to sell the concept to the up-scale Westside hospital from which he'd been suspended but they'd declined the offer. The procedure was a bit dangerous, the clientele a bit shady, and the hospital didn't' need the money, thanks. Middleman Hospital, a small for-profit place a couple of miles away, however, jumped at the chance.

So, Jerry happily gave up his anesthesiology practice and set up the Center for Addiction Recovery at Middleman. Security was tight and anonymity was guaranteed. It was an instant success. Rock stars, movie stars, studio executives and wealthy entrepreneurs with a 'drug problem' lined up. Patients flew in from the East Coast. Jerry was going to take his program nation wide.

Until the twenty-two-year-old son of a New York banker died. The young man had been using cocaine and heroin in heroic amounts, was diabetic, and had asthma. Probably not the best candidate for rapid detox, but both father and son had been insistent. The risks were explained, the consents were signed. The patient knew what he was getting himself into. He also knew that he stood a good chance of dying from his drug abuse, so what the fuck? Half way through the procedure he developed a life-threatening cardiac arrhythmia. A code blue was called but nothing worked.

News of the young man's death never made it to the local media, but word spread throughout the drug world. Jerry's business dried up.

For a while. But the promise of going to sleep one day and waking up the next with the monkey off your back was too seductive to ignore and within a few months things were rolling once again. It was time to expand. The San Gabriel Valley was far enough from West Los Angeles to have its own demographic but near enough for one doctor, Jerry, to keep a close eye on things. Saints', a small hospital in a nice area with money problems, looked like the right place.

"Come on, do we really want to get involved with Dr. Byner? The guy's a druggie!" Dr. Carter, Chief of Staff, shared the opinion held by most of his colleagues. Jerry wasn't exactly the sort of guy they wanted to have a drink with at the annual staff retreat.

"He's not a 'druggie', as you put it, he's a recovering substance abuser," Mr. Doyle corrected. "Besides, I've spoken to him about all that, and he feels that his experience with drugs and rehab make him uniquely qualified for this sort of practice."

"Right," Dr. Riegel chimed in, "like I should go out and get run over by a bus so I can be better qualified to treat trauma patients."

This elicited laughs from the physician members of the committee. Administration was less amused.

"I think you are all being a little narrow minded," Mr. Doyle said, trying to regain some control. "This hospital is a business, and like any business it needs to make money to stay alive. A program like CARE could bring in the revenue we need to continue doing some of the other things we do, like treating the poor and uninsured."

He had a point. Still, the idea of turning Saints' into a refuge for rich junkies under the care of a marginal character like Dr. Byner wasn't sitting well.

Chapter 16

Sunday night at the Thirteenth Step was pasta night. In the spirit of his Italian heritage, and in memory of his life as a child, Tommy insisted that Sundays be set aside for friends and family. Admission to the bar was by reservation only, and only those who'd been formally invited by Tommy could make reservations. It was a little unusual, but it was the Step and the unusual was to be expected.

The invitation list was short and getting a spot on it conferred a certain VIP status to the invitee. Tommy was not a VIP kind of guy. He hadn't been big on back stage passes or velvet ropes when he was touring. They were a necessary evil as far as he was concerned, used by the clubs and record companies to hype the product. But Sundays were his nights to relax, the kitchen staff was small, and he needed to keep the crowd intimate.

Fish was on the list and this Sunday he'd booked a table for four. Friends of friends had to cleared with Tommy. Fish's brother Danny and his girlfriend Ashleigh got the immediate OK. Danny was a lawyer doing mainly business litigation for a firm in San Diego. At thirty-one years old he was six years younger than Fish, but the two had similar personalities and attitudes, about life, women, work, whatever, and were closer than most siblings with that sort of age gap. Ashleigh was finishing her last year of pre-law at UCLA. She was twenty-four, the same age as Micky.

The two had met during Fish's malpractice trial. Ashleigh had been working as the 'assistant' for the plaintiff's attorney, one Barry Bauer, Esq., the self-proclaimed Silver Fox, King of Torts. She'd been hired because she was a Latina, fluent in Spanish, and gave her boss greater access to the large Hispanic population in LA. That she was a knock-out at five-five and a hundred ten with a pretty face, a world class body, and an ass that people who appreciate that sort of thing, like Barry, would practically die for didn't hurt.

Prior to meeting her Danny had been like his brother, a no commitments, lots of casual girlfriends, ladies man. One look at Ashleigh and that life was over. They started dating as soon as the trial ended. He took it slow, a departure from his usual M.O. When they finally got around to it the sex was unlike anything he'd experienced. He was a goner. Their relationship involved some commuting but that was fine. She was busy with schoolwork, he was busy earning a partnership at the law firm, and a week's worth of anticipation made the weekends that much more exciting.

The brothers hadn't seen each other in a while so when Danny called saying they needed to catch up Fish suggested dinner at the Step. Danny was spending the weekend at Ashleigh's place so it was easy. The doors opened at five P.M. and by five fifteen the Hooks' party of four was sitting at a table off to the side of the stage.

"Hey, Doc," Tommy said as he approached their table. He gave Fish a pat on the shoulder and bent down to give Micky a kiss on the cheek. He knew Danny and Ashleigh from previous visits and they stood to greet him. Danny got a handshake, Ashleigh got a hug. Even Tommy, minor rock star who'd pretty much seen and done it all, was in awe of Ashleigh. He wasn't sure what he enjoyed more, squeezing her or looking at her, so he did both with an enthusiasm that might have been offensive coming from just about anyone else.

"Man!" he said with a laugh when he finally let her go, "these woman are way out of your league. Can I get you something from the bar?"

Food service didn't start until sometime after six. Tommy respected the cocktail hour. When the girls each ordered Chardonnay Fish and Danny decided to forego the usual Martini's. Tommy knew a little about wine and with some help from Marla he'd put together a short list of moderately priced but respectable bottles running the gamut from pinot grigio to chardonnay, pinot noir to chianti and cabernet sauvignon.

"Make it a bottle, four glasses," Fish said.

Marla poked her head out of the kitchen looking for her brothers. When she found them she joined the group.

"So what's for dinner?" Danny asked after the hugs and kisses.

"Well," she began, "we have the usual antipasti and salad, of course."

"Of course," the four responded in unison. Tommy was a traditionalist, albeit an eclectic one, and certain things were better left unchanged.

"But for the main course we have two choices. The first is my version of Tommy's mother's penne with meat sauce, meaning tomatoes, meatballs, *and* sausages. For those of you who actually need to sleep tonight and have things to do in the morning we also have orecchiette with some crumbled Italian sausage and rapini. I made some cannoli for dessert. Really good."

Tommy returned with the wine and Marla headed back to the kitchen.

"Hey, Tommy," Fish asked as the wine was being poured, "you ever heard of something called 'rapid detox'?"

Tommy finished pouring and put the bottle down before answering. "Oooh, Doctor Jerry." He grabbed a chair from a nearby table and pulled it up to theirs. "Yeah. Couple of guys I know, pretty famous, went through it."

"And?"

"And nothing. They were about to go on tour in Europe and Asia and needed to get clean. They go see the good doctor, schedule the appointment. In one day, out the next. Cost 'em a bundle but it's peanuts to them. On the road five months then home and back using within a week. I think it's bullshit."

"Why? You just said it works."

"It's too easy. Drugs are powerful things. If you really want to get off heroin you need to fight to get off just as hard as it's fighting to keep you addicted. I'm not talking Ray Charles lock yourself in a room for a week and go cold-turkey but this take a nap and wake up sober is a little ridiculous."

"And what about Doctor Jerry? What's his deal?"

Tommy grunted. "The junkies love him because he gives them an easy out, and he's getting rich."

"Hmm," Fish muttered. The others at his table had no idea what this was all about. Danny was about to ask but Tommy spoke first.

"Why you asking? You got a problem I don't know about?"

"Well, yeah, uh, no, not what you're thinking," he began. He then went on to explain what he'd learned from Dr. Riegel.

"The world is changing," Tommy said, his tone suggesting that he'd prefer it wasn't. He then got up to visit with the other guests who by now had arrived and been seated.

Fish dropped the subject. He and Danny had more pleasant things to discuss while Micky and Ashleigh, who'd become good friends, had some catching up of their own to do.

Chapter 17

The big day finally arrived and the Walter clan was almost giddy with anticipation. The reading was scheduled for eleven A.M. and by ten-fifty everyone on Leo's list was sitting or standing in Mr. Wright's waiting room. The children, Elaine, Louise, and Leonard, Jr. did their best to appear calm, if not exactly nonchalant. The grandchildren, with the exception of Lauren, were nervously whispering among themselves and sneaking frequent glances at the two non-family members sitting in a far corner, Consuela Sanchez and Sister Dolores. Lauren and Amy sat together in the opposite corner involved in a conversation of their own, the substance of which completely unrelated to the upcoming reading.

Mr. Wright let them wait the additional ten minutes. At eleven sharp he had his office manager herd them into the large conference room. His office was in Beverly Hills, on the tenth floor, with large windows facing north and west. At this time of day the sun was not yet high enough to shine directly into the room so there was no need to close the blinds. The view provided was of the Los Angeles Country Club and the 'Hills' section of Beverly Hills.

Once every one had been seated Mr. Wright performed a mental roll call. The children and their spouses. Check. The grandchildren, Elaine's son Robert, 40, divorced, no kids, her daughter Lauren with her daughter Amy. Check. Louise's two sons Larry, 38, married to Karen, no kids, and Jack, 35, single. Check. Leonard's son Leonard, III, 33, single. Check. Consuela Sanchez. Check. And lastly, Sister Dolores. Fourteen in all. Check.

Mr. Wright took his seat at the head of the large rectangular table. In front of him was the sealed envelope he'd been given by the late Leo. He picked it up without opening it, and ran his eyes across the group.

"Before we get started," he began, "there's something you all should know." He let that lay there for a minute, per his instructions from Leo. A low murmur began to fill the room. The lawyer cleared his throat and the murmur subsided.

"This is the final will and testament of Mr. Leonard Walter, Sr. I have no idea what's in it, because I did not draw it up."

The murmur quickly reasserted itself, now louder. He had to clear his voice twice before order was restored.

"A few months before his death Leonard, Mr. Walter, came to this office to discuss some things with me, how he wanted certain things done. It was at that meeting he expressed his wish for a low-key memorial," he paused here while Elaine fidgeted, "and he gave me this," indicating the envelope.

"He told me he'd made some alterations to the will and he thought it best that I not know what they were. I tried to get an explanation from him but there was none forthcoming. He just smiled, shook my hand, and 'no' was all he said."

John Wright was a big fan of The Band and he couldn't help himself. This elicited a smile from Lauren. The others either didn't get it or were too agitated to appreciate it.

"Then he turned around and walked out the door. Never said another word about it."

All this was having the effect Leonard had hoped it would. Elaine, afraid of an accident, asked for directions to the restroom. When she returned a few minutes later the murmur had become more of a din. Fortunately Mr. Wright had a gavel handy, his prize for winning his case in Mock Court during the final year of law school, and he used it now to good effect.

"OK," he said when the group had settled down, "let's see what we've got."

He carefully opened the envelope, removed the document, and began to read.

Chapter 18

Back at Saints' Timothy Doyle, COO was taking advantage of Sister Dolores' absence to have a private conversation with Dr. Riegel. The topic was Dr. Gerald Byner, specifically his pending staff privileges, and Dr. Riegel's reticence to approve them. Dr. Riegel was a member of the Credentials Committee, as he was of just about every other committee the medical staff bylaws mandated. Although he didn't particularly enjoy the meetings his attitude was that it was better to attend and keep an ear open to what was being said, especially about the ER, than not to attend.

Over the years he'd learned that no matter the problem or the individuals involved an attempt would be made to blame the whole thing on the Emergency Room. If a patient's test results don't get sent to his doctor's office it's the ER's fault, not the fault of the computer system that can't be programmed to perform the routing. If a patient with a sore throat is given a prescription for antibiotics the ER doctor is declared incompetent by the primary care doctor because the sore throat is obviously a viral infection and antibiotics won't work. Until the next patient with a sore throat is sent out without the prescription and the ER doctor is castigated for not treating it. The ER is an easy and convenient target and taking pot shots at it is one of the most popular sports in just about any hospital. Dr. Riegel's presence made petty criticism and scape-goating awkward.

"We need to get this application out of Credentials and on to the Board this month."

Mr. Doyle was doing his best to be intimidating, but at five-eight and a hundred and forty-seven pounds, with thinning blond hair and thick glasses in painfully un-stylish frames it wasn't working. Dr. Riegel stared at him for a minute as though the man was some sort of lab specimen.

"You understand," he finally replied, "that Byner's application isn't exactly 'clean', right?"

"You're referring to the diversion, I presume?"

"For one, yeah. I'm also concerned that he's been on staff at about a dozen other hospitals in the area over the past twenty years, never for more than two or three years at any one of them. He just decides one day to resign and move on. Pack the wagons, break camp, pull in the lines. Doesn't that seem a little strange to you?"

"He's an anesthesiologist. It's common for anesthesiologists to be on staff at more than one hospital," Mr. Doyle countered.

"True. And the good ones generally stay on staff for a long, long time. They form relationships with the surgeons. They get the calls for the big cases. They don't just pull up stakes after a couple of years and move on, start over somewhere else."

The COO narrowed his eyes in an attempt to appear menacing. He managed to look like a Chinese albino. And not one who knows martial arts.

"What are you implying?" he asked.

"I'm not implying anything but I think that before we let this guy on staff and he starts running amok with his rapid detox we should get a little more background. You know as well as I do that if a doctor is having some kind of problem it's a hell of a lot easier for everybody if he voluntarily resigns from staff than it is to start a formal investigation. He starts acting a little goofy in the O.R., patients start waking up in the middle of their appendectomy, whatever. Resignation. Problem solved. No drawn out investigation, no reporting to the state Medical Board, no lawyers, it's over."

Mr. Doyle took a moment to digest what he'd heard. "There's nothing in his file to suggest he left any of those hospitals under anything but friendly circumstances. I don't see why we need to start looking for problems that don't seem to exist."

They both knew that if Dr. Riegel's suspicions were correct, there would be nothing in the file. Keeping his file clean would be the whole point of resigning.

"And I don't see why we need to rush this thing through committee. The guy's been flaky in the past. We need to be sure he isn't going to start getting crazy here. We need more information."

"We need to make some money! This hospital is on very shaky financial footing right now. A guy like Dr. Byner could save our necks. You need to get off your high horse and do the right thing here. Or else!" Mr. Doyle was red-faced and small droplets of spittle had formed at the corners of his mouth.

"Or else? OR ELSE? Or Else WHAT?" Dr. Riegel did not like to be threatened, and though he was pretty sure what the implication was he wanted the COO to say it out loud.

"Or else I'm going to have to find some other way to cut our losses," Mr. Doyle responded after regaining his 'cool'. "And the best way I can see to do that would be to close down your department. Save us a bundle. Might not need Dr. Byner. Then, when things are stabilized, we can think about opening it back up, but with a different contract holder, someone or some company that understands the needs of the hospital better than you seem to."

"That's blackmail," Dr. Riegle said, shaking his head.

"That's business, and that's life. I'd think a guy your age would have figured that out by now."

The director wanted to tell him to fuck himself. "I was here before they hired you and I'll still be here after your gone. Have a nice day," was how he worded it.

Chapter 19

All eyes were glued to Mr. Wright and no one made a sound.

"To my children, Elaine Baker, Louise Conroy, and Leonard Walter, Jr., I leave my business conglomerate, including all seven automobile dealerships and all commercial real estate, as well as my personal residence and all the contents therein, with each of my children entitled to one third of those assets."

Mr. Wright looked up. Tears of joy were forming in the corner's of Elaine's eyes and all three of the children wore expressions one might expect to see on the faces of people who'd just won the lottery. He let them bask in the glow for a moment before continuing.

"But before you wet yourselves, 'his words, not mine'," the lawyer said, "there are some financial details you need to consider. I refinanced all of my properties a while ago. It was hard to ignore the low interest rates and I'd been giving some thought to expanding my holdings. But, when my health began to fail I realized that involving myself in new ventures was unrealistic. I also realized, based on years of observation, that allowing you three to make those kinds of decisions was equally unrealistic."

The lawyer paused again to survey the room. The children's expressions of utter joy and gratitude had begun to deteriorate, replaced now by looks of cautious optimism. The others in the room, who'd thought they'd been snubbed, now sensed things could be looking up for them. They, too, were cautiously optimistic.

"So," Mr. Wright continued, "what this means is that all my holdings, the dealerships, the shopping malls, the office building, and my own home, are now heavily leveraged, eighty percent loan to value, to be exact. Your options are these: you can sell everything and realize about ten cents on the dollar after taxes, or you can actually run the businesses, pay down the loans, and make yourselves some real money. Up to you."

Elaine, her brother and her sister did some mental arithmetic. The numbers were not exactly what they'd hoped.

It also means I have a substantial amount of cash on hand. The question, then, is what am I going to do with all the money?"

A low rumble filled the room as people began whispering to themselves and to one another, trying to predict the old man's decision. Mr. Wright banged the gavel.

"I spent a lot of time thinking this over. In the end, the answer was clear. To each of my five grandchildren I am leaving a sum of one million dollars with the stipulation that you cannot access any of it until you reach your fiftieth birthday, at which time you will get half. If and when you make it to sixty, you will receive the second half, plus whatever interest has accrued. I am making an exception for Lauren. Because I believe she has the most sense she can have her inheritance in full as soon as it becomes available through probate."

This prompted considerable discussion, requiring several bangs of the gavel for order to be restored.

"Everyone, please!" Mr. Wright yelled above the noise. "We have a lot more to get through. There will be plenty of time for questions and discussion when I'm done. Thank you."

"To my great-granddaughter, Amy, I leave the sum of two million dollars. This will be placed in a trust until she reaches the age of thirty. Until then she can use whatever she needs for reasonable educational expenses. I have detailed what I consider those to be in a separate document.

"Next, to Consuela Sanchez I leave the sum of three million dollars."

There was a gasp from the far corner of the table where she sat next to Sister Dolores, accompanied by another outbreak of rumbling.

"That money will be placed in an investment trust. The earnings will be paid out in regular installments and should be sufficient to support Mrs. Sanchez and her family in a comfortable manner for the rest of her life. When the time comes the principle can be distributed according to her wishes as stated in her will.

"O.K.," Mr. Wright continued reading, "that accounts for ten million dollars. The balance of my estate, roughly seventy million dollars in cash, goes to Saints' Hospital Charitable Foundation, under the direction of Sister Mary Elizabeth Dolores, Mother Superior of the Sisters of Ineffable Sorrow."

There was a stunned silence, during which Sister Dolores made a discrete sign of the cross and raised her eyes toward heaven. Then all hell broke loose.

Chapter 20

"O.K., listen up, pay attention."

It was seven A.M. on Friday, three days after his meeting with the COO. Dr. Riegel had called an emergency meeting of his physician staff. There were some 'important things to talk about' was all he'd said in advance. All eight of his doctors were now crammed into his small office waiting to hear what the big deal was.

After his first conversation with Sister Dolores, during which the idea of closing the ER had been raised and dismissed, he'd decided to share that information only with his assistant director. Why upset the rest of the staff when there was no realistic chance of an actual closure of the department? But now things had changed. The threats from the COO and his subsequent private meeting with Sister Dolores the following day had been both worrisome and promising. It was time to get the troops mobilized.

"I don't know how much you know about what's going on around here," he began.

Looking at the mostly blank faces staring back at him, the exception being that of his co-director with whom he'd had a private conversation the previous day, he assumed the answer was 'not much'.

"That's what I thought. You show up for your shifts, see the patients, try not to piss anybody off, then go home and forget about it until the next time. Fine. You do a good job. But there's more to this business than practicing medicine and it's time you learned about it. First of all it *is* a business, right?"

There seemed to be a consensus on this point, so he continued.

"Good. We see patients, we send out bills, and we try to collect money. More like you see patients and I take care of all the rest of that stuff so we can get paid. Well, I see some patients, you know what I'm saying."

So far that seemed to be the case.

"But we're a business inside a business. You following me here?"

They were following, but the gap was widening a bit. Fish sensed the confusion.

"What Dr. Riegel is saying is that we work within the hospital. We have our own practice, the ER, but we depend on the hospital for support."

"Exactly," the director said. "The hospital pays for the nurses, the equipment, the medicines, the physical space we work out of, all of it. The only thing they don't pay for is us. So, if the hospital isn't making money then we as a group of doctors trying to make a living by working in the hospital have a problem. Got it?"

Heads nodded in the affirmative.

"Good. Actually, not so good, because for the last several months the hospital has been losing money. Lots of it. That's why Sister Dolores hired Mr. Doyle, our new Chief Operating Officer. You all seen him? Little pasty guy with the big glasses? Well this guy Doyle is supposed to be some kind of financial wizard. He's going to find new ways for the hospital to generate revenue and cut costs. And guess what his first big idea was."

He paused waiting for some feedback but the stares remained blank.

"He told Sister Dolores that she should close the ER. He said our patients were costing the place a fortune."

This caused a buzz in the room. The director let them mumble for a minute before continuing.

"And you know the worst part?" he then asked. "No? Well, the worst part is that he's right. With the laws the way they are and the economy the way it is we're seeing more and more patients with no means to pay for the care we provide. Used to be most people had some kind of insurance and the State would pay us a little something for the ones who didn't. Nowadays we're seeing cuts in reimbursement across the board and every time we admit an uninsured patient to the hospital we are digging a hole that's getting harder and harder for the hospital to climb out of."

He paused to let that sink in. Blank stares were being replaced by expressions of concern. Good, he thought.

"Fortunately for us we have a couple of things working in our favor," he continued.

"Like what?" Dr Graber asked. "Like we're still mostly young enough to find new careers?"

This earned a few nervous titters.

"There's that, sure, but there are a couple of other things. First, Sister Dolores would rather pull her own teeth out than close the ER. Treating the poor and sick is what her mission is all about, and nowhere in the hospital do we do more of that than in the Emergency Room.

"Another thing is that this guy Doyle is trying to bring some new programs to the hospital, the kind of stuff that people are willing to pay cash for, like a Rapid Detoxification program for drug addicts. Problem is that the guy who runs it is a little slimy and the medical staff isn't real comfortable with bringing that kind of business to Saints'. Still, if Doyle can drum up some paying customers for something that doesn't involve slime balls it would take some of the heat off us."

The tension that had been building in the room was now beginning to dissipate as the director injected some measure of hope into the conversation.

"But the biggest thing we have going for us, and this is huge and it stays in this room, right?"

Everyone swore himself to secrecy.

"The biggest thing is that the hospital's charitable foundation was just given a gift of seventy million dollars."

Loud murmurs ensued. Dr. Riegel let them talk for a minute.

"O.K., so what's the problem?" Bob Graber was by now one of the more senior members of the staff and his relationship with Fish, and his sister, conferred upon him a certain leadership status. With Dr. Hooks apparently already in the know, he took it upon himself to be the group's mouthpiece.

"Sister Dolores just got a fortune, the money problems just went away. Why are we having this discussion?"

"Because it's not that simple. Remember that case Fish was involved in a few weeks ago, the old guy who coded in the ICU, The Undead, Mr. Walter? That's where the money is coming from. He left it to the hospital in his will. Problem is his family went berserk when they found out about it. They're contesting the will. It could be months, years, before the thing is settled. Remember that case a while back, the one where this really old rich guy married some young hottie, then keeled over leaving her all the dough? People are still suing each other. By the time this is over we could be out of business, the ER, maybe the whole hospital, closed. We need a plan."

Chapter 21

The silence that followed Mr. Wright's announcement of the seventy million dollar gift to Saints' lasted about eight seconds. Elaine was the first to speak.

"WHAT!?" she managed to shout.

Then everyone began yelling, or almost everyone. Consuela slumped down into her chair trying to minimize the target for that part of the general invective aimed at her. Sister Dolores, not one to be easily intimidated, sat bolt upright, hands folded on the table, with the suggestion of a smirk on her face. No need, she realized, to add to the pandemonium by defending herself. There would likely be plenty of time for that later. Mr. Wright applied the gavel with vigor, which only added to the cacophony.

After several minutes with no end to the hysteria in the foreseeable future Lauren stood, motioned to Amy, and began moving toward the door. She'd been observing her family with a mixture of fascination and embarrassment, and when the latter became predominant she decided she'd had enough. Elaine noticed her impending departure and stopped shouting to inquire about it.

"And just where the hell do you think YOU'RE going, hmmm?"

This got the attention of the rest of the group who quieted down to hear the response.

Lauren stared at her mother, then glanced around the room at the others. "If I heard Mr. Wright correctly," she began, "each one of you has just become a millionaire. I'd think you would be happy about that."

Another outbreak ensued during which Lauren and Amy again made an attempt to leave. This time Elaine stood and physically blocked their paths.

"Sit back down and listen," she commanded.

No one moved.

"Please," she added in a more conciliatory tone.

Lauren considered the request and decided to honor it. She escorted her daughter back to her seat, and resumed her place at the table. The rest of the family members had by now regained a measure of composure and were quietly sulking. Elaine collected herself and sat.

"John," she said, addressing the attorney, "do you have an explanation for the manner in which my father's estate is to be distributed?"

The lawyer held up his hands. "Like I said before we started, your father only told me he made some 'alterations' but wouldn't tell me what or why."

"'Why' is going to be difficult to answer," Elaine said, "considering he's not here to tell us, but 'what' should be fairly simple considering you wrote up his previous will. Can you tell me, us, what sort of changes he *did* make in the will you *read* compared to the one you *wrote*?"

Mr. Wright thought about that for a moment. He'd saved a copy of the old will anticipating there might be a problem if Leonard had made drastic changes to it. As it turned out, he had.

"Ah, in your father's previous will, the one I drafted for him, he left, I believe, five million dollars to Saints' Hospital Charitable Foundation and the rest to you, Louise, and Leonard Jr. The other distributions remained the same. Except that for Mrs. Sanchez. In the earlier document he'd left her one million."

So much for peace and quiet. Elaine tried to restore order but was unable to be heard above the din. She then stood, walked to the head of the table, removed the gavel from Mr. Wright's hand, and slammed it down on the table.

"QUIET!"

That had the desired effect. She returned to her seat and locked eyes with the lawyer.

"John," she said softly, doing everything she could to seem calm and in control, "*surely* you agree that something must have gone terribly wrong with my father, there, near the end. His mysterious behavior with you, these irrational changes to his will, giving practically his entire estate to an institution that practically tried to kill him, *did*, in fact, kill him, not to mention an amount three times greater to his caretaker than to any of his grandchildren. *Surely* you can see that this was not really what he intended. And, I'm equally *certain* you understand that we as a family will not allow this to go unchallenged. My father's memory cannot be that of a feeble, confused man. *Surely* you know we are going to do everything we can to have this so called 'will' thrown out."

Of all the things Elaine accused him of being sure, this last was the only one of which he actually was.

Chapter 22

By eleven A.M. Saturday morning, the day after his meeting with the staff, Dr. Riegel's emergency room was on 'diversion'. This meant the ER was closed to paramedic traffic. The reason was there were no available beds. There was nowhere to put a new patient brought in by the paramedics. Rather than stay open and run the risk of having to keep the ambulance personnel tied up waiting for a bed to become free the decision had been made to 'close'.

Normally this was something the ER, and administration, tried to avoid. It was inconvenient for patients and paramedics who had to bypass Saints' and go to the next closest hospital. It was contrary to the hospital's mission statement, which promised to provide care to all in the community who required it, to the extent of the hospital's capability. And it was a large part of 'the plan' the director and his doctors had devised.

The people who ran the County's pre-hospital care system are able to keep track of each hospital's status by means of a centralized computer network to which all the County's ER's are connected. Is your CT scanner on the blink, are you having internal facility problems, like a flood, are you so crowded that you need to go on 'diversion'? If the answer to any of these questions is 'yes' you can click on the appropriate box and everyone in the system will know. This includes the various base stations, the larger hospitals with specially trained nurses who direct paramedic traffic.

Saints' base station was Memorial, the trauma center about five miles east. The nurse manning the radio noticed that Saints' was 'on diversion' and began routing patients elsewhere. The business of closing the ER to paramedic traffic was something that had drawn scrutiny from the County as well as from Sister Dolores in the past. A review of ER statistics had shown that the ER was frequently closed during the night shift. Nights were not particularly busy at Saints' and the closures were investigated. It was discovered that a certain night nurse preferred taking it easy, and closing to ambulance traffic was the simplest way to ensure peace and quiet. Once discovered the nurse was asked to 'knock it the fuck off' by Dr. Riegel.

At the time, closing the ER was not only a problem from a public relations standpoint, it was bad for business. The paying patients brought in by ambulance more than compensated for those who were uninsured, at least in the case of Saints' Hospital given its location and demographic. At the time.

But not all hospitals enjoyed the same set of geographic circumstances. Some realized they could shield themselves from unwanted business by going on 'diversion'. The walk-in patients were generally easier to take care of and more likely to have some means of paying the bill. Going on diversion allowed them to be more available for this group and less so for the homeless drunk found sleeping in the bushes and brought to you by the paramedics.

The County realized the system was being gamed, and changed the rules in an attempt to discourage the practice. If an ER was full to capacity it could go on diversion, but only for an hour. Then it would be automatically re-opened for fifteen minutes. Although it was not specifically stated in the new policy it seemed as though the base stations had been instructed to take full advantage of that fifteen minute window by dumping as many patients in the lap of the newly re-opened emergency room as possible in retribution for having closed in the first place. The fact that you might have been legitimately overcrowded notwithstanding. Still, closing and taking your chances for fifteen minutes was likely to work in your favor if keeping things slow was your goal.

Dr. Riegel's so-called 'plan' was to jam up the works, keep the beds full, and stay on diversion for as long as possible. Times had changed, as Mr. Doyle was fond of pointing out, and staying open no matter what was no longer good for business. This was, the director realized, not much of a plan but his options were limited. So, the uninsured accidental overdose from the rave was held in the ER for ten hours until she was suitable for discharge instead of being admitted to the hospital. Likewise the thirty-four year old man with chest pain. Serial lab tests and EKG'S were done over the course sixteen hours until the ER doctor could reasonably say the chest pain was non-cardiac and the man could go home. In an eight-bed emergency room you didn't need many boarders to keep the place 'saturated'.

"If we cut down on the number of uninsured hospital admissions from the ER, do more of the work-ups ourselves, we can stay off the radar, out of the line of fire, buy some time until that dork Doyle can figure out some way to increase revenues without turning this place into some kind of freak show," was how he'd explained it to his colleagues.

He understood his strategy was a bit flawed. Keeping the place full cut down on the number of patients that could be seen and increased the wait times. This was bad for patient satisfaction. Sooner or later angry letters would be written, complaints would be made, and Sister Dolores would want to know 'just what is going on down there'.

It was also probably illegal. According to the federal government, all patients presenting to an ER with a certain complaint must be treated in a similar fashion. So the thirty-four year old guy with chest pain and Aetna and the thirty-four year old guy with only chest pain should either both get admitted to the hospital or both get their complete evaluation in the ER. That, however, was very bad for business.

"Look, I know we're gonna get caught sooner or later, probably sooner, and hopefully by Sister Dolores and not the feds, but I'll say we were trying to be team players and do what was best for the patients. Why admit the uninsured guy and run up all these bills he won't be able to pay, put him in the poorhouse or on skid row or whatever? We can do the eval in the ER, save him a bundle. And the insured guy, if we keep him in the ER for all those hours he's just taking up a bed that we could be using to treat another uninsured guy. Right?"

There was a tortured logic in his explanation that was probably sufficient to keep the doctors out of prison. Still it was the unspoken wish of all in the room that things would be returned to normal ASAP.

Chapter 23

When Elaine finished her speech informing Mr. Wright of her, and the family's, intention to contest the will she stood and motioned to the others it was time to leave.

"There's more here," the lawyer said, "you might want to stay a few minutes longer."

"I think we've heard all we need to for now," Elaine replied. "We should be going. There's some work we need to do."

Mr. Wright knew it was pointless to respond. The relationship between him and the Walter family was different now. Radically so. He was the executor of Leonard Sr.'s will, and as such his duty was to see that it remain in force. Those who would challenge were adversaries. They would get their own legal counsel and a battle would ensue. There was a lot on the line. He was pretty sure the last thing Elaine and her siblings had intended to do after the death of their father was work for a living.

As the Walter clan filed out of the room no one made eye contact with him. No one except Lauren who gave him a sympathetic glance and what appeared to be almost a wink. He raised his eyebrows as though to ask, "Huh?" but stopped short of actually saying anything.

Consuela waited for the last of the family to pass, keeping her own eyes focused intently on her shoes. When it seemed safe she, too, made a motion to stand. Sister Dolores, sitting to her immediate left, placed a firm hand on her thigh, suggesting she might want to stick around a while. Consuela got the message and settled back into her chair.

The three sat, speechless, for almost five minutes. Speechless, because Consuela had no idea what to say, and because the other two had no intention of saying anything until they felt certain the others were in the elevator on their way to the lobby. Finally the lawyer broke the silence.

"So," he began, "I'm assuming that neither of you are intending to contest the will, right?"

Consuela shook her head 'no' and Sister Dolores smiled.

"Mr. Wright," she said, "I know a little about wills and probate. I've been running the Charitable Foundation for a long time and we've been remembered in people's wills before, though never with anything close to this level of generosity. But my guess is that regardless of the amount the procedure is the same. Correct?"

"Uh, by 'procedure', you mean what, exactly?"

"I mean that as the executor your job is to see that things get done the way Mr. Walter wanted them to."

"Yes, that's the basic idea."

"Good. You're an attorney. That's convenient. You're the executor, which means you are going to be on our side." She nodded toward the caretaker as she said this. "So Mrs. Sanchez and I don't need to go out and hire our own lawyers right now because we aren't contesting the will and you'll be working to protect our interests. Do I have this figured correctly?"

Mr. Wright smiled. Sister Dolores had figured it correctly. He was their de-facto attorney. They wouldn't have to spend a dime of their own money, at least not yet, hiring people to do what he had already agreed to do himself.

"Yes, Sister, you do," he replied. "Elaine is probably on the phone right now lining up her legal team. As soon as that's been done they will file papers contesting the will and I will begin the process of defending it, and by extension, your interests as well."

"Hmm. That's what I thought. How long do you think this is going to take?"

"Well, that's the seventy million dollar question, isn't it? Look, uncontested it would take close to a year to get this settled. It's just the way the system works. With an estate the size of Mr. Walter's it could take even longer. We have to verify the status of his holdings, the absence of liens, whether or not anyone is out there trying to sue him, it takes time. But with Elaine hell bent, excuse my language, on having the will annulled I really can't say how long it will be before anyone sees any money."

"Hmm."

A silence then settled which no one seemed anxious to disturb. Finally Mr. Wright took the lead.

"I understand that time might be an issue here, maybe more for you," looking at Sister Dolores, "than you," nodding toward Consuela. But there are things we can do to expedite this process. Nothing I want to go into right now. Let's see what position Elaine takes, then we can devise our strategy."

This seemed to satisfy the immediate needs of both the nun and the caretaker. Sister Dolores stood, taking Consuela with her. They all shook hands, and the women made their way to the elevators.

"Call me when you know something," was the last thing Sister Dolores said on her way out the door.

When he was alone Mr. Wright sat and picked up the will. "Jesus, Leonard," he said as he attempted to put it back into the manilla envelope from which he'd taken it. The document hit an obstruction. He looked inside and found a letter-sized envelope at the bottom of the larger one.

"What the...," he mumbled, taking it out. It was addressed to him. He opened it. Inside were two typewritten sheets.

"Dear John," it began. The lawyer began to read, then began to smile, then began to chuckle out loud.

When he was done he folded it back up, placed it back into the envelope, and got up to lock both documents in the office safe.

Chapter 24

"Do you ever ask yourself 'what am I doing'?"

It was Saturday night and Micky's weekend off. Fish had taken her to dinner at La Spiaggia, an Italian place specializing in seafood and one of her favorite restaurants. They hadn't had a romantic evening out in a while. Truth was they hadn't had a romantic evening in a while. Either their schedules conflicted or they were too tired or not in the mood. The mood issue, Fish realized, was mainly his. He'd been letting work and its recent problems preoccupy his thoughts. Tonight was his way of making up for lost time.

They'd started the meal with prosecco and crudo, Italy's version of sushi, thin slices of raw fish seasoned with olive oil, sea salt, and a little fresh pepper. Instead of a pasta course they shared a simple Margherita pizza with tomatoes, basil, and mozzarella made from buffalo milk. Micky then opted for the branzino from the wood-burning oven while Fish had the scallops and they washed it all down with a chardonnay blend from the Piedmont area. For dessert they shared a panna cotta and a single small glass of grappa, the clear, powerful distillate made from the seeds and stems left over from winemaking. It had all been perfect.

Conversation during the meal had drifted from the hospital, to various bits of gossip they'd heard, to the Step, (Why doesn't Tommy have a girlfriend? Do you think he has a thing for Marla?). Nothing about themselves, their relationship, or the recent lack of excitement. Fish had been thinking about those things but didn't want to ruin the mood. Micky had given no hint that those thoughts had ever crossed her mind.

They'd just gotten into bed and for some reason even he couldn't understand, those words popped out of his mouth.

"You're licking my neck. I'm pretty sure that's what you're do-ing," she said, adjusting her position to give him easier access.

"No, I mean you, do you ever, you know, wonder where this is going?"

Micky grabbed him by the sides of his face, which had made its way to her left breast, and forced him to look up.

"OK. You picked a weird time to have this conversation so I'm go-ing to keep this short. I'm young, you're older. I don't care. My mother says I'm wasting my time. I don't think so and she isn't the best judge considering she and my father got divorced when I was seven. I'm an only child, so I don't know that much about big families. I'm happy now. I'm not worried about later. And as far as where *this* is going," she said giving his face a gentle shake, "I can barely wait to find out."

She then returned his mouth to her breast and gave his head a slight push downward. He ran his tongue around her nipple then down over her belly, pulling the covers off her as he went. He moved to her inner thigh, first one side, then the other. She began to moan softly and arched her back. Finally she tilted her pelvis to signal she couldn't wait any longer. He was more than happy to oblige.

Chapter 25

"Ron? Yeah, it's me, Bill." Dr. Riegel had privately declared war on the COO and was calling Dr. Carter, the Chief of Staff, in an attempt to recruit him to the cause.

"Got a minute? Good. I need to talk to you about Doyle. Yeah, *that* Doyle. He's trying to blackmail me into supporting Byner's application. Says if I don't play ball he's gonna recommend that the ER gets shut down to keep the no-pays out. Right, right, Sister Dolores isn't going for it, at least for now, but this guy's slick so it's hard to know what could happen if the money situation gets worse. I need a little help. You in?"

Dr. Carter had been on the staff of Saints' Hospital for over thirty years. He was a well-known and well-respected member of the medical community. His relationship with Saints' lent a certain respectability to the place and the reputation of the hospital as a solid, no nonsense center for quality health care reflected that aura back onto him and the other physicians. He was reluctant to allow that image to be tarnished by the admission of a questionable physician to the staff or by the adoption of a program like CARE.

"What can I do?"

Dr. Riegel explained that as a surgeon in the community for many years he would likely know most of the other surgeons in the area. A discrete inquiry could be made about the work habits, and other habits, of a certain anesthesiologist. Completely off the record, of course.

"See if there's any fire behind all the smoke, find out why this guy needs to change hospitals every few years. If he's clean, fine, but if he's squirrely we need to know."

Fact was that Dr. Carter had already made a few calls of his own. He'd been uncomfortable with the idea of a rapid detox program at Saints'. He knew that one bad outcome, one celebrity death at the hands of Dr. Jerry, would get blown into epic proportions. A small hospital like Saints' would have a difficult time recovering from that kind of publicity.

Though no one would say as much he got the impression that his colleagues at the surrounding hospitals hadn't been particularly sorry to see Dr. Byner go. He couldn't get details but when his questions about ethics and character were answered by 'Oh boy,' he figured that the flames Dr. Riegel suspected were probably real.

Besides, he had another reason to join forces with the director. In his own private meeting with Mr. Doyle he'd been informed of another plan to improve the bottom line.

"I'm in negotiations with a surgical group to bring their bariatric program to Saints'."

Bariatric medicine is the treatment of obesity. When diet and exercise just won't do, there are a variety of surgical procedures available that can be used to help those with insufficient will power, or 'glandular problems', lose weight. Who qualifies for the procedure is based on body mass, though the selection process can get a little fuzzy depending on who's going to be paying for it. If it's the patient, cash up front, he or she might have a bit more to say about the need for surgery than if Blue Cross was on the hook.

Getting a surgical group to leave one hospital and join another generally involved the payment of bribes. The head of the group would get a 'directorship' with a stipend. The hospital would agree to supply office space, maybe staff, at a discounted rate. So far Saints' had maintained a no bullshit policy in this regard. If you were a physician and you wanted to work at Saints', fine, as long as your application was clean, but nobody was going to pay you for your business. Dr. Carter intended to do whatever he could to keep things that way.

"Gee, that's great," Dr. Riegel said, "he can call the program FATSO, the Fast Answer To Severe Obesity."

"Sorry I didn't think of that at the time or I'd have suggested it."

"Oh, Christ," had been all he could think of at the time as he walked out of the COO's office.

"So?" Dr. Riegel asked.

"I'm in," was the response.

Chapter 26

It took less than a week for project diversion to attract the attention of the County EMS director. Hospital closure hours were one of the statistics she kept a close eye on. All ER's closed once in a while, some more often than others, but in general each facility had a fairly predictable routine. Saints would close three or four hours a week. Memorial, because the types of cases they received and their patient volume, would close a few hours more. When Saints' began closing for ten to twelve hours a day eyebrows were raised.

The first to notice were the MICN's, the mobile intensive care nurses, at Memorial. These were the nurses who worked the radio and directed the ambulance traffic. Mention was made to the Paramedic Liason Nurse, the MICNS' boss, who then made a call to Elizabeth Rowland, the director of the County Emergency Medical Services. She in turn phoned Sister Dolores who then rang Dr. Riegel, inviting him to a meeting in her office.

"I got a call from Elizabeth Rowland this morning. You familiar with her?" The question was rhetorical.

"She told me our ER has been on diversion nearly twelve hours a day for the past week. She wanted to know what the problem was. I couldn't tell her because for some reason no one had bothered to let me know we had a problem. So, do we have a problem?"

"It's Doyle." The director had thought about this conversation since the day he'd devised The Plan. A good offense, he'd decided, would be the best defense. Sister Dolores tilted her head slightly.

"Mr. Doyle told you to go on diversion?"

"Not exactly. Remember the day you went to the lawyers office for the reading of Mr. Walter's will?" Another rhetorical question. "Well while you were gone Doyle calls me in for a little pep talk. Told me I needed to green-light that guy Byner's application 'or else'."

"Keep going."

"Says that without Byner's business this place is going to go under. Then he threatens to close the ER or get me fired, or both. Byner's file doesn't smell right, and I tell him as much. He doesn't care. Turns out that he had a talk with Dr. Carter, too. Something about moving a bariatric program to this hospital. Rapid Detox, bariatric surgery, what's next? Maybe we should get a liquor license or find some Indian we can put on the board and turn part of the med-surg ward into a casino. All I'm doing is trying to cut down on the number of uninsured admissions until we can figure something out that makes sense."

"Or until Mr. Walter's will clears probate," she added.

"Yeah, or that."

"Look, Bill, I appreciate your motives, but you know as well as I do that if the County comes in for an audit, maybe invites someone from the federal government to join them, and sees what you're doing, Doyle could be the least of your problems."

The director thought about that for a minute before responding.

"Remember years ago when all we did was take care of sick people? I mean people with infections, people who needed surgery, and I'm not talking about liposuction or tummy tucks. I think we were both happier then. I mean, we were younger then, so we were probably happier about that, but I think we enjoyed our jobs more than we do now."

"We also hadn't been doing them as long," she pointed out.

"That's true, but still, there's something else that's gone wrong. If I'm working in the ER taking care of some diabetic with a sugar of a thousand and a blood pressure of fifty I'm still having fun. Even now, though I can't do it as often as I used to. I'm not thinking about anything but the sick guy and what I need to do to turn the situation around. And when I do, I still feel that rush, you know, job well done and all that. So why is it a hospital can't make money doing what it was built to do in the first place? We haven't run out of sick people. There's plenty of them to go around. It's just that no one wants to pay the bills any more."

Sister Dolores was perfectly aware of all this but chose to stay silent and let her old friend blow off a little more steam. Dr. Riegel sensed the opportunity and decided to take advantage of it.

"So now, we take care of sick people for nothing, or next to nothing, and the hospital has to go out and hire a gerbil like Doyle to drum up some paying business. And the best he can do is dig up guys like Byner and some specialty surgical group, guys that have found a way to work the system, living well on the outer fringes of legitimate medicine. It's all billboards and magazine ads. And that's not even scratching the surface because so much of this so-called medical care doesn't even see the inside of a hospital any more. It's out-patient, office work, surgi-centers. There's nothing left for the hospitals to do any more."

He heard himself say it, and a second later it registered. Sister Dolores noted the moment of enlightenment.

"You done?"

The director grumbled, suggesting he was.

"Good. You're right. It's not like the old days, and it will never be that way again. We *are* competing with all those places you just mentioned and we have to find new ways to 'stay in the game', is how I think you'd put it. Mr. Doyle isn't the problem. We need someone like him who knows what's out there, what our options are, to help us stay solvent. It's up to him to come up with suggestions, it's up to me and the medical staff leadership to decide which of those things would be a good fit for Saints'. You getting me?"

"Yeah, yeah."

"So go back to the ER and get those patients admitted or discharged or transferred or whatever you have to do to get the place open again. I'll tell Doyle to back off on Dr. Byner's application until we can get more information and I'll talk to Carter about the bariatric thing. It might actually be OK, you know? Taking someone who weighs five hundred pounds and getting him down to two-twenty without killing him isn't necessarily contradictory to our mission statement. Oh, and tell your second in command, Dr. Hooks, that I'm keeping an eye on him.

Chapter 27

"So?"

Ten days had passed since the reading of the will, sufficient time for Elaine to enlist the services Dunham and Sykes, a high powered firm with offices in New York, London, Hong Kong and Los Angeles, specializing in business litigation and probate law. I had also been enough time for the first salvo of allegations and accusations to come crashing down on the offices of John Wright, solo practitioner. Mr. Wright had expected as much. With seventy million dollars at stake he doubted the family would scrimp on attorneys' fees.

Among the various complaints enumerated in the initial documents were diminished capacity on the part of the deceased, mistreatment, and possible malpractice, in the form of 'failure to treat' during the final code blue, on the parts of one Dr. Hooks and Saints' Hospital, and undue influence by the caretaker, Mrs. Sanchez, who obviously took advantage of the old man's frailty and somehow managed to get Mr. Walter to change his will, much to her benefit.

Sister Dolores was anxious for details, and she figured ten days was long enough to have to wait for them. It was she who'd initiated the call.

"Well, it's pretty much what I thought it would be. They're going to say Mr. Walter was getting senile and didn't understand what he was doing, and then they are going to go after you and Mrs. Sanchez."

"And how are they going to do that?"

"I can't give you all the specifics yet, but..."

"Yeah, yeah, yeah," she interrupted, "just give me some idea what you think they're up to."

Mr. Wright took a long breath before continuing. "OK. In the complaint they allege mistreatment by the hospital and specifically by Dr. Hooks. They say life-saving interventions were withheld at the very end causing Mr. Walter's death."

"That's ridiculous!"

"I'm sure it is," the lawyer replied calmly. "They haven't filed a malpractice case, at least not yet, and the firm they've retained doesn't do that sort of thing."

"So?"

"My guess is that they will try to raise doubts about the ethics of the hospital. Were there ulterior motives that may have influenced the doctor's decisions? They will try to impeach the reputation of the hospital. They will do whatever they can to convince a judge that you and Saints' are unworthy of the gift and that if their father had been in his right mind he would have realized all this and would never have altered his will."

"That's all just nonsense," Sister Dolores sputtered. "And what about Consuela? How are they going to try to ruin *her* life?"

"Ah. That's going to be a little easier. Whenever, or almost whenever, there's a will in which the caretaker or a domestic gets what seems like a disproportionate share of the estate and the will is contested, the family will claim the caretaker was guilty of applying 'undue influence'. In this case, my guess is they'll claim Mrs. Sanchez was with Mr. Walter every day for many years, which she was, and that Mr. Walter was dependent upon her for many of the basic activities of daily life, which is probably less true but will be difficult to disprove."

"And then they'll say that because of this relationship she was able to convince Mr. Walter to give her three million dollars and Saints' seventy million? If she was that much of a Svengali why didn't she get him to give her the whole thing?"

Mr. Wright allowed himself a short chuckle. "Good question, and probably one I'll be asking at some point. Look, we're at the very beginning of this suit and I don't think it is of any benefit to either of us to speculate too much. Suffice it to say they will be aggressive and it will get unpleasant, if not downright ugly, before it's over."

"Hmm," she replied. Then after several moments of dead air she asked the question the lawyer had been anticipating since he first picked up the phone.

"So, how are our chances?"

"Well, I wouldn't break ground on construction of the new wing just yet, but I'm optimistic."

"Hmm."

Chapter 28

Norman Pearl was a partner at Dunham and Sykes and head of the probate division for the LA office. Probate is one of the more Byzantine areas of the law and over his long career Mr. Pearl had become intimately acquainted with its idiosyncrasies. The Walter estate, though sizeable, and the Walter family, though petty and cantankerous, were neither the largest nor the most disagreeable he'd ever had to deal with. Not by a long shot.

The office was located in a downtown Los Angeles skyscraper and occupied half of the forty-third floor. The views were expansive, and expensive, as befitting a firm with the stature of Dunham and Sykes. The large corporate clients and wealthy individuals who comprised the bulk of the firm's practice found the environment 'homey'.

"Please, come in and make yourselves comfortable," he said, motioning toward the conference room.

The family, or rather Elaine, had decided that crowd control was going to be an important element of the legal proceedings. The fewer people voicing their idiotic opinions the more focused the discussions and the quicker the resolution. Had she been able she would have limited the crowd to herself and the lawyer. Louise, in her opinion, was a middle-aged ditz with little common sense and no business sense whatsoever. Her brother, though not as ignorant, was spineless. Still, the business had been left in equal shares to each of them, and the cash, should their challenge be successful, would also be split three ways. Her sister and brother had to be involved. The last thing she needed was to win the case and then get sued by her own family. Besides, the lawyer had insisted they be present.

It was going to be up to her, she knew, to hold the hard line, keep the others focused. Louise had wanted her husband, Larry, to be there. Larry was, after all, the property manager for the office building they owned. Elaine reminded her that Larry was at best lazy and a bit dim, and that he owed his title to the fact he was married to her. She also pointed out that their father understood this, which is why he'd hired the young man with the M.B.A. from Wharton to be Larry's 'assistant manager'. Elaine hadn't invited her own husband to attend for similar reasons. Though he was paid to oversee the shopping malls, most of the actual oversight was done by the same young man. Maybe *he* should have been invited, she thought.

"I've read the will," Mr. Pearl began, "and I think I have a fairly good idea what your objections to it might be. I also understand there was an earlier version of the document with quite a different distribution, and that the new one was drawn up only a couple of months before Mr. Walter passed away. Is this correct?"

Leonard, Jr. opened his mouth but Elaine turned her face toward him and he quickly closed it. They had decided to allow Elaine to be the spokesperson. "It will be simpler that way. We can discuss the various details among ourselves privately but it would be best if only one of us spoke during the meeting. We don't need to bother Mr. Pearl with a lot of chit chat," was how she'd presented her case. She also reminded them that at $900.00 an hour talk wasn't cheap.

"Yes," she responded, "those are the basic facts. It is also important for you to understand that my father gave no reason whatsoever for the changes he made. None. He wouldn't even tell his own attorney. He had someone else draw up the new will. My father was an intelligent and sensible man. Nothing about this seems intelligent or sensible."

"Yes, it does seem a bit peculiar, and I think that will work in our favor. There are a few other vulnerabilities I think we can take advantage of as well."

"Such as?"

"Well, the most glaring is his relationship with Mrs. Sanchez. How long did she work for him?"

"About sixteen years. Eight, sometimes more, hours per day, six days a week. He treated her like family, we all did, and now look what she's done!"

"Well, we don't know that she's 'done' anything, but the fact that she's a big winner in the new will is going to raise some suspicion that she might have had something to do with your father's change of heart. The question is whether or not we can make it seem suspicious enough to convince a judge."

"You said there are a few, what did you call them, vulnerabilities, I think?"

"Yes, well, we touched on your father's state of mind, that will need to be explored, and we certainly will have a lot to say about his relationship with Mrs. Sanchez, but we will also need to take a close look at the hospital and the nun who runs it, Sister Dolores."

"You know, or maybe you don't, that our father died in that hospital, and that he died under questionable circumstances?"

"Oh?"

"He was a sick man, we knew this, but he was always a fighter. We as a family wanted to give him every chance to live. We wanted the doctors to do everything possible for him right up to the end. As it turned out, they didn't. When father's heart stopped the last time the doctor taking care of him, some doctor from the emergency room, just let him die. In fact, he told the nurses that our father 'needed to be dead'. Sister Dolores knows about this and told me the medical staff was going to look into it. Something about an investigation by some committee."

"I'm not an expert in medical malpractice," Mr. Pearl said after thinking about what he'd just been told, " but it might be helpful to get an opinion from someone who is. We don't do that sort of work here at Dunham but I have an acquaintance at a reputable firm that specializes in personal injury cases. With your permission I can give him a call. He can subpoena the records from your father's hospital stay and look them over. If necessary he can have one of his physician experts review them as well. If there's a problem it would be good for us to know."

Elaine looked at her siblings and raised her eyebrows. "Well?" Louise and Leonard, Jr. both nodded in the affirmative.

"Fine. Go ahead." She paused a moment then added, "So what's this going to cost?"

"For a record review and an expert medical opinion, probably less that ten thousand dollars."

Elaine grunted.

"It's not cheap, but I think it's worth it. Now," he said, changing the topic, "it's time for you to get your business affairs in order. This process is going to drag on for a while and until it's been resolved you need to keep things going. I will be in touch with you by phone and by mail to keep you apprised of the progress being made. There will be some depositions that will need to be taken and a lot of behind the scenes activity between our firm and Mr. Wright. As soon as I get an opinion from the malpractice attorney I'll let you know."

Chapter 29

The telephone conversation with Mr. Wright had given a lift to Sister Dolores's spirits. Despite the lack of details she now believed there was a reasonable chance the seventy-million dollar miracle could actually happen. The hospital was still losing money, though not quite as robustly as it had been a few months earlier. This was due in part, she realized, to the recent decline in uninsured admissions from the ER. She'd had her talk with Dr. Riegel, she'd told him to resume doing business as usual. The closure hours were back to normal. Whether or not the director had found some other way to steer the bad business away from Saints' was something she decided she didn't need to know. At least not now.

She'd also had a talk with her C.O.O., Mr. Doyle. She'd managed to convince him that the credentials committee had a legitimate need for more information regarding Dr. Byner and his rapid-detox program before approving his application.

"We don't want to push this through without getting as much information as possible. What good would it do if we get his program up and running, attract some attention, make some money, and then find out he's checked himself into Daydreams Recovery Center for six weeks of rehab?"

Doyle reluctantly agreed to 'be patient' in the matter of Dr. Byner. But, he was adamant that his vision of bringing new programs to Saints' was the correct one for the hospital's long-term viability.

"The staff's getting old. Guys like Carter are going to retire some day. We need to look ahead, find the next big market, and position ourselves to be a leader in that arena. And, I think I know what it's going to be."

Sister Dolores stared at him. After rapid detox and bariatric surgery she couldn't imagine what he'd come up with now.

"Geriatrics!" he announced with a grin almost as big as his glasses.

It's true, the population is aging, the baby-boomers are applying for Medicare, and the demand for specialized health care programs to meet the needs of this group will grow. Elderly patients have a unique set of problems, from brittle bones to irregular heart beats, from the need to be on multiple medicines to the loss of visual acuity that can make taking the right pills at the right time a challenge. Programs designed to combine outpatient day care services for the majority of these issues with an in-patient unit staffed by experts in gerontology to handle the more severe illnesses and injuries would be an invaluable asset to almost any community.

The problem is that these patients are covered by Medicare, and Medicare reimbursement is insufficient to justify the expense of setting such a program up at most smaller, independent hospitals. Plus, patients covered by Medicare cannot pay extra to any particular doctor or hospital for a service covered by Medicare. Whether they can afford it or not. So if Saints' wanted to add a surcharge for geriatric out-patient services in order to make those services available to at least some of the seniors they would be legally unable to do so. Medicare has a fee schedule for such services, and if Saints' can't make ends meet on that amount of money, too bad.

Saints' was running in the red, and though a comprehensive geriatric medicine program would be a perfect match with the hospital's mission statement there was no way the hospital could afford one. Sister Dolores tilted her head and knitted her brow as she continued to stare at her C.O.O. He, of all people, should have understood this.

"Huh?" she managed to say in response.

Mr. Doyle stared back, confused. "You know, geriatrics, old people. There's a lot of them and more on the way."

"I know what geriatrics is, you nitwit! What I'm asking is what, exactly, do you have in mind?"

Mr. Doyle hadn't anticipated a hostile response to what he considered to be a brilliant solution to a difficult problem. He was taken aback. He was also aware that self-preservation required that he not make his resentment obvious. He collected himself for a moment before answering.

"I've been in touch with a Dr. Varna. He has a large geriatric practice in this area. He might be willing to move some of that business to Saints'." Mr. Doyle had decided to leave out the 'if we can provide a little financial support' condition Dr. Varna had mentioned.

Sister Dolores had heard the name but was having difficulty remembering the context in which it had been raised. The C.O.O. took advantage of her reverie to continue.

"I told him I thought you would be interested in hearing what he has to say and I'd set up a meeting for the three of us."

"Isn't Varna the guy with all the nursing home contracts?" she asked, her memory having cleared some of the dust that had settled in that particular corner.

"I believe that he does some nursing home work as part of his practice, yes."

"Doesn't he send his patients to Memorial and Valley for admissions?" The Dr. Varna memory niche was now clean as a whistle.

"I believe so," Mr. Doyle replied.

"So why does he want to start sending patients to Saints'?"

"I'm sure he'll tell us at the meeting. I think..."

"Let me tell you what *I* think," she said, interrupting him. "I know how these guys operate. They have contracts with a bunch of nursing homes, they're the doctor assigned to care for all the patients living there. Make rounds at least once a month or something. On any given day two or three of these poor people, with strokes, feeding tubes, urinary catheters, you name it, look sick enough to be admitted to the hospital. I mean they're a mess on a good day, right?

"So the staff calls Dr. Varna, he tells them to ship them off to the ER. The patient shows up looking awful, they do a bunch of tests, and sure enough they find something far enough out of whack to justify putting him in the hospital for a couple of days. Then, after he's been 'cured', they send him back to the Home until the next time. Am I close?"

"I think that's being a little simplistic, Sister, I mean..."

"Simplistic? The only thing simplistic here is your attempt to con me!"

"Sister!"

"Shut up, Doyle! The reason he wants to start coming here is one, he's looking for another 'directorship' to supplement his income, or two, he's having problems at Memorial and Valley, or most likely one *and* two. And what's this got to do with geriatrics? It's geriatric ping pong, that's what it is."

The C.O.O. was by now completely deflated and bore the expression of a puppy scolded for urinating on the carpet.

"Oh knock it off," Sister Dolores said in way of an apology. "Set up the meeting. I'll at least listen to what he has to say."

Chapter 30

"Hey, Tommy."

It was Wednesday evening, four days after his romantic dinner with Micky. Fish had just finished working the afternoon half of his boss's shift and had stopped by the Step for a beer and a bite to eat. Micky had also worked the day shift, but had agreed to stay a couple hours late to cover for one of the night nurses who was having last minute baby sitting problems. Fish figured it would be pointless going home to an empty house.

Tommy was working the bar and Fish had taken a seat at one of the stools. The place wasn't particularly busy so he'd decided to ask a few questions that had been on his mind for a while.

"Yeah?' was Tommy's response.

"Can I ask you something?"

"Uh, sure."

"How old are you? I mean, you don't have to tell me if you think I'm getting too personal or something."

Tommy laughed at that. "You know, Fish, you could probably Google me to find that out. A lot of what used to be 'personal' isn't any more. I'm thirty-six. How about you?"

"Thirty-seven. Well, thirty-eight almost."

"Oh yeah? When?"

"About six weeks. September seventh."

"No kidding! My birthday is September tenth. Maybe we should have a party or something."

"Yeah, maybe. Really?"

"Well, the tenth is on a Saturday. We could do it on the eleventh, Sunday, instead of the usual pasta night. Think about it."

"Wow. OK."

"Cool. But back to your question. Why did you want to know how old I am?"

"I guessed we were close, you know, in age, and I was wondering why you're still single."

Tommy smiled, poured a beer for himself and came out from behind the bar. He motioned to an empty table in a quiet corner and the two took seats on opposite sides.

"You mean," Tommy began once they were settled, "that you're wondering why *you're* still single and whether or not I have any deep insights into the subject of marriage and the aging single man."

Fish let out a soft laugh. "Yeah, I guess that's probably closer to it."

"Fact is, I *was* married once, long time ago, for what seems now like maybe five minutes. I was twenty, she was nineteen, we were young and crazy—about each other and just crazy in general."

"Mind if I ask what happened?"

"My career. When we met I was a nobody singer/songwriter/guitar player working in little clubs up north, where I'm from. Six months later I've got this band and a couple of decent songs. We started getting attention from the A and R people, the..."

"The who?"

"Sorry. A and R, artist and repertoire. They're the people who work for the record companies, go to clubs six nights a week looking for new talent to sign or new material they can use for their established acts. Anyway, we get a deal to do a record but first its show time. They want to send us out on tour to open for one of their bigger bands, give us some exposure and a chance to get the material super tight. In the middle of all this Donna and I decide to get married. Everything is happening fast and we just jump right on in. Time comes to leave for the tour and she can't come with me. It's a money thing. The label's paying for the tour and they don't want to shell out one more penny than they have to on a new act."

"Let me guess," Fish said. "Groupies!"

Tommy laughed. "Yeah, that was part of it. I'd never been on tour before and only heard stories, but a lot of what I'd heard turned out to be true. It's intense, different town every other day for three months, women throwing themselves at you, even if you're just the opening act. It goes to your head. By the time I got home we both knew we'd made a mistake. Still friends, though."

"And you never thought about getting married again? The rock and roll life too good to let go?"

"Hey, Doc, take a look around. I let that life go when I bought this place. Sure, I've thought about it. Just haven't met the One."

"The One? Shit, I've never seen you with Any One. What's that about?"

"Hey, just because I don't bring the girls I'm seeing to the Step, or maybe I do and don't make it obvious I'm seeing them, doesn't mean I'm home alone every night."

"Yeah, I guess that makes more sense. Micky and I were starting to wonder if maybe you had something going with Marla."

Tommy laughed and took a sip from his beer glass. "I love Marla, I do, but it's more important to me to have her in the kitchen than the bedroom. Besides, I'm pretty sure she has a boyfriend."

They sat quietly for a moment. A few new patrons had drifted in, Tommy knew he'd have to get back behind the bar soon. Fish opened his mouth, about to say something, but Tommy spoke first.

"Alright, so why don't we talk about what it is you came here to talk about, mainly why you're still single. Is Micky starting to make marriage noises?"

"No, that's the weird thing. She says she's perfectly content the way things are."

"But you're not?"

"I don't know. I mean, I've never had a long-term relationship before this, couldn't imagine it. But now I'm starting to wonder if maybe I'm missing something. Maybe it's time to move forward, be responsible,…"

"Get married and start a family?" Tommy said, interrupting.

"Yeah, maybe. Jesus, I can't believe I'm even saying this. What about you, don't you want kids, some little rock and rollers you could share your wisdom with?"

They both took drinks now.

"Mmm. Kids. You know, when I was younger I thought I'd never want that life, figured I'd suck at being a parent. I was too much of a kid myself. But I have to admit that the idea has a certain appeal to me now. I think I would be a good Dad, and God knows I'd have a lot to teach them. But I'm getting older. By the time I meet the One, go through the preliminaries, get married, I might think I'm too old to deal with starting a family."

"Yeah, I know what you mean. Lucky for me Micky's so young."

"No kidding!" Tommy said, laughing.

"Well hey, Tommy, maybe you'll meet the One and she'll already have the Little One. Package deal."

"Hmm. I suppose that would be OK. As long as the Little One's father was way out of the picture. Anyway, I've got to get back to work. Think about the party. I actually enjoyed this conversation. Don't get a chance to talk about this kinda stuff very often."

"Thanks, Tommy. I'll poke my head into the kitchen, say 'Hi' to Sis.

Chapter 31

The meeting with Dr. Varna took place the day after her conversation with the C.O.O. The only surprise was the amount of money he wanted to be paid as the Director of Geriatric Medicine for Saints' Hospital.

"Ten thousand dollars a month?" Sister Dolores asked, quietly, as though she was actually considering it.

"It's nothing, really, compared to the revenue this program will bring to the hospital. I have an A.D.C. of nine. That's well over ten thousand dollars a *day* in revenue."

A.D.C. is hospital-ese for Average Daily Census, the number of patients on average a particular physician has in the hospital on any given day. Nine, for a hospital the size of Saints' with a total bed capacity of ninety-nine, is a big number.

"Nine. Wow. And what's your L.O.S.?"

Length of Stay is more important than Average Daily Census. Medicare pays according to a system called D.R.G.'s—Diagnostic Related Groups—each diagnosis is allowed a certain number of in-patient days. If the patient has pneumonia, for instance, the allowable L.O.S. is something like 2.8 days. If the patient stays for four days, the hospital loses money. If the patient only stays one and a half days, it makes money because Medicare will still pay for the full 2.8 days. Go figure.

And, depending on the diagnosis, the allowable L.O.S. will be more or less long. The trick with Medicare is to pick the diagnoses with the longest allowable lengths of stay and get the patients out of the hospital in the shortest amount of time. This involves meticulous documentation on the part of the admitting physician, meticulous being the adjective he would use, fraudulent the one the government frequently invokes when auditing medical records in its attempt to deny payment.

"It's great! In and out, no problem."

"Hmm."

Sister Dolores was a firm believer in the adage that if something sounds too good to be true, it is. A skilled gerontologist can actually get most of his patients 'in and out' within the allowed time frame. A less skilled doctor can still get them in and out, but not necessarily cured. When this happens the patient will often end up having to be readmitted within a few days. Medicare is aware of this. Readmissions for the same diagnosis to the same hospital within a few days of discharge are tracked closely. Medicare considers such admissions to be the result of 'premature discharge' and will then deny payment for the entire first stay.

One of the countermeasures the doctor can employ is being on staff at multiple hospitals. If a patient is admitted and discharged from one hospital, but then relapses and requires a second hospitalization, he can be sent to a different hospital where no one will know he was sent home from the first one, having been treated for the same thing, only two days earlier.

"And how about utilization?"

This is the third element that will determine whether or not a patient's hospitalization will result in a net profit. If you are going to be paid a fixed dollar amount for a certain diagnosis, you don't want the admitting doctor blowing it all on expensive diagnostic tests and fancy drugs. You also don't want him calling an excessive number of consultants. Every new doctor brought in on the case feels obligated to add something to the evaluation and treatment process. More tests are ordered, more medicines prescribed, more time passes waiting for results and follow-up visits. It becomes a mess.

"I'm telling you, Sister, I know how to manage my patients. I have none of these kinds of problems you're referring to."

Sister Dolores stared at him for a moment, then shifted her glance to her C.O.O., who'd wisely kept his mouth shut during the interview.

"Well, Doyle?"

"It sounds good to me, Sister. A program like Dr. Varna's would give us a real boost."

"I agree," Dr. Varna felt obligated to add.

Sister Dolores agreed as well, in principal. If someone like Varna could keep eight to ten patients a day in the hospital, every day, manage them effectively, and minimize the readmissions, it would indeed provide a significant boost. The problem was, she knew from the very fact she was having this meeting it was unlikely, at best, to be the case.

A practice like the one Dr. Varna was trying to convince them he had would be extremely valuable to the hospital hosting it. Administration would do whatever necessary to keep the good doctor happy. They wouldn't want to run the risk of a defection. Dr. Varna was making a heroic attempt to defect. Chances were he was wearing out his welcome at Memorial and Valley.

"Here's what we should do," she said after considering the situation. "Go ahead and fill out an application to the medical staff. Once it's approved you can start sending a few patients to us. We'll have our utilization people keep a close eye on things, and if it all goes as smoothly as you say, we can talk about some sort of directorship down the line."

"But..." Dr. Varna began.

"But nothing. It was nice to meet you. Mr. Doyle will see you out."

Meeting over. After Dr. Varna was dismissed she called the C.O.O. back into her office.

"OK, Doyle. What's your take?"

"Well, it seems like a no-brainer to me. He's got the patients, he understands the management issues, and we need the business."

"Hmm. So why do you think he wants to start sending his patients to Saints'?"

"We're a good little hospital, not as big and impersonal as Memorial or Valley. Maybe he thinks he'd be a big fish in a small pond."

"Baloney. My guess is he's a disaster. I'll bet his numbers are terrible, his patients are a nightmare. He's probably being hounded by committees at both places and he needs somewhere else to go. If I'm right, he's exactly what we don't need. Business that loses money is worse than no business. I'll also bet he never fills out a staff application. He'll keep going to different hospitals until he finds one desperate or unethical enough to take him on. You're on a roll, Doyle. Keep up the good work."

She nodded toward the door and didn't bother to look up as the C.O.O. slunk out of it.

Chapter 32

"Hey, Danny, it's me."

"Hey, Bro, what's up?"

Fish almost never called his brother at the office. On the rare occasions he did, Danny had correctly assumed there was a problem of some sort.

"Remember the case I was telling you about? The old guy I had to resuscitate a bunch of times because the family wanted 'everything done'?"

"You mean the guy who left a ton of dough to the hospital in his will? What did you call him, The Un-dead? That guy?"

"Yeah, that guy."

Fish had mentioned the case during dinner at the Step on pasta night. He knew his brother wasn't a specialist in health law but he also knew he was smart and a very good lawyer. He wanted to hear his opinion on the subject of 'doing everything possible' and who had the authority to decide what 'everything' was. When the details of the will became public he'd called knowing his brother would be interested in the turn of events.

"Sooo?" Danny asked, wondering what The Un-dead could possibly be up to that would have prompted this phone call.

"So, some lawyer just subpoenaed his medical records."

"Uh, y-e-a-h?"

"Come on, Danny! It means the family's hired some malpractice shithead to sue me for not giving the old guy the full court press!"

"Whoa, Fish, slow down. That's an awfully big leap you're making."

Danny had stood by his brother's side during the previous malpractice suit and knew how much he despised the entire medico-legal system. He was also fairly certain his brother was seriously overreacting.

"Really? You think so? The guy dies at the hospital, the family thinks I bumped him off, says as much to Sister Dolores, demands an investigation, then finds out their father left almost his entire estate to that very hospital and you don't think they're going to want to sue me?"

"Well, since you put it that way..."

"See?! I knew it!"

"I'm kidding, for fuck's sake! Calm down. The family's contesting the will, right?"

"Right, and..."

"Shut up for a minute, OK?"

Danny took the momentary silence from the other end of the line as a 'yes'.

"Good. First, how do you know the medical records were subpoenaed?"

"Medical records, or 'Information Management', whatever they call it these days, told Sister Dolores. She told Riegel, and he told me."

"OK. Any idea who's representing the family?"

"Riegel said something about Dunman and somebody, I don't remember exactly. Why?"

"Dunham and Sykes? Does that sound familiar?"

"Yeah, actually. I think that's right. But what's the difference?"

"Dunham and Sykes is an old, large, powerful, and mostly ethical firm. They are going to look at anything and everything pertaining to their case. Certainly the old man's hospitalization is pertinent, don't you think?"

"Yeah, I guess."

"So their wanting to look at the medical records isn't something surprising, right?"

Silence.

"And when they look at those records what are they going to find? Wait, I'll tell you. They're going to find that The Un-dead was really old and very sick and that you and the hospital did everything within reason to keep him going. Peer review looked at the case. You told me so. They found nothing wrong with the medical care. In fact, if anything they thought the family was being overly aggressive. How am I doing so far?"

More silence.

"Good. So Dunham, or more likely Norman Pearl who's their probate guy, will do his job, turn over all the stones, and realize he's going to have to look elsewhere for damaging evidence against the hospital. That's what this is all about. It's got nothing to do with you. Really."

"How do you know so much about this Dunham and what's-his-face bunch?"

"I'm a business litigator, remember? I interviewed with that firm, met the partners, including Pearl, who's actually a good guy. They do business with big-time companies on a global scale. They aren't going to risk damaging their reputation by doing anything iffy on some nickel-dime probate case."

"Seventy million isn't exactly 'nickel-dime.'"

Danny allowed himself a short laugh. "It is in their world, Bro. Listen, forget about it, OK. If they even *think* about bringing in some tort litigator to rattle your cage I'll send them a letter making it perfectly clear that you would be delighted to be named in a lawsuit because you will win, without a doubt, and then you will countersue for malicious prosecution and harassment, you will sue the family personally, and *you* will be the one with the seventy million when it's all said and done."

"You can do that?"

"Yeah, I can. I'm a lawyer. I can do whatever I want. But I won't have to. This isn't going anywhere. OK?"

Fish grunted what sounded like an OK.

"Great. Oh, while I've got you on the phone I should give you the news. Ashleigh just found out she's been accepted to law school down here in San Diego. She's finishing up her last bit of course work in summer school now. I'm going to throw a graduation party for her up in LA sometime toward the end of August or beginning of September. I'll give you the date as soon as I know it so you can make sure the two of you are free."

"Wow! Congratulations! We wouldn't miss it."

"All right. Take it easy."

"Yeah, yeah."

Chapter 33

In addition to the regular cafeteria Saints' had a small coffee shop named Daisy's Café. The hospital leased the space to Mr. and Mrs. Choi who ran the place. Daisy was the Choi's dog, an old, crumpled Shar-pei. Whenever they ran a 'Daisy's Special' Dr. Riegel would wonder if their faithful pet had finally gone to its reward, its soul in dog heaven, its carcass on the Café's menu. Regardless, Saints' made some money on the lease, the Choi's made a decent living, and the hospital staff and guests had somewhere to go for lunch when it was liver and onions day, or really bad lasagna day, in the caf.

Today was fried chicken day, something Dr. Riegel actually liked when he allowed himself the indulgence, but he needed a spot with a bit more privacy than either the cafeteria or the small doctor's dining room adjacent to it could provide. He was meeting with Dr. Carter. The topic was Dr. Gerald Byner and his champion, Timothy Doyle, C.O.O.

The director had managed to secure a booth at the back of the room and waved to the Chief of Surgery when he saw him walk in. Once both were seated Mrs. Choi, who did the waitressing, came over quickly to take their orders. She knew the doctors generally had a limited time for lunch and in the interest of keeping them happy she paid them a little extra attention.

"So, I've been thinking," Dr. Riegel began once they were alone. "It seems like the heat's off a little bit on Byner's application. I haven't heard a word from that twerp Doyle in over two weeks. Sister Dolores must have told him to back off."

"Yeah, he hasn't been bothering me about it either. What do you make of it?"

"Hard to tell. Guy like Doyle isn't going to just give up and forget about it. He needs to show his boss that he can get things done, bring in some new horses, change the game around. My guess is it's only a matter of time before he starts leaning on us to push it through."

"You're probably right, and when it comes down to it I doubt we'll be able to deny privileges."

"Whataya mean? The guy's a fuckin' disaster!"

"You know that, and I know it, and probably every medical staff in the valley knows it as well as every staff in LA. Problem is there's nothing we're going to find in any of his files more incriminating than what he's already shown us. You know, the diversion stuff. He's done what the medical board asked him to do and technically he's clean. So unless we catch him doing something really stupid or illegal we're not going to have any legitimate reason to keep him off staff."

The conversation paused for a moment as Mrs. Choi placed their orders on the table, a grilled chicken breast and brown rice for Dr. Carter and a BLT for the director. "What the hell," he'd said, "it would have been fried chicken otherwise." After they'd taken a couple bites it was Dr. Riegel's turn to respond.

"You know, I think we *do* have a way to keep him outta here."

"Oh?"

"He's an anesthesiologist, right? And anesthesia is a closed department at Saints'."

"Meaning?" Dr. Carter asked.

"Meaning that no anesthesiologist can apply for privileges unless Silverman is sponsoring him."

Dr. David Silverman, and his company, Valley Anesthesia, had been given the contract to provide all anesthesiology services to Saints' Hospital and its medical staff. Anyone wanting to practice anesthesiology at Saints' had to be a member of his group, and only he could decide who that would be.

"You know," Dr. Riegel continued, "one of his guys leaves town or one of his women gets pregnant and needs, you know, three years of maternity leave or whatever till the kid starts preschool and he's short a doctor or two and needs to fill the spots, so he finds the people he wants and walks their applications through the system."

"OK…" the surgical chief said, not exactly sure where his colleague was headed. "But my understanding is that Byner isn't applying for general anesthesia privileges. He only wants limited privileges to do anesthesia on his detox patients."

"Yeah, well, that's where it gets a little murky. I was looking at the bylaws a couple days ago. I couldn't find any staff category called 'limited anesthesiology'. It's either you're an anesthesiologist or you're not. As far as I know, Silverman has a full house so Byner's out of luck."

"Hmm," Dr. Carter replied, chewing the last bite of his heart-healthy lunch. "So you're saying we'd have to create a new category of staff membership to accommodate this guy?"

"Looks like that to me."

"And that would require a change in the bylaws, which would require a majority vote of the entire medical staff," Dr. Carter mused, almost to himself.

"Which would take months, maybe a year," Dr. Riegle added, a smile now forming on his face, exposing a tiny piece of lettuce stuck between his upper front tooth and adjacent incisor. Dr. Carter made a discrete gesture to alert him to the problem, and the director made a not-so-discrete application of index fingernail partially hidden by dirty napkin to remove it. Once the offending morsel had been dislodged, Dr. Riegel continued.

"Yep. No way Byner's going to wait all that time to get his show on the road. Lost time, lost momentum, not to mention lost income while we're farting around in committee trying to figure out what this new category of doctors is going to be, who's qualified to apply, what the scope of privileges is gonna be."

Dr. Carter laughed. It was one of the few, if not only, times the excruciatingly slow process of medical staff governance seemed to be a potential ally. "Doyle's gonna shit when he hears this."

"No question there, but there *is* a question," the director added after a pause, "and it's why hasn't anyone thought about this before? I mean, Byner's application has been on our fucking agenda for three months. All that time we've been looking at the diversion issue, now the multiple medical staff membership and resignation thing. And nobody ever brought up the fact that we don't need another anesthesiologist. Doyle wants the rapid detox program but he never thought it through. He never understood that this guy would have to be admitted to a particular department, in this case anesthesia, and that it wasn't going to happen without Silverman's OK."

Dr. Carter and Dr. Riegel then just stared at one another a moment.

"Shit!" they exclaimed simultaneously, drawing the attention of the family of visitors at the adjoining booth.

Chapter 34

"Hey, congratulations!" Micky gave her friend a hug, then they both took seats at the bar. Micky was the second person Ashleigh called after opening the letter from the U. C. San Diego school of law that morning, the first having been Danny. To celebrate the two had decided to meet at the Step for a drink and an early dinner.

"Congratulations for what?" Tommy asked, walking up from behind the bar.

"Ashleigh's going to be a lawyer!"

"Wow! That calls for a hug," he said. He was around the bar, and around Ashleigh, in less time than it took her to get off the barstool.

"Watch it, Tommy, she can sue you for that," Micky teased.

"It'd be worth it," he said with a laugh. "Really, Ash, that's fantastic. Good for you! I think this calls for some champagne."

"Champagne? You have champagne at the Thirteenth Step?" Micky asked, truly amazed.

"I'm a romantic, what can I tell you. I figure you never know when it might come in handy. Go get Marla and I'll get the vino. And I think a table would be appropriate." He grabbed four flutes from under the bar and placed them on a table in the center of the room.

Marla was the second person Micky had called with the news, the first having been Fish, who'd already heard it from his brother. Marla's arrival prompted another round of hugs then the three women sat as Tommy returned with the bottle.

"I hope this will be acceptable?" he said, holding it so they could see the label.

"Jesus, Tommy!" Marla blurted, "Dom Perignon, 2005? Are you kidding? Where did *this* come from?"

"My secret, your treat," he replied as he popped the cork and filled the flutes. "Way to go, Ash," he said, raising his glass, "we're proud of you."

They each took sips. Marla, and, to a lesser extent Tommy, understood how good it was. Micky and Ashleigh had less sophisticated palates but realized they were tasting something special.

"My god, Tommy," Ashleigh moaned before going back for seconds.

"Whoa, it's been a while since anyone's called me that!"

"Don't be a dork," Marla said, punching him in the arm.

"OW! Man, it's been a while since anyone's called me *that*. Where'd you learn to hit so hard?"

"Three older brothers, remember?"

"I will now", he said, rubbing his arm. "OK, ladies, it's Thursday, you know what that means. I need to get back to work before it gets too crazy. I assume you'll be having something to eat?"

There were menus on the table and he slid one in front of both Micky and Ashleigh. The usual Ladies Night items were there, with the addition of a 'special'.

As Ashleigh read down the list of options her eyes got wide and her face got red. She'd never been to the Step on Ladies Night.

"'Fer Her Burger'? 'Lickety Split'? And what's this special, 'Pierced Poultry/Chix on Stix'?

"Yeah," Tommy replied a bit wistfully. "I couldn't decide so I kept both names. Marla can explain. Enjoy the rest of the Dom. I'll check in with you a little later."

While Tommy walked back to the bar Marla did her best to explain the menu, and Tommy's sense of humor. By the time she got to the special Ashleigh was actually enjoying the presentation.

"So it's basically a take on chicken satay. Marinated strips of chicken breast on skewers, grilled, and served with three dipping sauces. A traditional peanut based satay, a chimichuri, and my version of a sweet and sour thing."

"So," Micky began after the food decisions had been made and Marla had gone back to the kitchen, "you did it. You're going to be a lawyer. Your parents must be insanely proud."

"I haven't told them yet. Or my brother. He's the one who's going to be the happiest. We're having dinner at my parents' house on Sunday. I thought it would be better to wait and tell them all in person. Danny's going to be there, too. First time meeting Papi. I mean, they know I've been seeing someone, and that he's a lawyer in San Diego. And they're not stupid so they know I'm sleeping with him, or at least I'm pretty sure they have that figured out. But Papi is pretty old fashioned and it's going to be a little tough for Danny. I thought that if I give them the good news at the same time they meet my boyfriend it might all go a little easier."

They both laughed and Micky refilled their glasses.

"But what about you?" Ashleigh asked after another sip of wine.

"What do you mean, 'what about me'?"

"You know, you and Fish. You've been together for a while and you seem so happy, that's all."

"What's gotten into everybody lately? Everything's going fine and then the other night out of nowhere he starts talking about the future. It was a little weird. And now you. Is everybody worried I'm going to be some old hag pretty soon?"

"Hey, I'm sorry, really. It's not my business. I didn't mean…"

"It's OK. *Really*. Look, you and Marla are my best friends so I'm glad you worry about me. But I'm OK. My relationship with Fish is good. Really good."

"And you never think about the future? You're perfectly happy to let things, you know, just *happen*?"

Before Micky could respond Marla returned with their orders. "Stix for the chicks and some grilled marinated veggies. They weren't on the menu but I thought you might enjoy them."

She noticed the bottle was almost empty and poured what was left into their glasses. "You guys did a job on the DP. You need anything else?"

"Yeah, I think so," Micky said, draining her glass. "It's going to be one of those nights. But no more bubbles. Maybe some chardonnay."

"One of those nights? Sounds mysterious. I want all the details later."

"So?" Ashleigh asked after the new bottle had been opened and the new glasses filled.

"So, yes. That's basically it." She paused while Ashleigh stared at her, not wanting to push but clearly not satisfied with the response.

"OK. Fish is a great guy. He's a really good doctor, he's sweet, and I know he's nuts about me. But he's a dreamer, which is good, but that part of him makes it difficult for him to settle down completely."

"What do you mean? He seems pretty down to earth to me."

"He is, but he doesn't know what he wants. He has this great job, and he does it really well, but he's always talking about quitting, doing locum tenens, surfing, travelling, working *here*, for God's sake."

"What!"

"Yeah! Can you believe it? He said it might be fun to work in the kitchen with Marla and do some part-time ER work to make enough money to pay the bills. We're in bed, you know, fooling around and he goes, 'yeah, fuck all that administrative bullshit. I'll go work at the Step'. I started laughing. I couldn't help it. Total mood-kill. He's such a kid."

"Oh, God," Ashleigh said, laughing. They took a few sips from their glasses and Ashleigh refilled them. "But what about you? Do you know what *you* want?"

Micky was quiet for a moment as she stared at her wine glass, gently twirling the stem. Finally she looked up. "Yeah, I do. I'm a lot younger than Fish but I think I've experienced a lot more than he has."

"You want to expand on that a little?"

"All right. So you know, or maybe you don't, that my parents got divorced when I was seven. I was still Daddy's little girl and all of a sudden he was gone. I remember the arguments and the slammed doors, but when you're that age you can't imagine that your family is going to just go away one day. I lived with my mother and saw my dad on weekends, a couple of weeks during the summer, and it was good but it wasn't the same.

"My mother was able to stay at home with me for the first few years but when I was ten or eleven she had to get a job. I guess money was a problem. I saw less of my dad then, too. He had a new girlfriend and I don't think she liked having this pre-teen girl hanging around competing for my father's attention. Besides, I thought she was a bitch and I didn't particularly want to be around her, either.

"By the time I got to high school, right?, ninth grade, Convent, and the hormones fully kicked in, I just went wild. I was a latch key teenage girl with pretty good looks and a serious chip on her shoulder."

Ashleigh's eyes got wide. "You? Wild? You're so not wild!"

"Yeah, well, not any more. But then I was hanging out with guys a lot older than me, smoking a lot of pot, drinking, cutting classes,.."

"Having sex?" Ashleigh interrupted.

"Constantly. From the time I was fifteen until everything blew up just before my eighteenth birthday."

"What do you mean?"

"I got busted. I was in a car with some friends, driving around, getting high. The guy who was driving was my sort-of boyfriend. He was twenty-three, I was seventeen. He ran a light and a cop happened to be there to see it. Pulled us over, took one whiff, and that was that. He searched the car, found this bag of weed. He took us down to the station to book us for possession and whatever else he could think of. Luckily he figured out who I was and called my dad."

"Huh?"

"I forgot to mention my dad is a cop. He was a sergeant then, he's deputy chief now. Anyway, my dad came down to the station and man, was he pissed. Somehow he managed to get the charges against me dropped. I didn't have anything on and I was a minor. I think he wanted to kill my boyfriend, or at least charge him with statutory rape, but I denied that we'd ever 'done it' and dad knew it was better to leave it alone."

Ashleigh took another gulp from her wineglass, as though the act of swallowing would somehow facilitate the absorption of all this new information. "Oh my God..." was all she was able to say.

"No kidding. And it wasn't just the pot and the sex, but everything was a mess. I was practically flunking out of school. Actually, I *was* flunking out of school, I just hadn't bothered to tell anyone. I'd managed to intercept the letters the school was sending to my mother so she was clueless. After the bust, though, it all came out."

It was Micky's turn to have a drink. She hadn't told this story to anyone, and, except for her parents, she hadn't seen or spoken to anyone who'd known her then for years.

"But you seem so, so, I don't know, *normal* now."

Micky laughed. "Getting busted was the best thing that could have happened to me. My dad really stepped up. I thought he'd just go nuts, beat me up, ground me, go all cop on me or something. Instead he insisted that we go to counseling. I couldn't believe it. He never seemed like the counseling type. He was this tough Irish police sergeant that everyone was afraid of and there he was sitting in a room with me and my mom talking to this psychologist. Twice a week. I hated it at first. I was so mad at my parents for the divorce, for leaving me alone, for dad's girlfriend, mom's dates, all of it. And I was mad at myself for getting into the situations I'd let myself get into. I turned eighteen about three months into the sessions, and I could have quit, but luckily by then things had started to get better so I stayed with it."

She paused for another sip.

"But what about school? I mean, you're a nurse, so somehow you managed to graduate high school and go to college, right?"

"Another lucky break. My parents met with the nuns at Convent and arranged for me to get an incomplete for the last semester of my senior year, the one I was really screwing up. So instead of flunking out I was able to do a home-study course to get my diploma. I graduated after the fall semester of the next school year. My grades were good, my attitude was much better, and the principle wrote a nice letter of recommendation for me. I got into City College for the winter semester, and it was pretty smooth sailing from there on."

"Reminds me of Carlos," Ashleigh mumbled, almost to herself.

"Yeah, a little," Micky said, remembering what she'd heard during his testimony at her brother's malpractice trial a couple years earlier. "He had it a lot tougher than I did, though. I was just an angry little brat. Anyway, to get back to where this all started, I did a lot of living when I was younger and I had to make some conscious decisions about who I wanted to be when I grew up, so, yeah, at this point I think I *do* know what I want. Hey, I need to make a trip to the ladies room. All this wine, you know?"

"Me too."

They got up and Ashleigh had to hold on to the back of her chair for support.

"Whoa! I guess I overdid it a little. I'm kind of a lightweight when it comes to alcohol."

Micky was feeling it, too. She put her arm around Ashleigh's waist and together they managed to make the short trip down the hall. Not, however, without catching the attention of Tommy, who'd been keeping an eye on them from behind the bar, and of a number of women who'd come in during the time they'd been there. The two best looking women in the room, by a good margin, arms around each other, on Ladies Night at the Step. There was, Tommy knew, no better advertisement than that.

On the way back to their table they stopped by the kitchen to say goodnight to Marla. She took one look at them and made a decision.

"OK. Tommy will call you a cab to take you to my place. Ash, you can stay in my room. I'm going to Bob's when I get off. Mick, I'm sure you were planning to see my brother when he got home from work? Good. I'll come by tomorrow morning and give you a ride back here so you can pick up your cars."

"But…" Ashleigh protested.

"No buts," Marla replied, cutting her off.

It was a few minutes after eight when the two walked out the door onto the sidewalk, still with their arms around one another.

"Good friends?" a woman asked with a lascivious grin as she walked past them to go inside.

"Nah," Micky replied, smiling, "we just met."

"Damn! I'm going to have to start coming earlier," the woman grumbled.

Chapter 35

"What do you mean 'there's nothing there'"?

"Just that. There's nothing there."

"That's impossible. There has to be something there. Even *you* said that your colleague said that there's *always* 'something there' if you know where to look. Are you sure this guy knows what he's doing?"

"He's been doing this a long time and he's quite capable. If he tells me 'there's nothing there' I believe him. He had one of his experts review the entire record, took him over two full days, and he couldn't find anything either."

"But that doctor just gave up. He said my father needed to be dead, and then he just let him die. How can that be 'nothing'? It certainly sounds like 'something' to me! What's wrong with everybody?"

Elaine was having some difficulty understanding how her father could be admitted to the hospital one day very much alive, if a bit worse for wear, and then leave the hospital only three days later dead as a doornail, and have it be no one's fault. It was always someone's fault when something happened that you would rather had not. Wasn't it?

"Let me try to explain," Mr. Pearl said, trying to maintain a professional tone. "Your father had multiple organ failure. His heart, his kidneys, were failing. According to my colleague and his expert, the doctor, Hooks, I believe, did everything within reason to sustain him. At the end, when the doctor said 'he needs to be dead', he was making a somewhat flippant, though accurate, observation. No additional treatments or interventions would have prevented your father from dying. It was his time. It would have been inappropriate to subject him to any further discomfort or indignity."

There was silence on the other end of the line as Elaine tried to process the disappointing news. "So that's it? We just let it go?" she finally responded.

"We let this particular issue go, yes."

"So now what?" Elaine was beginning to question her choice of counsel. As far as she was concerned she'd just spent ten grand on a wild goose chase. That it had been a wild goose she herself had demanded be chased, was, in her mind, irrelevant.

"Excellent question!" Mr. Pearl heard the edge in her voice. Praising an obvious question was his way of dulling that edge. "So now we move on to the issues in the case most likely to produce the results we are looking for."

"Such as?"

"Such as you father's state of mind when he revised the will, and his relationship with Mrs. Sanchez."

"And how do you plan to do that? Are you going to give Connie a ring and ask her if she talked our father into changing his will, cutting us off for all intents and purposes? Maybe ask her if he was acting a little strangely, getting a little senile? Then I suppose she's going to say, 'yes, I'm so sorry, I took advantage of that poor old man. The nun made me do it. I don't want any money, here, please, take it back. I couldn't live with myself knowing I cheated you out of your rightful inheritance?' Is that your plan?"

"Mrs. Baker," the attorney began after pausing long enough to stifle his growing annoyance, "when you retained this firm to represent you I'm assuming you did so after considerable deliberation. Am I correct?"

"Of course! This matter is of vital importance to our entire family."

"Of course. And your decision was based in part on our reputation as being one of the best firms in the world in this area of the law. Is that also correct?"

"Yes, but…"

"Mrs. Baker, excuse me for interrupting, but let me explain. Dunham Sykes is, in fact, one of the top business litigation firms in the Country, and I, as the head of the probate division, pride myself as being at the top of my field. As such you would expect me to have a better understanding of how to proceed in this matter than would a layman, such as yourself, for instance. Would you agree?"

He was taking a chance but felt it necessary. Either his client would come to her senses and allow him to work the case as he saw fit or it would be a miserable experience for all involved until the matter was resolved, or more likely, until he and the Walter clan parted ways. He was, he believed, too old to be miserable.

There was silence on the line as Elaine considered her options. She wanted to tell Mr. Pearl to go fuck himself, something she hadn't allowed herself to say to anyone in many years, and language that seemed somehow liberating as she ran it through her head. But intellectually she understood he was right. He was the professional, and from what she'd learned from her research, the best in the business. If she fired him it would set the entire case back by weeks and whomever she then hired would likely be less capable.

"OK, Mr. Pearl, where do we begin," she conceded at last.

Chapter 36

"Come in, have a seat."

Sister Dolores was behind her desk and she motioned to the chair on the opposite side. Once her visitor was settled she wasted no time on formalities.

"Look, when you called I was surprised, to say the least. I was under the impression that I wouldn't be seeing anyone from your family outside an attorney's office or a courtroom."

Lauren smiled. "That's understandable, considering the way things were left the last time we were all together."

"Hmm. So what's the purpose of your visit?"

Sister Dolores was expecting a sales pitch, an appeal to her conscience, or possibly some sort of veiled threat to her or the hospital should she refuse to consider an annulment of the will. She was ready for a fight. Lauren detected as much in her tone.

"I'm here because I think what I have to say needs to be said in person. Face to face."

The Mother Superior's expression hardened and her eyes narrowed slightly. "Here we go," she thought. "And just what might that be?" she asked.

"I'm not your enemy," Lauren replied.

This was unexpected but Sister Dolores remained on guard. She was not going to be manipulated by some young girl. Certainly not one named Lauren Walter. She waited, saying nothing.

"OK," Lauren continued, "I understand why you might be skeptical. That's why I'm here. You need to see me, not just hear me. I'm on your side. I don't want to have the will 'thrown out' like my mother promised to do. My grandfather was sick, but he wasn't senile or crazy. I'm not sure why he changed his will the way he did, but I *am* sure he had a good reason. My daughter and I have been well provided for. We're happy."

Sister Dolores allowed her face to relax a bit and the fire that had been burning bright in her eyes a moment earlier dimmed to a smolder. "So why are you telling me this? Wouldn't it be a lot easier for you to just keep quiet? I mean, if you aren't contesting the will you have nothing to lose and possibly a lot to gain by doing absolutely nothing. Aren't you worried what you mother and the rest of your family would do or say if they found out about this little visit?"

"What they're doing is wrong and I won't be a part of it. And as far as what they might say or do, believe me, it's all been said and done before."

The old nun tilted her head, taking a slightly different view of the young woman before her. She wanted details, but, uncharacteristically, felt that asking would be overstepping her authority.

"I've always been the black sheep of the Walter family," Lauren offered, "to everyone except my grandfather. My parents, my brother, aunts, uncles, cousins, all of them, lived their lives with one goal in mind—cashing in on my grandfather's fortune some day. It's been their only ambition as long as I can remember. I went away to college because I wanted a good education, but mainly because I needed to get away from my family.

"They told me I was being flaky, that I was irresponsible, too good for the rest of the family, a hippie, like they even knew what that was. Then, when I got pregnant with Amy they used it as a justification for all their nasty comments. Now I was all those things plus I was a slut and an about-to-be unwed mother."

Sister Dolores raised her eyebrows and tilted her head to the opposite side. This, she thought, was getting interesting. Lauren saw her reaction.

"I'm so sorry, I didn't mean to offend you, really. I just got carried away. I'll stop," she said, mortified by her own outburst.

"Listen, I might be an old nun, but it's going to take a lot more than that to offend me," Sister Dolores said, a smile beginning to form at the corners of her mouth. "You have a beautiful little daughter. I think it's remarkable how well you've raised her all by yourself."

Lauren visibly relaxed and returned the smile. "Thank you. She was my grandfather's favorite. Everyone knew it. They've always treated her like a second class citizen."

"I'll tell you a secret," Sister Dolores said with a conspiratorial wink. "I was the black sheep of my family."

Lauren looked up with an expression of incredulity. "But you're a *nun!*"

"Yes, and it's the last thing my parents wanted me to become. I'm an only child. My parents wanted to see me get married, have children. When I told them about my decision to join the convent it broke their hearts."

"Wow, I never thought of it that way."

"I understand what it means to follow your dreams. I was meant to be a nun, to run this hospital, to help others. I have never regretted my decision, and I think my parents eventually came to understand that it was the right thing for me to do. At least I pray they did."

The two women sat quietly, each considering what had been said, and heard. Sister Dolores was first to break the silence.

"Lauren, I want you to know I appreciate your coming here like this. I'm sure it wasn't easy for you. You should also know that your grandfather's gift is vital to the survival of Saints'. From what you've learned about me today, I'm sure you understand I'm not going to give it up without a fight. A very big fight."

Lauren laughed quietly. "I wouldn't expect anything less." She then stood. It was time to leave. "Oh, before I go I want to ask you to say thank you to the doctor who took care of my grandfather that last day. I understand he worked very hard to make things as easy as possible for everyone, and now they're trying to blame him for his death. Tell him I'm on his side, too. And tell him my mother's lawyer hasn't been able to find anything wrong with the care my grandfather received."

"I can do that, but you can tell him yourself if you want. His name is Dr. Hooks. He's in his office, actually his boss's office, over by the ER. I'll call and tell him you're coming. OK?"

It was.

Chapter 37

"OK, Dave, start waking him up. I'll be done in a minute."

It had been a routine hernia repair, maybe the thousandth one Dr. Carter had performed. A small incision in the groin, the hernia sac reduced back into the abdominal cavity, the defect in the abdominal wall repaired and reinforced with mesh, and now the last layer of wound closure. Twenty minutes skin to skin.

Dr. Silverman began dialing back on the anesthetic. By the time the last suture was in place the patient would be awake and breathing on his own, enabling Dr. Silverman to remove the endotracheal tube, the tube connecting the ventilator to the patient's trachea, without the patient being aware that it had ever been there. Elegant and efficient.

"He's becoming tachycardic—heart rate is one-forty. His temp is rising. Shit! Get the cooling blanket on him!" the anesthesiologist barked at the circulating nurse. "Malignant hyperthermia. He had no history, no family history. Damn it!"

Dr. Carter was done with the surgery, which was now the least of the patient's problems. He began helping the nurse with the cooling blanket while Dr. Silverman began administering new medicines to control the patient's temperature and to prevent him from developing any life-threatening heart rhythm disturbances.

Malignant hyperthermia is an inherited condition often unmasked by general anesthesia. A detailed history taken prior to surgery includes questions designed to reveal the possibility such a condition might be present. Any problems with a prior surgery? Anyone in the family have a problem with a surgery or with anesthesia? Anyone in the family suffer an unexpected death during a surgical procedure? In the case of the hernia patient all the answers had been 'NO'.

"Let's get him down to the ICU," Dr. Silverman ordered. The breathing tube was still in place and he attached an inflatable bag to it to manually assist the patient's ventilation. "Page respiratory to the unit. I'll start a sedative drip when we get there and put him back on the ventilator."

Ten minutes after the crisis began the patient was wheeled into the ICU. His temperature had begun to stabilize, his muscles had become a bit less rigid, and his heart rate had not increased. Over the course of the next hour neither Dr. Silverman nor Dr. Carter left his bedside. Untreated the patient's condition would likely be fatal. With the best treatment there remained risks of permanent brain damage, muscle death, kidney failure, and heart rhythm problems.

"OK, his core temp is back to normal, lets turn off the cooling blanket. We'll keep him on the drugs for now. Call me if there's any sign of worsening." Dr. Silverman allowed himself a sigh of relief. The patient was responding well to the various interventions. His chances of making a complete recovery were good. The two physicians left him to the care of the ICU staff and walked back to the surgical lounge.

"Jesus! That guy scared the piss out of me," the anesthesiologist said, pouring himself a cup of coffee. "I haven't seen a case like that in years."

"Me neither. Good job in there. You saved his life," Dr. Carter added. "You know, I've been meaning to ask you something."

"Yeah?"

"Yeah. This case reminded me how even the simplest things can go very wrong sometimes."

"And?"

"And I'm sure you wouldn't want to put yourself at any unnecessary risk."

"Of course not. But what are you getting at, Ron?"

"Alright. Are you in cahoots with Jerry Byner?"

Dr. Silverman looked at him and raised his eyebrows. "I don't know if 'cahoots' is the term I'd use, but if you're asking me if I support his application to the medical staff, the answer is yes, I do."

"But the guy's a flake! Why would you want him to be a member of your group? You already have a full house."

"I do, and they're good, but it's getting hard to hold onto them."

"What do you mean?"

"I mean the volume of surgeries is down, or at least the ones we get paid for. Haven't you noticed?"

Truth was Dr. Carter had noticed that the overall surgical volume was down from the previous year. He also noticed that he was getting calls from the ER for a larger number of uninsured or under-insured patients. It's just that it didn't really bother him too much. He was winding down a long, successful career. He didn't really need the money. The decrease in volume and the deterioration of the payer mix wasn't a problem. At least not for him.

"Look, Ron, I've got a couple of young guys in my group. They're very good, but I'm having a hard time keeping them busy. They have families, mortgages. They need a good number of good cases to pay the bills."

"And how is adding another anesthesiologist going to help with that?" Dr. Carter was pretty sure he knew the answer but he had to ask.

"Simple. Byner has his own patients. He brings in new business and it's all cash up front. He handles the detox drugs and he uses another anesthesiologist to do the actual anesthesia part of the procedure. Even if it's only three or four cases a week it would make a big difference to our bottom line."

"That's what I figured. And you're not worried about a bad outcome? It's happened before and it's going to happen again. You willing to get sued?"

"You said it yourself. Even the simplest things can go wrong sometimes. There are risks involved with everything we do. The trick is knowing what they are, screening your patients to minimize them, and knowing how to manage the problems that do arise. I'm going into this eyes wide open."

"But..."

"But what? You're going to tell me Byner's a little off, his patients are a little slimy? Maybe, but I'm not getting married to the guy. It's business. These people need help and we need the work. By the way, the next credentials committee is in a couple of weeks and Doyle tells me Byner's application should be ready to go."

"Wonderful," Dr. Carter muttered as he walked out of the lounge and into the dressing room.

Chapter 38

"So why are you telling me this? I don't get it."

"Sister Dolores asked me the same question and I'll give you the same answer. I think what my family's trying to do is wrong."

"But you have to admit it's a little weird that The Uh—I'm mean, Mr. Walter, would want to give all his money to the hospital. Right?"

"My grandfather was a very intelligent man, right up to the end. I'm sure he had his reasons. It's not like he left us penniless. You were about to say something before you caught yourself. You mind telling me what it was?"

"What do you mean?"

"You know what I mean, just before you said 'Mr. Walter'. Come on. Out with it."

Fish stared at her. The whole visit had been a bit surreal, beginning with the phone call from Sister Dolores announcing her arrival, to the 'thank you for taking such good care of my grandfather', and finally the 'Mr. Pearl, the lawyer representing my family, says there was nothing wrong with the care my grandfather received at Saints'.' It was a lot to digest.

"Dr. Hooks," Lauren nudged, "I've been quite candid with you. I think I deserve the same consideration."

"It was nothing, really, I was…"

"Dr. Hooks?"

He thought before speaking. He was in the clear, she'd told him as much. This entire business no longer had anything to do with him. What the hell?

"Fine. I was about to say The Un-dead."

"The Un-dead?"

"Yeah. It's the nickname I gave your grandfather that last day."

Lauren didn't respond, but her expression indicated she wanted a few more details.

"He was critically ill, pretty much all day. He went into cardiac arrest three different times and each time I got called from the ER to do the resuscitation. I got him back twice. I'm not sure how. I mean, I know how I did it, but I wasn't expecting him to survive. Your family insisted that we go all out. I thought it was pointless, but it wasn't my decision. So Mr. Walter should have been dead a lot sooner than he actually was."

"The Un-dead. Hmm," Lauren mused. "It's actually the truth. I mean technically he's been dead for weeks but in a way he's been a bigger part of our daily lives since he died than he was while he was alive. I think he would have found that amusing somehow. And you know, it might explain why he did what he did, with the will I mean."

"You think so?"

"I'm starting to, yes."

"Hm," Fish grunted. "Sounds like your grandfather was quite the interesting guy. Sorry I never got the chance to actually get to know him. Mind if I ask *you* a question?"

"What's that?"

"Well, how does all this affect you?"

It was none of his business but she chose not to mention the fact.

"My daughter, Amy, she's ten, got two million dollars, or she will get it when she's thirty. I got one million, which I can have as soon as this probate thing is over."

"Any plans for the money?" he asked. He figured if he was going to be nosy he might as well be really nosy.

"I studied wine appreciation in college. Yeah, I know, what's that, right? But now I'm working on getting my master sommelier's certificate. I've been working in bars and restaurants for years. One of these days I'd like to have my own place. This money could make that happen."

"Wow! A wine expert! My sister's in the restaurant business. She's a chef. She's about your age. Maybe the two of you should meet."

"Maybe. Where does she work?"

Fish described the Step, as he called it, in the terms the Time's restaurant reviewer had used. Gastro-pub. He didn't want to ruin the chances of the two women getting together by going into too many details, such as the full name of the place or that of its owner.

Chapter 39

"All I'm asking is that you just *think* about it, OK?"

"There's nothing to think about. It's ridiculous. I'm not putting my name on anything even *close* to that."

"Fine. No problem. We can call it Tommy's Special. You can blame it all on me. I think we'd be doing the public a service. Especially in *this* neighborhood."

"I wouldn't do it in *any* neighborhood, but especially not in *this* one! Come on, Tommy, they'll burn the place down or something."

It was Saturday, a few hours before opening time. Tommy and Marla were having a discussion about possible new menu items. Tommy had long felt he'd been ignoring the vegetarian and vegan members of the community. He thought he'd figured out the perfect solution.

"It's road-kill, for Christ's sake! It's perfect! Just think of all those people out there dying for a burger or a steak but they're worried that it's cruel to animals. We can offer them a guilt-free carnivorous dining experience. I mean, the damn thing got killed by accident. There it was, living free and proud, and then one day it steps out of the woods and onto the black-top and wham! Never knew what hit it.

"Now the guy who mowed it down has a choice to make. Does he let it just lie there, dead, for other animals to feast on, or does he do something a little more creative? I'm not talking about strapping it to the roof of his car and driving it to LA, but what if we had a service, you know a number he could call, and some guy with a truck could come and pick it up, take it to a butcher shop or meat processing plant or whatever. They could do the dirty work and ship it directly to the Step. Overnight."

Marla couldn't tell if her boss was serious but she wasn't taking any chances.

"You're out of your fucking mind, Tommy. I'm pretty sure that even if you could arrange something like that it would be illegal for about a dozen different reasons."

"You know," he continued, undeterred by her lack of enthusiasm, "it would probably be pretty easy to find out where the greatest number of vehicle versus large, edible mammal collisions occur. I could probably get that info from the Auto Club. Then we could contact someone in each of those areas, a tow truck operator or a handyman or whatever, some guy, to be the point man for the harvest. We'd get a toll free number that people could call, like 976-ROAD KIL, and it would go to our guy.

"He goes out there, picks up the carcass, and hauls it to our processer. We could pay him by the pound or something. Then the processer does his thing, wraps it all up, and FedEx's it to the Step. It wouldn't be an everyday menu item, of course. It would depend on supply. But we'd have a sign we could hang behind the bar when we do have something. 'Tommy's Vegan Delight Road-kill Special', or 'Vegan's Choice—Pontiac Farms Road-kill', something catchy to let the squeamish know it was all just an unfortunate accident and eating it won't cost them their PETA membership or anything."

He was smiling, but Marla knew that didn't mean he was joking. "You can be a real jerk, you know that?"

"Or," he said, his grin getting wider, "we could just *say* it's road-kill. No guilt for them, no problem with the health department for us."

He saw it coming but couldn't move fast enough to avoid it completely. The right cross grazed his shoulder but it was well enough thrown to have the desired effect.

"Ow! Man, you gotta stop that!"

"Can we be serious now? For maybe two minutes?" Marla was having a hard time suppressing her own smile. "Can we get back to the venison concept? Traditionally sourced, not scraped off the interstate. Medallions, one to the order, peppercorn-red-wine reduction, with a couple pieces of grilled baby vegetables on the side. Bar food size, high-end restaurant taste. You can call it Bit 'o' Bambi if you want, whatever.

"I love that!"

"I figured. My brother's bringing someone in for dinner tomorrow," she said, changing the subject, "some woman he wants me to meet."

Tommy narrowed his eyes slightly.

"Don't even *think* it, you perv! She's a wine person, the granddaughter of the old dead guy he was telling us about."

"The Un-dead?" Mr. Walter was by now famous among the Step regulars.

"Yep. She's working on her master sommelier's certificate. Wants to open her own food/wine place some day. G thought I could give her a few tips, thought we'd have a lot in common. Her name's Lauren, so be nice."

"I'm always nice!"

"Then be less nice, OK?"

"Fine. I'm looking forward to meeting her."

Chapter 40

Once Elaine managed to accept the fact that the hospital, and that smart-ass doctor, Hooks, were not going to be held liable for her father's death she was able to turn her full attention to the larger picture. The probate battle was very much alive on other fronts. Mr. Pearl had assured her he was fully engaged and she had wisely deferred to his judgment on the matter.

Of more immediate concern, to her, and to the rest of the family, was the business, or businesses, her father had left them. While he was alive Leonard Sr. had kept himself at the helm. He'd given nominal titles to his sons-in-law, and to Leonard Jr., and he'd hired Michael Perino, a young business whiz with an M.B.A. from the Wharton school, to be his lieutenant. But it was the old man who made all the substantive decisions. He knew the balance sheets, the accounts receivable, the dealerships that were underperforming, the managers who were becoming lazy, and the ones who were trying to make names for themselves by working extra hard.

He understood the limitations of his family members and made sure Mr. Perino kept a close eye on their activities. Although he never intended to leave the business to his lieutenant he had hoped to make it obvious to his heirs that the young man was indispensable. Whether or not the family may have fully appreciated this while he was alive, he hoped they would come to that conclusion in a reasonably short time after the reading of his revised will.

Elaine had understood Mr. Perino's value for a while. Although she never got directly involved with her husband's business activities, she knew that left on his own the shopping malls would likely have gone under. In a good real estate environment it would have been difficult for Roy Baker to have maximized their potential. He just didn't have a head for that sort of thing. In the current, deadly, real estate environment…she preferred not to think about it.

The same was true for her brother-in-law. Larry Conroy was a nice enough guy, and good to her sister, but he was, for lack of a better term, a dummy. Had it not been for the oversight of Michael Perino, the office building would have been as vacant as Larry's stare more often than not. Her brother was only marginally more capable.

She was aware of Mr. Perino's value, from a distance. She became intimately aware of it that awful day in Mr. Wright's office when the will was read. A multi-million dollar business empire, mortgaged to the teeth, now in the hands of the three stooges. She'd allowed herself the luxury of pouting and posturing, fantasizing about a quick resolution to the probate mess, arguing with Mr. Pearl, but now it was time to get serious. It was time for her to get involved.

The phone call from Mr. Perino was no real surprise. The only thing she found somewhat surprising was the fact that he'd beaten her to it. He'd suggested a meeting. Just the two of them. There were things to discuss.

They agreed to lunch and Elaine was given her choice of restaurants. She chose the Silver Spur, an old, familiar place with large booths, a clubby atmosphere, and things on the menu like trout almandine and frogs' legs. It wasn't trendy, it wasn't noisy. Two people could share a meal and a conversation without shouting or having to listen to a ten-minute recitation of the day's specials. The fact that there was a full bar and a decent wine list had also been a consideration.

"So," Elaine began after their orders were placed and the drinks had been served, "what's on your mind?"

"I'm sure you have a pretty good idea, so I'm not going to waste your time with small talk. Your father hired me to take care of the day-to-day operations of his companies. All of them. He was very hands-on, amazingly so, considering his age, but he needed someone to 'manage the managers' is how he put it."

Elaine laughed. "Let me save *you* some time. I'm aware of your role in our company and I'm aware that without your continued involvement it will be difficult, if not impossible, for the company to prosper, or possibly even survive. I have no illusions about the abilities of my family, including my brother and my husband. What I want to know is what are you going to need in order to continue working with us?"

This was not what he'd expected. He'd always known that Elaine was intelligent, possibly as smart as her father, but he'd considered her to be aloof, condescending and arrogant. He understood that without her support there was no chance of making the kind of deal he felt was necessary for him to be successful at running the business. It was why he'd called for the private meeting. Still, he'd been dreading it.

"Uh, excuse me?" was the best he could do while he tried to process her remarks.

"Mr. Perino, Michael, listen. I have the reputation of being something of a bitch. Probably well-deserved, too. But I am every bit my father's daughter and now that he's not here to shield me from the harsh realities of life, and has for some reason chosen not to shower me with riches, I am ready to assume the responsibility of riding heard on the rest of the family. I'm assuming that's what you've come here to ask. Am I right?"

"I need your support, yes. But I also need some authority."

"I'm certain you've thought this through. Why don't you just tell me what sort of plan you've devised."

Over the next hour, and over grilled halibut with a lemon butter sauce, filet mignon wrapped with bacon, potatoes au gratin, green beans sautéed with slivered almonds, and a couple more glasses of wine, Mr. Perino laid out his vision of the future.

Chapter 41

Saturday afternoons were usually busy and this Saturday was busier than most. It wasn't just the volume of patients, but the kinds of patients that were gumming up the works. Two women with abdominal pain, one in her thirties the other in her eighties, both requiring extensive and time-consuming work-ups to establish their diagnoses. Two of eight beds monopolized for hours.

One teenage psych patient with visual and auditory hallucinations waiting for the county PET team, (the psychiatric emergency tech on call for the entire county), to evaluate him, place him on a 5150, (a 72-hour involuntary hold), and arrange for an admission to an in-patient psychiatric facility willing to accept uninsured patients. Another bed full for an indeterminate length of time, plus one nurse dedicated to keeping an eye on him. Of course, Dr. Graber could give him a shot of a powerful sedative or anti-psychotic medicine to calm him down, but if the patient was too calm, if the hallucinations stopped for a while, and the psych tech showed up during that interval to do the evaluation, the patient might be deemed 'un-holdable'.

In that scenario Dr. Graber would have to let the young man go, knowing full well that when the medicine wore off, the patient would once again become floridly psychotic. If, during that episode of psychosis, the patient, now ex-patient, decided to jump off a building or run out onto the freeway there would be serious questions raised as to why he was allowed to leave the ER in the first place. Better to lose one nurse for a few hours, allow the patient to remain delusional, than risk the alternative.

Bed four was home to a chest pain patient, an elderly man with high blood pressure and diabetes. His initial evaluation had been negative, meaning the EKG showed no evidence of an acute coronary event and his cardiac enzymes, chemicals released from heart muscle cells when they are damaged or deprived of oxygen for a significant length of time, were normal. Nevertheless, the man was at risk for a heart attack based on his age, symptoms, and co-existing medical problems and needed to be admitted to the hospital for at least a day for further testing. Easy. Except that the telemetry unit, where the patients who need cardiac monitoring are sent, was short a nurse. The patient was being held in the ER until the night shift arrived.

Beds five, six, and seven were occupied by patients with minor problems, a woman with symptoms of a bladder infection, a 2-year-old with a fever, running around the room chasing his 3-year-old sister, and a construction worker who'd whacked his thumb with a hammer. These cases were simple and could be dispatched quickly, once Dr. Graber got done taking care of the patient in bed eight.

This was an 83-year-old woman who'd tripped and fallen on uneven pavement, sustaining a large, deep laceration through her right eyebrow. A careful evaluation had failed to disclose any other injury so it was a matter of wound repair only. This type of laceration requires the use of two types of fine suture material, one that is absorbable and can be used on the deep layers and one that is not, for the skin. It also requires good lighting and decent instruments.

The overhead lights in the ER at Saints' were top of the line when the hospital was built, some forty years earlier, but were now tired and restless. What light they managed to produce was difficult to focus, as the fixtures tended to drift when not being held in place. With the ER full and the waiting room filling there was no one available at the moment to perform that task. Dr. Graber couldn't adjust them himself without contaminating his gloves, which he would then have to change. So his strategy had been to allow the lights to find a comfortable spot for themselves and then move the patient's head to be more or less in their glow.

This only worked for so long. Eventually the lights would get antsy and move to a spot beyond the reach of the patient's head, or assume an angle so oblique as to render them more of a nuisance than a help. "Could somebody get in here, please?" he yelled from the doorway.

"What're you yelling about?" Dr. Riegel was passing through the department on his way to the parking lot. He'd stopped in to take care of some paper work and his habit was to leave via the ER. It gave him a chance to see what was going on, and it gave the staff the chance to see that he was there. This behavior lent itself to the generally held belief that one could never be certain when the boss might be nearby, so it was probably wise to assume he was and to act accordingly.

He walked over to bed eight and without asking understood the problem. He adjusted the lights and held them while his younger associate returned to the business of fixing the wound.

"Thanks. This has already taken twice as long as it should have between these ridiculous lights and these crappy instruments."

The instruments were made in Pakistan and were disposable. No surgeon alive would even think of using them in the operating room. But they're cheap and ER doctors are expected to make do.

"I thought you said we were getting some new equipment down here," Dr. Graber said while trying to grab the whispy 6-0 nylon with the jaws of a needle holder that didn't quite come together at the tips.

"I've been after Sister Dolores for months. She told me she'd look into it and do what she could. Then she hired Doyle and put him in charge of purchasing. So, I went to his office with the same requests, explained that it's getting to be like a MASH unit down here, jungle medicine, why can't we get even a little cooperation, and you know what he says?"

Dr Graber looked up. He obviously had no idea what Mr. Doyle had said and assumed the director understood as much.

"Well, do ya?" Dr. Riegel pressed.

"Uh, no, no idea. What'd he say?"

"I'll tell ya what he said. He said, 'Even if we had the money I don't think it would be wise to make any capital investments in a department that may no longer exist in a few months'. THAT's what he said!"

"Oh, my!" The woman being sutured had been taking all this in and was clearly unhappy with the thought of the ER being closed. "Is it true? Is the hospital going to close the emergency room?"

"I'm sorry, ma'am," Dr. Riegel said, "I shouldn't have said all that with you in the room."

"Yeah, but now that you did I think we'd both like to know the answer." Dr. Graber was done suturing and removed the wet and bloody drape from the patient's face. Together they looked at Dr. Riegel, waiting.

"Truth is, I don't know. I thought Doyle was just yanking my chain, sorry again, ma'am. There's been no mention of it since that first time. But he's a devious little twerp, sor..." He was about to apologize a third time but the patient raised her hand and shook her head. "Bottom line, I don't trust him so I don't know."

"Well I think that would be terrible!" the patient replied. "I've been coming here for years. We need this place. I'm going to write a letter to the head of the hospital. Who would that be?"

"Sister Dolores, ma'am, and that's probably not a bad idea."

Chapter 42

The plan put forward by Mr. Perino made sense. With her father no longer alive there needed to be someone with real business acumen in control, and ideally someone already familiar with the various companies and their key employees. Michael Perino was clearly that person and Elaine agreed to his terms and conditions. The problem, she knew, would be getting the men in the family to buy in.

The will made it clear that the businesses were now owned equally by herself, her sister, Louise, and her brother, Leonard Jr. Roy Baker and Larry Conroy were not owners so although having them fully on board with the plan would be good for company morale, it wasn't actually necessary.

Elaine gave a good deal of thought to the matter and in the end settled on a divide and conquer approach. Another luncheon was arranged, this time with Louise.

"So what's this all about? You sounded so mysterious on the phone," Louise asked after they'd settled into their booth at the Silver Spur.

"It's about the business," Elaine began. "With Daddy gone, we need someone to fill his shoes, so to speak."

"Well, Larry said he was hoping for a larger role in the company. I think he'd be happy to assume more responsibility."

Elaine had anticipated this. Her sister had exactly no business sense and was the last person she would trust to gauge the abilities of someone else, especially her husband.

"Excellent! Roy has also made similar comments. And I'm sure our brother is looking for a chance to prove himself as well. Isn't it great? The whole family willing to tackle this terribly difficult task at a time when even the slightest mistake or error in judgment could cause the entire empire to collapse. Practically overnight."

A cloud passed behind Louise's eyes. What, she wondered, was all of a sudden so 'terribly difficult'? Elaine noticed her discomfiture.

"With the companies mortgaged to the hilt we have a huge debt service to pay each month. Hundreds of thousands of dollars, straight to the bank, before we can even begin to pay any of the bills, not to mention payroll. One bad month, one missed payment, and the entire company could go into default." She knew she was overstating things. She almost felt guilty about the deception. Almost.

"What does that mean, exactly?" Louise asked, the clouds getting darker by the moment.

"It means that if we lose a tenant in the office building and the space remains vacant for very long, we will be running in the red. In order to stay afloat the shopping malls and car dealerships would have to pick up the slack. Larry would be under enormous pressure. Same thing for the malls. If the economy gets any worse, if the companies leasing space from us can't pay the rent, or go bankrupt, we're done."

"But…"

"But what? When our father leveraged the businesses he basically put us in a position similar to the one he was in when he first started. There is no room for error, let alone laziness or incompetence. But, unlike our father's position at the beginning, if we fail now we take the entire family down with us. Do you really think that Larry or Roy or our brother have what it takes to get us out of this mess?"

"But the will, Mr. Pearl said…"

"Mr. Pearl said there's a *chance* we can get it thrown out. A chance. And even if we do it will take over a year for that to happen. A lot can go wrong in a year. In a year the business can go bankrupt. Then, if we *do* get the will tossed and we *do* get the money, it's all going to have to go to the bank. We'll be stuck with property we'll have to sell in one of the worst real estate markets we've ever seen just to keep our homes. And if we don't get the money? Are you prepared to move to skid row?"

A tear formed at the corner of Louise's right eye which she dabbed with her napkin before it had the chance to reach her cheek. Elaine sat back against the booth cushions. That, she thought, should do it.

"So what do we do?" Louise asked, dabbing at her left eye.

Elaine then explained the Perino Plan and Louise was only too eager to get on board.

Chapter 43

After leaving Amy with a sitter, something Amy considered unnecessary and somewhat humiliating, Lauren got in her car and headed off for the Step. The plan was to arrive no later than 5:30 so she'd have some time to visit with Marla before dinner service began.

Lauren rented a small cottage in West Hollywood, a town within a town just east of Beverly Hills known for its many bars and restaurants, decorating and design shops, Sunset Strip clubs and its large population of gay men. It was a lively neighborhood with most of what she wanted within walking distance or a few minutes' drive. One of the few drawbacks, and the one she was confronting now, was its lack of a nearby freeway. Knowing she would have to spend time navigating surface streets whichever way she chose to go she made sure the sitter was at her place by 4:30.

As she made her way east she thought about what, exactly, had made her agree to this meeting in the first place. Sure, Dr. Hooks was nice enough, but not her type. Besides she didn't get the sense he was hitting on her. She knew lots of people in the restaurant business so meeting another up-and-coming chef who worked in what sounded like a neighborhood bar, despite the spin he'd put on it, wasn't something in which she would normally invest a Sunday evening. Sunday was her day off. Sunday evenings were generally spent with her daughter either going out for pizza or having something fun at home.

But the circumstances of their meeting, the relationship it had to her grandfather, the whole Un-dead business, gave her a gut feeling that she should follow wherever things led. At least to a point. One Sunday evening and a drive to Silverlake didn't seem too much to ask, though she wasn't sure who was asking or what the question was, exactly.

By 5:20 she was slowed to a crawl checking addresses for the correct one. When she found it she had to do a double take. It wasn't the Step, it was the Thirteenth Step, much more interesting, and funny. She found a parking spot a few doors down, maneuvered her small Honda into it, checked the mirror one last time, (she wasn't big on make-up and wanted to make sure that what little she was wearing wasn't smeared, or on her teeth), grabbed her purse, and got out.

As she approached the front door she had to laugh. Who could possibly have chosen the name for this place and why would an allegedly good chef be working here? It appealed to *her* sensibility, but she knew she was in the small minority when it came to matters such as these.

She opened the door and stepped in. As her eyes adjusted to the dim light she heard someone calling her name. She turned in the direction of the sound as Fish approached with his hand extended.

"Hey, glad you made it! I was afraid you were going to change your mind and blow me off," he said, shaking the hand she reflexively offered in response to his.

"Dr. Hooks…"

"Call me Fish."

She gave him the look everyone gave him the first time they heard that.

"It's a long story, but that's what my friends call me."

"OK, 'Fish', good to see you, too," she replied after a brief pause. "You didn't tell me the name of this place was the Thirteenth Step."

"Yeah, well, Tommy, the guy who owns it, has a peculiar sense of humor. I didn't want to put you off before you had the chance to check it out."

"No, I like it. I want to meet this Tommy," she said smiling.

"You will, I promise. He's around here somewhere, probably in his office. Marla said she told him you were coming in, probably so he'd be on his best behavior."

"Not for my sake, I hope."

"Yeah, well…"

"Excuse me, can I get you something from the bar?" The question came from Karen, one of the regular Sunday night waitresses.

Lauren did a quick survey and what she saw wasn't promising. "A glass of white wine would be good, thanks," she said, choosing the one thing besides a shot of bourbon most likely to be at least drinkable in a place like this.

"Put it on my tab, Karen, thanks."

Fish and Lauren exchanged small talk for the two minutes is took Karen to return with the wine.

"Here you go," she said, handing Lauren the glass. "Enjoy!"

Lauren automatically gave the glass a swirl and brought it up to her nose. She realized what she was doing and stopped with a soft laugh. What, she asked herself, was she thinking? The chances of whatever it was in her glass having an interesting bouquet were negligible. Better to just hold her nose and take a swig. Then she caught the aroma, and smiled again. She took a sip to confirm her suspicion, rolling it over her tongue to the back of her mouth, pulling a little air through her lips as she did so, before allowing it to continue on its way on down.

"Spanish. Alberino. Nice."

"It's something new. Marla just put it on the list. She was hoping you'd ask for a glass of wine so I could have you try it," Karen said before returning to work.

"Speaking of Marla, why don't we go to the kitchen so you can meet her?" Fish suggested.

"Lets."

As they opened the kitchen door they were greeted by the unmistakable redolence of a well-made tomato sauce. Lauren treated herself to a deep breath.

"Wow, this place if full of surprises."

Marla was at the sink, her back to the door, but turned when she heard them enter. She had a clam in her left hand and a small brush in the other, both of which she dropped back into the sink before drying her hands on the small towel tucked under her apron strings.

"Hi, you must be Lauren. Welcome to the Step," she said with a smile.

"And you must be Marla. Your brother has been raving about your culinary skills, and from the smells in here I'd have to say with good reason. What's cooking?"

"Thanks, but it's pretty simple tonight. What you're probably smelling is the marinara. I used fresh tomatoes. The really good ones are just starting to show up at the farmers' markets. It's hard to mess up great tomatoes, fresh basil and some garlic."

"Hard, but definitely not impossible," Lauren replied with a laugh. "I've managed a time or two. What's going on over there?" she asked, nodding toward the sink.

"Ah. Scrubbing clams. Linguine alle vongole."

"With the marinara?"

"No, no. Penne with the marinara, parmesan cheese. Nothing else. For the clams I just sauté garlic and shallots in a little olive oil, then some red pepper flakes, a little thyme, white wine, and some water. Not much because the clams will contribute their own juice. Put the clams in and when they're all open I'll add a handful of chopped parsley and a little salt. The linguini goes into the pan with the clams, and maybe a little of the pasta water if it looks dry. That's it."

"Sounds great, I'm practically drooling. Oh, and this wine, what a nice surprise. It'll be perfect with the clams!"

"The alberino?"

"Yes. It was the last thing I expected to find in my glass after taking a look around."

"Yeah, I know what you mean," Marla said laughing. "I know a little about wine and I've been trying to expand the list with things that are interesting but not too expensive. Tommy's been supportive, but I don't think he'd want me to turn this place into a full-on wine bar. I wish I had the time to learn more."

"Maybe I could help with that, if you want."

"Really?"

Fish had been standing behind Lauren and realized he was no longer needed. The girls were doing just fine all by themselves.

"Uh, excuse me," he said, interrupting.

"Oh, sorry G. I didn't mean to ignore you."

"No problem. It's just that you two seem to be hitting it off so if it's OK I'll get back out there. I'll save a table."

"Thanks," the women said simultaneously.

"G?" Lauren asked after Fish returned to the bar.

"Huh?"

"You called your brother 'G'. He told me his friends call him Fish."

"Oh that. I guess he didn't tell you his real name is Gilbert, after our father. He never liked the name. Kids started calling him 'Fish' and it stuck. He actually likes it. Not me, though, so it's always been 'G' between us."

Lauren thought about that a minute and realized it would probably all make more sense when she got to know them better. "So, back to the food for a minute. Is Italian your specialty?"

"No, not at all. I guess G didn't tell you about pasta night."

"He didn't tell me much of anything. I think he was afraid he'd scare me off."

"Figures. OK, so Sunday the Step is actually closed to the public. Tommy comes from an Italian family and they always did big pasta dinners on Sunday nights. Tommy wanted to continue the tradition, so every Sunday we have pasta night for friends and family only."

"This Tommy sounds like quite the character."

"You have no idea. You'll get a chance to see for yourself as soon as he's done in the office."

"I can hardly wait."

"So about the wine, are you serious about teaching me a few things? I don't know if I can afford to pay for your time."

"How about this, I'll teach you about wine, and you'll let me watch you cook. Deal?"

"Really?"

"Really."

"Wow. Deal!"

The two continued talking while Marla returned to the clams. Conversation was easy given their shared interests. By the time the last clam had been scrubbed they realized they were becoming friends.

"OK, that's done. How about we take a look out there and see what sort of a crowd we have? And we can get you a refill," Marla said, noticing Lauren's now-empty glass.

It was an eclectic mix. Tommy's musician friends, a few regulars from ladies night, the waitresses' boyfriends. Tommy insisted on keeping the total number to something under thirty, preferably closer to twenty. Any more and it was too much like work. Fish had chosen a table in the corner near the small stage. He stood and waived as he saw the women entering from the kitchen, and he managed to catch Karen's eye as well, indicating refills were in order.

"So, what do you think?" Fish asked as the women approached.

"It's certainly not what I expected, but I didn't really know what to expect," Lauren replied with a smile. "I like it. I mean, good food, good wine, these people." She was sitting with her back to the room and turned, gesturing to the crowd, as she said this. Then, turning back, she added, "and the irreverence. I probably like that the best."

Karen arrived with the refills and Lauren raised her glass. "To you, Fish, thanks for inviting me."

They took sips from their glasses and as they did Tommy walked up behind Lauren.

"Oh, and here he is," Marla said, " the one and only Tommy."

Lauren stood and turned. She hadn't quite managed to swallow the wine she'd sipped to toast Fish. She looked at the face grinning at her, gasped, coughed, and sprayed wine all over Tommy's shirt.

"Lauren Walter, I'd like you to meet Tommy Traina," Marla said, as though nothing out of the ordinary had happened. "But something tells me you already have."

Chapter 44

Over in East LA another Sunday dinner was taking place. Danny and Ashleigh had been the last to arrive. Her brother, Carlos, the former Los Locos gang member, who called himself El Culebra for the elaborate tattoo of a rattlesnake that began around his navel and ended at his right fist with a pair of fangs and emerald green eyes, had gotten there a few minutes earlier.

Carlos's association with the gang had been short-lived. He'd joined because he felt he had no real choice. In his neighborhood he was either with them or against them. There was no such thing as neutrality. The night he got stabbed and wound up in the emergency room of the County Hospital he realized it really wasn't worth it. He'd been stabbed in the chest. Twice. Only luck, and the ineptitude of his attacker, had saved him.

His parents and sister had gone to the ER as soon as they got the call informing them of the situation. They were relieved to find him alive and with no serious injury, especially his sister who was only ten at the time, seven years his junior. She idolized her brother then. Unfortunately, or, rather, fortunately as it turned out, his father saw the gang tattoo on his neck, the block L's at an angle, which the flimsy hospital gown could not conceal. Enraged that his son had succumbed to gang life, and adamant that his daughter not be exposed to it, he threw Carlos out of the house.

With no money and nowhere to go, El Culebra had some decisions to make. He could stay in East LA, crash at one of the Los Locos guys' place for a while, deal some dope, steal some cars, and wind up dead or in prison, or he could get the hell out of there. He chose the latter.

He had cousins living in the San Gabriel Valley, far enough away to be out of Los Locos territory. They had a construction business and offered him some work in exchange for a place to stay. For a while he worked only when absolutely necessary. It was easier to sell pot than it was to haul lumber and bang nails. Besides, it's what he knew. He was content. He understood the benefits of low expectations, though he probably couldn't have verbalized his knowledge as such.

He missed his family, especially his sister, but she'd been forbidden to have any contact with him. He'd resigned himself to the fact that those people were from a different life and he'd have to go forward without them. Until the day he and Rosa, which was the name she'd been given by her parents, met unexpectedly. In a hospital of all places. She was grown up, beautiful, and working for a fancy, if a bit sleazy, lawyer. She was appalled to see the snake tattoo, which he'd gotten after being evicted from the family home, (he figured it made him look a little crazy and possibly dangerous, improving his chances of survival on the streets), and she refused to call him El Culebra. He was equally disturbed by her new name, Ashleigh. In his mind it was an abdication of her heritage. In hers it was a liberating departure from a stereotype.

Whatever. The two renewed their relationship and with the help of her influence and example he quit selling pot, then smoking pot, then calling himself El Culebra, then started thinking about forming his own construction business. She'd even gotten him back together with the parents.

This was the Carlos sitting at the family table with a slight smirk on his face that Sunday evening. He was no longer the main target for his father's suspicions and disapproval. That honor had been passed to Danny.

"So," Mr. Montes began as soon as the soup had been served, "you've been seeing my daughter."

Danny wasn't sure if the comment was rhetorical and fidgeted with his soupspoon for a moment trying to formulate a response. "Uh, yes, sir." Keep it simple, he'd decided. Ashleigh had warned him of the impending third degree. He'd thought that his experience as a trial lawyer would render him impervious. The beads of sweat dampening his armpits informed him he was not.

"I see. She tells me you're a lawyer."

"Yes, sir."

"Uh." Mr. Montes took a sip of the soup. Danny took advantage of the pause to do the same.

"Excellent soup, Mrs. Montes. Albondigas, right?"

"Thank you. Yes, I'm glad..."

"Don't change the subject," Mr. Montes interrupted after dabbing his mouth with his napkin.

"Gabriel! Be polite," his wife admonished, using his full name to emphasize her disapproval.

"I'm sorry, Marta, but this is serious. Lawyers can be tricky. What kind of lawyer are you?"

"Business litigation."

"Hmm." More soup was consumed while Mr. Montes considered his answer. "You know, my daughter, Rosa, used to work for a lawyer," he continued. "Some maricon named Barry Bauer. Has his picture in the paper all the time. Ambulance chaser. Is that what 'business litigation' is?" He picked up his napkin to dry his lips and to hide any expression that would allow the now visibly rattled Danny a chance to relax. Carlos, a chip off the old block in many ways, was loving every minute of his father's interrogation.

"Uh, n-no. No. Barry Bauer is a personal injury lawyer. I, we, my firm, we don't do anything like that. We work with..."

"OK, Pappi," Ashleigh interrupted, "I think you should let Danny finish his soup. He works for large businesses, corporations. I'm pretty sure you already knew what business litigation was. He's very good, in case you were wondering."

Her father put down the napkin. He opened his mouth, about to quash this minor insurrection, but Ashleigh raised her hand to cut him off.

"There's something else I wanted to tell you," she said. "Something important."

Now she had everyone's full attention. Was she pregnant? Are they getting married? She knew what they were probably thinking, and let them think it for a few more seconds.

"I've been accepted to law school. The University of California in San Diego. I start in the fall. I'm going to be an attorney."

A brief, stunned, silence ensued, followed by a gasp from her mother and a soft 'all right' from Carlos. No one in the Montes family had ever gone to college, let alone law school. Danny was off the hook. A flurry of questions, hugs, and kisses followed. Why hadn't she told them before? Why was it such a secret? When was she moving to San Diego? Was she planning to move in with Danny? This last question from her father, who'd managed to regain his composure and refocus his attention on what really mattered.

"No, Pappi. We talked about it and decided I should have my own place. I'm going to be busy and I'll need to concentrate on my studies. I didn't say anything earlier because I didn't know if I was going to be able to do it, you know, get accepted. I didn't want you to be disappointed. Danny helped a lot. I got to work in his office and the senior partner wrote a letter of recommendation for me."

Carlos had gotten up and stood behind his sister. He gave her a hug around the neck and whispered in her ear, "So this is the 'big plans' you told me about, huh? Way to go."

"So, Carlos," Mr. Montes said. Carlos heard the tone and realized he had resumed his role as favorite target. "What's going on with you? Any big surprises, or just the same thing, working and getting by?"

He did have a surprise and had planned to reveal it before being upstaged by his sister. It no longer seemed quite so big. He considered his response and decided 'what the fuck'.

"I've been going to night school," he mumbled, almost under his breath. Ashleigh heard him clearly. He was still draped around her neck.

"What?" she yelled, jerking her head back and almost colliding with his chin.

"OK, it's no big deal, all right?" he said dodging the head butt. "Finishing my high school stuff. I want to maybe get a contractor's license."

The smile on Mr. Montes' face, the reaction to his daughter's news, got impossibly wider. He'd always known Rosa would make something of herself, he just hadn't known what that would be. His son, on the other hand, had been at best a question mark.

It was Ashleigh's turn to hug her brother, and wipe the tears on the collar of his shirt.

Chapter 45

The Perino Plan was simple. Why, he wondered, were these people having such a hard time understanding it?

"Could you run that by me one more time?" Larry asked, a look of bewilderment and consternation on his otherwise handsome face.

"Sure," Mr. Perino replied. "No problem."

The meeting had been called by Elaine and it was being held in her late father's office, a spacious though modest room at the oldest of his car dealerships. The office was dominated by a large oval table, at the head of which sat Mr. Perino. This had caused Leonard Jr. a bit of discomfort. Since his father's death he had assumed he would be the one in charge, certainly of the auto business, if not the entire company. The big chair at the head of the table should, he felt, be his. Mr. Perino was already ensconced when the others arrived and gave no indication he was going anywhere.

"As I said," he began in response to Larry's question, "when Mr. Walter was alive he functioned as the CEO and chairman of the board. There was never any question he was in charge. You, (nodding toward the men in the room), were given specific titles and responsibilities as well as generous compensation packages. What you did not have was autonomy. You were asked to do things the way Mr. Walter wanted them done. I was hired to make sure you did. With Mr. Walter gone someone needs to fill the management gap. I apologize for being blunt, but the only one in this room qualified to do that is me."

He paused to allow them to process what he'd said. Leonard opened his mouth but Elaine raised her hand, her usual gesture suggesting he'd be better off keeping it shut.

"Why don't we let Michael finish outlining his plan before discussing specific details," she said calmly. Her use of the familiar address was not lost on Leonard Jr. who was beginning to sense he'd been led into some sort of trap.

"My plan is this: I will take over as the CEO with overall responsibility for the management of the entire company. In effect, I will be assuming the job that Mr. Walter did so well for so long. You, Leonard, will be president of the automotive division. Roy and Larry, you will be co-vice presidents of the commercial real estate division, with Roy overseeing the malls and Larry handling the office building.

"As for compensation, I propose base salaries commensurate with the responsibilities each of you will assume with bonuses semiannually based on performance. In the past most of the income you drew from the business came from company profits, which were substantial due to the lack of debt. Going forward, highly leveraged as the company now is, there won't be that kind of profit and your incomes will have to be looked at as operating expenses.

"Assuming you all work hard and meet your performance goals the company should thrive. In that scenario there will in fact be profits which will be distributed equally to the owners at year-end. So, although Leonard will be earning more each month due to the complexities of his job, overseeing seven dealerships, each of you has the potential to do quite well with the year-end distribution."

"And what about yourself, how do you envision getting paid," Elaine asked, anticipating the question that should have been on the minds of the others.

"I will draw a salary, just like everyone else, and I will also be eligible for profit sharing at the end of the year. I will want a golden parachute, something that will discourage you all from firing me after a couple of years if we get this company out of some debt and you think you can manage on your own."

"And the board of directors?" again from Elaine.

"Ah, good question. In the past Leo basically *was* the board of directors. As the sole owner he didn't see the need for a lot of 'outside interference'—that's how he described it to me when I asked the same question. Now, obviously, things have changed. There are three equal owners, and each of you should have a seat on the Board. As the CEO I would also have a seat. In addition we should have at least one other member, someone from outside the company, an attorney or head of some large, successful business with no conflicts of interest. As for the officers, I would like to nominate Elaine as Board Chairman. She is an owner and has demonstrated a keen insight into the needs of this company over the past few weeks."

"And what if we don't want to accept your so-called plan?" Leonard suspected this entire scheme had been concocted in advance between Mr. Perino and his sister. He didn't appreciate being manipulated. "This whole thing sounds like something the two of you cooked up and were planning to shove down our throats."

"How perceptive of you, Leonard," Elaine responded with a smile. "Yes, we did discuss this in advance of the meeting. And as for what would happen if we choose to turn down his offer, I'll let Michael answer for himself."

She turned toward the head of the table. Mr. Perino was cool and calm.

"It's simple. You either agree to the terms I've outlined, or I quit. Remember, there are three owners. Only two need to agree."

Leonard looked at Louise. She'd been unusually quiet during the entire meeting and sat now looking at her hands, folded in front of her on the table. He realized then that she had to be in on the scheme.

"Louise?"

She glanced up briefly but said nothing. Larry and Roy were also beginning to get the picture.

"Louise?" they asked in unison, a hint of panic in their voices.

She was beginning to tremble slightly, but the look on her face betrayed a growing anger, not the fear the others had expected. She looked up, first at her husband, then squarely at her brother.

"I'm not going to let you destroy this company. I'm not going to live on skid row."

"What the…" Leonard began but Elaine cut him off.

"Great! I think it's time for a vote. All in favor of accepting the plan outlined by Mr. Perino, raise your hand."

Elaine and Louise raised their hands.

"OK, two out of three. The plan is accepted."

"You can't do that!" Leonard, Jr. shouted.

"We can, and we did," Elaine responded quietly. "If there are people in this room who feel as though the jobs offered them are too difficult, or if the money being paid is insufficient, you are welcome to seek better employment elsewhere. However, considering your ages, and your lack of qualifications, I'm fairly certain this offer is by far the best you are likely to find."

"I'm going to talk to a lawyer! This is blackmail!" Leonard fumed.

"I've already done that," Elaine said calmly. "What we're doing is perfectly legal and now that we've voted to accept the plan the attorney will be drawing up all the necessary documents."

"But…"

"And another thing," she continued, not waiting for her brother to complete his sentence, "keeping your jobs will require your actually doing them. We cannot afford incompetence or laziness. The board of directors has a responsibility to this company to see that all management positions are filled by capable people. As Mr. Perino mentioned earlier, there will not be sufficient profits in the first couple of years to allow lavish bonuses. One way or another, either here or somewhere else, you are all going to have to work for a living. Unless, of course, you've managed to save enough money over the years to be able to retire comfortably right now."

They hadn't. Their retirement nest eggs were currently earmarked for the Saints' Hospital Charitable Foundation.

Chapter 46

Marla grabbed a napkin off the table and began blotting the wine off Tommy's T-shirt. It was one of his favorites, with a wild-eyed Ted Nugent on the front holding a guitar in one hand and a crossbow in the other. Fortunately the wine was white and no significant harm would come to Ted, the shirt, or Tommy.

While she worked Tommy studied the face from which the wine had erupted. Familiar. Hmm. Lauren. Hmm. Hot. Hmm. "Whoa! *That* Lauren! Wow, it's been what, ten years? Man, you look great!"

Lauren, already blushing, got a shade redder. "Hi, Tommy. Sorry about that. I just, you know, didn't expect the famous Tommy to actually be the famous Tommy. It was a surprise. To say the least. You look pretty great yourself."

Marla was done with the mop-up and stepped back. Tommy took the opportunity to give Lauren a hug. Marla noted with some interest that the hug was reciprocated.

Tommy held Lauren by the shoulders and took another head to toe look. "Geez," he said, letting her go, "what happened to you? You just vanished. Poof. And the number you gave me was bogus."

Lauren looked around nervously, first at Tommy, then at Fish, and finally at Marla, who said, "Yeah, what happened? We're dying to know." Lauren looked back at Tommy who shrugged his shoulders and raised his eyebrows. She took it to mean it was up to her what and how much to divulge.

"OK, fine. We're all grown-ups." She took a seat and the others followed her lead. Tommy waved to Karen and when she approached the table he whispered something in her ear that made her smile before walking away.

"So?" Marla asked when they were settled. She really *was* dying to know.

"There's not that much to tell, really. Tommy and his band did a couple of shows at UC Santa Cruz just before Christmas break during my senior year. I was a big fan. I mean 'Bite Me' was *my* song. It was pretty much how I felt about things at the time. So I got tickets for myself and a girlfriend. We were up front, close to the stage, and I got the feeling he was looking at me. A lot. I was going through a wild and reckless phase, so after the show I asked my girlfriend if she wanted to try to get backstage to meet the band. She chickened out but I decided to go for it. I talked my way past the bouncer found Tommy, and, well, picked him up and took him home with me."

Marla sat back, eyes wide. "You mean you were a groupie!"

"I don't think I qualify for groupie status. It was the first and only time I did anything like that. Honest. I'd broken up with a boyfriend not long before and I was feeling not so sure of myself. I did it partly to get back at him, though I doubt he ever found out about it, and partly as a way of regaining my confidence. And, you know, partly because, well, Tommy is Tommy." She said this last bit with a quick glance in his direction and another blush.

Marla looked at Tommy, who was looking at Lauren. "So, Tommy, that's what happened? And you haven't seen each other since?"

"Well, not exactly. She's leaving some stuff out."

"Please, you don't need to go into the details," she said with a slight shudder.

"Not *those* details," he said with a grin, "though as I recall they were pretty great. What she's not telling you is that I actually sent one of the roadies to find *her* but she found me first. She also forgot to mention that we spent three whole days together and that I invited her to come back to LA with me. Oh, and when it was time to go and I asked for her phone number so I could stay in touch she gave me the wrong one."

He turned toward Lauren. "You know, I always wondered about that. I thought we'd connected, I mean mentally. I was hoping to see you again."

"Come on, Tommy," she replied, "it was all so spur of the moment and crazy. I did it for myself, mostly. It was selfish. I had no idea what kind of person you really were when I made my move. It was supposed to be a one-night thing, or a few hour thing."

She paused and looked around the table. This was an awful lot of information to be sharing with people she just met, she thought, and started laughing quietly.

"What's so funny?" he asked.

"Me, you, this whole situation. I barely know Fish and Marla, I haven't seen you in over ten years and thought I never would again, and here I am at the Thirteenth Step going on and on about all this personal stuff that I probably wouldn't tell my best friend."

Just then Karen returned with a bottle of the same Dom Perignon he'd opened to toast Ashleigh's acceptance to law school. Lauren saw the label and sat up straight. "OK, first the Albarino and now DP 2005. This just keeps getting weirder and weirder."

"And better, I hope?" Tommy added.

Lauren smiled. "Yeah, and better."

The glasses were filled and Tommy raised his. "To old friends."

"And new ones," Lauren added.

Marla stood. "I've got to get back to the kitchen. Dinner's just about ready. G, why don't you come with me. I could use a hand getting things plated."

"Uh, sure." He'd been listening and watching with growing fascination. He knew Tommy pretty well by now, and had seen him interact with lots of women. Something about this seemed different somehow. Reluctantly he got up and followed his sister to the kitchen.

"So," Tommy said when they were alone, "what have you been up to all this time? Married?"

She shook her head 'no'.

"Steady boyfriend?"

She shook her head again. "No," she said softly. "What about you?"

"Me, nah. Still single."

They were quiet for a while, sipping on the champagne.

"All right," Tommy said, breaking the reverie, "this may sound a little strange after all this time, but I was serious when I said I was hoping to see you again. No one was more surprised than me when a one-nighter turned into three days. Three really great days. I thought we maybe had something, you know?"

She looked up, a hint of a smile forming on her lips, and nodded again. "Yeah."

"How about this, then. You give me your number, the real one, so I can call you and take you out for coffee, or lunch. It seems like it would be a huge waste of a perfectly good coincidence not to."

Her smile got wider. "A perfectly good coincidence *would* be a terrible thing to waste. Besides, I already gave the number to Marla. Before realizing this place was yours we'd agreed to a swap—I'm going to help her with the wine list and she's going to teach me about food. So it looks like you're going to see me again whether you want to or not."

She took another sip of champagne. "This is *so* good!"

"Yes, it is," Tommy said, grinning.

Chapter 47

"Mrs. Sanchez, I realize that this is probably new to you and you might be feeling frightened or intimidated, but I assure you the purpose of this meeting is to make what's ahead as comfortable and easy as possible."

John Wright was doing 'client prep'. He'd been notified a week earlier that the offices of Dunham and Sykes would be scheduling the deposition of one Consuela Sanchez. Today was Monday. The deposition was set for Wednesday. Although she had known from the beginning that this was likely going to happen, that knowledge had done nothing to mitigate her fears. She didn't trust lawyers, she'd never been involved in a lawsuit, until this one, and she was fairly certain the system was rigged to provide the worst possible outcomes for her and those like her.

She sat in a leather-upholstered club chair, hands folded in her lap, legs crossed at the ankles, knees almost imperceptibly shaking back and forth. The glass of mineral water provided by Mr. Wright's office manager sat untouched on the small occasional table adjacent to her chair. There were about a million places she would rather have been at that moment, including the dentist's office, and she really hated going to the dentist.

"A deposition is no big deal. You will be asked a number of questions about the work you did for the Walters and about the relationship you had with them. You will answer as simply and honestly as you can. I will be right there at your side. If I think the question being asked is inappropriate I will make an objection and advise you not to answer. So, one of the things you will need to do is wait a few seconds before answering any question. That will give me the time to object if I think I have to.

"The other thing you will need to do, and this is extremely important, is listen very carefully to the question being asked. If you are not sure what the lawyer is asking, say so, and the question will be asked in a way that makes it more clear. Once you are sure you understand the question you may give your answer.

"But, here is the third thing you need to remember: only answer the question being asked. Don't go off on any tangents. Keep your answers brief and to the point.

"For example, if he asks you, 'Did Mr. Walter give you vacation time?', the answer is either 'yes' or 'no'. You don't want to say, 'yes, he gave me six weeks a year'. Do you understand so far?"

"Yes". Consuela had considered waiting a few seconds to give him a chance to object but knew he would likely not get the joke. As for keeping her responses brief, that was perfectly fine. She was not in the mood for chitchat.

"Excellent! Then let's get started. I'm going to pretend that I'm Mr. Pearl, the lawyer who will be taking your deposition. I will ask you questions and you will answer them the best you can. OK?"

"Yes."

Over the next hour Mr. Wright was able to establish that Consuela had worked for the Walters for close to sixteen years, first for both Leonard and his wife, then, after his wife's death, just for Leonard. Her duties consisted of grocery shopping, preparing meals, light housekeeping, (an agency sent a small crew in every Saturday to do the heavy work), taking care of the laundry, and providing the occasional livery service when one or the other of her employers needed to run an errand.

After Mrs. Walter's death her role changed. She still prepared the meals, but instead of serving and leaving the room, she was sometimes asked to join Mr. Walter at the table. He didn't like eating alone. She was also consulted on wardrobe choices, which necktie with which shirt, French cuffs or buttons? As the years passed she also assumed more of the driving duties. She would chauffeur him to and from the office, to appointments with the lawyer, the doctor. She became more than his housekeeper. She was his companion. As Elaine had noted the day of the reading, she was like family.

Because he had been Leonard's attorney for many years, Mr. Wright already knew this. He asked the questions to allow his client a clear view of what she was likely to experience during the actual deposition. He also wanted to establish the limits of his own knowledge before getting into areas about which he was less informed.

"OK, Connie, that was great. Now I'd like to ask some questions that might seem a bit more personal. So far everything we've discussed has been a matter of common knowledge. I mean, we've known each other a long time and I'm sure we both have a general sense of what our roles were over the years."

She narrowed her eyes slightly, not sure where this was going, exactly, but not liking the general direction in which he seemed to be headed.

"Remember when I brought up that question about vacation time?"

"Yes." Brief and to the point, with an edge of suspicion in the tone.

"Good. Could you tell me now how much vacation time you were given?"

"Yes."

"Good, right. I'm sorry. I didn't make myself clear. We're done with the practice deposition. Now I'm acting as your real lawyer. There are things I need to know so we don't have any surprises on Wednesday. So please, say as much as you can now. Remember, I'm on your side, and there's a lot at stake."

Consuela took a deep breath and let it out with a sigh. She then took a long sip from her glass of mineral water.

"I got four weeks of vacation plus holidays off, like Christmas, Easter, Thanksgiving. But I didn't always take that much time."

"Meaning what?"

"Meaning they needed me and I felt bad leaving them alone. Especially after Mrs. Walter died. My family didn't need to take long vacations and it was hard for my husband to get time off when the kids were out of school. You know he has a landscaping business. Summer is his busiest time. So I would take maybe two weeks off. I would work the other two and Mr. Walter would pay me double."

"OK. How about sick time?"

"We never talked about that. If I was sick, or if one of the kids was sick and I couldn't come to work I just called him and told him."

"So there weren't a specific number of days per year you could call in sick and get paid, whether you were really sick or not?"

"That's crazy! Why would I say I was sick if I wasn't?"

"Right. Good. Now we need to discuss your financial arrangements. What kind of salary were you paid?"

"It changed over the years."

"Yes, I'm sure it did. But, at the end, how much were you being paid, say, for the last year before Mr. Walter died?"

Consuela fidgeted in her chair. She didn't like talking about money, though she realized this entire meeting, this whole mess, was about money.

"Fifteen hundred dollars a week."

"Plus the extra for working during your vacation time, right?"

"Right."

"Any bonuses?"

"Yeah, for Christmas. Every year."

"How much?"

"It depended on the year. If it was a good year, maybe fifteen thousand dollars. If it wasn't so good, maybe ten."

"Any benefits?"

She gave him a hard glance. "What do you mean, 'benefits'?"

"You know, like health insurance, a pension contribution, things like that." Mr. Wright noticed her reaction and thought he might have discovered a sore spot.

"Oh, OK, that kind of stuff," she responded, visibly relieved. Mr. Wright realized he'd discovered nothing of the kind. "Yes. He paid for our health insurance."

"Were you, are you, on the company's policy?"

"No. I was employed by Mr. Walter personally. He bought a separate policy for me and my family. My husband is self-employed, so this helped us a lot."

"Thank you. Was there a pension or a 401k plan?"

"No."

"So there was nothing there for your retirement, no savings?"

"We saved what we could. We have an account for the kids, you know for college. The one Mr. Walter had you help us set up, remember?"

"Yes, Connie, I remember. But…"

"Look, Mr. Wright, I don't want to be rude, but you already know everything there is to know. You were the lawyer. You knew all his business. What are you driving at?"

"OK, fine. Did you and Mr. Walter ever discuss his will?"

"You know, you could've asked me that an hour ago. Saved a lot of time. Yes. He mentioned his will from time to time. He said there would be something for me. Something to help us get by after he was gone. He never said how much and I never asked. I didn't like to think about it. It was money I was going to get when he died. I never wanted him to die."

Consuela began to cry and Mr. Wright offered a tissue. She quickly regained her composure and continued. "He was like a father to me. I spent more time with him than his own kids. I think the only ones he cared about more than me were his granddaughter, Lauren, and his great-granddaughter, Amy. He really loved that little girl."

"So you never discussed the size of your inheritance?"

"Never."

"And you never suggested he should leave the bulk of his estate to the hospital?"

"No. But I'm glad he did."

"Why's that?"

"Because his children always took advantage of him. They were lazy and mean. They didn't deserve to get the money he worked so hard to make all his life."

"OK. One last thing and we're done. What's your relationship with Sister Dolores?"

Consuela reached for the water glass and took another long drink. Then she slumped back into her chair.

Chapter 48

"All in favor?"

Everyone in the room raised his hand. Except Dr. Riegel.

"Bill?" the chairman asked.

"You know what I think, but just in case you forgot I'll tell you again. I think this is a bad idea, a terrible precedent. We let one guy like this on staff and pretty soon we'll be running an old time medicine show. Maybe I'll start selling snake oil out of the ER, hire a witch doctor to do triage. It would save us a bundle in nursing salaries."

"So noted. All opposed?"

Dr. Riegel raised his hand.

"OK, Dr. Byner's application has been approved. That's it for new business. Can I get a motion to adjourn?"

The Credentials Committee meeting was over. On his way out of the room the director stopped Dr. Silverman and pulled him aside. "You know, Dave, this guy fucks up and it's on you."

"For Pete's sake, Bill, you gotta stop it already! Even Carter finally figured out we need the business. Byner isn't the only guy in the world doing this procedure. He just happens to be one of the busiest. We're lucky to have him."

"We'll be lucky if he doesn't kill somebody and the entire credentials committee doesn't end up in jail with him. *Then* we'll be lucky."

Dr. Siverman shook his head and walked out of the room, empty now except for the director and Timothy Doyle, C.O.O., who'd remained in his seat. Dr. Riegel looked at him, and the smirk on his face. "Congratulations, Doyle. You did it. Saints' is now one step closer to being the shit hole you've been trying to turn it into. Nice job."

The pasty white complexion of the diminutive C.O.O. began to take on a pinkish hue, and the eyebrows, magnified by the large glasses, moved closer together. His mouth opened but the director was already out the door before any words were able to escape.

As Dr. Carter had predicted, his informal investigation into the practice habits of Dr. Gerald Byner had unearthed a lot of innuendo, head shakes, and sympathetic glances. But nothing concrete, beyond what everyone already knew and for which Dr. Byner had done his penance, had been found. A denial of staff membership could not be based on innuendo or even common knowledge. There needed to be documentation of substandard practice or as-yet-undiscovered felonious behavior, and there wasn't.

"Fucking Byner," the director mumbled as he walked into Sister Dolores' office.

"Excuse me?" she asked, looking up from whatever it was she'd been studying on her desk.

"Oh, Jesus, I mean, Christ, I mean aw hell, you know." He took a seat opposite hers.

"What's the problem?" she asked, shaking her head and rolling her eyes in response to his entrance.

"Credentials just approved Byner's application."

"Over your strenuous objection, I assume."

"Damned right! Sorry."

"Look at this," she said, handing him the short stack of papers she'd been poring over before the interruption.

He took them and began to read. "What's all this?"

"It's the financial report I have to bring to the Board later this week. See all those big numbers in red ink? That's how much money we lost just last month. Now look at the next page."

He did. There were even bigger numbers in red ink.

"That's a projection of where we are headed by year's end unless something changes. Mr. Doyle did the math. Don't say it," she said raising her hand, "I don't care what you think about him. His numbers are accurate. Now look at the last page."

The red ink was gone. The numbers were small, very small, but they were black.

"Guess what that is."

"A projection of how great things are going to be with Byner and his rapid detox?"

"No. We can't project things we don't have any hard data for. Guess again."

The director studied the page more closely. He sat back in his chair and shook his head.

"Ah, you figured it out. Yes, this is a projection of where we would likely be at year's end if we closed the ER tomorrow. Either closed it, or downgraded it to urgent care status, meaning walk-ins only, no ambulance runs, no paramedic traffic."

"You're actually going to present this idea to the Board? You're going to go along with that weasel Doyle and close the ER?"

She paused before answering. He deserved it, she thought, after the way he came barging into her office.

"No. I'm going to present the financial report and I'm going to recommend we approve Dr. Byner's application to the staff. Then I'm going to let Mr. Doyle describe the CARE program."

The director sagged in his chair, defeated.

"Oh quit being a baby!" she said, taking the papers out of his hand. "Don't you have a department to run?"

Chapter 49

"My husband comes from a very big family." Consuela paused, as though that statement alone was sufficient to answer any further questions Mr. Wright might want to ask.

"Sorry?"

"His father had eleven brothers and sisters."

"Uh, that's a big family alright, but…"

"And all of his aunts and uncles got married and had their own children. Mostly big families, too. Not ten children each, but, you know, three or four anyway. So he has maybe thirty-five or forty cousins. And they all live in this general area, and now they're married and have their own kids. I mean the holidays are crazy."

Mr. Wright was finding the Sanchez family tree to be mildly interesting, but climbing it was not what he'd planned for today. "I can see how it could be a little hectic, but…"

"So, you know, with a family as large as ours, and I'm not even talking about my side, which is pretty big, too, how do you keep track of everybody?"

There was silence for a long moment. Consuela helped herself to another sip of mineral water while Mr. Wright considered the possible implications of missing persons.

"I'm sure it must be difficult trying to keep in touch with everyone," he conceded finally, "but what does this have to do with our meeting here today?" He was afraid he had an idea, but didn't want to jump to any unpleasant conclusions.

"OK, look, I didn't know, all right?"

"Uh, know what?"

"Fine. My husband's father, my father-in-law, was one of the youngest kids in his family. The oldest was a girl. Linda. She married a gringo. The family wasn't real happy with that. I mean, it was a long time ago and people didn't do that sort of thing. So Linda and her husband were a little like outsiders. Plus, they only had one child during their entire marriage, which also made them different from all the rest. I mean I never even met them. They're both dead now."

"There's more, right?" The lawyer didn't want to be overly forceful but it was time for full disclosure.

"Yeah, there is. So Linda and Jack had a daughter, and the story is that this daughter became a nun. I guess the whole family was shaken up one way or the other when this happened. I mean, some thought it was great, devoting her life to God, and some thought it was terrible that their only daughter would be selfish like that and not get married and give them grandchildren."

"Let me guess," Mr. Wright said, resigned to what now seemed fairly obvious. "The nun we're talking about is Sister Dolores. Am I right?"

"I had no idea. I promise. I didn't know until after the business of the reading of the will. I told my husband all about it when I got home. I mean first I told him about the three million dollars for me, but then I told him about how Mr. Walter left almost all his money to the hospital and about how the hospital is run by this nun named Sister Dolores, and how nice she was to me. Then Juan, my husband, gets this surprised look on his face, and starts asking me to describe Sister Dolores, but there's only so much I can say because, you know, she had her habit on and she's all covered up. But I describe how old she seems, how tall, you know, what I can."

Consuela paused to catch her breath. She'd been anxious tell the lawyer about the connection since she first learned of it, but hadn't know whether it would be better to remain silent, and assume no one would ever find out. Now that she was talking she was finding it difficult to stop.

"So Juan says he has a cousin who became a nun, and that nobody in the family had seen or heard from her in years, but it sounded like Sister Dolores could be the same person. He starts calling his aunts and uncles, asks a bunch of questions. Turns out one of the uncles *had* kept in touch over the years. Christmas cards, like that. He said that the family pretty much disowned her when she joined the convent. But he said it was definitely her."

Mr. Wright had seen this coming for several minutes so the shock of hearing it was less than it might have been. "So, let me be clear," he began. "If I'm hearing you correctly, Sister Dolores is your husband's first cousin. Am I right?"

"Yes."

"Hmm," the lawyer grunted, thinking it over. "Tell me, does Sister Dolores know who you are? Does she know that you're married to her cousin?"

Consuela sat back in her chair. She hadn't considered this possibility and felt a wave of relief wash over her. "Wow. I really doubt it. I'd never met her before the reading. Juan had never spoken about her, and I certainly haven't told anyone about this until today. So, I'm pretty sure she has no idea."

"Hmm," Mr. Wright concluded.

Chapter 50

"What do you think about kids?"

Micky was lying on top of him enjoying a moment of post coital bliss when he decided to interrupt her with the question.

"Hmm?" she replied dreamily, giving him a gentle squeeze with her pelvic muscles. He readjusted himself to keep from sliding out.

"You know, kids, children."

She lifted her head and looked at him. "What are you talking about?"

"It's just a little weird, that's all. I mean aren't most women your age obsessed with the idea of having children? The biological clock and all that?"

She made an attempt to roll off him but he grabbed her by the hips and managed to roll with her, maintaining the connection, but now he was on top looking down. He raised himself up on his elbows increasing the pressure against her lower body.

"Mmmm," she purred.

"Well?"

"Well what?" She wiggled, just enough to keep him in place.

"Come on, Micky. Don't tell me you never think about it."

"OK, I won't." She smiled and wiggled a little more.

Fish was having a difficult time maintaining his concentration and found himself doing a little wiggling of his own. But this was a question he'd had on his mind for a while and he wasn't going to let her seduce him out of asking.

"I'm serious. Do you think you want to have kids some day?"

"Do you?" she asked.

"What's that got to do with it?" The wiggling was becoming more intense and the erection that had almost died after the first go-round was finding a second life.

"I'd say it has a lot to do with it. So, do you?"

"I don't know, I mean, I never thought about it much. It wasn't something I ever planned on or anything. I always figured maybe some day, you know."

"So what's the deal now? Your 'biological clock' starting to run down or something? Oooh." He was by now fully aroused and she sensed this conversation would soon be over. Or at least postponed.

"Yeah, maybe, I don't know. Mmmm."

"That's good. Ohhh," she moaned, grabbing his head and pulling him down onto her. He was about to say something else but she covered his mouth with hers. By the time the kiss was over he'd forgotten what it was.

Chapter 51

"Sister Dolores, hi, it's John Wright."

After his meeting with Consuela he realized there was some damage control to be done. He believed her when she told him she'd never met her cousin, the nun. But in case she had and forgot, or had but hadn't realized it, he thought a conversation with Sister Dolores was in order.

"Mr. Wright, good to hear from you. I'd been thinking of giving you a call. How are things going with the probate?"

He filled her in on the progress to date, including the up-coming deposition of Mrs. Sanchez.

"I understand Mr. Pearl ran into a dead end, so to speak, in the matter of any possible wrong-doing on the part of the hospital and Dr. Hooks," she added at the end of his presentation. "I got a surprise visit from Lauren, one of the grandchildren, the one with the young daughter. She told me we were in the clear."

"Hmm. That's correct. It was one of the things I was calling to tell you. She's interesting, that one. She's the only person in the entire family who seems genuinely satisfied with the will as stated."

"So what else do they think they have to support their case? We should be getting close to wrapping this up, right?" She said it, but she didn't really believe it. Still, it never hurt to keep positive thoughts.

Mr. Wright chuckled. "I'm pretty sure you know we have a ways to go yet. There's the question of Mr. Walter's mental capacity at the time he revised the will. That needs to be explored, and though I'm fairly certain we will be able to show that he was of sound mind, we're going to have to jump through a few flaming hoops to prove it. A little trickier is the relationship he had with Mrs. Sanchez, Consuela. They were very close during the last years of his life. The family will try to convince a judge that she exercised undue influence and had him change the will for her benefit."

"But he gave almost all his money to the hospital. How does that make sense?"

"Right, we discussed that a while ago. I'm sure her motive is something Mr. Pearl is working very hard to establish. We should get some idea what he's come up with at her deposition."

"Hmm," was all she said in response.

"The main reason I called, though, was to get some background information about you."

"Oh? Such as?"

"Well, let's start with your family. Were you born around here? I mean, not 'here' in Beverly Hills, where I'm calling you from, necessarily, but, you know, the LA area?"

"Yes. Covina."

"And do you have any family in the area?"

She laughed. "You wouldn't think so, considering I never see or hear from them, but I have a lot of relatives nearby. Or at least I used to."

"Meaning…"

"Meaning I haven't kept up with the comings and goings of my family. Or, more to the point, they haven't kept me in the loop."

"Could you explain that little?"

Sister Dolores was quiet a moment. "Fine. Why not," she said. "I told Lauren some of it. I might as well tell you. I joined the convent right out of high school. I was eighteen. It was my choice to make. My parents didn't see it that way. I was an only child and they wanted me to have a more traditional life. Marriage, children. I tried to explain to them that I felt a real calling and that they should be glad for me. They weren't buying it. They said they would disown me if I went through with it, and they pretty much did.

"I don't know if you understand how it works. I mean, you don't just decide to become a nun one day, join a convent, and that's it. It's not like running off to join the circus."

She paused to allow the attorney a moment to stop laughing. "I never thought of it quite like that," he said.

"Right. I doubt you've thought of it at all. Anyway, there are a number of steps you have to go through, stages, before you take your final vows. They want to be sure you know what you're doing, and that you are suited to the life. Soon after I joined I was sent to a convent in Philadelphia. I did my novitiate, took my preliminary vows, and eventually my final vows. I also went to school. I got a college degree and an MBA in hospital administration. The Order I chose runs hospitals. It's a big reason I chose it. After getting my degree I started working for one of their, our, hospitals in Philadelphia. I tried to contact my parents from time to time, but they never returned my letters. The only information I got was from my favorite uncle, Jaime. He was my godfather. We wrote each other, not that often, but enough for me to get some idea what was going on back home.

"One day, maybe eight years or so after I'd joined, I got a letter from him telling me my father was sick. Very sick. I petitioned the Mother Superior for a transfer back to the LA area so I could see him before he died. She was sympathetic and said she'd try to help but I would need to be patient. Patience is a big deal in the nun business.

"It took a few months but a position opened at Saints' Hospital, I always suspected it was created for me, and I was approved to fill it. By the time I got out here my father was in the hospital and wasn't expected to live much longer. He had lung cancer. I called the hospital administrator and introduced myself. I wanted to visit but I didn't want a room full of people there when I did. I needed to be alone with my parents. I thought maybe after all the time that had passed we could start over, as a family. Maybe they would be able to see how happy I was. Maybe they would be able to accept me for who I am."

A long pause followed. Mr. Wright heard her breathing and chose to allow her time to process what had to be difficult memories.

"Anyway," she said, breaking the silence, "I was able to see him after normal visiting hours. Only my mother was allowed to be there through the night."

She paused again. Mr. Wright had almost all the information he needed. He decided to try to wrap things up.

"So, were you able to get the closure you were after?"

"Hm. Not really. I saw him a few more times, always just the three of us. As sick as he was I could tell he was still angry at my decision. I think my mother might have even blamed me for him getting sick in the first place. He held my hand but never told me it was OK. He died a few days later."

"And you never saw the rest of your family?" He needed to be sure.

"At the funeral. I came in late and sat in the back. I saw them but I don't think they saw me. I left before they rolled the casket back down the aisle. Now I need to ask you a question."

"Uh, OK. What's that?"

"What does any of this have to do with the probate?"

Mr. Wright had anticipated she might ask this but hadn't formulated a pat answer. He needed to improvise.

"As your representative in this matter it's important for me to know something about you," he began. "Your character speaks for itself, you're a nun and you run a not-for-profit hospital. I just wanted to fill in some of the blanks regarding your background to make sure the other side isn't going to have any surprises for us down the line. I asked Mrs. Sanchez many of the same questions during our preparation for her deposition." It was more or less true and, he hoped, more or less plausible.

"So?"

"So what?"

"Are we going to get any surprises?"

"I don't think so, no."

"Good."

"Yes."

The conversation ended and Sister Dolores sat back in her chair. She suspected there was more to the interrogation than that to which the lawyer had admitted, but she sensed from his tone that whatever it was would not be a problem.

Chapter 52

"Hey, you busy?"

"Not yet, but the day is young. So?"

It was the morning after his dinner with the Montes family and Danny had been given instructions to call his big brother with the details as soon as he got the chance. He'd spent the night at Ashleigh's place and was in the car on his way back to San Diego and the office. It was seven-fifteen. He knew his brother started his shift at seven, and figured, rightly, that calling him early would give him the best odds of having at least a few minutes of uninterrupted conversation.

"It was rough."

Fish laughed. "Are you surprised?"

"Yeah! I mean no. I mean I knew her father was going to give me a hard time…"

"Because you're banging his daughter?" Fish jibed, still laughing.

"I don't know that he knows that," Danny replied, an edge of indignation in his tone.

Fish laughed even harder. Tears were beginning to form in his eyes. The laughing was making it hard for him to speak. "Right," he managed between fits. "His gorgeous, young, Latina daughter brings this older, white lawyer she's been dating home to meet her family but it's only platonic. I'm sure that's what he was thinking."

Danny waited for a minute to allow his brother to compose himself. "You done now?" he asked when the laughter stopped.

"Yeah, OK, I'm done. Until you say something else as hysterical as that."

"Fine. OK, so maybe he suspects it's not platonic."

Fish bit his lip. He wanted to hear the details and knew another outburst on his part could induce Danny to hang up on him.

"Anyway, he waits until we're sitting at the table, about to start dinner, and then he lets me have it. I'm seeing his daughter, he knows I'm a lawyer, what kind of law do I practice, am I a scumbag like the guy his daughter used to work for? I mean, he wants to know if I'm fucking Barry Bauer in disguise! I'm trying to stay cool, compliment her mother on the soup—albondigas in case you're interested, fucking delicious, too—and he tells me 'don't change the subject'. I'm starting to sweat a little. And her brother, Carlos, is sitting across the table from me with this shit-eating grin on his face. He's loving it 'cause now *I'm* the bad guy."

"Geez, Danny. But you knew it wasn't going to be a love fest, right? I mean, Ash gave you a big heads up. At least that's what Micky told me."

"Yeah, she did, but I had no way of knowing how intense her father is. Though you'd think a smart guy like me could have figured it out knowing how intense his son and daughter are."

"So, was it, you know, a total disaster?"

"Actually, no. After the Barry Bauer comparison Ashleigh figured it was time to cut him off. She told them about the law school acceptance, gave me some credit for helping her make it happen. They were stunned at first, and then there was all the hugging and kissing and I was pretty much off the hook."

"Hey, glad to hear it. You don't need to start a feud with your future father-in-law before you even get engaged."

"Huh? What father-n-law? Who said we were getting married?"

"You did, remember? The day you first met her in the court-house and told me she was the future Mrs. Daniel Hooks?"

"Oh come on, that was just me being a smartass."

"I don't know, it sounded serious to me," Fish teased. "Anyway, so that was it, everybody happy, life goes on?"

"No. It got even better. Her father gets the news about Ashleigh and he's beaming he's so proud. Then he looks at Carlos and asks him what's new in *his* life in this tone of voice that makes it clear he has the lowest of low expectations. Carlos catches the tone and doesn't say anything for a minute, then he mumbles that he's been going to night school to get his GRE. Says he wants to get his general contractor's license."

"Really?"

"Really. I thought the old man was going to pass out he was so happy. I could have probably dragged Ashleigh under the table for a quicky at that moment and gotten away with it."

"Uh, probably not," Fish replied after running the scenario through his head.

"Yeah, I guess you're right. Anyway, when everybody calmed down I told them I was planning on throwing a party for Ashleigh, the graduation-going away thing I told you about. I'm thinking about the weekend of September 10th. You and Micky free?"

"Yeah, I think so." Then, after a pause, "Oh! That's the week-end Tommy mentioned something about having a party at the Step in honor of our birthdays. We're a year and a few days apart, it turns out. He said we could do it on Sunday, the eleventh."

"9-11?"

"Hmm. I hadn't thought about that, but I think the Step is a pretty low-priority target. Any chance you'd be interested in having a combined party? You know graduation-going away-birthday kind of thing? It would be a lot of the same people anyway."

"It's OK with *me*, but I'll have to check with Ashleigh. I don't want her to think she's going to be taking a back seat to Tommy, or anyone else for that matter. I kinda wanted it to be her night, you know?"

"Yeah, I completely understand. If she's not cool with it Tommy and I can do a birthday party next year. I figure we have at least a few more birthdays left in us, but you only graduate college and start law school once. Hopefully."

Fish looked at the patient board. Three new ones had signed in during his conversation with Danny. Abdominal pain, shortness of breath, and a possible broken ankle.

"It's starting to get busy so I've got to run. Let me know what she says. I'm fine with it either way. Really."

He hung up and reached for the first chart. Female, 23, lower abdominal pain, vomiting, dizziness. "And away we go," he said to himself as he walked toward room seven.

Chapter 53

"Look, I don't want to seem like a stalker or anything, but I was wondering if we could maybe meet for lunch."

It was eleven A.M. on Monday, the day after his re-acquaintance with Lauren. He knew Mondays were one of her days off work. He also knew that their first 'date', if that's what this was going to be, should be lunch, not dinner. So it was either going to have to be today, or he'd have to wait an entire week to see her. That was unacceptable.

"Uh, sure. When did you have in mind?"

"Great! How about one o'clock?"

"One o'clock? Today?"

"Yep, that one o'clock."

"Geez, Tommy, I..."

"I know we just re-met and all that," he interrupted, "but if we don't do it today we won't get another chance until next Sunday. And, I know it's been, like, ten years or something, so what's another week, but the way I see it is it's already been ten years so what's the point of wasting even more time?"

It had been obvious to both of them that there was a mutual attraction. Tommy had been right when he said he thought they might have had something. Lauren had been expecting him to call. She just hadn't expected the call to come this soon. She'd wanted time to think things through.

"Come on," he continued, "our relationship was founded on spontaneity. Why change things now?"

"Uh, because we're older and more mature now?" she offered.

"Speak for yourself. Seriously, it's just lunch. I'll drive to West Hollywood. I can pick you up if you want."

"Are you telling me resistance would be futile?"

"Exactly."

"OK, fine."

She didn't want him to pick her up, though. She wanted her own car and she wanted her home address to remain a secret. For now, anyway. Given their history, their spontaneous tendencies, her self-imposed celibacy of late, and the fact that Amy was spending the week at day camp, she needed to minimize the possibility of any rash behavior.

She chose a place close by that served an eclectic mix of Mediterranean-inspired dishes. Something for everybody, she figured, though if the menu at the Step was any indication Tommy was not a picky eater and anywhere would have been fine. She walked in five minutes past the hour. She didn't want to seem too eager by being early, or right on time, but five minutes was the most she was able to manage. Being fashionably late was not in her nature.

Tommy was already there, and had been for ten minutes. He hadn't thought about whatever message being early might send. He was anxious to see her, and the sooner the better. He'd chosen a table in a quiet corner and stood when she walked in. She was wearing faded jeans and an oversized white blouse, her hair pulled back in a ponytail. Simple, casual.

Tommy greeted her with a hug when she got to the table. "Wow, you look even better than you did yesterday," he said with a smile. She felt her face get warm and hoped the subdued light in the restaurant would keep him from noticing. The waitress approached with menus. Lauren declined. She was familiar with it and knew what she wanted. Tommy took a quick look and handed it back.

"I'll have the grilled salmon salad and a bottle of Pellegrino," Lauren said. The waitress looked at Tommy, a hint of recognition in her eyes.

"I'll have the same," he announced. He'd been in situations like this enough times to know the look. It was best, he'd learned, to pretend he didn't and avoid awkward conversations.

"So. What have you been up to for the past ten years?"

She told him about school, about her various jobs, her interest in wine, and her current studies to acquire her sommelier's certificate. Things she'd mentioned the day before about which she could now expand. She talked about her grandfather.

"The Un-dead?" Tommy asked.

"Yes. And you have no idea how true that is."

She talked about the will and how it was being contested. "Not by me, I'm fine with it. But everybody else in the family has been losing their minds trying to get it thrown out."

The subject of the will led to a brief explanation of how she met Fish, and through him Marla, "and, you know, you."

She lied about why she was still single. "I just never felt like settling down." And she made no mention whatsoever of Amy.

He told her about his life on the road, his failed attempts to track her down, and his decision to get out of the music business and buy the bar. "I didn't want to spend my golden years doing oldies at some Indian casino."

He told her a half truth about why he changed the name of the place to The Thirteenth Step, "My warped sense of humor," but told the whole truth about why he'd never gotten remarried, "I never met the One."

By the time dessert arrived, a panna cotta they agreed to share, it was clear there would be a second date.

Chapter 54

The board meeting had been over for almost half an hour. Dr. Byner's application to the staff had been presented and approved. Reluctantly. Dr. Riegel had voiced his objection to it, the same one he'd made at credentials committee, and again his concerns were duly noted, then ignored. As Chairman of the Board Sister Dolores had been the one to tap the gavel indicating it was a done deal, but not without a few comments of her own.

"OK. I think we all know who and what we're dealing with here. Under normal circumstances I would have to agree with Dr. Riegel— we are setting a potentially dangerous precedent and we are soliciting fishy business from a fishy character, no offense meant to Dr. Riegel's assistant director."

This got a few chuckles, and even a smile from the director, who hadn't found much to be happy about for the past two hours.

"But," she continued, "these are obviously not normal circumstances. As you all heard in the financial report Saints' is flirting with bankruptcy. The Diocese has been generous, making contributions to our Charitable Fund and allowing us to keep our creditors more or less at bay. But that generosity has its limits and believe me when I say we are testing them now.

"Our mission is to provide the very best medical care possible to every member of our community who needs it. Period. I will not allow that mission to be compromised either by restricting access to care, (a glance in the direction of Mr. Doyle), or by allowing any member of the medical staff to practice sub-standard or unethical medicine."

She took another hard look at the C.O.O., a small figure on any occasion, now trying to make himself even smaller to escape the scrutiny.

"So, we may have let the fox into the henhouse, but the wolf, (both index fingers pointing to herself), knows he's there and will not hesitate one instant to do him in if even a single feather gets ruffled."

The allegory was meant for Dr. Riegel. A page out of his play-book, she'd thought when composing it. She understood his misgivings and wanted to be sure he knew she shared them. A discrete glance in his direction, undetected by the director because he was now staring at Mr. Doyle with something between a smile and a sneer on his face, confirmed he did.

The remainder of the meeting was devoted to a flustered Timothy Doyle's presentation of the CARE program. In general terms he described the patient population, (unfortunate men and women who find themselves drug-dependent and want a second chance), the treatment process, (the patient is placed in an intensive care environment under anesthesia and the recovery medications are administered over a twenty-four hour period in the safest possible manner), the conditions of admission, (the patient is responsible for the entire cost of the procedure, much of it in advance), the absolute need for discretion, (this is a sensitive area of medicine and the patients expect complete and absolute privacy), and finally a brief bio of the program director and his first lieutenant, (Dr. Gerald Byner is well-known in the area of addiction medicine, and he will be assisted by our own Chief of Anesthesia, Dr. David Silverman).

When it was over a less-than-enthusiastic Board filed out of the room. All except Sister Dolores who motioned to the C.O.O. indicating he, too, should stick around a while.

"Alright, Doyle," she began once they were alone, "I think it's time for a job performance review."

"But..." His contract clearly stated when and how such reviews were to be conducted. Off the cuff and after a Board meeting weren't clauses he was able to recall.

"Never mind the 'but'," she growled. "Let's look at what you've managed to accomplish these past few months. There was the bariatric surgical program, which failed to materialize when I refused to pay the head surgeon a 'director's fee' of fifteen grand a month plus a dedicated nurse practitioner to follow his patients post-op. Then there was Dr. Varna, the patron saint of geriatrics, who disappeared without even filling out a staff application when I refused to give *him* a bribe. And now we have Dr. Gerald Byner and his rapid detox. I'm surprised *he* hasn't asked for a little cash on the side. Makes me wonder if maybe no one else in town wants him."

She paused to give him a chance to respond, but Mr. Doyle had been through enough of these 'discussions' to know that anything he said would truly be used against him. He wisely kept his mouth shut.

"Good idea," she said when she understood he was exercising his right to remain silent. "Either you come up with some other plan to enhance revenue or your fate is in the hands of Dr. Byner. He screws up and you're both out of here. Go."

He went.

Chapter 55

Consuela arrived at the offices of Dunham and Sykes a full fifteen minutes before her scheduled ten A.M. deposition. Mr. Wright was waiting for her when she arrived. He'd anticipated her anxiety and desire not to be late. He'd also anticipated that whatever fears she'd demonstrated during her 'prep' would be magnified in proportion to the grandeur of the Dunham-Sykes suite. Even the reception area had a view of most of Los Angeles. He knew she would need to see a familiar face when she walked through the large, thick, slab of frosted-glass with the Dunham and Sykes logo etched into it that served as the door to the office. He'd been sitting there drinking decent office coffee since nine-thirty to make sure that face would be his.

He stood to greet her when she arrived. She wore an expression of impending doom as she pushed through the door, but relaxed noticeably upon seeing her attorney.

"Mrs. Sanchez, good morning," he said, shaking her hand. "We're a little early. Can I get you some coffee?"

"Good morning. No, thank you. Coffee gives me the jitters and I'm nervous enough already."

"I understand, but it's going to be fine. Really."

She took the seat next to his and listened as he reviewed what they had discussed during the prep session. "Don't rush your answers, listen to the questions, if you don't understand something ask him to repeat it, and, above all, keep your answers short and to the point."

At ten A.M. the receptionist led them to the conference room. Mr. Pearl was already there and he stood to shake hands with opposing counsel. The stenographer was also there, ready to begin. Mr. Wright had given Consuela a description of the scene so the stenographer was not a surprise. The video camera, cameraman, and microphones, however, had not been anticipated. Her eyes got wide as she scanned the room. She turned to Mr. Wright, also a bit taken aback, who then turned to Mr. Pearl.

"Really, Norman?" he asked, waving his hand in front of the video equipment.

"John, you know as well as I that body language is sometimes more eloquent than the spoken word. I just want to make sure we get all the information we can from this witness."

"A moment with my client, please."

"Certainly," Mr. Pearl replied, a beatific smile on his face.

Mr. Wright ushered Consuela to a far corner of the room. "OK, no problem," he began, immediately acknowledging the problem. "This happens all the time. It doesn't change anything. The only difference is they will be taping you. They will clip a small microphone onto your blouse and you just have to speak normally. Don't worry about looking into the camera. In fact, don't think about the camera at all. You don't have to do anything more or less than what we've already talked about. OK?"

She nodded 'yes' but it was clearly not OK. Mr. Pearl had correctly assumed that Mrs. Sanchez would be uncomfortable with having her deposition taken. He'd also correctly deduced the camera set up would compound her anxiety, hopefully un-doing much of whatever calming Mr. Wright had managed to accomplish during his prep. An anxious deponent can be a flustered deponent, and a flustered deponent might say something she would later wish she hadn't. Also, an anxious deponent looks less believable on videotape than a calm one, even when she's telling the truth.

When everyone was settled at the conference table, and Consuela had been wired for sound, Mr. Pearl began.

"For the record, could you please state your name?"

Consuela looked to Mr. Wright who simply nodded.

"Consuela Sanchez."

So far, so good.

"Thank you, Mrs. Sanchez. Now, is it true you were employed by the late Mr. Leonard Walter?"

A brief pause, then "Yes."

"Good. Can you tell me in what capacity you were employed?"

Another look to her attorney, but this time one of confusion. A brief, whispered conversation was had between them.

"I don't understand the question," she replied at last.
"I'm sorry. I just want to know what you were hired to do."

"I did a lot of things."

"Yes, I'm sure you did. Would it be fair to say you were hired to be a caretaker?"

Mr. Wright considered objecting as too vague but chose instead to let her answer. He sensed this deposition was going to take a while. No use getting it bogged down over the definition of 'caretaker'.

'Yes."

Consuela was beginning to perspire. Mr. Wright noticed and placed a nearby box of tissues in front of her. She took one and between glances at the camera, Mr. Pearl, and her lawyer, dabbed her brow.

Over the next two hours Mr. Pearl was able to elicit much of the information Mr. Wright had prepared her to provide. Length of employment, specific duties, salary, her relationship with other members of the family and theirs with hers, and her relationship with Mr. Walter, pre- and post the death of his wife. She kept it simple and to the point. Finally the issue of the will was raised.

"Mrs. Sanchez, did you know before he died that Mr. Walter had a will?"

"Yes."

"Did you know that you were a beneficiary?"

A pause, and then "Yes."

"Yes, I'm sure you did. You stated previously that things changed a bit after the death of Mrs. Walter, is that correct?"

"Yes."

"In fact, you said that after her death you became more than a caretaker, really, more like a companion. Is that right?"

Consuela began to fidget. She didn't like where this was headed. She looked at Mr. Wright.

"You can go ahead and answer, Connie," he said. They'd been over this.

"I suppose."

"You suppose, or you know. Earlier you said it as though you knew." Mr. Pearl needed to get her off balance but needed to do it gently. His voice was on the videotape, too. It would be disadvantageous to give the impression he was browbeating the witness.

"Yeah, I guess."

"You guess? I don't want you to guess, Mrs. Sanchez. Take a moment to think about the relationship you had with Mr. Walter during the last few years of his life, then tell me whether or not you considered yourself to be a companion or merely a caretaker. I'll give you a little help. For instance, did you share meals with him?"

"Sometimes. He didn't…"

Mr. Wright reached out and touched her wrist. "That's enough, Connie. You answered his question."

"That's OK. I'd like to hear what she has to say. Go on, Mrs. Sanchez."

"Objection. That's not a question."

"Mrs. Sanchez, can you please tell me what it was you were about to say?"

"Objection, relevance."

"John, we can't know if it's relevant until she says it. My assumption is *she* thinks it's relevant or she wouldn't have wanted to say it in the first place."

"I renew my objection and I'm advising my client not to answer."

Consuela was watching this back and forth with an increasing sense of anxiety. She didn't like arguments and this was beginning to sound argumentative. Mr. Wright was objecting in part to give her a chance to collect herself. He noticed it was having the opposite effect.

"OK," Mr. Pearl said, a hint of annoyance in his voice. "Let's try this: is it fair to say Mr. Walter didn't like having his meals alone?"

She looked at her lawyer who simply nodded.

"Yes."

"And is it fair to say that during those meals together you had conversations with Mr. Walter?"

"I suppose."

"You suppose?"

"OK, I mean yes, yeah, we talked sometime." Beads of sweat were forming on her forehead and she was beginning to flush. Mr. Wright offered her another tissue.

"OK, good. So you had meals together, you had conversations. Is it also true that you drove him wherever he needed to go?"

"Of course! He was old. How was he supposed to drive himself?"

Mr. Wright saw she was beginning to come undone but feared any intervention on his part would only exacerbate the problem. He needed to get this finished soon.

"Of course," Mr. Pearl agreed. "Did Mr. Walter sit in the front seat or the back seat during these car trips."

"The front! It's not like I was his chauffeur."

"Exactly. What sorts of things did you talk about while you were driving him around?"

"I don't know. All kinds of things."

"Might you have discussed his health?"

"Maybe, if I was taking him to the doctor."

"Did he talk to you about the business?"

"Sometimes."

"What about the business?"

"I don't know. Usually stuff about how he had to keep an eye on the family to make sure they didn't mess anything up."

"OK. Did you discuss his will?"

"No."

Mr. Pearl paused a moment and stared at her. "Really? You never discussed the fact that he was leaving you money?"

"Look, he mentioned it from time to time. I didn't like to talk about it."

"OK. So let's review what you've said. You had meals with Mr. Walter, you had many conversations with him, he confided in you, told you personal things about the family, his health, his will. Would you say he treated you more like a caretaker or more like a companion?"

"We were close, OK?"

"Would you say like family?"

"Object..."

"Yes. Like family!" she responded before allowing her attorney to speak.

"Did he trust you?"

"Ob..."

"Yes!"

"Did he value your..."

"Objection!"

"I haven't finished the question."

'I object to this entire line of questioning! You're asking the witness to speak for another person's opinions and state of mind."

"So noted. Did he value your opinion?"

"OBJECTION! Don't..."

"YES!"

"Thank you, Mrs. Sanchez. One last question and we can wrap this up. What's your relationship to Sister Dolores?"

They'd gone over this in detail during the prep. She was ready.

"I never met her before the day the will was read."

"That's not what I asked you. Listen carefully. What's your relationship to Sister Dolores?"

She looked at Mr. Wright. He nodded.

"I don't have a relationship with her. Like I said, I never met her before that day."

"OK. Again, that's not what I asked you. Let's try it another way. Are you related in any way to Sister Dolores? Remember, you are under oath. If you lie it's perjury—a crime."

She looked at Mr. Wright again. He shrugged. "How the fuck did he figure it out?" he asked himself.

"She's my husband's cousin," she mumbled.

"I'm sorry, could you say that a little louder so we can be sure we have it on tape?"

"She's my husband's cousin!"

"Wow!" Mr. Pearl said in mock surprise. "You were the trusted confidant of Mr. Walter, he mysteriously changes his will a few months before he dies and leaves almost all his money to you and your husband's cousin. No wonder the family is contesting it."

"I never met her before the day the will was read. I didn't even know my husband *had* a cousin who was a nun," Consuela said softly in her defense.

"Oh? And how is it you know that now?" Mr. Pearl was taking a chance. He had no idea what she would say. Mr. Wright thought about objecting but decided instead to allow his client to answer. He did know what she was going to say and knew it would be difficult for Mr. Pearl to discount it.

Chapter 56

"Thanks for meeting me here. I didn't want to have this conversation at the hospital. Too many ears, if you know what I mean."

Fish rarely knew what his boss meant early in any conversation with him so was unconcerned about his lack of understanding now. The last time they'd met at the Step to discuss 'important business' the topic had been the possible closure of the ER. He assumed this was a follow up.

They were seated at the small table near the stage nursing beers, compliments of Tommy, and nibbling on plates of olives and Marcona almonds, courtesy of Marla's kitchen assistant. It was 5:30 and they had the place pretty much to themselves.

"So, what's the big secret?" Fish asked. "Doyle trying to shut us down again?"

"Huh? Doyle? Nah, this has nothing to do with that rodent. You know he got his boy Byner's application approved, right?"

Fish nodded. Of course he knew. The director had told him all about it the day after the Board meeting.

"He and Silverman have their first case tomorrow. Fucking freak show. But this has nothing to do with that. Or at least nothing directly to do with that, except for the fact that that kind of stuff is partly why I'm doing what I'm doing. You get me?"

Fish nodded 'yes', now more confused than before.

"Anyway, it's time for some changes, different scenery, shake things up a little. Only a matter of time, really."

Fish took a long drink from his beer and motioned to Tommy to bring a refill. A dull pain was forming behind his eyes. He needed to knock it down before it grew into a fully fledged headache.

"Bill, what the fuck are you talking about?" he asked after the second round had been delivered.

"It's obvious, isn't it?

Fish just stared at him.

"Aw c'mon Fish! We've discussed it about a million times. It's just now it makes the most sense."

More silence from across the table. Tommy, who'd returned to the bar and had been eavesdropping quietly stepped around it. This was shaping up to be a classic and he didn't want to miss anything.

Dr. Riegel stared back at his younger colleague. "You telling me you have no idea what I'm talking about?"

"Not a fucking one."

"Retirement! Hasta la vista, happy trails, gold watch, golf! Except I don't play golf. Stupid fucking game. And I don't need another watch."

Tommy pulled up a seat at the table. "Whoa! Congratulations! That's great!"

"WHAT?!" Fish yelled.

"Don't act so surprised. I've been telling you for years, at least a few years anyway, that I wasn't going to do this job forever, get dragged out of the ER in the middle of a shift in a body bag."

"But..."

"But what? Who's going to run the ER? That's one of the things I needed to talk to you about."

"Hey, slow down," Fish said, trying to get a grip on what he'd just heard. "When are you planning to do this, exactly?"

"Good question. That's the other thing I wanted to talk to you about."

They both took drinks. "So start talking," Fish said when the glasses were back on the table.

"So remember when I told you this business was getting harder and harder to run as a single-hospital ER group? We're competing with these large multi-hospital outfits and it's getting to be near impossible."

"Uh, how's that?"

"We have no economies of scale. Our insurance costs are higher than theirs, our billing costs are higher, recruitment is tough and we can't offer the same set of benefits because we can't afford it. You following me?"

He was, finally. "Yeah, but we have this good group of doctors and we don't have all the corporate bullshit to deal with that those big groups put you through. That's gotta be worth something, right?"

"Less and less all the time. Ultimately, it's all about money. Remember when the old guy died, what was his name, Mr...."

"The Un-dead?" Tommy offered.

"Yeah, him, thanks. Anyway, you asked me why we had to take the case to Peer Review and I told you he was a big donor to the foundation and you asked if it was all about money and I said everything was all about money. Remember that?"

"Yeah, but what's *that* got to do with *this*?"

"Nothing, really, except that it *is* all about money. Anyway, I was looking into the future and it wasn't looking real good. Sooner or later some big group was going to come in and try to get the contract away from me. Promise the hospital better utilization, better revenue, whatever. So I started nosing around. I know a lot of people in this business. I called a guy I've know for over twenty years, runs an ER group, has something like fifteen ER contracts scattered around, mostly in the greater LA area.

"Anyway, we're talking and he mentions he's trying to expand his operation and would I consider selling out to him. I said I would, if I could get Sister Dolores to go along with it. I spoke to her yesterday. She's thinking about it but I'm pretty sure she'll say OK."

"So then what?" Fish asked, a vague sense of dread creeping up his spine.

"So, if it happens it happens like this. They pay me for the contract—which is a big deal because it gives me the extra money I need to actually retire. I stay on for a year to run it for them, smooth the transition, take my victory lap. Then I turn it over to the new director."

"And who is that?"

"Obvious choice is you, if you want it. You'd be working for them, but I've already outlined the kind of deal I'd want you to have and they've agreed to all the terms."

Fish sat back in his chair. His head was spinning a bit so he took another sip of beer to slow it down.

"Did you consider talking to me *first*, before you talked to your 'guy' with the ER contracts? Maybe ask if *I'd* be interested in buying you out, maybe get my own ER group together?" he asked after thinking it over.

"Yeah, actually, I did, and I decided not to because I thought there was a chance you'd be dumb enough to do it."

"What's that supposed to mean?"

"Just what I said. Look, I've been doing this for a long time, right? I understand how the business works and I've seen the changes over the years. Will you agree to that much?"

Fish grunted to indicate he would.

"Then you should believe me when I say it's become a giant pain in the ass. When I first started out I was basically working for the hospital. We saw the patients but the hospital did the billing and paid for our malpractice insurance. Then, every month they wrote me a check for a percentage of our gross billing the previous month. I paid the doc's a fair hourly rate and I kept some for myself. I had the best job on earth."

"So what happened?"

"The government happened. First it was Medi-Care and the DRG's where they started paying a fixed amount based on the diagnosis. Hospital revenue took a dive. Then the other insurance companies figured if we'd take it from Medi-Care we'd take it from them, too. Another big drop in revenue. The hospital starts looking for ways to save money and it takes them about three seconds to figure out they could save a bundle by cutting us loose, make us fend for ourselves, no more free lunch.

"So now we have to do our own billing and collecting, buy our own insurance, but we still have to see whoever walks through the door whether they can afford to pay us or not. The best job in the world got a lot harder and a lot less fun. Plus, the government keeps coming up with new ways to fuck with us, new guidelines for care, some of which are really ridiculous I gotta tell ya', and it won't lift a finger to protect us from bullshit lawsuits."

The director stopped to take a drink. Fish remained silent. He had heard him talk about all this in bits and pieces over the years but had never heard him talk about it with this much emotion. He was not going to interrupt him now.

"So," Dr. Riegel continued after wiping beer foam off his lips, "I didn't ask you if you wanted to buy me out because I didn't want you to say yes. It's not worth it. You'd have to go to the bank, put your house up as collateral for a line of credit, take on a big financial risk plus all the headaches that go with running a small business. This way my 'guy' as you called him can handle the business stuff. He's already got the people in place, the credit line, all the other crap you'd have to put together from scratch. Then you could just be the director, the clinical guy, see some patients, go to some meetings, have lunch with Sister Dolores once in a while, get decent money, have a life. You get me?"

"Yeah," Fish said after a pause. He actually did get him and it was a little unnerving to have to admit it to himself.

"Wow," Tommy said, "Fish becomes the Kingfish."

"Pretty much, except for the part where he doesn't have the contract," Dr. Riegel added. "Look, I gotta go. You've got a lot to think about. I don't need an answer right away, but the sooner you decide the sooner I can get you introduced to everyone and get you in shape."

He drained his glass, stood and walked out. Tommy and Fish watched him go.

Chapter 57

"Elaine? Hi, it's Norman Pearl."

The deposition of Consuela Sanchez had gone better than he'd hoped. In preparation for it he'd had several in-depth conversations with his client. She'd been able to give him valuable information regarding Mrs. Sanchez' job description and her relationship with her father, Mr. Walter. They'd discussed the Sanchez family as well. Husband and wife, two young children, a landscaping business that had its ups and downs, and their dependence on Connie's income to keep themselves above water.

It was common knowledge that Consuela had been named a beneficiary of Mr. Walter's will. The old man had mentioned it on a number of occasions, generally in the context of a conversation involving the words 'I don't know what I'd do without her'. Elaine realized Connie was indeed deserving of some consideration but had always been uncomfortable with not knowing what that would be, exactly. She'd assumed her father would do as he always had done, namely take care of his children. But she knew Connie didn't hold her, or the rest of her family, in the highest regard and worried she might be able to convince her father to take a little less care of them than he might otherwise have been inclined to do. It now appeared that could be the case.

"The information you provided was extremely helpful. I want to thank you again. I also want to share with you something else I was able to learn that I think will be quite useful as we go forward with this lawsuit."

In addition to interviewing Elaine, and various other members of the family, Mr. Pearl had placed one of Dunham and Sykes's best private investigators on the case. It was he who'd managed to uncover the background of Sister Dolores. How he'd managed was of no particular interest to Mr. Pearl. P.I.'s had their ways and it was often best not to question them. Regardless how the knowledge had been obtained Mr. Pearl knew in advance of the deposition that there was a good chance Sister Dolores was Dolores Marialinda Carter, only daughter of Jack Carter and Linda Sanchez, aunt of Juan Sanchez, husband of Consuela.

"Oh?' Elaine responded.

"Yes. It turns out that Consuela's husband, Juan, and Sister Dolores are related to one another."

"WHAT?"

"First cousins, in fact," the attorney replied calmly.

"Are you serious?"

"Completely."

Elaine was momentarily speechless. "Then it's over, we win," she said at last. "Consuela used her relationship with my father to get him to rewrite the will. It's obvious."

"Not so fast. Mrs. Sanchez said she'd never met Sister Dolores until the day the will was read. Says she had no idea such a person even existed."

"Of course she's going to say that. Who's going to believe it? Besides, when you depose the nun she's going to have to admit they're related, right? I mean, she's a nun after all. She can't commit perjury, can she?"

"Well, technically, she can, but I don't think she will. That's the problem."

"Uh, excuse me?"

"Let me explain. When I began the deposition I had information suggesting there might be a relationship between the nun and

Mr. Sanchez. My investigator was 'pretty sure' but not positive. My plan was to push the issue to see whether or not I could get confirmation. I pushed and I was able to get Mrs. Sanchez to admit her husband and the nun were cousins."

"So what's the problem?" Elaine was becoming impatient. Why was her lawyer, at nine hundred dollars an hour, spending a lot of expensive minutes trying to explain the obvious?

"The problem is this: Mrs. Sanchez said she'd never met Sister Dolores prior to the reading and the way she said it made me think she was telling the truth. She claims she found out about it when she was going over the details of the reading with her husband. The name rang some kind of bell with him, he did some digging and realized Sister Dolores was his estranged cousin.

"You see, from what I've learned, when Sister Dolores ran off to join the convent she was essentially abandoned by her family. There's a chance Mr. Sanchez never met her himself, and it's almost certain he's had no contact with her in the last forty years even if he *had* met her at one time. It is not unreasonable to assume that Mrs. Sanchez didn't even know there was a rogue nun in her husband's family."

Mr. Pearl paused to let the significance of his comments sink in.

"So," he continued, "what happens if I take Sister Dolores' deposition? Any ideas?"

"No, tell me. What happens?" Elaine grumbled. She had enough of an idea to know that whatever it was wouldn't be good.

"My guess is she will tell the truth, and if the truth is that she had no idea she and Consuela's husband were related it's going to damage our case. She's a nun, and in the minds of most people nuns don't lie, much less commit perjury. So, that makes taking her deposition a big gamble. If we get lucky, and she admits she knew of the relationship, great. But if Consuela was telling the truth and Sister Dolores confirms it, we've got a problem."

"But you said earlier you had some information that was going to be 'very helpful' for us. Now you're telling me we have nothing. Which is it?"

"We do have something. We have a plausible theory of motive— why Mrs. Sanchez may have wanted to influence Mr. Walter. The fact is her husband and the nun are cousins. Whether or not she was aware of it prior to the reading is still something of an open question. The last thing we want to do is have Sister Dolores swear under oath that she had no idea she and Consuela are related by marriage."

"I'm sorry. I'm not following. We know they're related but we can't prove they knew it before the reading. In fact, from what you're telling me it's possible the nun still has no idea. How is that helpful?"

"Look, Elaine, everything is a negotiation. It's not always winner-take-all. I'm sure Mr. Wright has his own doubts about who knew what when. In the end it may seem advantageous to all concerned to settle this matter, divide the money. How it gets divided will depend on who seems to be holding the better cards. This relationship is a good card to be holding. We just have to be sure we play it correctly."

"So what's next?"

"I'll be calling Mr. Wright in a few days to discuss just that."

Chapter 58

"So. You're gonna be the Kingfish now. That's a pretty big deal, right? More prestige, more money?"

"I guess."

"So why do you look like your dog just died?"

"Jesus, Tommy. Look, I don't know, alright?"

Dr. Riegel had been gone only a few minutes. Tommy and Fish were still sitting at the table.

"Don't know what?" Tommy asked, popping an almond in his mouth.

"It's complicated."

"Maybe if you tried to explain it to me it'll get less complicated."

"Think so?" Fish snorted.

"Worth a shot."

"OK. Fine. I don't know a lot of things, and one of them is whether or not I want to be the Kingfish. When I got into this business part of the attraction was the freedom it gave me. Work *when* I want, *where* I want, as much or as little as I needed to pay the bills. No office to manage, no employees to worry about, no hiring, no firing. But since then I've gotten more and more tied to the job. I mean I've been working at the same place since I finished my residency and I'm the assistant director now. I'm responsible for all the other doctors, I have to deal with their attitude problems, their customer service issues, the complaints. I have to go to meetings, deal with the politics. It's everything I thought I was going to avoid by being an ER doctor."

Tommy had his elbows on the table, his chin resting in his hands. "Keep going."

"So if I take this job, become the medical director, it's going to be even more responsibility. I'll be this regular 'doctor' guy."

"Instead of what?" Tommy asked, the makings of a smile on his lips.

"I don't know, surfer guy who's a doctor on the side maybe? Whatever. The point is…"

"The point is," Tommy interrupted, "you need to take the thirteenth step."

Fish sat back in his chair, surprise and concern on his face. "What?"

"You need to take the thirteenth step," Tommy repeated calmly.

"What are you talking about? Are you selling the bar?"

Tommy laughed. "No, I'm not selling the bar and that's not what I'm talking about. The thirteenth step isn't a thing or a place. It's more of a decision, an idea. Something you do that makes you free."

"Like getting a divorce?"

"You're not even married yet, so no. Plus, that just makes you broke."

They shared a laugh then Tommy continued. "I'm going to tell you something but I'd appreciate it if you keep it to yourself, OK?"

"Sure."

"Several years ago, while I was still performing, I had a bit of a drinking problem. I wasn't falling off the stage or forgetting lyrics or anything like that, but I was drinking a lot. Too much, I decided. So I turned myself in to rehab."

Fish pointed toward the bathrooms and the picture of the Betty Ford Center.

"Yeah. I hung the picture as a reminder. Anyway, I went through the program, got clean, went to a few meetings, learned about the twelve steps, and realized my life was still being controlled by alcohol. The only difference was instead of being controlled by using it I was being controlled by not using it. I had to watch where I went, who I saw. It was like avoiding booze was my new career.

"Finally one day I said 'Fuck it'. I didn't want to be that asshole any more. I wasn't going to let alcohol run my life, one way or the other. I refused to be a recovering addict for the rest of my life. I made the decision to quit being that kind of jerk. That's when I took *my* thirteenth step and bought the bar. I was going to prove to myself that I could be around alcohol, drink once in a while, and not be controlled by it."

"The thirteenth step, huh?"

"Yep. And it's different for everyone. For me it was buying the bar. One of the best things I've ever done."

"And me?"

"Only you can know for sure, but I have some ideas if you want to hear them."

Fish nodded.

"OK. You're afraid to commit to your job because you have some image of yourself as this carefree, footloose guy. Meanwhile you do your job very well and seem perfectly happy doing it. You're afraid to commit to your relationship with Micky for the same reasons—you see yourself as this bon vivant, single guy, ladies man when in reality you haven't been on a date with anyone but her in over two years and when she's not around you're miserable. Am I right so far?"

Fish made a wry smile. "Yeah, pretty much."

"So, maybe *your* thirteenth step is taking another look at yourself, who you actually are, and accepting what you see. Once you do that, the rest will fall into place."

Fish smiled again, a real smile, and shook his head.

Just then the front door opened and Marla walked in with Lauren close behind carrying a box filled with wine bottles.

"Hey, G! What are you doing here?"

"Hey, Marla, hi Lauren. Nothing much. I had a meeting with Riegel. You just missed him."

"He's just being modest," Tommy said after taking the box from Lauren and giving her a 'hello' hug. "You're looking at the new Kingfish."

"What?" both women asked simultaneously, Marla because she wanted to know the details and Lauren because she had no idea what Tommy was talking about.

"Hey, it's nothing, at least not yet," Fish offered in way of an explanation. When they continued to stare at him he realized he'd need to provide a few details. "OK, so Dr. Riegel, my boss, better known to Tommy as the Kingfish," he began, looking at Lauren to make sure she was following, "told me he's thinking about retiring. Said he's been working on a deal to sell the ER contract to a larger group, and when he leaves he wants me to take over as the director."

"Wow, G, that's great!" Marla said.

"Yeah, that's what Tommy says. It's a big step, you know, a commitment," he gave Tommy a subtle conspiratorial wink, "and I need to think about it before I say yes. Probably need to talk it over with Micky, too. Which reminds me, she'll be home, well my place anyway, soon and I'm going to have to get going so I can have dinner ready when she gets there. By the way, where have you two been all afternoon?"

"Lauren took me to a wine tasting. Italians." She smiled at Tommy before continuing. "Now we're going to do some work in the kitchen to develop dishes that compliment the flavor profiles of some of these wines. Gimme a hand with that?" she asked, nodding toward the box.

Tommy beat him to it and carried the wine to the kitchen. Fish was waiting for him when he returned. "So, tell me something."

"I already told you plenty, did you forget already?"

"Very funny. But since we're on the subject of commitments I was wondering how things were going with you and Lauren. I heard you've been seeing a fair amount of each other."

"You know, I'm not sure. It's a little weird because we have all this chemistry but she's kinda keeping her distance. She says there's someone I have to meet before we can take the relationship to the next level."

"You mean the *sex* level?"

"Yeah, that one, which is also a little weird when you consider the fact the relationship started on that level in the first place."

"So who is this person you have to meet?"

"Don't know. She won't tell me. I hope it's not the parents. That would be awkward."

"And when is this supposed to happen?"

"Don't know that either. All she said was 'soon'.

Chapter 59

Micky couldn't help smiling as she drove toward the beach. Her boyfriend had become quite the romantic lately. When she got to his place the previous evening after a hectic day in the ER there was a hot bubble bath waiting for her, a cold glass of champagne next to the tub, and the aroma of a roasting rack of lamb wafting through the house. Three of her favorite things.

"Wow! What's the occasion?"

"Does there have to be an occasion for me to do something nice? I'm just happy to see you, that's all."

She'd decided to leave it at that and enjoy the moment. If there was something on his mind he'd say it soon enough. Midway through dinner he mentioned the possibility of Dr. Riegel's retirement.

"Even if the deal goes through he'll be the director for another year, so nothing much changes for a while. But once it's done there's going to be some pressure on me to decide whether or not I want the job. And", he added, "none of this has anything to do with the bubble bath and champagne. I really am happy to see you."

She'd been careful not to seem partial. Whatever he chose to do, work-wise or otherwise, the decision had to be his. As for being happy to see her, there was little doubt about that. They had barely finished doing the dishes when he practically carried her to the bedroom, pulled open her robe, and helped himself to dessert.

She had the day off and was driving into town to meet Ashleigh for lunch. They hadn't seen one another for a while and there was much to discuss. They'd chosen a place in Santa Monica near the beach. It was a hot, late August day in Los Feliz but a pleasant seventy-five degrees and sunny near the shore. When she got off the freeway at Fourth Street she opened the windows and turned off the air conditioning. She was in a good mood already and the ocean breeze only made it better.

She found a spot in one of the City-owned parking structures and walked the block and a half to the restaurant. It was a French styled bistro with an authentic menu executed well. Ashleigh, and a glass of champagne, were waiting for her when she walked in.

"More champagne? What's gotten into everyone lately?"

She filled her friend in on the previous evening's pleasant surprises, including the attentive after-dinner sex.

"I'm not sure what's gotten into him but it's like it was when we first started dating."

Ashleigh gave her a recap of the Sunday dinner at her parents' place. Micky had heard it from Fish, but hearing it again from one of the principals added a new dimension.

"He actually tried to compare Danny to Barry Bauer?"

"Yeah. That's when I decided enough was enough. Pappi was doing what he thought he had to do, you know, watch out for his little girl, chase away the bad man trying to take advantage of her. But I'm not a little girl any more and Danny is a really good guy. If anything, I think I take advantage of him once in a while."

Micky raised an eyebrow. "Oh?"

"Nothing evil! But like that night, after we got back to my place, he was pretty exhausted. I guess the anticipation of meeting the parents, the whole third degree, the big emotional scene when they found out about law school and about Carlos going for his GRE, all he wanted to do was get in bed and go to sleep. My reaction was completely the opposite and all I wanted to do was, you know."

"And?"

"I kept him awake for almost three hours. I felt a little guilty about it afterward. I knew he had to get up early to get to work."

"Come on, Ash. I'm pretty sure most guys, most straight guys anyway, would love being taken advantage of like that, especially by someone who looks like you."

The waitress had come and gone and their plates had just been placed in front of them. Moules frites for Micky and a croque madame for Ashleigh. All the sex talk had given them an appetite and they dug right in.

"Danny wants to throw a party for me, a graduation, acceptance to law school thing," Ashleigh said between bites. "He wants to do it the weekend of September tenth."

"I heard, so?"

"So it's the same weekend Tommy and Fish were thinking of having a birthday party for themselves at the Step. Danny asked what I thought about having a big party to celebrate all of it, the birthdays, the graduation, everything. He tried to discourage the idea, though. I think he's afraid I'll be taking a back seat to the boys and he wants it to be more about me."

"What do you think?"

"Actually, I like the idea. I don't think I want to be the center of attention. It would be a little, I don't know, too much like my quinceanera and I'm way past fifteen. It would be fun to have everyone there, my family, Tommy's friends, people from the hospital. It would give my parents a chance to see who I've become. We could do it at the Step on the eleventh, Sunday, instead of pasta night."

"You sure? I know Fish would love it but he's perfectly fine doing a birthday party thing with Tommy next year. No big deal, really."

"Yeah, the more I think about it the better is seems."

"In that case, there may something else to celebrate."

Ashleigh dropped her French fry and her eyes got wide. "No! Don't tell me! He proposed!"

Micky laughed. "No, but the way he's been acting lately who knows? It's a little scary. No, it's about his job. Dr. Riegel, Fish's boss, says he wants to retire. He wants Fish to take over as the director when he does."

"Wow, that's great!"

"It wouldn't be until a year from now, and Fish being Fish, he's going to torture himself for a while trying to decide what to do, but yeah, it would be a good thing."

"OK," Ashleigh said, munching on the previously dropped French fry, "so we have a graduation, an acceptance to law school, two birthdays, a retirement, and a job promotion. This is going to be some party."

"I'll let Fish know you're OK with it and he'll work it out with Tommy."

"Good. I'll tell Danny and then we can start putting together the guest list."

Chapter 60

"John? Hi. Norman Pearl here."

He'd waited two days to make the call. It was enough time for Mr. Wright to consider what had been revealed during Mrs. Sanchez' deposition but probably not enough time for him to have discussed it at any length with his clients. Mr. Pearl wanted an offer on the table when that conversation took place.

"Norman, always good to hear your voice. What can I do for you?"

"I thought we could talk a little about the Sanchez deposition and how it might help us move things along with the case."

"It's a little soon, don't you think. I haven't even received the transcript yet. Or a copy of the video tape," he added, a hint of sarcasm in his voice.

Mr. Wright had been anticipating this call. Having established the relationship between Sister Dolores and Mrs. Sanchez, and thereby having formulated a plausible motive for the application of 'undue influence' by her, Mr. Pearl would naturally want to get some idea of the advantage he had.

"I thought about that," Mr. Pearl replied, "but you know, other than seeing the exact words and the fidgeting your client was doing the transcript and the tape aren't going to change the fundamental facts, and those are that Mrs. Sanchez and Mr. Walter treated one another like family, and Mrs. Sanchez and Sister Dolores *are* family. I'm fairly certain a judge would take a rather jaundiced view of all that internecine kindliness and generosity."

John Wright allowed himself a short laugh. "Norman, that's some of the most eloquent bullshit I've heard in a long time. So, what, exactly, is it you want to talk about?"

"Well, I had a chance to speak to my clients, and I broached the subject of a settlement. Now, I haven't recommended they settle because I think we will win this case if it goes the distance. But, somewhat to my surprise, I found that they might be amenable to settling for the sake of expediency."

John Wright was quiet for a moment, as though he was giving the idea deep thought.

"So, let me see if I understand correctly," he said at last. "You spoke to Elaine, you told her about the relationship between Connie and Sister Dolores, she thought the case would now be a slam dunk and authorized you to throw a few dollars at us to make us go away before spending any more of her hard-inherited money on legal fees. The rest of the family has no idea what's going on. Is that about right?"

It was Mr. Pearl's turn to laugh. "I sometimes forget you worked for them for so many years. Yes, that's about it, except for the part about the others knowing what's going on. Elaine is the spokeswoman and it's her responsibility to keep them informed. Whether or not she does is something I can only guess."

"OK. But before you tell me what you think a reasonable offer would be, understand that I don't consider Mrs. Sanchez' testimony to be particularly damaging."

"With a little luck and some negotiation we may never have to find out if you're right about that," Mr. Pearl responded.

"OK, Norman, what are you offering?"

"Look," he began, "I feel for Mrs. Sanchez and I think the Charitable Foundation is a worthy cause. Elaine, and I'm assuming the others, too, feel the same way. So I suggest we allow Mrs. Sanchez to keep the three million. I'm sure she's earned it over the years. And as for the Charitable Foundation and Sister Dolores, I think I could convince my clients to donate five million dollars. I think you would agree that's a significant endowment."

"And the balance?"

"The balance would go where it should always have gone, to Mr. Walter's three children in equal portions."

"Hmm. Five million instead of about sixty-five million. I'm not sure Sister Dolores would consider that a reasonable offer. Especially considering that it is the exact amount she was going to get before the will was re-written."

"I mentioned that to Elaine. She might be willing to go as high as six if we can get this done quickly."

"I'll bet she might. OK, Norman, I will present your offer to my clients and get back to you."

"Thank you, John. That's all I'm asking."

Chapter 61

"Code Blue, ICU. Code Blue, ICU."

Dr. Riegel was half way through his half shift and until now it had been unusually peaceful. He'd seen only five patients, and only one of them had actually been sick enough to require hospitalization. She was an elderly woman with shortness of breath and a history of emphysema. He'd suspected pneumonia as the cause for her sudden decompensation, though the chest x-ray hadn't shown a definite infiltrate. Nevertheless his experience told him that once she was given some intravenous fluids and her hydration improved the infection would blossom and a repeat x-ray would confirm his diagnosis.

He'd advised the admitting physician to put her in the ICU for at least the first day 'just to be on the safe side'. The admitting doctor had been reluctant to do so. Putting her in the ICU meant he would have to come to the hospital and see her within two hours of the admission time. He had an office full of patients and would have preferred to wait until the end of the day to make hospital rounds.

But the director had been insistent. "Her oxygen saturation is only in the mid eighties and because of the emphysema we can't give her too much or she'll stop breathing altogether. Then she's in the Unit *and* on a ventilator."

In people with normal lungs carbon dioxide levels in the blood drive the respiratory rate—the higher the level the more rapid the rate in order to get it down to normal. People with emphysema tend to have low oxygen levels in the blood, and in these people low oxygen becomes the principal driver. If you put someone with emphysema on too much oxygen, and increase the blood level, the drive to breathe will be suppressed. In that scenario carbon dioxide levels can rise to dangerous levels causing the patient to become unconscious and stop breathing.

The admitting doctor knew Dr. Riegel was right, and full office or no full office he was going to have to find a way to get to the hospital within the mandated two-hour window.

"Code Blue, ICU. Code Blue, ICU."

The director had been sitting in the ER workstation reading the paper when the first Code Blue had been paged. He was already on his way to the Unit when the second call was announced. "Christ!" he mumbled to himself as he walked quickly down the corridor. "I'll bet it's the old lady. I told him she wasn't stable."

Entry to the ICU required punching a pass code into the door lock. Dr. Riegel had a problem remembering pass codes and tried to use the same one for all applications. The code for the ICU door had been set by someone in the hospital maintenance department and his usual 1-2-3-4 wasn't going to work. Fortunately, the director realized his shortcomings in the area of pass codes and had written the one for the ICU on a piece of tape which he'd then affixed to the back of his I.D. badge.

The Unit, a little frenetic under normal circumstances, was now practically chaotic. The center of attention seemed to be Room One, off to the side and isolated from the other patient rooms. As he pushed his way through the crowd of nurses, techs, and respiratory therapists he saw a patient on the bed, unconscious, intubated, and presently being ignored. He saw Dr. Silverman standing off to the side of the bed, a horrified look on his face, staring down at the floor.

When he finally got to the bedside he was able to see what the commotion was all about. Lying near the bed, supine, wearing a doctor's lab coat, shirt and necktie in shreds, with defibrillator electrodes on his chest and looking much like a corpse was a familiar face.

"It's Byner," Dr. Siverman announced. "We're about four hours into the rapid detox procedure, everything's going fine, and then he grabs his chest and keels over. The nurses put the quick-look defibrillator paddles on him, shows he's in V-fib, and gives him a shock. He converts back to sinus and he has pulses but he hasn't woken up."

Meaning—Dr. Byner had an episode of ventricular fibrillation, an abnormal heart rhythm that causes the heart to stop pumping blood. As a result, no blood, and no oxygen, was getting to his brain and he passed out. The nurses correctly applied the defibrillator paddles, which correctly diagnosed the problem, and delivered the electrical shock that returned the rhythm to normal, restoring Dr. Byner's circulation. Given the rapidity with which he'd been diagnosed and treated he was expected to be waking up shortly.

"Christ!" Dr. Riegel mumbled for the second time in five minutes. "Get him on a gurney and wheel him down to the Emergency Room."

"But we're already in the ICU," Dr. Silverman said.

"Yes. And we need to get him to the ER so I can treat him and make arrangements for a transfer to the cath lab at Memorial. He's probably having an MI. We need to move fast so let's go."

"But what about our patient?" Dr. Silverman asked, pointing to the comatose middle-aged man on the bed.

"He's not *our* patient," Dr. Riegel replied as he began moving toward the ICU door, "he's *your* patient. And as for what to do about him, that's up to you. I don't know the first thing about rapid detox."

"But..." Dr. Silverman began.

"But nothing," Dr. Riegel interrupted as he accompanied the gurney, and the now awake but confused Dr. Byner, down the hall.

Chapter 62

"OK, start paddling. Hard! Good! OK, NOW!"

There were two distinct cliques among young white kids growing up in Southern California, the surfer types with longish, sun-bleached hair and perpetual tans, and the greaser types, with pasty complexions, jeans, T-shirts, and jean jackets with the sleeves cut off. Both groups were into cars, though no self-respecting greaser would be caught dead in a Woody.

Fish had been of the surfer persuasion, a basically wholesome kid who spent as much time as possible in the water. Micky, though, had been drawn to the dark side. During her rebellious teen years she'd preferred the company of 'bad boys'. Her association with them stopped the night she got busted, and though she didn't identify with the type any longer she still had a difficult time imagining herself on a surfboard.

Nevertheless that is exactly where she found herself the morning Dr. Gerald Byner was having his difficulties. For two years Fish had been trying to get her to try it and for the same length of time she'd resisted.

"I'm a little old to start something like that, don't you think?"

"Oh, please."

"The water's freezing, I'll catch pneumonia or something."

"I'll get you a wet suit. You would look very hot in a wet suit."

She had to admit he'd been right, at least about that. He'd dragged her to the surf shop several days earlier where she'd tried on a number of models before settling on a long one reaching from her neck to her ankles, black, with red inserts over the shoulders and upper arms. It fit her like a second skin and Fish had had a difficult time keeping his mind on the purpose of the outing as she posed in front of the full-length mirror before making her decision.

"I might not be able to avoid drowning, but at least I'll be warm when it happens," had been her rationale.

Late August was prime hurricane season and a tropical storm had been kicking up the surf off the tip of Baja for the past few days. LA beaches were just beginning to reap the benefits. Fish had been scheduled to relieve the director that afternoon but he'd managed to talk Bob Graber into taking the short shift. Micky had the day off and he wanted to spend some time with her. What better way, he thought, than her first surfing lesson.

He picked a spot he knew would be relatively empty. The waves were coming up from the south, so the south-facing beaches would see the biggest surf and that's where most surfers would be. The stretch of beach he'd chosen was angled more to the west lending itself to a gentler break and a lot less traffic.

This was her third attempt at catching a wave. The first had rolled under her board and on to the beach leaving her bobbing too close to the shore to catch another. She gamely paddled back out.

"You have to get your board moving at the same speed as the wave," Fish instructed.

Micky just grunted and tried to catch her breath. If the actual surfing was as difficult as the paddling, she thought, it was going to be a very long morning. When she had recovered sufficiently to try again Fish got her lined up and ready. When he gave the order she began paddling furiously. This time is was different. She felt the wave catch the board, propelling it forward. No more paddling necessary.

Now it was time to stand up. They'd practiced the maneuver on the beach prior to hitting the water. Hands on the edges of the board, a quick jump into a crouch, left foot in front of the right, then let go and stand. She braced herself, got into the crouch, and realized she was still on the board. She let go and tentatively raised herself to a standing position. She was surfing! She turned to make sure Fish was watching. He was, and he just shook his head. "Keep your eyes forward, don't look back," had been the other instruction he'd given her between waves.

As soon as she looked backward she became disoriented and lost her balance. She went off the board sideways, at least she'd remembered not to go off head first, and got caught in the break. It was a relatively small wave so the rolling around under water was limited to only a few seconds. Still, the experience was sufficiently unpleasant to etch any further instructions clearly in her mind.

She was practically to the beach and had to paddle all the way back, through the next set of in-coming waves, to get to the catch zone. Her shoulders were aching and she was breathing hard when she got there, but the momentary exhilaration she'd experienced between standing and falling off had given her the motivation to try again.

"Mick, that was great! You did it on your second try! Next time, just keep your eyes forward and enjoy the ride. I'll be watching you the whole way."

The sets were coming in at about four-minute intervals and she let three go by before turning her board toward the shore. Fish was scanning the horizon and as the next set approached he did a quick assessment. The first wave seemed about right, and there were two more behind it.

"OK," he yelled. "Start paddling!"

She did, and when she felt the wave take over she repeated the jump, crouch, and stand. This time she knew the board would support her—it was an old style long board perfectly suited for beginners and very stable in the type of surf she was riding. She kept her eyes forward and felt the unique rush of gliding on the water, with no sound but the roar of the surf, and nothing to see but water, foam, and the beach ahead. She understood why Fish loved it.

He'd watched her take off, and when he saw she was up and doing OK he paddled and caught the third and last wave of the set, riding in behind her. She had a little problem with the dismount, taking the wave closer to the sand than might have been optimal and getting caught in the shore break. Fish hopped off his board, put it under his arm and waded to where she was sitting in the surf trying to collect herself and her board, attached to her ankle by the tether and bobbing toward the beach. He got there in time to prevent her from getting dragged by the board or pummeled by the next set of waves.

"Wanna go back out?" They'd been sitting on the beach for fifteen minutes. Fish knew the perfect conditions wouldn't last longer than another hour or so and wanted to take advantage of them. Micky was breathing easily, staring into the horizon, a small smile on her face, oblivious to his question. "Mick?"

"Huh?"

"I asked if you wanted to go back out. You seem like you're a million miles away. What are you thinking about?"

"Um. I don't know. I don't think I was thinking about anything. It's weird, but my mind was completely blank."

Fish smiled. Surfing and skiing were about the only things besides sex that could clear his head of everything but the moment, and sex, as great as it was, rarely did so for more than an hour. He knew Micky had just discovered the same truth.

"So?"

"So, I can't believe I'm going to say this, but yeah."

Chapter 63

News of Dr. Byner's collapse spread quickly and the small group that left the ICU moving toward the ER grew larger the closer it got. Dr. Carter had heard the Code Blue page in the surgeons' dressing room and had gone to the Unit to see if the victim was one of his post-op patients. Upon learning it was Dr. Byner he strode off in the direction of the ER.

The ICU nursing director had called Sister Dolores to inform her of the incident, and to apprise her of the fact that the patient undergoing rapid detox was now in the questionably capable hands of Dr. Silverman, who, she noted, appeared to be none too happy about it. Sister Dolores then called Timothy Doyle, C.O.O.

"Doyle, your friend Dr. Byner just had a cardiac arrest in the ICU."

"WHAT?"

"You heard me. He was in the middle of one of his detox procedures when it happened."

"Is he…"

"No, he's not dead. They shocked him and got him back. They're taking him to the ER."

"Oh thank God."

"Yeah, well maybe not so fast."

"What's *that* supposed to mean?"

"It means he's not out of the woods yet. And there's another problem."

The C.O.O. knew what she was about to say and beat her to it. "Oh, God, the detox patient."

"Bingo. Silverman's in charge. Anything goes wrong I'm holding you responsible."

"ME? But..."

Click.

After hanging up both Sister Dolores and Timothy Doyle left their offices and headed toward the ER. They arrived just as Dr. Byner was being wheeled through the doors.

"Get a 12-lead!" Dr. Riegel barked at the first nurse to approach the entourage. He needed a twelve-lead EKG to determine whether or not Dr. Byner was having the sort of event that would qualify him for a lights-and-sirens ride to Memorial and an emergency cardiac catheterization.

While the electrodes were being attached to his chest, Dr. Byner was having blood drawn from from an IV catheter in one arm, a blood pressure cuff wrapped around the other, oxygen tubing applied to his nose, and a pulse oximeter clamped onto one of his fingers to measure his blood oxygen concentration.

"You having any chest pain?" Dr. Riegel asked as he was handed the EKG. It was the first time since passing out that anyone wanted any information directly from him and Dr. Byner was momentarily at a loss.

"Uh, what's going on?" he replied.

"You had a cardiac arrest in the ICU. Actually V-fib. The nurses got you back with one shock. You're in the ER. Are you having any chest pain now?" the director offered in way of explanation.

"It just feels a little tight."

"I'll bet it does. EKG shows you're having an MI. Anterior. And a lot of PVC's." Premature ventricular contractions could predispose an ailing heart to go back into ventricular fibrillation. "Get him an aspirin, some nitro and 300 milligrams of Amiodarone. Fax this EKG to Memorial. As soon as they've seen it call 911."

Aspirin prevents blood from clotting, a useful function in cases of blocked coronary arteries. Nitroglycerin can dilate blood vessels, allowing blood to flow more freely to the area currently being deprived. Amiodarone was the current first-line antiarrythmic drug used to suppress the PVC's. Whether it worked better than last year's favorite was a little murky but in situations like these it was probably wise to go along with the American Heart Association's recommendations.

The nitroglycerin was sprayed under Dr. Byner's tongue and the Amiodarone was pushed into his IV. A few minutes later the tightness in his chest began to subside.

"Uh, what are you doing?" Dr. Jerry was still having a hard time processing all the information. "You say I'm having a heart attack."

"'Fraid so. Paramedics are on their way now. They'll take you to Memorial, get you up to the cath lab, and hopefully this can all be fixed with a stent or two."

"But the tightness is practically gone. Are you sure all this is really necessary?"

"Come on, Jerry. You know better than that."

Dr. Byner was quiet a moment. "Yeah, I guess I do. Hey, Bill?"

"Yeah?"

"Thanks. Really. You saved my life."

"Hell, I didn't do much, but you're welcome. It's going to be OK."

They heard the paramedic siren approaching. In all, Dr. Byner would have been in the ER for less than twenty minutes. Diagnosed, treated, and transferred for definitive care in well under the ninety minute goal currently established for the treatment of acute heart attacks.

As he was being loaded onto the paramedics' gurney Sister Dolores and Timothy Doyle approached.

"You gave us a scare," she said, shaking her head.

"Sorry," he said with a slight smile. "Oh, hey! We were doing a detox when this happened. What's going on with that?"

"Dr. Silverman's handling things."

"But…"

"There's a protocol, right? It went through all the committees. Mr. Doyle has assured me that Dr. Silverman is familiar with it and should be able to handle the case without any problems." She smiled in the direction of the C.O.O. as she said this. He looked as though he was considering joining Dr. Byner on his trip to Memorial.

Chapter 64

John Wright waited a day before calling his clients. There was more to discuss than the low-ball offer put on the table by Mr. Pearl and he wanted time to think about how he would present it. In person and in a comfortable environment was what he'd decided. Sister Dolores had the most at stake, financially and possibly emotionally, so the meeting was set to take place the following afternoon in her office.

Connie had been early, as was her habit when dealing with what she considered to be formal occasions. She'd been advised not to discuss any of the details of her deposition prior to Mr. Wright's arrival. She was having a little trouble making small talk and was relieved to see him when he walked in a few minutes later.

"So, there must be something important going on for you to drive all the way out here," Sister Dolores said after everyone was settled.

Mr. Wright smiled. No beating around the bush. "A couple of things, actually."

"So let's hear them." It had been days since Connie's deposition and she hadn't heard a word from her attorney until now. She wasn't sure what to make of the silence but found it unnerving. Whatever it was he had to say she wanted him to hurry up and say it.

"Well, the first bit of news, and I think it is good news, is that this case can probably be settled without a trial."

The nun and the caretaker both raised eyebrows upon hearing this.

"I spoke to Mr. Pearl, the family's attorney, and he said they are anxious to get this behind them and would be interested in a settlement. He made an offer which I'm obligated to present to you. Before I do, though, there are a couple of things I want you both to understand. First, it's his initial offer and I don't expect it to be his final offer. Secondly, I want you to know that although I would not be opposed to a settlement I feel that we have a strong case and I would discourage you from accepting less than that to which I think you are entitled. Understood?"

Consuela nodded. "OK, out with it," Sister Dolores said.

"Mr. Pearl has been authorized to offer three million to Mrs. Sanchez and five million to the hospital's Charitable Foundation. Possibly six million if we settle this quickly."

There was a small gasp from Consuela. She'd left her deposition feeling beaten and off balance, despite Mr. Wright's attempts to ensure her that no great damage had been done. Until this instant she'd felt it was unlikely she would ever see the one million left to her in the original will, let alone the three million in the revised document.

Sister Dolores was less in thrall. Six million wasn't enough to save the hospital but it would buy some time. To refuse it could turn out to be at least a one million dollar mistake, possibly worse. Plus, she saw the strategy behind the offer and understood Mr. Pearl knew what he was doing.

"So," she began after considering what had been said, "Mrs. Sanchez gets everything she was left in the new will and therefore has no reason to object. The Foundation gets a million more than we were originally going to receive. If I refuse and insist on taking this to a trial I could be costing Consuela a fortune plus I could further jeopardize the ability of Saints' to continue to operate. There seems to be a bit of gamesmanship here. Am I right?"

"No doubt getting you two on opposite sides of the issue was a consideration when this offer was devised. But there's something else you need to know."

Connie looked down at her hands resting in her lap and quietly bit her lower lip. Sister Dolores narrowed her eyes and stared at the lawyer.

"Well, it turns out that the two of you," waving his hand from one to the other, "are related by marriage."

"Excuse me?" Sister Dolores sputtered, looking back and forth between Mr. Wright and Mrs. Sanchez.

"Connie's husband, Juan, is your first cousin."

Sister Dolores slumped back in her chair. "Juan. Sanchez. My mother was a Sanchez," she mumbled to herself. "I haven't spoken to anyone in my family in over forty years. Are you sure you have the right Sanchez family. It's not an unusual name, you know."

"We're sure."

"Connie?"

"I swear, I had no idea," she began, shaken. She then went on to explain how it was she learned of the relationship. When she was done she wore an expression that seemed to beg for forgiveness. "I'm really sorry if this is going to cause trouble for you and the hospital," she murmured.

"Please, it's not your fault my family decided to disown me. Tell me, Mr. Wright, how does all this affect our bargaining position?"

"I need to be clear on something before I can answer that. From your reaction here today, and from what you've said, my sense is that you had no idea you and Mrs. Sanchez were related. Is that correct?"

"Of course that's correct!"

"Good. Mrs. Sanchez has assured me that she was equally unaware. Mr. Pearl's theory is that Connie used what we call 'undue influence' to convince Mr. Walter to change his will making you and the Foundation the big winners. He will say she did this because you and she are family. The problem he is going to have is that both of you make very credible witnesses and each has said she had no idea that any such relationship existed until after the death of Mr. Walter. It will be difficult for any judge to understand why someone close to the decedent would exercise undue influence to convince him to leave almost all his money to a complete stranger."

"So what do we do now?"

"We make them a counter offer."

"And what do you suggest that should be."

"I think it should be the same offer they made us, with the roles reversed. Connie gets her three million, you authorize five for the family, six if they act quickly, and the Foundation gets the rest."

"Do you think that's going to work?"

"No, but it's a lot closer to where, in my opinion, we are going to end up than what *they* offered."

Sister Dolores let a moment pass. "You really think so?"

"Yes, I do," the lawyer replied, giving her a look suggesting he meant business.

"OK. Do it."

Chapter 65

The Zen of surfing had been a pleasant surprise. An empty mind, Micky realized, could be a happy one. The physiology of surfing had been a surprise of a different sort. The sore muscles in her shoulders and back and a gnawing hunger preoccupied her thoughts on the ride home.

Once there they stayed long enough for a quickie, ("it's the wet suit, I can't help it," was his explanation for the impulsive behavior), a shower, and a change of clothes. Then it was off to the Step for lunch and some party planning.

Marla and Tommy were huddled at one of the tables when they arrived. Each had a sheet of paper in front of them and a pen with which they were scribbling notes.

"Hey, it's Frankie and Annette," Tommy remarked when they walked in. Fish had told his sister about the surfing lesson and she'd obviously shared the information with Tommy. "So?"

"So what?" Micky replied. "And who are Frankie and Annette?"

Tommy shook his head. "I really am getting old."

"It was great, she got up on the second try and surfed the third one all the way in. Caught a bunch more rides after that. She's a natural," Fish said pulling up two chairs.

"Wow! I mean I guess 'wow' since I never tried it myself. Kids didn't do much of that where I grew up."

"I thought I was going to hate it but it really was fun, and relaxing in a way. But now I'm starving. And seriously, who are Frankie and Annette?"

"Really?" Tommy asked. Micky just stared at him. "OK, fine."

While Tommy gave Micky a brief history of the Beach Party movie series Marla went into the kitchen. By the time she returned with burgers and fries he was up to Beach Blanket Bingo.

"It was even before *my* time but I caught one of those movies on late-night T.V. We were in some beach town in Florida, on tour, staying in this cheesy surf-themed motel. I turned on the tube and there it was. I got hooked immediately. It was so not San Francisco. Eventually I saw all five of them."

While Micky and Fish attacked their food Marla and Tommy went over their notes. Keeping the guest list to a reasonable number had been the biggest problem. It was supposed to be about Ashleigh, whether or not she wanted that to be the case, so she'd been given a certain latitude. There were four in her immediate family, plus a dozen assorted relatives and friends. There were others but Ashleigh had been able to pare her list to the essential sixteen.

Then there was the Hooks contingent. Gilbert, Marlene, Danny and Micky, Marla and Bob Graber. Billy sent regrets. He'd be in Hawaii that week. Dr. and Mrs. Riegel had somewhat surprisingly agreed to come. The director wasn't much for parties and large groups but he liked Tommy and the Step was his kind of place.

Lastly there was Tommy's list. Lauren, of course, was at the top, followed by an assortment of musicians, their significant others, a few of the ladies' night regulars, ("It's not a party without those gals," was his explanation.), his agent, road manager, record label execs, and former band members.

"I talked to the guys about a week ago, asked them if they'd be into doing some playing. Kind of a Train Wreck reunion. They were a little iffy at first but when I told them it would be at the Step for a roomful of friends, and that is was my fucking birthday, they agreed to do it. I get the honor of paying for the rehearsal space, and keeping them fed and happy, of course."

"And we decided to out-source the food," Marla added. "I lined up this cool catering company that's going to do a Tex-Mex kind of thing. They'll provide kitchen and wait staff plus a bartender so none of our employees will have to work."

"So how many people altogether?" Fish asked as he polished off the last of his burger.

"Looks like sixty, more or less," Tommy replied.

"Geez."

"Yeah, I know. And that's pretty much just the inner circle."

"It's only about two weeks away. You sure all these people are going to be able to make it? It's a little short-notice."

"We've been making a lot of phone calls and yeah, they're all gonna be here. It'll be after Labor Day, summer's over, the kids are back in school. The timing worked out."

"And we're splitting it three ways, right?"

"That's what we figured initially, but it's turning out that my list is a lot longer than yours or Ashleigh's, so maybe we should reconsider."

"No, Tommy. You might have the longest list, but you're providing the space and the entertainment. Three ways is more than fair."

"You sure?"

"Yeah, I'm sure."

"OK, then. We won't know the total cost until after the party, you know, see how much drinking this bunch does. I'll count the bottles and charge the booze at wholesale."

'Cool. Hey, and thanks for lunch."

"Gotta take care of my favorite kahuna and his wahine, dude."

"Oh, God," Fish moaned.

Chapter 66

"Good morning, Dave. You look like shit."

It was the day after Dr. Byner's collapse. Dr. Riegel had stopped at Daisy's Café for a quick bite and saw a haggard looking Dr. Silverman sitting in the back of the room. He decided to join him.

"Thanks, Bill, have a seat," he replied to an already-seated Dr. Riegel. Mrs. Choi had noticed the director enter and was quick to place a cup of coffee and a menu in front of him.

"How about an egg white omelet with spinach and mushrooms, wheat toast, no butter?" the director asked without bothering with the menu.

"Ooh, you're on a diet again?" Mrs. Choi was familiar with his routines, including the intermittent bouts of more-or-less healthy eating. The director just grunted in response.

"Worried about your heart?" Dr. Silverman asked when they were alone.

"I'm not worried, just trying to be sensible. Watching Byner try to check out yesterday put a crimp in my appetite. Any news?"

"Yeah. I called over there a little while ago, got a hold of his cardiologist."

"And?"

"And it's not great. He took him to the cath lab right after he got there and found multiple partial blockages that he couldn't get stents into. He's scheduled for bypass surgery later this morning."

"Jesus!"

"No kidding. He said they're going to have to do at least three grafts, maybe four. He'll be in the O.R. most of the day."

"What's the rehab look like?"
"Months. If everything goes well."

"Hm. I guess that puts you in charge of the CARE program for now."

"Yeah, but I don't think so. That guy we were treating when Byner went down?"

Dr. Riegel nodded.

"I was up all night with him. Blood pressure was all over the place, he had a seizure. I finally got him settled about an hour ago, got a CT of his head, which was normal, thank God, and he's off the ventilator, but I'm not anxious to do another case like that."

"Does Doyle know?"

"I don't think so. At least I haven't said anything to him yet. I'm going to have to tell Sister Dolores the program's going to be on hold for a while. I'll let *her* give Doyle the news."

"I'd love to be there for that. The little fucker's going to freak out. It's the one piece of new business he actually managed to recruit, sketchy as it is, and now, poof, gone."

"Yeah, not good for Doyle, but not good for me, either. Or you, for that matter."

Mrs. Choi returned with the director's order and placed it in front of him. "We'll see how long *this* lasts," she said before leaving.

Dr. Riegel stared at his plate for a moment. The pale omelet with bits of green poking out the ends and the two sad pieces of dry toast stared back, daring him to eat them.

"Fuck it," he mumbled to himself. Then he grabbed his fork, lopped off a piece of the omelet, and put it in his mouth."

"Does it taste as bad as it looks?" Dr. Silverman inquired.

"No. But considering how bad it looks, that would be tough. What were you saying about how all this is going to be bad for us?"

"Surgery volumes are down and I'm having trouble keeping my guys busy. The CARE program, whether you liked it or not, took some of the heat off the ER. It shuts down, Doyle starts looking for ways to cut expenses. As I recall, one of his pet projects was closing your department."

"Never happen," the director responded, crunching on a piece of toast. "Keeping the ER open is Sister Dolores' pet project."

"Maybe, but the Board has a larger responsibility."

"Namely?"

"Namely keeping the *hospital* open. If there's a way to trim your operation in a way that will allow Saints' to survive you can bet they're going to consider it."

The conversation, combined with the health-conscious breakfast, was giving Dr. Riegel heartburn. He flagged down Mrs. Choi.

"Can you get me an order of hash browns to go with this, please?"

"Diet lasted five minutes. That's a new record!" she said with a slight smirk before leaving to place the order.

Chapter 67

"What are *you* doing all dressed up?"

Marla had been putting menus on the tables when Tommy walked in. He was wearing his good jeans, the ones without the holes over the knees, a real shirt with a real collar, and a sport coat.

"You know, it's Thursday, Ladies' Night?" she reminded him. "Not a good chance your gonna get lucky."

"We'll see about that," he replied with a sly smile.

"OH?"

"I've got a date. With Lauren. Not that it's any of your business. I just stopped by to pick up a bottle of wine."

"Ooh!" she teased.

Tommy walked behind the bar and started pulling bottles from the rack. "What would you recommend?"

"Wow! Buying wine for the wine expert. Very brave. Well, it depends where you're taking her and what you're going to be eating."

"Not taking her anywhere. She invited me to her place. She's cooking. Said she's making something Italian that you taught her."

Marla considered that for a moment. She and Lauren had had only five sessions together in the kitchen so the list of possibilities was short. Pasta with a lamb ragu seemed a good guess. She nudged Tommy to the side and pulled a bottle from under the bar.

"Brunello di Montalcino, 2006. This should do the trick," she said, handing him the bottle.

"I don't remember ordering this. Where'd it come from?"

"From the tasting we went to, remember? I was saving it for one of our pasta nights. Lauren picked it, so I'm pretty sure she's going to like it."

"Hey, thanks."

"Who's going to be taking your place behind the bar?"

"Oh, yeah. I spoke to Karen yesterday and she said she could handle it. It *is* Ladies' Night after all."

"So," Marla drawled after a pause, "you think tonight is, you know, the night?"

"Good question. A little nosy, but good anyway. I don't know. I mean, I've never been to her place before, so that's promising. But she told me a while ago that there's someone I have to meet before we can move our relationship forward and whoever that is I'm pretty sure I haven't met him or her yet."

"That's kinda mysterious."

"Yeah, and I'd like to get it over with soon."

"I'll bet you would," Marla said with a lascivious grin.

"OK, that's it. I'm going. Have fun with the girls. I hope they like the new dish."

Marla shook her head as he walked out the door. The new dish was Diver Scallops. Tommy didn't even need to rename it.

As he made his way from Silverlake to West Hollywood he considered the possibilities. If this *was* the night, then whoever it was he was supposed to meet would be there, at Lauren's place. He ran the scenarios through his mind, one more disturbing than the next. A husband, disabled and confined to a wheelchair, wanting to meet his wife's potential new lover before giving her his blessing?

"Nah," he said out loud with a shudder, "she told me she'd never been married. She wouldn't lie about something like that. I think."

An elderly parent living with her, confined to a wheelchair, for whom she was the primary caretaker? "Hmm," he mumbled. It was an idea a little harder to dismiss.

"Christ!" he blurted. "She probably has a big, goofy dog and wants to make sure I like animals. That's gotta be it. I should have bought a toy for it. I wonder if it sleeps on the bed?"

He realized his train of thought needed to be derailed and switched on the radio. It was set to an oldies station. He wasn't much for hip-hop and it was fun to hear one of his tunes get played from time to time.

Fifteen minutes later he was in her neighborhood looking for a place to park. Included in the directions she'd given him was a detailed description of the likeliest places to find a spot that would not result in a ticket or his car being towed. After one lap around the block he found one.

He located the address half a block away, walked to the door, and rang the bell. A moment later it opened and he was face to face with a little girl.

"Uh, is this Lauren Walter's house?" he asked tentatively.

"Hi, Tommy," the young girl said holding out her right hand. "I'm Amy."

"Uh, hi, Amy," he replied, shaking her hand.

"Come in. My mom's in the kitchen."

Tommy stared at her a moment, his mind once again beginning to spin. He forced it to stop and stepped inside.

Chapter 68

Mr. Wright's counter offer had not been particularly well received.

"Is this supposed to be some kind of joke?" were the words Elaine had used.

Mr. Pearl assured her it was not.

"It appears he thinks he has a strong case. It also appears he recognizes that regardless of how strong his case may be his clients are best served by trying to negotiate a settlement."

"You call this a negotiation? This is an insult! We made a good-faith offer, better than what they would have gotten in the original will. That bitch Connie sabotaged our family and we *still* offered her a fortune. I say screw 'em! Take the offer off the table. They don't deserve a penny."

Mr. Pearl waited a full minute before responding. It took that long for the breathing coming through the other end of the phone line to slow from hysteria to mere anger.

"Are you done? No response, but a noticeable uptick in the respiratory rate. "Good. Listen. We don't want to go to a judge with this. You yourself once told me your father was an intelligent, thoughtful man. As far as we can tell he remained so up to the time of his death. We have found nothing to suggest he'd become demented or in some other way mentally incapacitated. Are you following me so far?"

"Yes," she hissed through partially clenched teeth.

"Good. That means there was probably a good reason for him to change the will. Any judge would be able to see this, and the judge to which this case has been assigned is a real pro. He is not going to let an emotional outburst by the petitioning family members sway his judgment in their favor. In fact, a reaction like the one you just had is most likely to work against you."

More audible breathing ensued. "What, then, do think is the appropriate response?" she finally said, the petulance clear in her tone.

"You need to understand what and with whom we are dealing. Mrs. Sanchez is not the person you should be focusing on. The offer we made her is the same as what she was left in the new will. I am certain she is more than delighted with it. Sister Dolores, on the other hand, is the person we need to appease. This is where it becomes a bit complicated."

"What's so complicated about a nun walking off with all our money?"

"It's complicated because she isn't the one actually *getting* the money. The money is being left to the Charitable Foundation of Saints' Hospital. She is Chairman of the Board and C.E.O. of the hospital. My investigator has done some poking around. It seems Sister Dolores is quite devoted to the hospital and to the concept of providing health care for the less fortunate. It is her mission. It also seems the hospital is in serious financial straits. It is actually close to bankruptcy."

"How did your investigator find all this out?"

"I don't know, nor do I want to. What I do know is that over the years the information he has provided has always been accurate."

"And expensive, I've noticed."

"Yes. But back to Sister Dolores. Your father's gift to the Charitable Foundation, if left in place, would likely be sufficient to keep the hospital open indefinitely. Five or six million would merely get it out of debt. Then, given the current climate for health care, the debt would once again start piling up and a couple of years from now she and the hospital would be right back on the brink of insolvency."

He paused to allow his client to absorb what he'd told her. Elaine didn't like where this seemed to be going and her breathing reflected her discomfiture. She was unable, though, to find anything to say.

"So," Mr. Pearl continued, "in order to satisfy Sister Dolores we are going to have to make her an offer she will find difficult to refuse."

Elaine found her tongue. "And just what the hell is *that* supposed to mean?"

"It means," the lawyer responded calmly, "we need to offer an amount that will not only retire the hospital's debt but that will provide additional investment capital from which the hospital can draw a steady income."

"And just how large an offer do you think we need to make," she asked skeptically.

"I think twenty million would be sufficient."

"WHAT!"

"Sister Dolores would have a difficult time turning down an amount that large and it would leave you and your siblings something in the neighborhood of forty-five million or so to split among yourselves. That's something like fifteen million each. It's a lot of money."

"But if we go from six million to twenty million in a single leap they'll think we're weak! They'll just come back and ask for more. Forty million, fifty!"

"Elaine. We can spend the next six months going back and forth with offers and counter offers and the only people who will benefit from the exercise will be Mr. Wright and myself. Between us you are paying close to two thousand dollars an hour. If we were to make this offer I would do it in a way that makes it clear to the other side it is our final offer."

Elaine was silent and Mr. Pearl could hear her breathing gradually slow.

"I can't do this without discussing it with the family."

"Nor should you. My advice is for you to sit down with your brother and sister and talk it over. I think you understand the issues well enough to present a clear picture. When you've made your decision give me a call and we will proceed according to your wishes."

The call ended and Normal Pearl sat back in his chair. Nine hundred dollars an hour, he thought, was probably not enough.

Chapter 69

Upon hearing the news of Dr. Byner's heart condition and the suspension of the CARE program Sister Dolores called an emergency meeting of the hospital leadership to discuss options.

"OK, Doyle, the first thing I want you to do is find out whether or not there's anyone else in the area doing rapid detox and whether or not they'd be interested in expanding their practice to our hospital."

Timothy Doyle had already done that research prior to bringing Dr. Byner on board and knew the answer was 'no, there isn't anyone else'. He didn't think this was the appropriate moment to share that bit of information with his boss.

"Will do."

"The next thing I want you to do is look for some other practice or type of business we can recruit to Saints'. CARE was set to bring in over two hundred thousand a month in revenue. We have to find a way to offset the loss."

"Yes, Sister."

His job was practically impossible. He'd done what he could to attract various lucrative practices but had failed, due in large part to Sister Dolores' reluctance to pay for 'directorships' to the physicians in charge. He understood why she felt the way she did. Paying what essentially amounted to bribes to doctors in exchange for their business was morally wrong, and, more significantly, illegal.

In order to justify such payments it must be obvious to an outside auditor that the physician receiving the money is actually doing something to earn it beyond funneling his patients to the hospital writing the checks. It isn't enough for him to merely be the titular head of a department. There needs to be a job description and an accounting of work done. At a hospital the size of Saints' there just wasn't enough of that sort of work to do to justify the amount of money the doctor would demand for his loyalty.

"And while you're out there," she continued, "keep in mind that my previous stance on directorships might be a little flexible if you can find some legitimate way to structure that kind of deal."

It was the first ray of sunshine to break through the clouds that had been hanging over his head since he heard about Dr. Byner's by-pass surgery. He'd walked into the meeting expecting to be fired. He'd only agreed to do what she'd asked to buy himself some time. Now there was an actual possibility of success and his body language communicated his newly found optimism. Sister Dolores noticed.

"Don't get too excited. We don't have a lot of time to make any of this happen and the next place I'm going to look to make budget cuts is our payroll."

Dr. Riegel was sitting near the opposite end of the table. He, too, had come to the meeting with low expectations and a sense of foreboding. He hadn't needed Dr. Silverman to remind him that the loss of the CARE program would draw attention to the ER. So far, he thought, so good. He even managed a smirk at the not-so-subtle threat regarding Mr. Doyle's continued employment.

"There's something else I'm going to do that you should all know about.
It's something I've refused to seriously consider, until now, and it goes against my most strongly held beliefs regarding the purpose of this hospital and its role in the community."

The director didn't like what he was hearing and stiffened in his chair.

"As most of you already know, the emergency room is a significant financial liability for us. We see everyone who comes without regard to their ability to pay, we accept paramedic runs from our immediate area and beyond, often bringing us patients so sick they need to be admitted to the hospital for intensive medical treatment or surgery, again with no financial questions asked."

The others in the room stole glances at Dr. Riegel who sat with his eyes fixed on Sister Dolores. It was all Mr. Doyle could do to suppress a grin.

"While I consider this type of work to be at the core of our mission," she continued, "it is becoming increasingly difficult to support. For that reason I've decided to contact the County to inquire about a change in our emergency designation. We are currently a Level II. That means we are open 24/7, we have a certain number of nurses and a physician on duty at all times, and we have on-call doctors to handle admissions and surgeries. This qualifies us as a paramedic receiving facility. If we were to downgrade to a level III we would still be able to see the walk-ins but we would lose the paramedic business, which, when we analyzed it, is what's costing us the most money."

"But..." Dr. Riegel began, not exactly sure what he was going to say but certain he had to say something.

"We can discuss this in depth privately," she said, cutting him off. "Understand, there is no guarantee the County will allow us to downgrade. We've lost a significant number of ER's due to financial problems already and the people downtown are not going to be happy to get my call. It will take months of reviews and hearings to get this request through the system, which is why I want to start the process now. If somewhere along the way we find new revenue and our financial outlook improves we can just tell them we've changed our minds. I don't think they would object to our keeping our current designation."

There was a buzz in the room and, she noted, a lot of grim faces, though none quite as grim as that of the director who continued to stare at her.

"Any questions?" she asked loudly. The buzzing stopped and the faces turned toward her. No one had anything to say.

"Good. We're adjourned." She then turned toward the director, meeting his stare. "Dr. Riegel, my office."

Chapter 70

Lauren's front door was at the opposite end of the cottage from the kitchen. As Tommy followed his young escort he noticed things were as he'd imagined. Simple, tasteful, comfortable. He also noticed a familiar, appetizing aroma wafting down the short hallway. The source became clear the moment he arrived at his destination.

Lauren, dressed in jeans, short-sleeved pale blue blouse, and a large red apron was at the stove stirring a pot of what Tommy recognized as a pasta sauce Marla had created one Sunday night.

"Wow! Smells great in here," Tommy said. He moved toward the stove to give the cook a hug but stopped short. He wasn't sure whether physical contact was appropriate in front of her daughter.

"Hi, Tommy," Lauren said, smiling as she turned away from the pot. She put down the spoon and extended her arms. Tommy awkwardly offered the bottle of wine, glancing briefly toward Amy as he did so. Lauren laughed and gave him a hug.

"Thanks, it's Marla's lamb ragu."

She took the bottle and glanced at the label. "Good choice. Marla?"

"Yeah. I think she figured out what you were going to make and pulled it out from under the bar."

"This is going to need to breathe a while," she said, handing the bottle back to him. "The opener's over there," pointing toward the counter opposite the stove. "Why don't you do the honors? While you're at it, there's a bottle of prosecco in the 'fridge. I thought we could start with that while I finish getting dinner together."

As Tommy removed corks and poured the prosecco Amy watched with an expression of mild amusement. She sensed his discomfort and knew she was the cause. When Tommy finished pouring he handed a glass to Lauren.

"Here's to…"

"Excuse me," Amy interrupted.

"Uh, yes?" Tommy replied.

"Where's mine?"

"Um, aren't you a little young to be drinking wine?"

"Yes, of course I am. But I always get to taste it."

Tommy narrowed his eyes and stared at her a moment. She stared back, expressionless. Tommy tried to keep his poker face but couldn't and started to smile. He glanced at Lauren who nodded almost imperceptibly.

"Forgive me, young lady, of course you do." He poured her a sip and handed her the flute.

"As I was about to say, here's to old friends," nodding toward Lauren, "and a new one," smiling at Amy.

"Well?" Lauren asked after they'd drunk the toast.

"Good!" Tommy replied taking another sip.

"Dry, crisp, with apples and pears," Amy said, swirling her glass and dribbling the last drops onto her tongue.

"Very good!"

Tommy raised his eyebrows. "Are you sure you're not a midget?" he asked.

"That's *so* un-PC. You mean short person, and yes, I'm short but only because I'm ten. I'll be tall eventually."

"Actually, I meant midget. I'm not the PC type."

"I know. I think that's partly why my mom likes you. And no, I'm not a midget."

"Amy, why don't you show Tommy around while I finish up in here. OK?"

"OK." She turned and led Tommy back down the hall. "I've been teaching myself to play the guitar. I'm not very good yet but I was hoping you could show me the chords for 'Bite Me'."

"What?"

"Yeah, it's kind of our theme song around here."

Tommy just shook his head. "Sure. It's pretty easy."

Two hours later they were sitting in the living room finishing the last of the sauterne Lauren had served with dessert, a pear tart. The adults had been on the sofa in a semi-snuggle when Amy decided to join them. Lauren was about to remind her of her manners but Tommy interceded.

"There's plenty of room for the three of us," he said, patting the empty space to his right.

"Thanks for showing me those chords. That 'G' thing is kinda hard, though."

"Just takes practice."

Amy inched closer until the two were almost touching. "Do you think you could give me another lesson some time?"

"Amy!" Lauren scolded.

"Mom, I'm pretty sure he's gong to be coming over again, so it wouldn't be that difficult."

"Amy!"

Tommy laughed. "I'd be happy to."

"Gee, thanks!" she said throwing herself around his neck.

"OK. Why don't you start putting things in the dishwasher and I'll walk Tommy to his car."

Amy gave him another hug and got up. "Good night, Tommy. It was great meeting you."

"It was great meeting you. Really."

Amy turned toward the kitchen while Lauren and Tommy walked to the door.

"What a great kid. Is she the person I had to meet before we could, you know, 'move our relationship forward'?"

Lauren opened the door. "Let's talk out here." There was a walkway leading to the front door flanked by a garden. On one side was a small metal bench. She led him toward it and they sat.

"So?" Tommy asked.

"So, yes. She's the one."

"So how'd I do?"

Lauren sniffed. "Are you kidding? She never throws herself at people she's just met."

"Well great! Everything worked out. We can 'move the relationship forward'."

"It's a little more complicated than that."

"What do you mean?"

"Her dad."

Tommy sagged. "What about her dad?" He'd wondered who the mystery parent was since meeting her, but when no mention had been made by either of them he'd allowed himself to believe it was a non-issue.

"Tommy, she's ten."

"Yeah, she mentioned that. But what's that got to do with her dad?"

"She's *ten*, Tommy."

"OK, but I..." His face clouded as he tried to make sense of what Lauren was trying to tell him. "Wait a minute," he said at last. "We met ten years ago. There was no baby that I remember, and no physical evidence you'd ever had one, either," he said glancing at her belly.

"We met eleven years ago. Eleven years and eight months. Amy's going to be eleven in three weeks."

It took Tommy less than fifteen seconds to do the math. "WHAT!" "ARE YOU..."

Lauren put her hand over his mouth. "Shh!" When she was fairly sure he'd regained a measure of his composure she removed it.

"Are you telling me she's my *daughter*!" he asked in a loud whisper.

"If you promise not to interrupt me I'll tell you everything. OK?"

He nodded 'yes'.

"Remember when I told you I was going through a 'phase' when I met you, you know, wild and reckless? Well, there were two other people besides you I had flings with around that time. One was this gorgeous guy in my dance class. I was pretty sure he was gay but I wanted to see if I could convert him. The other guy was my poetry professor. He was brilliant, and he was married. It was one time only with each of them.

"Then there was you. I did feel a connection with you and figured I'd look you up at some point to see if there was anything there but when I found out I was pregnant it changed everything. I mean, I didn't know if you were the father and I had no idea what your reaction would be. I wasn't going to get an abortion and I didn't want to drag anyone into a paternity suit. My grandfather was wealthy and he was thrilled about having a great-grandchild. I didn't need support from her father.

"Besides, one of the possible dads really was gay, so that wouldn't have worked out very well, and the other was married. I didn't need to be in the middle of all that. So, what I'm telling you is that you *could* be Amy's father. I'm sorry for dumping this on you now. I never thought I'd ever see you again. When we met that day at the Step I almost passed out.

"I think we both realized there was a chemistry between us. I thought about just disappearing again but it wasn't going to work this time. Fish and Marla both knew where to find me. I didn't say anything about this sooner because I wanted to see if we really liked each other. I mean, there's chemistry and there's reality, right? If we were just going to be casual friends with a history there would be no point in dredging all this up."

She stopped talking and waited for Tommy to respond. He sat, silent, for several minutes.

"Are you OK?" Lauren asked.

"Does Amy know anything about this?"

"She's so smart it's a little scary sometimes. I don't know what she knows. She *has* asked about her father in the past, but only a few times. I tried to be honest. I told her he was someone special who was a part of my life for only a short time before we went our separate ways and that I have no idea where he is now or how to find him. You know, it's strange, but she's never asked me for his name."

Tommy was quiet again for a while.

"You know," he said at last, "it would be pretty easy to find out."

"Find out what?"

"If I'm her father. We could do a DNA test. Simple."

"What?"

"It's no big deal. A blood test. We get the results back in a week"

"I know how it works, Tommy. It's just, I don't know, I figured that by the time we got to this part of the conversation you'd be running for your car and making plans to leave the country or something."

He laughed. "You know, it's weird. I've actually never had one of these conversations, which is remarkable considering the business I was in all those years. But I figured if I ever *did* have one my reaction would be pretty much what you figured it would be. But now that it's happening I don't feel that way at all."

"How *do* you feel?"

"Calm. Calm and a little excited, but in a good way. Look, I'm still interested in taking the next step with you. I guess it would be the fourteenth step."

"Huh?"

"Never mind, I'll explain it later. Anyway, you said there was someone I had to meet, and now I've met her and she's this terrific kid who might actually be *my* kid. It's like a bonus. So, yeah, I'd like to know."

Lauren was quiet now. She'd actually thought about this scenario, unlikely as she believed it would be, and realized it would not be the best move.

"What if the test shows you're *not* her father?"

"OK, what are the chances of *that* happening? You said it was a one-time thing with those other guys. We were together for three days and we were out of bed for maybe five hours, long enough to eat and take showers. And we did it in the shower, too."

Lauren smiled. "You're right, but still it's possible. It wouldn't be fair for Amy. She likes you and I have a feeling she'd be very pleased if you turned out to be her dad. But I wouldn't want to raise the possibility and take the chance of it not being the case."

"She wouldn't have to know. I saw this on TV. We could take some hair from her brush and send it to the lab with my blood sample."

"Yeah, we probably could. But that wouldn't be fair to *us*. One way or the other."

They were both silent for a while. Lauren heard the front door open and turned to see Amy standing in the threshold. How long, she wondered, had she been there and what, if anything, had she heard? Tommy turned toward the door, too, and took a long look at the little girl he'd just met, and saw her in a whole new light.

"OK," Amy said, "I finished all the dishes and went to find you but you weren't here so I got a little worried. Are you going to sit out there all night?"

"Sorry, sweetie," Lauren said with a smile, "we were talking and lost track of the time. We're almost finished so why don't you get yourself ready for bed and I'll be there in a minute.

"OK. Goodnight, Tommy."

"Goodnight, Amy."

"So what do you think we should do?" Tommy asked when they were once again alone.

Lauren sighed. "I think we should take it one step at a time."

"The story of my life," Tommy replied, shaking his head.

Chapter 71

"What's *he* doing here?" Leonard, Jr. asked with a scowl, pointing a finger at Mr. Perino. "I thought this was supposed to be a meeting for family only to discuss dad's will. This has nothing to do with him."

Leonard, Jr. still harbored significant resentment toward the new C.E.O. of Walter Industries Inc. stemming from the way in which the title had been acquired and, in his mind, how he stepped over the person in line to assume control of the company after his father's death, namely, himself. Elaine had convened the meeting in her father's old office, the same room in which the Perino plan had been unveiled. She'd made sure Mr. Perino got there before the others and took his place at the head of the table. She knew she was in for a tough fight and she wanted it to be clear who was in charge.

"He's here because I invited him," Elaine responded coolly. "This meeting *is* about our father's will but any decisions we make here today are, I think, going to be influenced by our overall financial condition. That means we need to know how the business is doing and what the outlook is for the near and distant future. No one has a better understanding of that than Michael."

After thinking it over she'd come to the conclusion that Mr. Pearl was correct. A trial was unlikely to produce the results for which she and the others were hoping. A series of escalating offers was only going to run up exorbitant legal fees and would likely get them to the exact place he had asked her to go. Getting her family to agree to a twenty-three million dollar offer, though, was not going to be easy.

Elaine had also asked their spouses to attend the meeting. It was, after all, about business as well as the inheritance and they all, with the exception of her brother's wife Karen, worked for the company.

"First," she began, "I want to thank you all for coming. We have some important things to discuss and a big decision to make. I want you all to be comfortable with whatever it is we decide to do today so there will an opportunity for you to ask as many questions as you want and to offer any suggestions you might have before this meeting is over. Now, though, I would like Mr. Perino to begin with an assessment of the company, present and future. Michael?"

In front of him was a stack of thin binders. He picked them up, stood, and walked around the table placing one in front of each person. When he was done he resumed his place in Leonard, Sr.'s big chair.

"These folders contain analyses of our entire company, broken down into different sub-sections for the automobile business, the malls and the office building. The auto business is further broken down to the individual lots. If you would please open the folders to the first page we can get started."

For the next forty-five minutes Mr. Perino led them through a detailed review of the company's performance over the past 3 months and a projection for the following quarter. What they learned was something of a surprise.

"As you can see from the graph, profits from the auto business are up twelve percent over the preceding six months. I have to give Leonard a lot of the credit for this. He has incentivized the sales staff and has worked with me to increase our lease sales. This is going to allow us to move into the pre-owned business as these cars come out of lease down the line. This, we think, will boost our profits further."

Leonard, Jr. had been sulking in his chair. He knew things had improved but had fully expected Mr. Perino to claim it was due to his leadership. Being called out as the one responsible was a pleasant surprise and his scowl softened upon hearing it.

"Roy has done a terrific job with the malls. With the economy the way it is we were looking at defaults and vacancies but Roy got in there, helped renegotiate a few leases, and made the tenants understand that we want them to succeed. We're making a little less than we were a couple of years ago, but we have no vacant storefronts and we are making money."

It was true. Roy was no genius but he was extremely genial. His simple, friendly approach was what the tenants needed to convince them they could ride out the economic storm. He responded to the praise with a broad smile.

The news was similar with the office building. While he was alive, and when conditions were more favorable, Leonard, Sr. had been of the mind that bigger was better. A larger company leased a greater number of square feet, the more square feet per company, the fewer companies he had to deal with to keep the building full. The problem with that approach became obvious when one of the big companies got into trouble and shut it's offices down. It left a lot of empty space to fill.

Together, Larry and Mr. Perino worked to attract smaller businesses. It involved more legwork but in the end would be less risky. Larry was good at following orders and things at the office building were moving in the right direction.

"In summary, the company is doing much better than anticipated. I expect to be able to make a profit distribution at the end of this year, and though it will not be nearly as extravagant as what you have experienced in previous years it is much more than what I'd initially thought it would be, which was, basically, nothing. Your father was a great man, but he was wrong about some things. While he was in control of this company he felt the need to micromanage. He called the shots and relied upon me to make sure his wishes were carried out. I think we have proven that you are all far more capable than he was willing to admit, and with proper direction there is no limit to what we can achieve."

It had the ring of a pep rally but it also had the desired effect. Leonard, Jr. was actually smiling, an expression he hadn't worn in the presence of Mr. Perino since the day he was installed as C.E.O. Elaine, who'd had a preview of Mr. Perino's presentation, was satisfied that the table had been properly set for what it was she needed to do.

"Thank you, Michael. Are there any questions for Mr. Perino before we move on to our other piece of business?"

No hands were raised.

"OK."

Mr. Perino stood, and to everyone but Elaine's surprise, left the room.

"As you pointed out before the meeting was called to order," she said, looking at her brother, "the discussion of our father's will is family business, and no one but family needs to be here."

Leonard, Jr. nodded.

"I have been the spokesperson for the family throughout this entire unpleasant affair. I have had frequent contact with Mr. Pearl and I believe I have a clear understanding of our position. As you know, we made an offer to the other side of three million for Connie and up to six million for the Charitable Foundation. We felt this was fair based in part on our newfound knowledge of the relationship between Connie and Sister Dolores. That offer was refused."

Murmurs erupted which she allowed to continue for several moments before continuing. She'd decided not to share anything from her most recent conversation with the lawyer until today.

"A counter offer was made," she said when order had once again been restored. "I don't think you are going to find it acceptable."

She then presented the counter, essentially their offer in reverse, and waited for the anticipated uproar to die down.

"Mr. Pearl does not think we should proceed with a series of offers and counter offers. His investigation so far leads him to believe that our father was of sound mind when he revised the will, and that he did so for some good reason, although what that might have been remains a mystery to me. He also believes that both Connie and the Charitable Foundation are worthy recipients of our father's generosity, that it is likely Connie and Sister Dolores were unaware of their relationship prior to our father's death, and that a judge, particularly the one assigned to this case, could very well decide in their favor. In that scenario we would be, pardon my language, fucked."

Elaine practically never swore but she'd decided now would be a good time.

"So," she continued, "he has suggested we put a final offer on the table that would be impossible for the other side to refuse. We give up more than we want to but we eliminate the possibility of losing everything if we go to trial."

She paused to allow them to absorb the information.

"Ok," Leonard, Jr. said, "let's hear it."

"Three million for Connie, twenty million for the Charitable Foundation."

The ensuing cacophony actually exceeded her expectations. She sat back in her chair, waiting for a return to sanity.

Chapter 72

The door to her office had barely clicked shut before the director began his protest.

"Downgrade the ER? Stop taking paramedic runs? You're going to turn my department into an urgent care center? Great! We can do blood pressure checks for the community, well-baby exams, give flu shots, or maybe if someone stubs his toe and it's not too bad we can put a bandaid on it, or maybe even get an x-ray, unless you're going to shut down radiology too while you're at it!"

Sister Dolores was unfazed. She'd expected as much.

"Sit down, Bill, before you have a stroke."

"Yeah, well we wouldn't want that to happen, would we? Shut down my ER and I have a stroke, which is certainly not out of the question here, you'd have to call 911 so the paramedics could haul me out of my own department and take me to some *real* hospital with a *real* ER that can handle *real* sick people."

"Sit!"

He sat, red-faced and a bit wild-eyed.

"Look at you," she said, shaking her head. "You're acting like a maniac and nothing's been done yet. I told you months ago we were in bad financial shape and since then things have not gotten any better. There was a glimmer of hope with the CARE program but, well, you know what happened with that."

"It's Doyle, right? The little twerp finally got to you. He's been trying to shut us down since the day he got here. Moron."

"The only thing this has to do with Mr. Doyle is the fact he's been unable to develop any new revenue streams except CARE…"

"Idiot."

Sister Dolores sighed. "…and now we are forced to look at ways to cut costs that would have previously been out of the question, including but not limited to a downgrade of our emergency status. Bill, you know as well as I do that eighty-plus percent of your business is walk-in. Downgrading to Level III and marketing to the walk-in crowd could actually work to your benefit."

She paused, anticipating another round of invective directed at her C.O.O.

"Sister," he began in a measured tone, "we go down that road and we risk losing a lot more than the paramedic runs."

"Such as?"

"Such as most of my doctors for starters. They are Emergency Medicine specialists, trained to handle the whole gamut of what comes through the door. They are not going to want to spend their careers taking care of runny noses and sprained fingers. They quit, I'll have to hire a bunch of non-board certified bozos, or maybe some family practice types, or maybe just a couple of nurse practitioners. Yeah, why bother having doctors at all? The HMO guys are already doing it. Make an appointment to see one of them and you get to see Dr. Patty or Dr. Mike, some PA or NP or whatever who's not a doctor at all. So I'll get a few of those people to staff the place and the next time someone codes in the ICU *they* can go down there to run it, except they have no idea how, so now you've got people dying."

Sister Dolores said nothing. She knew he wasn't done yet. No use rebutting until he ran out of steam.

"So then you have a situation where the rest of the medical staff gets nervous. They like to bad mouth the ER, but they *love* the fact we're there twenty-four hours a day to back them up, take care of their patients when bad things happen. No ER, no ER doctors, at least no real ones. One of their patients goes south in the middle of the night the nurses are going to be calling *them* to come in and deal with it. No more, "call the ER doctor" because there won't be one. A few calls like that and they're going to think twice about admitting patients to this hospital. Now you have no ER and no patients."

"Don't you think you are being a little overly dramatic?"

"Dramatic? Dramatic?! What's going to be *dramatic* is how fast the community figures out we're not a real hospital any more. You said it yourself, 'the ER is our window to the community'. Close the window and it's hasta la vista, baby."

"There's a big difference between 'closing the window' and a downgrade," she replied. "I think the people in this community are intelligent enough to know that."

The director snorted. The intelligence of the public in general, and the people in 'this community' in particular, was, in his mind, dubious at best. He sat, speechless for a moment.

"What about my retirement?" he asked finally, almost under his breath.

"Excuse me?"

"My retirement," he repeated in full voice.

"What retirement?"

"You know, the one where I sell the ER contract to that other group, hand the reins to Fish, sail off into the sunset. *That* retirement."

"I told you I thought we could work that out."

"That was before you decided to downgrade us. I was trying to sell an ER contract. If there's no ER, there's no contract to sell, no sale, no money, no money, no retirement."

"Hm," she said after a pause. "Look, between you and me, there's not much of a chance we're going to be changing anything, except maybe the number of people I have working for me. I think it's a little premature for you to consider drastically revising your life plans."

"Then why did you bring it up in the first place?"

"The Board is worried. As chairman it's my duty to consider all possible options. I had to be on record with this. Again, between you and me, I have a feeling things are going to work out. Until I'm certain, though, I have to go through the motions."

"What, you think Doyle is actually going to come through, find new business, resurrect the CARE program?"

It was Sister Dolores' turn to snort. "I sincerely doubt it. I already know there's no one else around here doing rapid detox, and I'm fairly certain there's no other cash practice we're going to be able to attract without committing a felony."

"So what was the point of sending him on a hopeless mission? Wait, let me guess. More going through the motions, right?"

She nodded. "Plus, I'm a nun. I believe in miracles."

Dr. Riegel rubbed his chin. "So, we're expecting a miracle here? Uh, with all due respect, Sister, miracles are, you know, by definition, kind of a long shot. I mean, between you and me and all that, can you give me a little something more to hang my hat on?"

She sighed. "The will."

"The will? You mean the old guy, The Un-dead?"

"His name was Leonard Walter. He left us a fortune. The family is contesting but they've already put an offer on the table. Our attorney thinks we will eventually get a considerable amount. Not everything, but enough."

"Jesus. Sorry. Why the hell didn't you tell me this right off the bat?"

"And deprive myself of one of your famous tantrums? I live for that stuff. And I was hoping maybe you wouldn't lose your mind and I could keep things to myself for a while longer. When I realized you really might have a stroke I decided to fill you in. But now you have a different problem."

"Oh, what's that?"

"If anyone else learns about this I know it will have come from you. That happens, you really *can* kiss your retirement goodbye because I'll cancel your contract and *give* it to that other group. If you're lucky they'll let you stay on and work for them."

"What will?" he said with a grin.

"Exactly."

Chapter 73

Micky was working and it was his day off, a situation that normally called for a drive to the beach and some surfing. Today, though, the drive was toward downtown, specifically the jewelry mart. After swearing her to absolute secrecy he'd confided his plan to Marla and enlisted her aid in its execution.

"If you breathe a word of this to anyone, and I mean *anyone*, I swear I'll find a way to completely ruin your life. I'll fire Bob. I'll tell Tommy to fire *you*."

"Oh, yeah, like *that* would ever happen," she said mockingly.

"Seriously. This has to stay a secret until after the party."

"Relax, G. I can keep a secret even though I think she already knows you're going to do it."

After his conversation with Tommy, and learning about the thirteenth step, Fish had done a little soul searching. What he found proved Tommy had been right, at least about his somewhat distorted self-image. He was a doctor, plain and simple. Whatever else he did, including surfing, had taken a back seat to medicine since the day he entered medical school. He'd always known it. Now he accepted it.

What Tommy might have gotten wrong was what his 'thirteenth step' ought to be. True, taking a closer look at himself was important. Necessary, really. And embracing his career was something long overdue. Accepting Dr. Riegel's offer to take over as medical director then became the obvious choice. It didn't rise to the level of a 'step'. Not to do so would be idiotic.

No. His thirteenth step was something else and he and Marla were going downtown to get what he needed to take it. They were off the freeway on surface streets, a convolution of one-ways and two-ways, two lanes and four, cars, busses and pedestrians that never failed to get him thoroughly lost. This time, at Marla's insistence, he'd entered the address into the Lexus' GPS, and they were closing in on the intersection of 6th and Hill Streets, the epicenter of the jewelry district.

"What's the deal with guys and asking for directions?" she said as she got in the passenger side. "It's a computer, for God's sake. It's not like she's going to think you're some kind of loser."

"You will have arrived at your destination—in one hundred feet," the robotic female voice informed him twenty-five minutes later.

"Thank you," he replied.

"Wasn't that better than driving in circles for the next half hour?"

"It would be really good if she could find us a parking spot."

It took less than one trip around the block to find an open space. The meter allowed two hours and he fed the maximum number of quarters into it. Having never done this before he had no idea how long it would take. He'd done some research on-line and had written the names and addresses of the shops that seemed most likely to have the sought-after item on a piece of paper which he now removed from his shirt pocket.

He'd also done some research into the item itself and had become familiar with the lingo. Carats, color, clarity, cut, certification—the five C's. Plus choosing a setting. He'd brought Marla along for both moral support and her opinion. Women, it seemed, had an innate ability to recognize good jewelry. Especially when it involved diamonds and engagement rings.

Three hours, four shops, and one trip back to the car to feed the meter later they were done.

"So?" Marla asked as they pulled away from the curb.

"So what?"

"How do you feel?"

"You mean, besides poor? OW!" he yelled in response to her punch to his shoulder.

After much deliberation he'd chosen a round, brilliant-cut stone, nearly flawless, and a hair less than two and a half carats mounted in a simple six-prong platinum setting. The price was twenty-two thousand dollars. He'd known what ballpark he'd be playing in from his research. Still, when the time came to hand over the American Express card he'd experienced a moment of sticker shock.

"OK! Geez. I feel good. Do you think she's going to like it?"

"You're kidding, right?
"No, but I take it that was a stupid question. Hey, when we left the house this morning you said something I've been meaning to ask you about."

"Oh?"

"Yeah. You said you thought Micky already knew I was going to do this. How could she know? I haven't said anything to anyone but you, and you haven't been out of my sight since I told you."

"Girls talk, G. She told me about how romantic you've become lately, how comfortable you seem. She's noticed the change in the way you see things. She knows you appreciate her. That wasn't always the case. I've noticed. Even Ashleigh's mentioned it."

"Lauren, too, I suppose?"

"Lauren's been too busy trying to figure out what's going on between her and Tommy, but except for her it seems you're the last person to get it."

"Hmm. So——do you think she's going to say yes?"

"If you'd have asked me that question a year ago I'd honestly have to say I don't know. You were a different guy then. I don't think she would have thought you were ready. But now, absolutely. Congratulations! You're getting married!"

Chapter 74

The meeting at Walter Industries ended with no decision being made. Despite her reasonably eloquent and quite accurate description of their position Elaine had been unable to convince her brother that giving up twenty-three million to save forty-five was a good idea. The others, she'd sensed, could have been swayed but Leonard Jr.'s insistence that the money, all the money, was rightfully theirs was seductive.

"Besides," he'd added, "no matter what Mr. Pearl said, agreeing to this offer will surly expose us to an even more outrageous demand down the line. I think it's time we *all* meet with the lawyer. He needs to hear from all of us, not just Elaine, and we need to hear from him, directly, how he thinks we should proceed."

The insubordination took Elaine by surprise. Apparently, she thought, the compliments paid him by Mr. Perino had gone to his head.

"Leonard, you are asking us to waste a lot of money and take a terrible risk. I have been honest and diligent in this matter. The offer I put forward was well-conceived. It would be a tragedy to allow ego and greed get in the way of a comfortable future for all of us."

"Really?" he replied, "who's ego are we talking about?"

The discussion, such as it was, deteriorated rapidly. Larry suggested a ten million dollar offer as a compromise. Leonard Jr. accused him of being a dumbbell and asked if he even knew how to write 'ten million', in words or numbers. Larry offered to 'beat the snot' out of Leonard Jr., saying he'd had it coming for years and that it might actually do him some good. Louise had to physically restrain him from acting out on the offer. Roy remained silent. He was married to Elaine, after all.

"Knock it off!" Elaine screamed. It got their attention. "Everybody sit down. Please." They sat. Elaine took advantage of the uneasy truce to attempt to salvage the situation. "Clearly we are not going to be able to come to an agreement. Perhaps my brother is correct. A meeting with Mr. Pearl with all of us in attendance might be helpful. If it's OK with you I'll call him now. If he's in maybe we can put him on speaker and make it a conference call."

She knew he was in. The plan had been for her to broker an agreement and call him as soon as discretion would allow so he could tender the offer to Mr. Wright before someone balked and asked to reconsider. The fallback, should a deal prove elusive, was the conference call. Plan B, as it were.

"Fine. Give him a call," Leonard Jr. said smugly. He was clearly enjoying the recent discovery of his testicles. His wife gave him an admiring glance. Elaine's eyes narrowed for the briefest of moments, but he noticed and it was enough for him to subconsciously drop his hands to his lap and remove some of the smugness from his expression.

She dialed the number, explained the nature of the call to the secretary, and was put through to Mr. Pearl.

"Good morning, Elaine. What can I do for you?"

"Hello, Norman. Before we get started I want you to know you are on speaker. I'm in the main office with my brother, sister, and our spouses."

The lawyer understood this to mean she'd failed.

"Well, then, good morning to you all. How may I be of service?"

"We've been meeting this morning to discuss business, Walter Industries, and to consider our counter offer in the matter of our father's will," she replied.

"And how is that going?"

"The business is doing quite well. We are ahead of projections and the outlook for the future is positive."

"Excellent!"

"Yes. But we are having a problem agreeing to the counter offer you suggested."

"I see. Is…"

"Excuse me, Mr. Pearl. This is Leonard Walter, Jr.," he interrupted. "If I can have a moment."

"Please." The lawyer now knew who had thrown a wrench into the works.

"Thank you. As you know, my sister, Elaine, has, up to this point, acted as the spokesperson for our family. I'm sure she's done a good job and we all appreciate her efforts. But now we're at a point where we are being asked to give away a huge sum of money, and I think I speak for everyone when I say we're more than a little uncomfortable with the idea."

He paused, expecting Mr. Pearl to begin a defense of his offer. Instead he was met with silence. When the silence became awkward he broke it.

"Uh, Mr. Pearl? You still there?"

"Yes. You were saying you were uncomfortable. I was waiting for you to explain what it was, exactly, you were all uncomfortable with."

"Well, come on. It's obvious. When this all first began you gave us the impression it was going to be easy. You said there were weaknesses or something we could exploit, that a judge would be able to see my father was tricked somehow into changing his will. When we made the initial offer I thought we were being more than generous. Now you're saying we need to give them four times as much. It doesn't make sense. We are his children. We are his heirs!"

More silence.

"Mr. Pearl?"

"Yes, Leonard," he began, using the familiar address. Leonard Jr. needed to be cut down a peg or two, and it was an effective way to begin the process. "Let me start by apologizing. If I gave any of you the impression that breaking your father's will was going to be easy, I am truly sorry. What I recall saying is that I thought it might be possible and that there were several avenues we could pursue to that end.

"For instance, early on there were the issues surrounding Mr. Walter's death, whether or not the physicians caring for him might have used poor judgment. That turned out not to be the case.

"Then there was the relationship between Mrs. Sanchez and Mr. Walter, and the question of undue influence. While there is no doubt they had more of a familial relationship than an employer-employee one, Mrs. Sanchez vehemently denied in her deposition that she in any way influenced him regarding the will. She is a believable witness. In addition, it is hard to explain why she would use her position to have the bulk of his fortune diverted to a complete stranger, that being Sister Dolores and the Charitable Foundation."

"But they're related! They're first cousins! I mean, come on!" Leonard Jr. was not ready to concede.

"Correct," the attorney responded. "But our investigation suggests neither of them knew it until the day the will was read."

"Then he must have been insane! There's no other explanation. Any judge should be able to see that."

"What the judge is going to see is a struggling Latina, mother of two, and a non-profit general hospital run by a group of nuns on the brink of insolvency on one side, and the owners of Walter Industries, a multimillion dollar a year company with, as you said, a positive future, on the other. And we've not been able to produce any evidence that Mr. Walter was 'insane' or in any other way of less than sound mind."

Another, longer, silence followed. Mr. Pearl could hear throats being cleared and the sounds of people shifting in their seats.

"So," Leonard, Jr. said, "you're saying our best move is to simply give them twenty-three million dollars?"

"Leonard, you are viewing this the wrong way. I'm not asking you to *give* them anything. What I'm advising is that you cooperate with me to see if we can get them to *accept* something far less than what they have already been given by your father. They have a strong position but there are no guarantees here. I'm hoping that if we put a large enough sum on the table they will take it rather than risk an unfavorable decision at trial. Are you following me?"

"Yes," he responded glumly.

"Good. It's Friday. Why don't you take the weekend to think it over. Elaine?"

"Yes?"

"Please call me on Monday with your decision. We have a trial date set for November eighth. That's just about two months from now. If you choose not to make a large offer I will have to start preparing for it next week."

Chapter 75

By noon on Friday Tommy thought he'd found the answer and called Lauren to give her the news.

"We need a short vacation," he said after they'd exchanged hellos.

"Huh?"

"Time alone, you know, so we can sort things out."

"Oh." She knew he was probably right. She'd given him a lot to think about and it seemed only reasonable he'd want some time alone to process the information. Still, she was a little disappointed and it could be heard in her voice. "OK. I understand."

"Great! Pack an overnight bag and I'll be by to pick you up in about an hour."

"What!"

"Nothing too fancy, but nice. And your hiking shoes, if you have hiking shoes. If not we'll get you a pair. No problem."

"Tommy, slow down. Five seconds ago you said we needed a vacation, time alone, and now you want me to start packing for some kind of trip?"

"Sorry. What I meant was that you and me, us, together, need to get away for a couple of days so we can be alone, together, and see how it feels. You know, drop Amy off at your parents' place for a couple of nights, and spend the time getting to know each other better, not that we don't already know each other pretty well."

Lauren took a moment to readjust her perception of the situation, from being dumped to being asked on what sounded like a romantic weekend. "Um, don't you think this is rushing things a little? I mean, you only found out about Amy and everything last night."

"Yeah, and I've given it a lot of thought. Look, we both know there's something going on with us. We knew it when we first met, what, eleven years ago..."

"Almost twelve," she corrected.

"Right, almost twelve. And we knew it the minute we met again a month or whatever it was ago. We need to see if it's just chemicals or if there's more to it than that. There's a lot at stake and what you said about Amy last night is right. If we're just going to be pals it probably wouldn't be fair to pursue the paternity issue. I can still give her guitar lessons and take her out for ice cream once in a while. But if we're going to have a real relationship, well, that's different. I think we should start trying to figure that out sooner than later."

"Gee, I don't know, Tommy."

"Look. We both know where our relationship is headed, so why put it off for some arbitrary reason."

"Like propriety?"

"Exactly. Besides, if we don't do it this weekend we'll have to wait at least two more weeks because the party is next weekend and I'll need to be around to help Marla set things up. Then school starts and you might not be able to get away. So, really, this is the perfect opportunity."

"Is this another one of those resistance is futile situations?"

"I hope so."

"OK. Suppose I say you're right. What do you have in mind?"

"I made a few calls before calling you and we got lucky. There's a place near Santa Barbara, very exclusive, very private, very nice. They have these little bungalows, with fireplaces, private hot tubs, gourmet restaurant that will bring food to you if you don't want to go out. Plus it's at the foot of the mountains with all sorts of hiking trails."

"Are you talking about the San Ysidro Ranch?"

"Yep."

"Isn't that where the Kennedy's went for their honeymoon?"

"Yeah, I think so. Anyway, they had a cancellation so I booked it. Two nights in our own private bungalow with a view. We can drive back Sunday afternoon, in time for pasta night."

"Geez! Are you always this impetuous?"

"Only when I'm sure I'm doing the right thing."

Chapter 76

Fish had assumed that making the decision to buy the ring, and then actually buying it, would be the most difficult parts of the engagement process. He'd been wrong. The hardest part was keeping it a secret. He couldn't tell his parents because they would tell Danny, who would tell Ashleigh, who might tell Micky. He couldn't tell his brother Billy because he'd probably tell his parents. He couldn't tell Dr. Riegel because there was no telling what he'd do with the information, and if one person at the hospital knew, everyone at the hospital would know in a matter of hours. Just like everything else that happened there. The one person he could trust to keep it to himself was Tommy, and Tommy was nowhere to be found.

"I don't know," Marla said when he called the Step looking for him. "All he said was that he was going out of town for a couple of days and could I handle the bar. I asked where he was going and he wouldn't tell me. He said I could call him on his cell if there were any problems."

"That's a little weird, don't you think. He's not the kind of guy who just disappears like that."

"Yeah, it is. But I had a hunch so I called Lauren to see if she wanted to do something together this weekend since Bob's working. Turns out she's going out of town, too."

"Oh really?"

"Really. Something about visiting an old friend from school."

"Tommy?"

"That's my guess. They met when she was in college and she's the type that really can't tell a lie. I know he was at her place for dinner last night. He stopped here first to pick up a bottle of wine. I was teasing him about whether or not it was going to be *the* night and he said something about there being someone he had to meet first."

"Yeah, he mentioned that to me once, too. Some mystery person. It was driving him a little nuts trying to figure out who it was."

"Well, they must have met last night. I guess we'll find out what the story is when he gets back."

"And when is that?"

"Sunday afternoon. Said he'd be here for pasta night. Should I book a spot for you and the future Mrs. Hooks?"

"Ooh, that sounds so, so…"

"Grown up?"

"Maybe that's it. But, yeah, definitely. I wouldn't miss it for anything. What are you making?"

"Lasagna. It wasn't the original plan, but if my hunch is right the occasion demands something a little special."

"Can't wait."

"I know. Tell me, why were you so anxious to speak to Tommy, if you don't mind my asking?"

"Because he's the only person besides you I can talk to about the ring without the whole world finding out. I want to wait until after the party before, you know,…"

"Popping the question?"

"Yeah, that. I don't want to upstage Ashleigh or Tommy and turn this into something for me and Micky."

"You worry too much. And, besides, it's probably not as big a se-cret as you think it is, not that I've said anything, because I haven't, but you're not exactly the most inscrutable person, you know? But, fine, whatever you want."

"Thanks."

Chapter 77

Though she'd asked the members of the Board and the medical staff leadership to keep the details of their emergency meeting confidential she knew hospital secrets were short-lived. That it took three full days for the news to leak into the community and boomerang back to her was the only real surprise.

Shortly after her meeting with Dr. Riegel, Sister Dolores had made the call to Elizabeth Rowland, the director of the County EMS. She inquired about the process of downgrading the department. Her questions were received with more than the anticipated amount of alarm.

"LA County has lost fifteen ER's in the past three years. We cannot afford to lose another," Ms. Rowland had said. "If we *had* sufficient bed capacity for all our patients the process would take roughly three months. Given our current situation, I can guarantee you the wheels of bureaucracy will turn much more slowly in your case."

Sister Dolores assured her that she was making a preliminary inquiry only, that there were no concrete plans to move forward with a downgrade, and that all other options would be explored and exhausted before such a move would be made. She was calling on behalf of the Board of Directors, "who are insisting we consider everything", and, given the length of time needed to effect a downgrade, are asking that the initial steps be instituted now.

"It would be far better for the County to have a hospital with a stand-by Emergency Room than no hospital at all," she'd said in summary.

"Hmm," was Ms. Rowland's response.

After hanging up, Ms. Rowland called the Paramedic Liaison Nurse at Memorial, the primary base station for Saints' Hospital. Base stations receive calls from paramedic units in the field and direct those units to the most appropriate receiving hospital. Were Saints' to downgrade to stand-by status it would mean there would be one less option for the base station and a hole in the pre-hospital care grid. Before considering Sister Dolores' request the impact of such a change would need to be assessed.

"We send them anywhere from seven to ten runs a day," the PLN informed her. "It's not a huge volume but if they drop out of the system it's going to put significant pressure on the surrounding hospitals, not to mention on the paramedics who will have to travel out of their normal catchment areas. Response times and transport times will increase. We've already got just about all we can handle here and even a few more patients coming in by ambulance could force us to close even more often than we already do, which will just make things that much worse for everyone."

It's what Mrs. Rowland already knew, having heard the same story fifteen times in the past three years, but she needed to hear it again each time another hospital considered changing it's emergency status.

"I'll discuss it with my medical director and I'll get back to you with his in-put."

The ER medical director of Memorial Medical Center, Dr. Samuel Davis, was on vacation and not scheduled to return for three days. Like Dr. Riegel he was an old lion of the specialty and the two had enjoyed a casual relationship for many years.

"Jesus Christ," he said on hearing the news his first day back. "They're going to downgrade Bill's ER? He's gotta be going fucking nuts. Let me call him to find out what the real story is."

He made the call and got the party line—"no definite plans, just evaluating all the options, you know, trying to protect what's left of the bottom line, I'll keep you in the loop, no need to worry yet, good to hear from you".

Dr. Riegel then went to Sister Dolores' office to let her know the cat was officially out of the bag and that it hadn't been he who'd set it loose.

"Got a call from Sam Davis over at Memorial. Seems you called Rowland, she called the PLN, and she spoke to Sam. If he knows, everybody's going to know, and soon."

"I wonder why it took so long."

"Because Sam was on vacation, that's why. So now I'm going to have to tell my guys before they hear it on the street."

Sister Dolores said nothing for a moment. She knew this would be the likely scenario and she knew a certain amount of damage control was going to be necessary.

"That won't be necessary," she said.

"What do you mean? My guys hear we're going stand-by and they'll start heading for the lifeboats, you know, abandon ship, get out of Dodge, every man for himself. I'll be lucky if Fish sticks around. We can alternate twenty-four hour shifts. I won't have to worry about retirement because I'll be dead in a couple of weeks."

She looked at him, sighed, and shook her head. "You done?"

No response.

"Good. I knew something like this was going to happen, and I also knew it was my responsibility to control the reaction, since I'm the one who put the ball in play, to borrow a phrase. Yesterday I sent out a letter to every member of the medical staff clarifying our actions and motives. After my conversation with Elizabeth Rowland it became clear that it would be many months before a downgrade would take place, if it would be allowed at all. In the letter I said there will be absolutely no change in operations here in the foreseeable future. I also explained that our inquiry is merely one of the things we are doing to ensure that Saints' Hospital remains a viable operation despite these challenging economic times. I have advised the staff not to overreact to whatever rumors they may hear and that I will send regular up-dates."

"You think they're going to buy it?"

"They don't need to buy it, they only need to rent it for a couple of months."

"What the hell is that supposed to mean? Sorry."

"The Walter probate case is set for trial on November eighth."

"So we sit tight for two months, is that the plan?"

"At the outside. Our attorney has told me he's got a very strong feeling we won't need a trial to settle this. In fact, he thinks that some-time in the next week or so there will be a conference to discuss a resolution."

"Hmm."

"Right. So all you have to do is keep a positive attitude, keep your troops calm, go on with business as usual, and let me handle the rest."

Chapter 78

"Well?" Elaine asked after ending the conference call with Mr. Pearl.

There was a palpable tension in the room. Larry glared at Leonard Jr. who did his best to ignore him and stared at the ceiling. Louise shuffled the pages of the business report, pretending to read them, while Roy wisely sat still and kept his mouth shut. No one spoke for a long minute, then everyone started speaking.

"Please! One at a time!" Elaine ordered.

"Who put you in charge?" Leonard Jr. asked.

Elaine shook her head. It was, she thought, going to be a long, unpleasant weekend. She was about to respond when her cell phone rang. She looked at the incoming number and recognized it as Lauren's. The ringing phone gave the others in the room something to focus on besides one another and they all turned toward Elaine.

"Excuse me, I have to take this," she said and walked out of the room.

The door hadn't closed before the bickering started and there were no signs of it letting up when she re-entered the room a few minutes later. She let them continue a while. It was entertaining in a way. What had begun as an argument about the will and the settlement offer had degenerated into a free-for-all character assassination. Larry's IQ, Leonard Jr.'s lack of a spine, Louise's passivity, Roy's subjugation by Elaine, and Karen's aloofness were ridiculed by one or the other, as years of frustrations and irritations, for so long made tolerable by the balm of Leonard Sr.'s money, spewed forth. She took her seat at the table and her brother took the opportunity to resume his interrogation.

"You didn't answer my question," he said accusingly.

"I'm sorry, what question are you referring to?"

"The one I asked before you left the room."

She thought a moment, then smiled. "Oh, the one about who put me in charge. Well, I did, of course, and from the things you've been saying about one another it seems it was the right thing to do."

"You had no business..." her brother began, but she raised her hand the way she had so many times before and he stopped in mid-sentence. Her smile was gone.

"Let me finish," she said. Her tone suggested it would be wise to let her do so. "During this entire—mess, for wont of a better description, I've done my best to represent our interests, *all* of our interests. It now seems as though we are running out of options. What you heard from Mr. Pearl is the unvarnished truth. Our father was sane and he chose to leave his money to charity.

"So now it's like poker," she continued, "you all understand poker, right? Well, we got dealt these bad cards and our last move is a bluff. If we put a big stack of chips on the table we might get lucky and the other side will fold, leaving us with enough money to retire on comfortably. If we don't make the pot rich enough, or if we take this to a trial, we stand a better than even chance of losing the hand.

"You know my position. I say we do it Mr. Pearl's way. The rest of you have the weekend to make your decisions. That phone call I got was from Lauren. It seems Amy will be staying with us for the weekend so Roy and I will be busy. Louise, Leonard, I'll call you Sunday evening for your answers."

With that she stood, took her husband's hand, and together they left the room. As before, the sniping resumed before the door latch clicked.

As she had predicted, it was a long and unpleasant weekend for all involved but her, her husband, and her granddaughter. While phone lines hummed, arguments were made and countered, and emotions smoldered, bursting into flames from time to time, Elaine let her answering machine handle the traffic. She neither bothered to pick up the phone nor listen to the messages. She was done with it.

Instead, it was the movies on Saturday afternoon, followed by dinner at *Il Pagliaccio,* veal picatta for Roy, gnocchi for Elaine, and pizza Margherita from the wood-burning oven for Amy. Sunday morning the answering machine was adjusted to pick up on the first ring and the sound was shut off on the cell phone. Waffles and bacon for brunch, then a trip to the zoo.

By late Sunday afternoon Elaine was feeling almost peaceful. As she watched her daughter and granddaughter drive off she considered postponing the phone calls to her brother and sister and preserving the mood. But even thinking about them was depressing and she realized that getting this bit of business over with quickly would be best. As soon as she lost sight of the car she picked up the phone and started dialing.

Chapter 79

While the rest of her family fought through tumultuous negotiations, Lauren and Tommy were engaged in a tumult of a different nature. During the drive north she'd decided to be pro-active about 'moving the relationship forward', barring, of course, any sort of deal-breaking behavior on Tommy's part or some unforeseen catastrophe.

As they wound their way up the long driveway to the resort she felt more certain she'd made the right decision. Their conversation had been easy and enjoyable, she found herself smiling almost constantly, and more than once she found Tommy's free hand on her knee or her shoulder in an affectionate, non-aggressive way, and she'd made no attempt to remove it.

Their bungalow was situated toward the top end of the property, surrounded by trees and a dense hedge. There was a view down the hillside, lush and green, with the ocean in the distance. A fire was burning in the fireplace when they entered, and a bottle of champagne was chilling in an ice bucket.

There were two rooms, separated by the large fireplace, open to both. The sitting area was furnished in an up-scale country casual style with scattered antiques, a sofa, desk, and small dining table upon which sat the ice bucket holding the champagne. The second room was dominated by a large canopied bed covered by an extravagant down comforter and oversized pillows. There was a door leading to the bathroom, featuring a shower with multiple showerheads, a Jacuzzi tub in which two could comfortably soak, his and hers sinks, and plush robes. It was into this room that Lauren decamped after unpacking.

"I need to freshen up a bit. Why don't you pour us some Champagne?" she'd said before disappearing.

When she emerged several minutes later she found the glasses full and Tommy standing at the window staring at the scenery. She quietly walked up behind him and put her arms around his waist. He turned and saw she'd put on one of the robes.

"Enjoying the view?" she asked coyly, letting the robe fall open just enough for him to understand it was all she was wearing.

"I am now," he said with a smile.

She pulled him close and pressed her lips to his. It was the first kiss they'd shared since that weekend on campus. She'd been worried things would be awkward, the signals unclear, fumbling through the afternoon and evening, wondering how the inevitable would evolve. It was why she'd decided to be the one to make the first move.

The kiss was another proof her instincts had been correct. It was easy and familiar, but also exciting, causing a tingle that spread from her mouth to her breasts and down between her legs. She pulled back and reached for the glasses. She handed one to Tommy and raised hers.

"To us," she said, "we deserve it."

They clinked glasses and drank. "C'mon," she said, grabbing his hand and leading him toward the bed. He'd already kicked off his shoes and Lauren helped him with the rest, leaving a trail of clothes on the floor. By the time he was down to his boxers he was fully aroused. Lauren noticed the bulge and slid a hand inside.

"Ooh, I remember him," she said, running her fingers along the entire length.

"Hey, no fair, you're still all wrapped up," he said reaching for the sash of her robe. He gave it a tug and the loose knot unraveled. She shrugged her shoulders slightly and the robe fell to the floor. His hands were on the sides of her face and he held them there long enough for a second kiss. Then he moved them down her body, following with his eyes.

"Wow," was all he was able to say.

She took the elastic band of his boxers in her hands and slowly lowered them to his ankles, taking a visual inventory of his anatomy on the way down, and giving a particular part of it a playful lick on the way back up, eliciting a twitch from the recipient of her tongues attention and a soft moan from its owner.

The remainder of the afternoon and evening were spent in hedonistic bliss, interrupted only by a trip to the shower, (where they staged a reprise of their first encounter years ago), room service, (lamb chops for Tommy, duck breast for Lauren, locally produced pinot noir for both), and a soak in the Jacuzzi.

She awoke the next morning with a smile on her face and a full bladder. She quietly slipped out of bed, trying not to awaken Tommy, who, she noticed, also seemed to be smiling in his sleep. When she returned he was wide awake and waiting for her.

"Good morning," he said as he pulled her close.

"Didn't you get enough last night?" she asked teasingly.

"I don't know what it is about you, us, but I don't think I could ever get enough."

Morning sex was something she'd always thought was overrated. Bad hair, bad breath, just not like it was the night before. But for some reason she had to agree with Tommy and she rolled on top of him. Later, lying next to each other, she asked the obvious question.

"Are we going to spend the entire weekend in bed?"

He laughed. "You know, that would be fine with me, but we really should go out. For a little while anyway. Give the maids a chance to change the sheets."

She lifted the one partially covering them and did a quick assessment. "Good idea."

By Sunday it was clear to both of them there was more to the relationship than 'chemicals', and though neither would admit it out loud, it felt a lot like falling in love.

"What are you going to say to Marla?" she asked as they drove home.

"I'm pretty sure I'm not going to have to say anything," he replied with a grin.

Chapter 80

The plan was to drop Lauren off at her place where she could unpack her overnight bag and pick up her car. She would then drive to her parents', get Amy, and meet him at the Step. It was not, they'd decided, the right time to introduce Tommy to mom and dad nor did they want to make it even more obvious to Amy they'd spent the weekend together. Before being dropped off on Friday she'd asked her mother to say 'hello' to him from her, and to let him know she'd made sufficient progress on 'Bite Me' to warrant another lesson. Lauren had responded with a simple, "What are you talking about?" to which Amy had replied, "Oh, please."

"How was your weekend?" Lauren asked once they'd cleared the driveway.

"It was fun, except for the phone ringing every five minutes. Grandma turned it off. She didn't answer it once. I asked her what was going on but she wouldn't tell me. She said it was just business."

"Hmm. That's a little strange."

"That's what I thought. I mean if it was business and if it was important enough to have all these phone calls on the weekend you'd think she'd want to answer them, right?"

"Right."

They drove without speaking for a while, Lauren wondering what sort of business her mother was involved with, and Amy thinking about how she was going to broach the subject she really wanted to discuss. She decided to be blunt.

"So," she began, "how was *your* weekend?"

"Uh, nice. Very nice."

"That's good," Amy said with a smile. "So you and Tommy had fun?"

"What makes you think I was with Tommy?" It was worth a shot, but she didn't expect it to work.

"Come on, mom. I'm almost eleven. I know stuff."

Yes you do, Lauren thought. There was no point trying to deny what was going to become obvious soon enough. "Yes, we had a really nice time."

"I'm glad."

"You like him, don't you?" Lauren asked.

"Uh huh."

"Good. We're going to his place, actually to his bar, restaurant, whatever, for dinner tonight. We'll be there in a few minutes."

"The Thirteenth Step?" Amy asked excitedly.

"That's it. Some of my friends will be there and I think it's time you met them."

It was shortly after six when they arrived. It was a smaller crowd than usual and they spotted Tommy immediately. He'd been sitting at a table visiting with Fish and Micky, keeping one eye on the front door. When it opened and he saw Lauren step inside he stood to greet her. She walked toward him, arms open for the anticipated hug, but Amy beat her to it. In the short distance between the door and the table she'd managed to get past her mother and was now dangling from Tommy's neck. He, too, had been preparing for a hug and when he realized who he'd be getting it from he bent down to meet her. She threw her arms around his neck, he put his around her waist, and stood up.

"Hi, Tommy," she said with a laugh as he gently swung her back and forth. "Mom says you had a nice time this weekend."

His eyes widened and he looked at Lauren who shrugged and raised her eyebrows. Then she took a step forward and planted a kiss on his mouth.

"Hi, Tommy. She's right," she said. Might as well get it all out there at once, she thought.

Fish and Micky sat with their jaws slack trying to process all the information. Lauren noticed their confusion.

"Micky, Dr. Hooks, I'd like you to meet my daughter, Amy."

Tommy had lowered her to the ground by this time and she'd somewhat reluctantly let go of his neck.

"Amy," Lauren continued, "this is Micky and Dr. Hooks."

"You can call me Fish," he said, shaking her hand. "Wow."

"Come with me," Tommy said after the introductions, "there's someone else I want you to meet." He then ushered Lauren and Amy toward the kitchen.

When they were out of ear shot Fish turned to Micky. "She has a daughter? And she never mentioned it 'til now?"

"And she spent the weekend somewhere with Tommy?" Micky added.

"So I guess that's the person he had to meet," Fish mumbled, more to himself than to Micky. They were momentarily speechless. "Is it just me," he asked more loudly, "or does Amy look more than a little like Tommy?"

Micky, who'd taken a large sip of chardonnay, choked, and grabbed a napkin to absorb the wine trying to exit her mouth via her nose.

Chapter 81

She made the call to Louise first. What she heard was disappointing.

"Where have you been all weekend?" Louise asked. "Leonard and I called you a hundred times and you never picked up or returned our calls. We have a very big decision to make and instead of discussing it with us you just disappeared. Leonard is furious."

Elaine took a deep breath and exhaled in an audible sigh. "Louise," she began, trying to remain calm, "when I left you two on Friday I made my position clear. There was nothing for us to discuss. You had all the information you needed to make an intelligent decision. I told you we would be busy taking care of Amy."

"Taking care of Amy!? There are millions of dollars on the line and you spend the whole weekend playing with your granddaughter?"

"That's correct. But I didn't call you to talk about what *I* did, I called to find out what *you* did. So, tell me, did you come to a decision?"

Silence.

"Louise?"

"I don't know," was the barely audible reply.

"Excuse me?"

"I don't know!"

"What do you mean, you don't know? That's ridiculous! It's not that complicated. You either decided to accept Mr. Pearl's suggestion or you decided to reject it. What's not to know?" Elaine was quickly losing her patience and her composure.

"I don't know because you wouldn't talk to us!"

"What? You're saying it's my fault you couldn't make a decision?"

"Yes! We talked about his offer and we talked about a compromise but we weren't sure what a good compromise would be. Leonard wanted your opinion and the more he tried to reach you the angrier he got. The last time I spoke to him all he could say was how you were trying to screw him somehow and he was sick of it and he wasn't going to put up with it any more."

"WHAT!"

"You heard me."

"Leonard is a paranoid fucking idiot!"

"Maybe, or maybe not. Either way you're going to have to talk to him to straighten this out."

CLICK

Elaine stared at the phone and shook her head. "That dumb bitch just hung up on me," she muttered to no one. Then she called her brother.

"It's about fucking time, don't you think?" were the first words out of his mouth. "Where the hell have you been?"

She repeated what she'd already said to Louise.

"Yeah, well, I think that's bullshit!" was his response. "I don't know what kind of game you're playing here but I'm going to find out, and when I do it's going to be all over for you!"

She didn't say anything for a moment because she couldn't make sense of what she'd heard. "Are you saying I've somehow been trying to undermine you during this process?"

"You thought I was too stupid to figure it out, but I'm on to you."

"No. I think you've lost your mind."

"Nice try, but I think I've finally found it and I think we'll let a judge decide how this is going to go."

CLICK

The next morning she called Mr. Pearl to report the breakdown of negotiations. When that call ended he placed another to Mr. Wright.

"Hello, Norman. What can I do for you?" (pause) "Hmm." (pause) "Yes, I agree with you, that would have been best. But let me make a suggestion. Before this goes to trial we are going to have to have a mandatory settlement conference. I have some information you and your clients need to hear before that happens." (pause) "Sorry, I can't do that. My instructions were clear. What I have to say has to be said in person with all parties present. (pause) "So why don't we do this—why don't we have an informal settlement conference sometime this week. I'll give you the information at that time, you can discuss it with your clients, and maybe we can come to some mutually agreeable compromise. (pause) "Thursday or Friday would be fine. Call me after you've spoken to your clients and we'll set the time. (pause) "Good. You too."

That done, Mr. Wright dialed another number. It was time to show *his* clients, particularly Sister Dolores, *all* the cards he'd been holding.

Chapter 82

That Tommy and Lauren were officially an item was no real surprise. It seemed inevitable. The surprise was Amy. Questions about the young girl's sudden introduction and Lauren's now somewhat mysterious past preoccupied Fish's thoughts to the extent he almost forgot the real reason he'd come to dinner in the first place. While the lasagna plates were being cleared in preparation for dessert he'd noticed Tommy heading in the direction of the rest room. He realized it was probably the only opportunity they'd have to speak privately so he followed him inside.

The rest room door hadn't fully closed before Fish pushed it back open, walked in, the latched it shut. Tommy turned and looked at him with an expression of amused confusion.

"OK, Tommy, I don't know what you're thinking, but whatever it is you're wrong. I need to show you something."

He reached into the pocket of his well-worn leather jacket and pulled out the small jeweler's box. "I took the step," he said, opening it.

Tommy stared at the ring and made a soft whistle. "Wow, I knew when it finally happened the moment would be special, but I never thought it would be like this," he said with a grin.

"Very funny. Come on, what do you think?"

"I think you've made me the happiest girl in the whole world!"

"Oh for fuck's sake, can you be serious for maybe thirty seconds?"

"It's killer, Fish, congratulations. She's a great girl and you're a lucky son of a bitch. When are you going to ask her?"

"I wanted to wait until after the party, so, you know..."

"So you don't steal anybody's thunder? Very considerate."

"Yeah, but it's been making me nuts not being able to tell any-one. The only other person who knows is Marla and I figured you were the only *other* person who could keep the secret."

"Thanks for that, and yeah, I'm good with secrets. So tell me, you said you took the step. Is it the step we were talking about a while back, you know, the thirteenth step? I thought that was going to be about the job."

"Me too, but when I started thinking about it I realized you were right. I mean, I was already doing the job. I've made a lot of incre-mental commitments to it over the years and the chances of me not making one more were pretty slim. I was just bullshitting myself about that. The big step I needed to take was embracing the future, the real future, and I realized that future was Micky."

"Bravo. So, how does it feel?"

"I've never been so sure I was doing the right thing before in my life."

"Like me buying the bar."

"Yep. Now you tell me something."

"What, about me and Lauren?"

"No, that's obvious. About Amy."

"Ah, the Little One."

"Yes."

"What do you want to know?"

"Well, is she in fact the Little One?"

"Do you mean am I cool with the fact that Lauren has a daughter?"

"That's part of it."

"Sure. She's an amazing kid. I really like being around her. No problem. What's the other part?"

"OK, I know this is pushing it, but she looks an awful lot like you."

"Gee, you think so?"

"Yeah, I do."

"We do have the same hazel eyes. Lauren's are that sexy dark brown."

"Yeah."

"So?"

"So, is she *really* the Little One?"

Tommy looked at him for a moment, trying to decide. "OK, you want me to keep a secret, now you have to swear to keep one. This stays between you and me. Promise?"

"Promise."

"OK. Maybe."

"Maybe?"

"Yeah, maybe. Lauren was going through a period of, let's call it, 'limited discretion' when we met. There are a couple other contenders but it seems I'm the favorite."

"Wow."

"Yep."

Chapter 83

Three hours into his shift on Tuesday morning he got the call.

"Are you sure about this?"

"Positive. Dr. Davis had a meeting with the staff this morning to talk about what the impact might be on our place."

"And where did he get his information? Did he say anything about that?"

"Yeah. He got it from our PLN who got it from Rowland downtown who got it directly from your CEO. So what are you going to do?"

Fish was at a loss for words on that subject. He'd made the decision to take over as director when his boss retired, but he hadn't agreed to be the director of an urgent care center.

"I guess I'm going to talk to Riegel."

"Davis knows I'm calling you. He wanted me to let you know we have room on the schedule for another full-time doc, especially one with your experience."

"Thanks. I'll keep that in mind."

It was a slow morning, and as soon as he hung up Fish made his way to the director's office. He didn't appreciate being out of the loop on something as important as this and his expression showed it when he stormed in without knocking.

"What the fuck's going on around here?" he asked as he walked through the door.

The director looked up from the stack of papers he'd been poring over and noticed the agitation on the face of his assistant.

"Come in, good morning, what the hell are you talking about?"

"I just got a call from a guy I know at Memorial. He told me we're going stand-by and that you know all about it. When were you planning to let *me* know?"

The director removed the reading glassed that had been sitting on the tip of his nose and gestured to the chair opposite his. "Sit down."

Fish glared at him a moment, then yanked the chair away from the desk and sat. "So?"

"So nothing."

Fish leaned forward and clenched his fists. "Look, I'm working, OK? I don't have time for one of your cockamamie explanations. I have it on good authority we're downgrading the ER and I'm here to tell you I am not going to spend the rest of my career working in some fucking clinic! You got that?"

"Jesus Christ, Fish, calm down. You're getting to be worse than I am. Spending too much time together or something. Maybe you shouldn't take this job. Gonna give you a heart attack or something. I wouldn't want to be responsible for that. Micky'd kill me, your brother'd probably sue me, my whole fucking retirement would be one big goddamn mess."

"Calm down?! What do you mean 'calm down'? That's all you have to say?"

"Nothing's gonna happen. Nothing's gonna change."

"Then why is Sister Dolores talking to the EMS director about applying for a down-grade? Hmm?"

"The Board asked her to do it, you know, turn over all the stones, look at it from all angles, that kind of thing. But it's not going to happen. You have to trust me on this."

"How are you so sure?"

"*I* have it on good authority but I promised to keep it a secret. So that means *you* have to keep it a secret. Can you do that?"

Fish sat back in his chair, the familiar sense of confusion he always felt after a few minutes of conversation with his boss beginning to take over. "Keep what a secret? That Sister Dolores is looking into a down-grade or that she is but it's not going to happen?"

"Yeah, all of that. And if any of the other guys asks you tell them, hell, I don't know, tell them it's just a nasty rumor. Besides, Sister Dolores sent a letter out to the medical staff explaining things. It should be in your mailbox today.

"Dr. Hooks, please call extension 2740. Dr. Hooks, please call extension 2740."

The overhead page came through the speaker in the ceiling of the director's office.

"Shit," Fish mumbled.

"That's the ER looking for you. Time to get back to work. And remember, everything's gonna be OK," the director said, placing the reading glasses back on his nose.

"Jesus," Fish said as he got up and left the room. First the ring, then the thing with Tommy, and now this. How many secrets was he supposed to be able to keep, he wondered?

It wasn't until he was back in the ER that he realized the director hadn't really told him anything,

Chapter 84

At about the same time Dr. Riegel was asking his associate to keep a secret he didn't really have Sister Dolores was having a discussion with her C.O.O. about a problem she now knew might not exist.

"Mr. Doyle, I'm sure you are aware we continue to run in the red."

He nodded in the affirmative.

"And I'm sure you know the Board has asked me to investigate every possible option for lowering our operating costs and increasing our revenue, including a down-grade of our emergency department to stand-by."

"Yes, Sister. I've always believed the ER was a significant liability for us and that eliminating it, or at the very least converting it to a walk-in clinic, would be in the hospital's best interest."

He was beginning to feel better. The Board's suggestion validated his position, proved he was a man of insight, a force to be reckoned with.

"Good. Then I am also certain you realize one of our largest fixed expenses is payroll."

His moment of euphoria was officially over.

"We cannot afford to maintain any non-essential personnel, and by non-essential I mean employees who are not contributing their fair share. We need value for our money, don't you agree?"

His normally pasty complexion turned another shade whiter as he again nodded 'yes'.

"Excellent. So why don't you bring me up to date with the progress you've made in the area of business development. Let's start with Dr. Byner and the CARE program."

"Uh, I spoke to Dr. Byner just yesterday. They released him from the hospital a few days ago and he's starting his cardiac rehab."

"And how long is that supposed to last?"

"Three months, I think."

"And will he be resuming his medical practice once he's completed the program?"

"Uh, he mentioned something about retirement. He said he wasn't sure yet, but the heart attack was a wake-up call or something and he needs some time to sort things out."

"I see. That makes sense. How about some of the other programs you were looking into? Anything look promising?"

The C.O.O. considered giving her a story, dragging out the inevitable as long as possible, but realized he was tired. He took a deep breath, blew it out slowly, and sat forward in his chair.

"Sister Dolores," he began, staring directly into her eyes, "I think we both know there just isn't much good business out there these days. Hospital medicine has changed and small places like Saints' are going to find it increasingly difficult to keep the doors open, ER or no ER. I've done what I could, despite what you or some of the others around here might think, and I'm out of ideas. So, rather than put you and the Board in the awkward position of having to fire me, I think it would be best for everyone if I resign, which I'm prepared to do right now."

Sister Dolores sat back in her chair and looked at the man sitting in front of her. He appeared larger somehow, and a bit flushed. Then she smiled.

"Mr. Doyle, I appreciate what you've done for us and I know your job was difficult and often thankless. I also appreciate your offer, and

I agree with your decision. Will three months severance pay be sufficient? It will get you through the holidays."

"That's more than generous. It'll give me some time to sort a few things out, too."

With that they shook hands and he left the office. Her conversation with Mr. Wright the previous day had made her fairly certain Mr. Doyle's position wouldn't be needed for much longer and his unexpected resignation was the best way of eliminating it. The informal settlement conference was scheduled for Thursday morning, just two days from now. It was, she thought, going to be a long two days.

Chapter 85

By Tuesday evening word of Mr. Doyle's departure had spread throughout the hospital, in large part thanks to Mr. Doyle himself. When he told Sister Dolores he was willing to submit his resignation, effective immediately, it was exactly what he meant. After leaving her office he made the short trip down the hall to his own, collected the few personal effects he kept there, then proceeded to the ER. He wasn't going to leave without getting some closure.

His relationship with the director had been contentious and unpleasant. He'd convinced himself it was due to Dr. Riegel's inability or refusal to understand the harsh realities of the medical business in modern times. But there was more to it than that. It had become personal. Rather than slip out the door unnoticed, allowing his detractors to gloat and speculate about the circumstances of his departure, he wanted to set the record straight.

The ER clerk told him the director was in his office. He walked to the door, knocked, and walked in after being informed "It's open". He found him at his desk, staring through his reading glasses at a stack of papers.

"Doyle, what are you doing here?"

The C.O.O. had not been in the habit of making visits to Dr. Riegel's office. "I've resigned. I wanted you to be the first to know, other than Sister Dolores, of course."

The director removed his reading glasses and narrowed his eyes. "You what?"

Mr. Doyle then calmly explained that he'd been hired to develop new business, that in the course of the past several months he'd learned that there was no such new business to be found besides the CARE program which was now most likely finished, and that he'd come to the conclusion it would be best for himself and for the hospital if he were to resign.

"It was my decision, and I'm happy with it. So, it seems you were right. I'm gone and you're still here. I hope it works out for you."

The ex-C.O.O. stuck out his hand and the director reflexively shook it. Then, with his head held high, the small man turned and walked away.

It took a full five minutes for the reality of what just happened to sink in. Dr. Riegel then picked up the phone and punched in a familiar extension. "Hi, it's Riegel. I just got a visit from Doyle." (pause) "Jesus! Sorry. Yeah, I just wanted to see if it was really true. Thanks."

After getting confirmation from Sister Dolores he walked to the ER to give Fish the news. After their earlier conversation he didn't want him to hear it from someone else first.

Later that night Mr. Doyle's sudden departure was the main topic of conversation at the Hooks' residence. Though he couldn't go into details per his promise to the director, not that he was sure he had any details to divulge in the first place, it was nevertheless satisfying to bounce his thoughts off Micky for her insights into what it all might mean. The discussion had begun during dinner and continued after they'd gotten into bed.

"Why does it have to mean anything?" she said finally. "Maybe he just found a better job."

"Or maybe he knows the ship is sinking and he wants to be the first rat to get off."

Neither spoke for a while. Fish realized his comment was a bit of a mood killer and decided to change the subject. "Wanna back rub?" he asked with a wiggle of his eyebrows.

Chapter 86

The settlement conference was scheduled for 10:30 A.M. in the offices of Mr. Wright. He considered allowing it to occur downtown, a more central location for just about everyone involved, but he chose instead to retain the home field advantage and whatever psychological edge it might confer. By ten Sister Dolores and Consuela were sitting with him, reviewing what he'd told them over the phone three days earlier. He also wanted to be certain they were committed to the strategy he'd devised. They were.

By 10:20 everyone invited was in the waiting area. Unlike the previous meeting during which the will was read, Mr. Wright had no instructions to 'make them squirm'. As soon as the last person walked through the door, who happened to be Leonard Jr., he had them ushered into the conference room.

There were no spouses this time, no children or grandchildren. Only the principals had been asked to attend. The money was either going to go to Leonard's children, in which case it would be their personal asset, or to Consuela and the Charitable Foundation via Sister Dolores. No one else needed to be there, no one else had an opinion that really mattered.

Once everyone was comfortably seated Mr. Wright walked to the wall safe, opened it, and removed the envelope he'd found at the bottom of the large manila envelope in which the will had been placed. He returned to his seat at the head of the table, opened the envelope, and removed the letter.

"This," he began, waving the document in front of him, "is a letter addressed to me written by the late Leonard Walter Sr. It was at the bottom of the envelope containing the will. I found it shortly after you left the day of the reading. I think you will find its contents interesting."

"Excuse me," Mr. Pearl interrupted, "are you saying you have information pertinent to this case that you've withheld from us until today, and that you are planning to reveal whatever it is without opposing counsel getting a chance to see it first?"

"Sorry, Norman, but yes. Those were my instructions."

"And just who's instructions are you referring to?"

"Mr. Walter's, of course."

"This is outrageous! What makes you think I'm going to allow something like this to happen. We have a trial date, we have rules of discovery. The judge is going to take a very dim view of these antics. I think you've really crossed the line here and it's going to hurt your case."

As the lawyers bantered the eyes of the others moved back and forth, from one to the other. Leonard Jr. even managed a smirk when he heard the remark about the judge's likely response. Sister Dolores and Connie stayed calm. They'd been advised this would likely be Mr. Pearl's reaction.

"I understand your concerns, Norman. But if you allow me to read this now you will understand why I've waited." He paused briefly then added, "You have all wondered what Mr. Walter's motive was for rewriting his will. I wondered myself until I read this. One way or another this document will be entered as evidence. The judge will see it. My sense is that your clients will be well-served to know its contents before that happens."

Mr. Pearl narrowed his eyes and stared at him. He knew John Wright was a straight shooter and he grudgingly admitted to himself that he was unlikely to be lying now. There probably was something in the letter that would be best seen in an informal context.

"Give me a minute, please."

"Of course." Mr. Wright stood and motioned for Connie and Sister Dolores to do the same. Mr. Pearl noticed.

"Sit down, John, that won't be necessary."

Norman Pearl moved to the far end of the table and had a brief discussion with his clients. Shortly after he began there was an unintelligible outburst from Leonard Jr. followed by a perfectly intelligible 'Oh grow up, Leonard' from Elaine. Soon thereafter the conference ended and Mr. Pearl returned to his seat.

"OK, John. Let's hear it."

Mr. Wright picked up the letter, cleared his throat, and began to read.

"Dear John,

"My guess is that by now you've had the reading of the will and things are somewhat chaotic. My children are no doubt running around like chickens without heads in search of legal representation and yammering about contesting the will, having me declared incompetent, and accusing Connie of God-knows-what. I can only imagine what they are saying about Sister Dolores. I'm sorry I'm not there to see it, though if even half of what the Church says is true I should have a pretty good view from where I am.

"I apologize for being so cryptic with you. I never gave you an explanation for why I decided to change the will, and I'm certain the family is interested to know what I was thinking. So here it is:

"I worked hard my entire life to build my business and make my family secure. I didn't coddle my children but I made sure they had what they needed. Over the years I tried to get them to be more self-directed. I hoped they would see me as an example of what they could accomplish with their own lives if they were willing to do the work. Instead, they saw me as an excuse to do as little as possible knowing I wouldn't let them fail to the point of destitution.

"But then I realized I had one more chance to get things right. All along I wanted to use my money to do the most good. Simply giving it to my children was not going meet that goal. In fact, it would probably make things worse. Money, especially if it's the kind that comes easily, can do terrible things to people. So, I mortgaged the business and gave the bulk of the cash to Sister Dolores' Charitable Foundation. The hospital does great work for the less fortunate in our community, and now it will hopefully be able to continue doing so for years to come. Connie's worked long enough. It's time for her to relax a bit and be home for her family. The three million should be enough to make that possible.

"As for my children, I've given them the business and a chance to prove to themselves they can run it well and make their own fortunes. But, it's going to take some time for them to figure that out which is why I'm going to ask you to go slowly. Don't rush anything. My hope is the longer it takes to resolve the probate the greater the chance they will realize they don't really need my money at all. Who knows, they might even learn to like working for a living, though if they play their cards right they shouldn't have to for very long.

"So please don't share this letter with them until you feel it's absolutely necessary. Let them think I was a crazy old man, or senile, or under some kind of spell or whatever for as long as possible so that by the time they have to face the fact that I was none of those things they will have come to the understanding that I was merely a father trying to do the right thing for his children.

"Oh, and as far as you're concerned, I feel quite certain that the legal fees you will run up during this affair will take you a little closer to your own retirement. That's my gift to you.

Sincerely,

Leonard Walter Sr."

Mr. Wright looked up for the first time since he began reading. "He had the letter notarized and there's another original copy at Schaeffer-Deutsch, the firm he hired to revise the will."

Chapter 87

"Norman?" Mr. Wright said.

The room had gone eerily silent after the reading of the letter. Sister Dolores and Connie sat poker-faced as they had the entire time, while Elaine, Louise and Leonard Jr. shot nervous glances at one another and at their attorney.

"Uh, yes, John?"

"There is an offer on the table, our counter to yours, to which you have not as yet responded. I think now might be a good time."

"A few moments in private with my clients, please?"

"Certainly." Mr. Wright ushered Sister Dolores and Connie out of the conference room and into his office. "I don't think this will take too long," he said after getting them settled.

"OK," Mr. Pearl began. "How would you like to proceed?"

"Maybe we should go with the idea you had last week," Leonard Jr. suggested. "You know, make them an offer they can't refuse."

Elaine rolled her eyes. "Come on, are you really that dim?"

"What are you talking about? You thought it was a great idea last week. You couldn't wait to throw twenty-three million dollars at them then," he responded angrily.

"Weren't you listening? Didn't you hear anything that was in that letter?"

"You know, I've…"

"Enough!" Mr. Pearl said loudly, staring at Leonard Jr. "Let me explain something to you that Elaine seems to have grasped. We are no longer in a good bargaining position. We may never have been, but we certainly are not now. We've been unable to produce any compelling evidence that your father was in any way impaired, we have not been able to provide any good rationale for why the money should go to you rather than to the Charitable Foundation and Mrs. Sanchez, other than the fact you want it and you don't want to work. If we go to trial, and this letter goes into evidence, there is a very good chance we will get laughed out of the courtroom."

"But…" Leonard Jr. offered meekly.

"But what?"

"But we're his children!"

Mr. Pearl had had just about enough of the spoiled whining. "Maybe you should have thought about that forty years ago before deciding to become his greatest disappointment."

Leonard Jr. crumpled in his chair while Elaine glared at him. Finally it was Louise who spoke.

"What do you suggest, Mr. Pearl?"

"I suggest you start begging. The offer is six million dollars. I think we ask for ten, and we ask very politely. If we are lucky, and if Sister Dolores isn't as fed up with you as I am, maybe she will meet us half way."

"Elaine?" Louise asked.

"Our father said something interesting in that letter. He said a lot of interesting things, but one in particular that is important to us now. He said if we play our cards right, we shouldn't have to work for very long."

"What the hell is *that* supposed to mean?" Leonard Jr. grumbled. "We are in our sixties. Is he implying we'll be dead soon?"

"You are a real ass, you know that? What he meant was this: we need to work long enough for the business to begin generating enough profit for us to survive on the profit-sharing distributions. In the past few months alone we've gone from a projection of zero dollars to a five-figure year-end bonus for each of us. With Mr. Perino's leadership and our continued diligence we could be out of the woods in a couple of years. Plus, our children, except for Lauren, are all working for the company. The money our father left them is not going to be sufficient for their retirements. The only hope they have lies in the success of Walter Industries. I think if we put it to them in those terms they would be motivated to step up, take some of the weight off us, and eventually take over the day to day operations."

"Then I say we do what Mr. Pearl suggested," Louise said.

"Good," the lawyer responded.

"Does anyone care to hear *my* opinion?" Leonard Jr. asked petulantly.

"NO!" the other three answered simultaneously.

"I'll call them back in," Mr. Pearl said, walking toward the door.

When everyone was once again seated at the table, Mr. Pearl began his appeal.

"John, we have considered your offer, and while it is quite generous there are certain circumstances that would, I think, warrant increasing the amount a bit. Without boring you with too many details..."

"Seven point five," Sister Dolores interrupted. "I'm too old to spend what's left of my life going around in circles with you."

"Uh, Sister..." Mr. Wright began. The plan had been to allow the other side to grovel and make their counter offer. The expectation was they would settle for the original amount rather than go to trial.

"Seven point five and the offer is good only until you leave the room today. I want this done now. If you drag your feet or hem and haw the deal is off."

"I was going to counter at ten," Mr. Pearl replied. There are…"

"Good, that means you were hoping to get seven point five. You got it. Do we have a deal or not?"

Mr. Pearl looked at his clients. Elaine and Louise nodded, while Leonard Jr. sulked.

"We have a deal. And thank you for your generosity."

"Don't mention it. Mr. Wright, draw up the papers. No one leaves until it's signed and official."

"Yes, Sister."

Chapter 88

The following day an emergency meeting of the hospital leadership was held. Though the settlement agreement reached with the Walter family would need the judge's approval before any distributions could be made, Sister Dolores had been informed that the approval was guaranteed and she'd decided to share the news with the Board and Medical Executive Committee. 'Why not let everyone have a nice weekend', had been her rationale.

"It's a little over sixty-one million dollars. At a modest four percent it will generate nearly two point five million a year. We are currently running close to one point eight million per year in the red. So, we're OK for now."

There were smiles all around and bursts of congratulatory chatter among the attendees.

"But," she continued loudly, quelling the festivities, "we must continue to be careful. The economic climate is harsh. We are facing new cuts in reimbursement from Medicaid and Medicare and we are seeing increasing numbers of patients with no insurance at all. The long-term viability of Saints' is still somewhat in question."

"Meaning what, exactly?" Dr. Riegel asked. He'd anticipated the announcement, having had the insider information given him by Sister Dolores, and he'd assumed that when it became official he could once and forever dismiss the idea of an ER closure or downgrade and move on with his plans. Her tone suggested otherwise.

"Meaning we can continue to offer the full array of services we are currently providing to the community, including a full-service emergency department. But we will need to ratchet down our expenses even further and maximize our utilization. I am also in the process of developing a more aggressive program for attracting private donations to the Foundation. This experience has made it clear that for us to survive in the long term we will need the support of the people we serve. So, is there an announcement *you'd* like to make?"

"In that case, yeah, I guess so. Uh, you all know I've been doing this a long time and you were probably wondering why I was still doing it, and some of you were probably hoping I'd stop doing it sooner than later because, you know, I can be a pain in the ass sometimes, sorry Sister, and my wife was wondering the same thing, though I have a feeling it was because as long as I was doing it she had some time to herself and if I stopped she have to find something else for me to do so I wouldn't drive her crazy, and I know some of my doctors were looking at me and wondering if that's what was going to happen to them if they did it for as long as I have, and so I figured maybe it's time to stop doing it."

Dr. Carter, who was better than most at interpreting the director's language, thought he had the gist. "Uh, Bill, are you saying you're going to retire?"

"Well yeah, wasn't that obvious?"

A roar of laughter ensued. When it died down Dr. Carter continued. "Then congratulations are in order! When, exactly, is this going to happen?"

Dr. Riegel went on to explain the pending sale of the ER contract, his one-year retainer to effect a smooth transition, and then the assumption of the directorship by his protégé, Dr. Hooks. "So you're not done with me quite yet."

Several miles away another conversation was taking place on a similar subject. Elaine wanted to let her daughter know that the issue of the will had been resolved and that soon she could move forward with her own plans.

"You know," she said, "when this all started I was mortified. I mean, to think my father would leave us in this kind of position at this stage of our lives. But it's interesting. Over the past few months I've actually come to enjoy being involved in the business, being chairwoman of the board. When your grandfather was alive there was no need, and really, no room for me. Now, well, it's quite different."

Meanwhile, in Silverlake, Tommy was leading Train Wreck through a rehearsal in advance of the up-coming party gig, and breaking in a new rhythm guitar player.

Chapter 89

"So that's it? Everything worked out for the best?"

"That's it for me. I can sell the contract and be retired a little over a year from now. It's not 'it' for you, though."

After the emergency meeting of the hospital leadership Dr. Riegel returned to his office to call Dr. Hooks. He wanted to move things along and needed to be sure Fish was still committed to assuming the directorship.

"What's *that* supposed to mean, it's 'it' for you but it's not 'it' for me? If it's 'it' then it's 'it' for both of us, right? You retire, I take over, the ER stays open, the hospital has money. How much more 'it' can it be?"

"It's 'it' for me because I'm retiring, done, finished, hang up the white coat, get the stethoscope bronzed, let my specialty board certification lapse. But it's not 'it' for you because you're still going to be working. In case you haven't noticed things are changing, and not necessarily for the better."

"So if it's not 'it' for me, what the hell is it?"

"It's 'it' for now."

"Huh?" Fish had allowed himself the fantasy that once the business of the hospital's financial viability had been resolved certain things, like convoluted conversations with the director, would no longer be a part of his life. That was not, he realized, going to be the case for the foreseeable future.

"Look, Fish, it's simple, OK? Things worked out. For now. The hospital has enough money to keep the doors open. For now. You're going to be me, Christ that's a scary fucking thought, and everything is going to be fine. For now. But the business of medicine is a mess and as far as I can tell the people trying to fix it either don't have the faintest idea what they're doing or they are purposely trying to make things worse. So what I'm saying is you have to keep your eyes open for the changes that are coming and have a plan for adapting to them. I was lucky. I got forty-plus years out of this career and most of them were pretty good. You might not be so lucky."

As far as explanations from Dr. Riegel were concerned, this one was actually understandable. Most made sense eventually, but this required little decoding.

"So you're saying I should have a back-up plan, something else I can do if medicine goes completely down the toilet?"

"What I'm saying is that you need to manage your expectations. I don't know that the job should be the center of your life, and that's what it's becoming, a job. It was a lot different when I was getting started, but I've told you that before and it doesn't really matter now."

There was silence on the line. Maybe, Fish thought, he'd been right all along. Maybe he should have never allowed himself to get sucked back into the job, the meetings, politics, the director's stipend. He'd been so close to walking away from all of it before his father's heart attack. And now?

"Hey, Fish, I know what you're thinking," Dr. Riegel said. "You're thinking you should have stayed in Hawaii, but you're wrong."

"Really?"

"Really. You're a good doctor, Fish, and just because the profession has been roughed up and will be some more, it doesn't mean you have to walk away. It just means you have to put it in perspective."

"And you know what that perspective should be, right?"

"Actually, I think I do. I think you do, too."

"Oh?"

"Yeah. Medicine is the engine that provides the juice for you to do the really important things. It's not an end in itself. At least not anymore. You already know that. I mean, what's more important to you, Micky or the job?"

"Micky, of course."

"Exactly. So do the job so you and Micky can have the life you want, and when it gets to the point where it doesn't do that anymore, then get out and do something else."

Fish realized the momentary lucidity with which the director had been blessed was fading fast. It was time to get off the phone.

"OK, Bill, I get it. Thanks. Go make your deal."

Micky had wandered into the kitchen during the middle of the conversation and was quietly eavesdropping.

"What was that all about?" she asked. They'd slept in since they both had the day off and she'd just gotten out of the shower. Fish turned and noticed she was in her bathrobe.

"That was Riegel," he said, walking toward her. "It's over."

"What's over?" she asked as he gently grabbed the front of her robe.

"The probate, the will, the whole Un-dead thing. Sister Dolores got the money and Saints' is out of trouble."

"That's great!" she replied, trying to keep her robe from falling open. "Stop that, Marla's in the other room."

He slipped his hand inside and moved it down her belly and between her legs. "No, that's good, this is great."

"Fish!"

Just then the door to Marla's room opened and she walked into the kitchen. "Am I interrupting something?" she asked with a lewd grin.

Fish reluctantly removed his hand and Micky managed an embarrassed giggle before running back down the hall.

"Yeah, but only for a minute," her brother replied, running after her and making it to the door before she had a chance to close it. Marla poured herself a cup of coffee, shook her head and smiled as Micky's giggling continued in the bedroom.

Chapter 90

He'd stashed the ring in the last spot he thought she'd ever look—inside an old snakeskin cowboy boot with a phoenix inlay of red and turquoise leather, lying in the very deepest recess of his bedroom closet. The left one. He was superstitious and figured that the ring would eventually be worn on her left hand so it should be hidden in his left boot.

The boots were a fashion statement he hadn't dared make in over a decade and had been standing in the back of the closet the entire time, waiting patiently for the next Urban Cowboy phenomenon to give them their well-deserved freedom and recognition. Beside them was an equally proud and ignored pair of in-line roller skates.

It was a quiet neighborhood. Nothing much happened and there was little, if any, turnover. There had been a momentary rush of excitement the day Fish dug into the closet and grabbed the left boot. Was this it? A return to glory? Fish dusted it off and took a moment to admire the leatherwork, and to reflect on days gone by. There was no denying the disappointment when the small box was placed inside and the boot returned to its spot on the floor. Still, the fact he remembered they were there at all was enough to allow them to keep the faith.

It was Saturday morning, the beginning of what Fish knew would be a long weekend. To fill the time, and to keep his mind off the ring and any chance of a premature popping of the question, he'd scheduled a number of activities. Among them were the mundane, like catching up on the laundry, the practical, like organizing the garage so it could actually accommodate the two cars it was designed to house, the co-operative, mainly consulting with Tommy and Marla about last minute party chores, and the romantic, specifically dinner at La Spiaggia and dessert at Ca' Hooks, with a little luck.

Nowhere on his list was there any mention of 're-arrange the bedroom closet'. Yet as he walked out of the bathroom wearing only his bath towel that was precisely the activity in which Micky seemed to be engaged. She was on hands and knees, in her robe, which hadn't been designed to provide adequate coverage to one in the down dog position, heading straight for the boots.

He took about five seconds to admire the view, then rushed forward, grabbed her by the pelvis, and pulled her back into the room.

"What are you doing?" she asked, suspicious she was about to once again fall victim to his overactive libido.

"What are *you* doing?" he asked, letting go, trying to make it clear no such violation was forthcoming.

"I'm trying to make some room in your closet. I've been spending a lot of time here, if you haven't noticed, and there's no room for my stuff. It's a pain having to go back and forth for clean clothes every day or so. I need some closet space, and drawer space, of my own."

He stared at her a moment, appreciating the irony that if things went well she'd have all the space she could possibly need in a couple of days.

"Hey! It's not like I'm trying to move in on you or anything," she said, misreading his expression. "And what's with the cowboy boots? Nobody except real cowboys have worn those things since I was, like, in junior high school."

"Yeah, well that's about how long they've been there. But never mind the boots, OK? And I promise I'll clear out the closet and the drawers this week. I just don't want to do it this morning, if that's all right with you. We have a lot of other things to deal with, like the party tomorrow."

She stood with her right hand resting on her cocked right hip. "You know, it would only take me about fifteen minutes," nodding in the direction of the boots.

"I can think of a better way to spend fifteen minutes," he replied with a wink.

"Geez, Fish! What's gotten into you lately?"

Chapter 91

The party was scheduled to begin at five P.M. It was Sunday, after all, and some of the invitees had things to do the next morning. The band had been there since three getting set up and doing a sound check. Marla had gotten there an hour before the band to meet the caterers. The food was going to be made on-site and getting people orientated to the kitchen was an important part of ensuring a successful dining experience. By five o'clock everything was in place.

By five-0-five Fish, Micky, Dr. Riegel and his wife, Ashleigh, Danny, Bob Graber, and Lauren were there as well. Fish knew the director and his wife would arrive pretty much at five on the dot. He had no patience for lateness, fashionable or otherwise, and Fish wanted to be there to greet them. Ashleigh, as the titular guest of honor, also felt the need to be first on scene, and Lauren wanted to keep an eye on Amy, who'd been hanging out with Tommy and the band.

By five-thirty the party was in full swing. The Montes clan and assorted relatives had been slightly taken aback by the name of the place but Tommy, in his inimitable way, made them feel welcome and at ease. The ones young enough to know who Tommy Traina was were having a great time mingling with Train Wreck and the other musicians, famous and not so famous, while Ashleigh's parents had latched onto Gilbert and Marlene Hooks. Carlos, who'd also felt out of place initially, soon discovered the gals from Ladies Night and was busy comparing tattoos.

Margheritas, mojitos, bite-sized tacos of various types and fajita skewers were passed among the guests under Marla's watchful eye. She wasn't cooking but it was her kitchen and whatever came out of it had to meet her standards. Dinner was served at six-thirty. Carne asada, chile verde, carnitas, chile rellenos, rice and beans.

"So?" Marla asked, walking up behind Carlos.

408

"El sabor autentico," he replied with a smile. "You know what that means?"

"Yeah, I took Spanish in high school. Plus I'm a chef, so I can recognize a compliment in just about any language," she replied laughing.

As the dinner plates were being cleared Fish stood and announced a toast. Glasses of champagne were distributed, ("no, not the D.P.", Tommy had assured Marla when the idea was first mentioned), and Fish walked onto the small stage. He turned on the microphone, the one Tommy would be using later, and after an awkward 'testing, testing, one, two, three' and a loud 'hey, Fish, it's working, OK?' from Tommy he began his speech.

"OK, first I want to thank you all for being here and I want to thank Tommy for letting us take over the Step for our little bash."

He raised his glass and tipped it in Tommy's direction.

"I guess you all know there are a few things we're celebrating tonight. There's Tommy's birthday," (a cheer ensued), "then there's *my* birthday," (another cheer). "Thanks! Also, we want to acknowledge my boss, Dr. Riegel's, retirement. What's it been, Bill, forty-four years or something working in the ER, trying to keep the young doc's out of trouble?"

"Christ! If my memory was good enough to know that I'd probably keep working," the director said loudly.

"There's someone else we need to make a toast to," Fish said when the laughter died down. "He's not here, at least physically he's not here, but he is very much here nonetheless. Without him, and his donation to Saints' Hospital's Charitable Foundation, Dr. Riegel wouldn't be retiring and it's possible both he and I would be looking for new jobs. Without him Tommy and Lauren wouldn't have gotten reacquainted and we'd have been deprived of one of the great love stories of our time."

A few wolf whistles ensued from the part of the room occupied by the musicians.

"So, I want to make a toast to Mr. Leonard Walter, Sr., Lauren's grandfather, better known to us as The Un-dead."

Most of the people in the room had heard of The Un-dead at one time or another and applauded loudly in his recognition. It took a few minutes for the room to quiet sufficiently for Fish to continue.

"But the big deal," he began, "and the real star of the show is Ashleigh and her acceptance to the University of California, San Diego school of law. Stand up and take a bow."

All eyes turned towards her as she rolled her eyes, blushed, and stood.

"Congratulations, Ash!" Fished raised his glass. "I think we can all drink to that." He took a sip of the champagne and the others followed his lead. "So," he continued, "if a few years from now one of you needs a lawyer, and from the looks of this crowd I would have to say that would be a safe bet, she's going to be your gal."

Another toast was drunk and requests for Ashleigh to say a few words were made. As much as she would have preferred not doing so she'd anticipated the situation and was prepared. She walked to the stage and took the microphone from Fish.

"There are a lot of things to celebrate tonight, and trust me when I say my getting accepted to law school is not the most significant. But, it was a good excuse to throw this party and I want to thank you all for being here. I especially want to thank my parents for doing what they had to do to make sure I got an education, and my brother, Carlos, for providing the inspiration I needed to keep going when things got tough. And, Danny, here's to you." She tipped her glass in his direction, then handed the microphone to Fish and stepped off the stage.

"OK, so Marla is going to be doing a dessert thing a little later, you know, after you've had time to make some room for it. Meanwhile we're in for a treat of a different kind. Ladies and gentlemen, please welcome Tommy Traina and Train Wreck!"

Tommy and the band took the stage and grabbed their instruments. The band consisted of guitar, bass, drums, and keyboards. Tommy did the singing and he was a good enough musician that a second guitar had never been needed. Tonight, though, a second guitar sat on a stand next to his.

"Before we get started," Tommy said, "I want to introduce the newest member of the band. On rhythm guitar, Miss Amy Walter."

Amy jumped up amidst whoops and applause and took her spot next to Tommy. She slung the guitar over her neck, an old Fender Telecaster, small enough for her to handle and loud enough for a room much larger than the Step. With their matching eyes and guitars dangling in front of them there was an eerie similarity between them hard to ignore. Tommy was about to cue the drummer when Amy stepped in front of him. She got on her tiptoes in front of the mike.

"Actually, it's Amy Walter *Traina*," she announced.

The din that preceded her comment died instantly. Tommy's jaw dropped and he looked over at Lauren who was equally stunned and who shook her head and mouthed the words 'not me'. Amy noticed the horrified look on her mother's face.

"It's OK, mom. I heard everything you guys said that night Tommy came over for dinner. I mean, you didn't think I was going to do the dishes and miss out on what was going on, did you? And you know he's going to ask you to marry him sooner or later, so I'm going to be Amy Walter Traina one way or the other and I figured why not start now?

A din of a different nature ensued. Amy nonchalantly turned to Tommy. "Well," she said in a loud voice, are we going to play or are we going to just stand here?"

This brought a laugh from the drummer. "A chip off the old block," he said, clicking his drumsticks to set the tempo for 'Bite Me'. Tommy, pro that he was, recovered his composure in time for the downbeat.

The band played three songs, it was all Amy was able to absorb in the short time she'd had to practice. Each was composed of no more than five chords and in keys that were easy for a guitarist. Tommy dragged out the songs with extended solos for himself and the keyboard player, giving Amy a chance to stay on stage a while longer.

"Ok," Tommy said at the conclusion of the third song, "we're going to take a little break now so we can have dessert."

He removed the guitar strap from around his neck and helped Amy with hers. They walked hand in hand back to their table where Tommy took his seat next to Lauren and Amy planted herself in his lap. She put an arm around his neck and her mouth next to his ear. "Thanks——-dad," she whispered. He gave her a soft squeeze and put his free arm around Lauren.

Just then Marla pushed open the kitchen door and rolled out a food cart upon which sat a large, two-layer strawberry shortcake covered in whipped cream and decorated with three candles and the word 'Congratulations!' in red icing. She looked over at Tommy, who had his hands full.

"I was going to ask Ashleigh, Fish and Tommy to blow out the candles, but all things considered I think I'll do it myself," she said, and did just that.

She then set about cutting slices and putting them on plates which the wait staff served to the guests. Fish and Micky were sitting with the Hooks contingent at a table next to Tommy's. When the last piece of cake had been delivered Micky stood and tapped on her glass with her fork.

"Excuse me, please," she said, getting the group's attention. "I know there's been a lot of excitement and a few, uh, surprises this evening, so I hope you won't mind one more."

With that she reached into the stylish Channel bag hanging on the back of her chair, a gift from Fish on *her* last birthday, and removed the small jeweler's box.

"What the…" Fish said when he saw what it was.

Micky calmly opened the box and gasps erupted from those close enough to see its contents. "Gilbert Hooks, Fish," she asked, "will you marry me?"

Fish just stared at the ring, then at Micky, speechless.

"Well?" she said when no immediate response was offered.

"Well, yeah, of course! But how…"

"Oh come on. I found the ring hiding in your stupid cowboy boot, like, the day after you put it there. I've been rummaging through the closet for weeks trying to figure out how to make some space for myself and one day I noticed that one of the boots didn't have any dust on it. I thought that was weird so I picked it up and found the ring. I didn't know what to do so I asked Marla and she told me what you were up to. Then I called Ashleigh to tell *her* about it and ask if it was OK to get engaged at the party. She talked to Danny and then she told me it would be great."

"So everybody knew about this but ME? And I was the one trying to keep all these secrets. Geez!"

"Marla had to ask Tommy if it would be OK and Tommy said you already told him about it. He told Lauren. I called Billy and he told mom and dad, so, yeah I guess you're right. When you caught me digging around in the closet yesterday I was actually putting it back in the boot. I'd taken it to a jeweler to get it sized."

Fish shook his head and looked at the director. "Did you know about this, too?"

"Nah, nobody tells me anything."

"Well, then give me a chance to do this right," Fish said, standing and taking the ring out of the box. He got down on one knee and looked up at Micky. "Michelle Riley, would you do me the great honor of being my wife?"

"Absolutely," she replied.

He placed the perfectly sized ring on her finger and gave her a big, wet kiss, accompanied by a loud ovation from the crowd.

The party that followed went on for much longer than originally planned, and it is safe to assume that a number of things that needed to be done the following day by a number of people in attendance were left for another time.

Chapter 92

Thanksgiving at the home of Gilbert and Marlene Hooks had always been simple. Simple in the sense that all the Hooks children were expected to be there enjoying one another's company and a meal that was decidedly elaborate. This year the logistics were a bit more difficult.

Danny had been invited to join Ashleigh for dinner at her parents' place. The significance of the invitation was not lost on him and a refusal was out of the question. They'd been asked to arrive at three P.M., precisely the time they were supposed to be in Lakewood.

Marla was also facing a similar conflict. Bob Graber wanted her to spend the day with his family. She'd met the parents on a couple of occasions but this was an opportunity to meet the other relatives. A coming-out of sorts. Their relationship was officially 'serious' and mention of 'the future' had been made on more than one occasion.

Since announcing her engagement Micky had been receiving more attention from her parents. There was going to be a wedding, she was their only child, they wanted to be involved. Surely, spending some time together during the holidays would be the perfect way to renew their relationships.

The only person without a conflict was Billy. He was single and not involved with a steady girlfriend. It was he who suggested the compromise. Over the course of many phone calls and much negotiation a plan was eventually devised and it was this—all non-Hooks festivities would begin no later than one P.M. Then, at six, everyone would convene in Lakewood. It would involve a lot of running around and significantly more calories but there was no other way. At least not this year. Everyone realized that in the future they would have to decide on a schedule, Thanksgiving with one set of relatives, Christmas with the other. But this year it was all too new, and except for Fish and Micky, still undecided. Covering all the bases for all the holidays seemed the best approach.

Things were a bit awkward for the Walter clan as well. Though it had been over two months since the business of the will had been resolved there remained some bruised feelings and battered egos. The business was doing well, and the money each received from the settlement was substantial. Still, there had been enough vitriol during the process to leave some deep scars. Thanksgiving, it was decided, was too soon for a family reunion. Maybe, they hoped, by Christmas things would be better.

Elaine and Roy had decided to host the holiday meal for their immediate family. Son Robert, daughter Lauren, granddaughter Amy, and Tommy. Tommy had met the parents. Lauren had arranged a lunch at the Silver Spur. A public venue, she'd felt, would minimize the possibility of any untoward behavior. That fantasy lasted less than a minute when Amy introduced Tommy as her dad.

"So my real name is Amy Walter Traina, and I'd appreciate it if you would call me that in the future," is how she'd put it.

No determination of her paternity had yet been made. Tommy and Lauren had decided not to do the DNA testing. At least not yet. Their relationship was still in it's infancy and though they each believed the other was The One, they hadn't said as much. Why throw a wrench in the works? Amy, though, had been of a different opinion. As far as she was concerned they looked alike, they thought the same kinds of things, and they both played the guitar. Clearly, she felt, given what she'd heard the night she eavesdropped on their conversation, he was her father and she was glad that he was.

Her announcement at the Silver Spur caused a scene beyond anything Lauren had feared. Questions, many of them embarrassing, were asked. Evasions were offered but not accepted and a demand was made by Elaine to 'get to the bottom of this immediately'.

"You've kept this secret for over twelve years and it's time to know the truth!" was her attitude.

Lauren knew there would be no peace until the issue was settled. She and Tommy had wanted to wait until Amy was old enough to make a thoughtful decision on her own. Amy informed them she was old enough now, (I'm eleven, OK?). Two days later, on a Monday, blood samples were drawn. Two weeks later the results were in. Amy Walter was officially Amy Walter Traina.

Lauren was then made to endure a crusade of a different sort. "So when are you two going to get married?" became the first words out of her mother's mouth each and every time they spoke. Thanksgiving was no different. There were the pleasant 'hellos' and the usual hugs followed by the predictable "Have you two set a date yet?"

"Not yet, mom," Tommy replied with a smile. "Mmm, smells good in here!" he added, changing the subject.

Thanksgiving dinner was a two P.M. event at Elaine's. The timing allowed Lauren, Tommy, and Amy to get to the Hooks' residence by the agreed-upon six. Marla and Lauren were business partners and close friends. Spending the holiday together seemed the natural thing to do.

The site for the new restaurant had been chosen. It was only a few blocks from the Thirteenth Step which would allow Marla to keep an eye on both places, though the Step was pretty much on autopilot by now and Marla's assistant was capable of running the kitchen alone. They hadn't settled on a name for the new place yet. Tommy had made a few suggestions to which they'd responded "Thanks, but no". He then suggested calling the place "Thanks, but no" to which Marla responded with a straight right to the shoulder.

The concept was to serve high-end food backed by a deep wine cellar in a warm, non-stuffy environment. Though the choice of a name had still not been settled upon, both women liked the idea of calling it 'Leo's'.

Thanksgiving for Sister Dolores meant spending most of the day downtown serving free meals to the residents of skid row. It's what she'd done for many years and it was what she had done again this year. Normally, she would then return to the small convent adjacent to

Saints' and enjoy her own holiday meal in the company of her fellow nuns, the Sisters of Ineffable Sorrow. Today was different. Instead of returning home she'd driven the old Ford to Covina, to the home of Juan and Consuela Sanchez.

The Walter affair had done more than rescue the hospital. It had put her back in touch with her family. Consuela had visited her at the hospital a few times since the settlement, and had brought her husband along on the most recent visit. Connie was of the mind there was more than coincidence involved in the entire business, and Sister Dolores, believer in miracles, had to agree. She had been happy to meet her cousin, Juan. She hadn't been sure she was ready to take on the entire family. Connie had insisted that Thanksgiving would be the perfect time to begin the end of her exile.

She parked across the street from the address she'd been given and sat a while. There were a million reasons to start the engine and drive back home. She'd been abandoned by these people and forgotten. Despite her best efforts to suppress them there were still feelings of anger and resentment that surfaced whenever she thought about how she'd been treated. But she knew Connie was right.

She took a deep breath and let it out slowly. Then she stepped out of the car, walked across the street to the front door, and rang the bell.